For Simon, my nephew, with love

The wish to hurt, the momentary intoxication with pain, is the loophole through which the pervert climbs into the minds of ordinary men.

Jacob Bronowski 1954

Chapter 1

Sunday, May 9, 1971

It was ten o'clock as Thomas Taylor Coltman slipped his feet into Wellingtons, took an oiled-coat from the rack by the back door, slung his leather bag over his shoulder, and stepped out into the night. All was quiet in Orford. He turned the iron key and placed it under a plant pot at the back of a rosemary bush. The plant's sharp smell brought saliva to his mouth: he remembered his mother lifting a crackling leg of lamb, spiked with the herb, from the oven. The thought of the semi-rare meat, pink juices oozing from the cut flesh, turned his mouth acid, choking him. He spat onto the garden path leading into Doctor's Lane, looked round, and guiltily smeared it away with his boot.

The moon was in its first quarter, fresh against the black sky; he gazed up, imagining the Apollo 15 astronauts who, in a few months, would be circling it. Brave men. Once, he'd been brave like them.

He thanked God, if there was one, the longer days were here, and would be for the next few months. He was filling the short nights with walks over the fields, lanes and beaches, with no one to see him but the nocturnal animals. As he walked down Doctor's Lane, east towards the North Sea, he savoured the smells of the night: grass, flowers and the tang of salt. A seed of joy started to grow in his heart. A movement of the air, hardly a breeze, touched his face, caressing his greying curls. His heart swelled as he remembered how Audrey used to stroke his hair, pushing it back from his ears as she looked up into

1

his face, her eyes full of love, lips parted in a sweet smile. Tears pricked his eyes. With head lowered he walked on; the familiar pain of losing Audrey and John never lessened, stretching his heart until he thought it would burst. The seed in his heart shrivelled. He moved his head from side to side, like a caged, flea-bitten tiger seeking escape. He must hurry. Find something to put in the bag. Keep moving, always moving.

He turned from Doctor's Lane down a pinched track called Doctor's Drift, which led to the River Ore, and then to the sea. A barn owl, white and silent against the starry sky, glided over the fields on its regular beat; head fixed, wings pressing down the air. He wished he was back flying in his Hudson plane, back before it all happened. Back before the war, back before being posted to the Malang base in Java. Back before defeat; they were totally underpowered with too few planes, and all out of date – no match for the Japanese air force.

Move on. Stop thinking. Find something for the bag. As he neared the river, where his rowing boat was anchored, alders and willows appeared. As a child he had come with his family every year from London to Orford for holidays in their Victorian summer cottage. The cottage was now his home. He'd grown to love the sea, crabbing, fishing and learning to row a boat. When he had returned in 1946 the boat was in the cottage's garden, rotting. He'd worked on it, replacing planks, caulking the seams until it was water-worthy again.

He bent over, pulled up the anchor, wincing as his back creaked. God, he wasn't sixty yet, but sometimes he felt like an old man. He pushed an oar against the bank and the boat glided over the stagnant water of the shallow inlet. He pulled on the oars, his muscles warmed and the movement of the boat soothed him. He thought of the uncompleted work in the kitchen cupboard. Tonight, he must finish it.

At the hamlet of Shingle Street the river emptied into the sea; tonight, it was calm, with a pleasant swell. He pulled hard on the oars and turned the boat north. To his right was Orford Ness, a wide shingle spit, linked to the shore by a narrow strip of land south of Aldeburgh. When he'd been a lad, it had been a place of mystery and fascination: a military site since 1918 and later used for secret research. He'd disobey his father and creep to the barbed wire guarding its perimeter and lie in the marram grass watching planes come in from Felixstowe; sometimes they'd drop test bombs which exploded in the sea. Often, they'd land, usually on the Ness's North Airfield. His dad warned him to never go onto Orford Ness. Not only was it forbidden, but it was littered with unexploded bombs and artillery shells. Soon after he was posted to Java he got a letter from Mum telling him poor Mr Laughton, the lighthouse keeper, had been blown to bits when he was beachcombing on the shingle ridges of Orford Ness.

Now it was deserted, the demolition crews had left years ago; it was rumoured they'd return next year and finish clearing it as there were still many unexploded bombs. From his boat he'd watched the Ordnance men working; he knew which areas were clear of explosives, and since they'd left, he often came to the Ness at night, ignoring the sagging barbed-wire and wind-worn wooden notices, bleached by salt-spray, their lettering faint against the pale wood.

LANDING FORBIDDEN
DANGER UNEXPLODED BOMBS

As he neared the shore, water from the oars splashed his face; he licked his lips, tasting salt as the keel ground against the shingle beach. He clambered out, his Wellingtons slipping on the pebbles, pulled the boat above the water line and threw the anchor onto the beach. He opened the leather bag and took out a torch and switched it on; its beam glinted off desired objects, which he picked up and put in the bag.

After working the beach for half an hour, he turned the torch off, straightened up and rubbed the small of his back. The red-and-white striped lighthouse was in front of him. Reluctantly, unable to stop himself, he turned and looked at the pagodas. There they sat, their black silhouettes squat and menacing against the night sky, their heavy, concrete roofs supported by thick pillars. As always, his stomach clenched with an absurd fear. They were shaped like pagodas, but they weren't pagodas, he told himself. This was Suffolk, not Java. He forced himself to look at them, always hoping the fear would fade. But it didn't. Never sleep at night, they said, for if he did, the nightmares came stealing from the recesses of his brain and he would wake up screaming, quivering, his pyjamas soaked with sweat.

Always the same dream: he was lying on bare earth, unable to stretch out his body, his head forced to his chest, knees bent, back rounded, confined by the bamboo cage, reeking of his own piss and shit. The nights were worse than the days. The darkness was absolute, the noises perpetual: the droning of mosquitoes as they approached his nakedness, the harrowing calls of night birds, the flapping of bats' leathery wings, the slither of snakes and the wind plucking the bars of his cage and flailing the leaves of the wild banana trees.

It was four o'clock, and the air redolent with the dawn chorus when Coltman laid the bag on his kitchen table, opened it and carefully extracted what he'd picked up from the shingle ridges of Orford Ness. There were tiny sea-snail shells, their nacred surfaces shining with rainbow colours; small ridged scallop and other bivalve shells, some veneered with pale blue lines; pieces of driftwood, grooved by the sea; glass pebbles, dulling as they dried; and rectangular dog-fish egg-cases, like the backs of black cockroaches.

He brought the work he must finish from a cupboard. It was the base of an empty chocolate box which he'd taken from a waste bin in one of the chalets in the holiday camp when he'd been sent to replace a light bulb. He didn't think the chalet occupiers would notice its absence. He'd reinforced the base with plywood and covered the insides with wallpaper he'd found in the attic. In the centre he'd pasted a picture of a young woman: pretty, with brown curls, a smile and happy, deep blue eyes. He'd cut her from a woman's magazine, he remembered it was a shampoo advert, sourced, like the chocolate box, from another waste bin. Round her he'd glued rings of shells.

He washed and dried the new shells, got a glue-pot from the cupboard and, using tweezers and a fine brush, completed the intricate pattern. From a drawer in the table he took out an envelope which contained lengths of fine wire. With a scalpel, its blade glinting, he made minute incisions round the edge of the box. He glanced at the clock on the wall. Five thirty. He'd time to finish it. He couldn't leave her like this – unprotected.

The pile of wires diminished. He looked at the clock again. Ten to seven. He needed to leave for the camp soon. He looked at his work and felt at peace. He'd got through the night and now she was safe. She smiled out

5

behind the wire bars. No one could harm her and she couldn't escape. He took the work upstairs to his bedroom, opened the wardrobe and placed the box with all the others.

Chapter 2

Monday, June 7, 1971

Laurel Bowman glanced at herself in the hall mirror. She'd put her hair up into a chignon and chosen a crisp white blouse to go with her new suit. She hoped Frank wasn't wearing a t-shirt and jeans. Sam Salter was the most important person to consult The Anglian Detective Agency so far, and she felt they ought to try and make the right impression.

She bit her lip and gave a rueful smile. No one could tell Frank what to do. The best she could hope for was the leather jacket and clean shoes. She pushed open the door of the dining room of Greyfriars House, which also served as their office and meeting room.

Frank Diamond, former Detective Inspector, was staring out of the window, rubbing his chin. It was the leather jacket. He still looked more like a rock star than a private detective. It was the hair – black, curly and too long.

'Still obsessed with your stubble, Frank?' She found the grazing of his bristles on her cheek when he occasionally, far too occasionally, gave her a friendly kiss, mildly erotic.

He turned, still caressing his face. 'Someone's got to be. I shaved at six and I swear it's grown an eighth of an inch already and it's only ten thirty.'

'Too much testosterone,' she said.

He shook his head. 'Tut, tut. Far too early to be talking sex.'

'What's all this?' Stuart Elderkin, formerly Frank's Detective Sergeant, came into the room. 'Good job Mabel's not here. You know she's sensitive about... you know what.'

'What's she doing married to you, then?' Frank quipped.

Stuart parked his bulky body onto a chair. 'She's going all domesticated, that's what she's doing. As agreed, she's supervising the new kitchen being installed and won't be at the meeting with Salter.'

'Dorothy's upset about that,' Laurel said.

'She's been rather sharp lately. Perhaps you'd better have a word, Laurel?' Frank said.

She shook her head. Not a good idea.

'I'm glad to get away from all the mess and Mabel moaning about the rising price of food, especially bread. Says she'll have to start baking if the price of a loaf goes up to 15p.'

Laurel sat down. 'Let's get down to business. Stuart, have you found out any new facts about Sam Salter? All I know is he runs several holiday camps.'

'Nothing juicy. He was a bit of a lad, used to mix with the East End gangsters in his teens and early twenties, but nothing serious, never charged with any crime. He settled down, one son, wife died when the kid was about five. He's made a great success of the holiday camp business and he's well-heeled.' He glanced at his notes. 'He's 51, never re-married. That's about it.' He smiled at her. 'You look terrific, Laurel. New suit? Grey suits you. You remind me of one of those Scandinavian film stars, you know, cool, blonde and unattainable.'

'Can't see you as Anita Ekberg,' Frank said.

She gave him a frosty look. She certainly couldn't compete with the Swedish film star in one respect: the star of La Dolce Vita was a 40DD at least in the bosom stakes. She chose not to rise to the bait. 'What height is Salter?' She pointed to her high heels. 'I don't want to tower over him.'

Frank laughed. 'Let's hope he's over six feet, then he'll be able to look you in the eye.'

'I wonder why Salter wants to keep this meeting hush-hush?' Stuart said.

'I've no idea,' she replied. 'I was hoping we'd meet at one of his holiday camps. I've never been to a holiday camp. Have you?'

Stuart smiled. 'Yes, went to one once. Must have been in the 1950s. I didn't like it, too many people all determined to have a good time and to let everyone else know they were having one.' His smile broadened. 'Not like last week in London, it was packed, but that didn't worry Mabel and me, we did what we wanted, when we wanted. Best holiday I've had in a long time.' He let out a long, slow sigh of satisfaction.

Dear Stuart, he looked happy and relaxed; it was good to have him and Mabel back, even though they'd only been away for a week. 'It wasn't a holiday, Stuart, it was your honeymoon. I know Mabel loved it; she certainly did a bit of shopping.' She raised her eyebrows and pulled a face.

He laughed. 'We've made a big dent in our savings, especially after this new kitchen we're having fitted. Just as well the firm's doing well; let's hope Sam Salter has a nice big, fat juicy case for us.'

The sound of a car pulling up on the drive drew them to the window. Through the lingering sea mist, which they'd woken up to, a dark silver car with a Jaguar mascot on its bonnet manoeuvred between her Ford Cortina and

Frank's Avenger. 'Gosh, the holiday camp business must be doing well,' she said.

Stuart pursed his lips. 'A 420G,' he said. 'Warwick grey; bet it's got red seats.' His eyes shifted to his car, parked nearer the round pond; his mouth turned down.

'I thought you loved your old car?'

'I do, but I could be persuaded to love that one even more,'

A tall, well-built man, dressed in a camel-hair coat and dark suit got out of the car, took a briefcase from the passenger seat, and walked towards the house. They stepped back from the window, like schoolchildren who'd been caught peeping at a courting couple.

Dorothy Piff, owner of Greyfriars House, one-time school secretary, now administrator of the agency, came into the room and looked at the layout of the table; she primped an arrangement of roses in its centre, sending a heavy scent into the air. The front door bell rang, and she looked at her wrist-watch. 'Eleven o'clock. He's punctual.' She squared pencil to blotting paper and pushed up her blue-framed glasses with a forefinger. 'I'll let him in. Frank, sit down. All of you, try and look alert. Stuart, wipe that moony smile off you face. The honeymoon's over, it's back to business.' She stomped off.

'What's got into her?' Stuart asked. 'She's always been bossy but that's border-line rude.'

Laurel patted his hand. 'She went to Emily's grave this morning; her death is hurting more than ever, and I think she missed you and Mabel when you were away. When Mabel said she wouldn't be here for the meeting, I don't think that went down well either.'

Dorothy's twin sister, Emily, had been murdered last September, by Nicholson, the headmaster of Blackfriars School.

'Welcome to The Anglian Detective Agency, Mr Salter. I'm Dorothy Piff, the administrator. Can I take your coat?' A deep voice rumbled a reply.

Frank rolled his eyes and Stuart sniggered. Laurel shook her head.

'Through here. The rest of the team are in the main office.'

Dorothy held the door wide as Sam Salter came into the room. He was tall, about six two, and divested of his coat, the well-cut suit couldn't quite conceal he was beginning to run to fat. Thick blond hair, darkened by age and silvered at the sides, sprang from a high forehead on which were traced faint lines – of worry? overwork?

Dorothy introduced them. He silently nodded and grasped each hand in turn. 'Our fifth associate, Mrs Mabel Grill – sorry, Mrs Mabel Elderkin – has another assignment.'

Salter looked quizzically at Stuart. 'A newly married man? My congratulations, Mr Elderkin.'

Stuart reddened, wriggling his shoulders. 'Thank you, Mr Salter.'

'Please take a seat.' Dorothy indicated the chair at the head of the table.

Salter's small, blue eyes stared at each of them in turn. His nose was neat, his lips full and there was a faint cleft in his chin. Not unattractive. He remained silent.

'How can we help you, Mr Salter?' Frank asked.

He took a deep breath, his barrel chest pushing against the expensive white shirt. 'Before I explain the reason for my being here, I must be assured all I tell you will remain within these four walls.'

What on earth was he going to say? They'd all been intrigued when he'd insisted he must meet them here, at

Greyfriars House, and they mustn't tell anyone he was seeking their help.

'We've had plenty of practise in keeping silent lately,' Frank said.

Stuart raised his eyebrows and Dorothy twisted her lips.

'Ah, something to do with that missing boy you found? I thought there was more to all those deaths than appeared in the press.'

She held her breath, but Frank kept a straight face and didn't say anything.

'That's why I'm asking for your help. I was very impressed when you found David Pemberton.' He turned to look at her. 'And I must say, Miss Bowman, I'm full of admiration for the way you fought off the mad headmaster last September.' His eyes twinkled. Perhaps he admired more than her fighting abilities.

'I can assure you of our complete discretion,' Frank said, casting a swift glance at the other three, who nodded in agreement.

'Would you like some coffee before you tell us why you came, Mr Salter?' Dorothy asked.

He shook his head. 'Perhaps afterwards. I need your help. I don't want to involve the police, not at this stage. If you discover what I fear, then of course, they'll have to be told.'

Frank leant forward, his green eyes gleaming with interest. 'What is it you're concerned about?'

Salter placed his hands on the edge of the table and leant towards them. 'I don't know if you're aware, but I mainly live at Selbourne Park, near Orford. Five years ago, I built an exclusive holiday camp in the grounds. It's different, adults only, no one below eighteen years of age allowed. The entertainment is more sophisticated.'

12

What did sophisticated entertainment mean?

Frank's eyes widened and a slight smile appeared.

Salter laughed. 'I can see what you're thinking, Mr Diamond. Nothing like that.' His face darkened. 'In the last two years, 1969 and 1970, during the holiday season, two young women, both staff members, suddenly disappeared, one each year. We notified the police, but they weren't interested, as they both took all of their belongings with them. They haven't been seen since, and they haven't contacted their parents.'

'Is there anything to connect them?' Frank asked.

Salter looked down at his hands; his knuckles shining white through the stretched skin. 'Yes. Me. I'm a widower, and I have to admit I'd taken a shine to both the girls. I know they were much younger than me, but they were – are, nice girls, they reminded me of...' He broke off, looking as if he wished he hadn't said that. 'I didn't think too much of it when Lucy went, although I was upset, but when Bobby, Roberta, disappeared last year, I began to wonder.' He paused. 'Do you mind if I smoke?'

Dorothy pushed an ashtray towards him. He took a gold cigarette case and lighter out of an inner breast pocket. As he opened the case, diamonds in the form of his entwined initials, S and S, caught the light. He saw Stuart staring at it. 'Cost me a packet. I lost one just like it a few years back. I had to replace it: my late wife gave me the original.'

He lit a cigarette and greedily sucked on its untipped end, then blew a stream of blue smoke towards the ceiling.

The smell of cheap tobacco filled the room.

Frank wrinkled his nose.

'Sorry, I got used to gaspers in the war. Can't stand these new mild, tipped cigarettes.'

'Woodbines?' Frank asked.

He nodded.

'What do you think has happened to the girls?' Laurel asked.

He turned to look at her, the lines in his forehead deepening. 'I'm not sure, but something makes me think... they've been murdered. I'm worried sick another woman might go missing this summer.'

Chapter 3

Frank looked at Salter, trying to make up his mind about him. There was a sheen of sweat on his high forehead, and he'd had difficulty framing the words about the missing women. As soon as Salter wanted to meet them Frank had contacted Detective Inspector Revie, who they'd worked with on the David Pemberton case, to ask if he'd any background information on Salter. Whenever Salter was in the news, the press always mentioned he had mixed with criminals in his youth, and married the sister of a well-known London gangster. Revie had said Salter had mended his ways and was now a respectable member of society, well known for charitable work.

'Can you tell us a little about the missing women, Mr Salter?' he asked.

Salter gulped and fiddled with the knot of his tie. 'Yes. The first to go missing, in 1969, was Lucy Milne. She was working as part of the entertainment team; you know, the ones who organise games and activities. They wear striped jackets, green and white, a cut above the jackets of other holiday camps. We call them Stripeys.'

'How long had she worked at the camp?' Laurel asked.

'She'd been with us three years, but it was her first year at Sudbourne Camp. She came in February, 1969. I have a policy: only the key workers stay in one place for any length of time, all the juniors rotate round the camps.'

'Keeps them on their toes, does it?' Stuart asked.

Salter inclined his head. 'Stops them forming cliques and getting more interested in each other than in the campers.'

'What did Lucy look like?' Frank asked.

'I'll show you a photo. All the staff have photos taken at the beginning of the season; we put them on the main notice board so campers can see who they are.' He bent down, picked up his briefcase and, holding it on his knee, opened it so the contents were hidden. He took a coloured photo, four by six inches, from it.

'How old is she?'

'She was twenty-two when she went missing.'

'So, twenty-four now.'

Salter nodded, gazing at it for several seconds before he passed it to him.

She was a lovely girl with an oval face, a pale smooth complexion, a small straight nose and beautiful almond-shaped eyes, clear blue with dark eyebrows matching her almost black hair. Frank's heart contracted. She reminded him of Carol Pemberton, the mother of the missing boy, David. He'd been strongly attracted to her, and let their relationship go too far. Lucy had the same blue eyes, black hair and porcelain complexion. There was a slight smile on her face, but she looked a serious girl, and although he shouldn't make a judgement based on a photograph, she looked honest and trustworthy. He passed it to Laurel.

'Lucy looks a nice girl,' she said. 'Have you a photo of Roberta?'

Salter nodded. He was becoming more uncomfortable by the minute and he wiped his forehead with a handkerchief. 'Very warm in here.' He took out another photograph from the briefcase and passed this to him. 'Roberta Dodd, Bobby. She worked in the camp's office.'

This girl had the same colouring as Lucy. The face more elongated and the lips fuller, but the similarities between the two girls were striking. It couldn't be a coincidence, could it?

Frank passed the photograph of Lucy to Stuart and looked at the one of Roberta. 'Mr Salter, you said these girls reminded you of someone; it sounded to me as if this was someone you were fond of. Who did they remind you of?'

Salter glanced down at the briefcase he was still hugging. 'I, er...' He raised his head and looked at him. 'My late wife, Patsy.' His head dropped again. 'I'm sorry, I find this difficult to talk about.'

'When did Roberta go missing?' Frank asked.

'Er... last September, towards the end of the season.'

'Why have you left it until now to bring this case to us? It's the beginning of June; the camps must be busy already,' Frank said.

Salter put his briefcase on the floor and sat up straight. He looked offended, his small eyes narrowing. 'I have my reasons.'

'I suppose you were waiting to see if Roberta turned up?' Laurel said, smiling at him.

She obviously thought he was being too blunt, and was trying to retrieve the situation. There was something about the man he disliked; he couldn't put his finger on it, but was the man honest? Was he telling the complete truth?

Salter smiled back at Laurel. 'That's right. In fact, it was my son, Stephen, who persuaded me to take some action. He could see it was preying on my mind. He suggested bringing the problem to you.'

Salter seemed attracted to Laurel, but then who wouldn't be? Since she and Oliver Neave had started seeing each other, there was a new radiance about her. Was it Dr Neave, or Dr Neave's Labrador, Billy, that was the main attraction? He hoped it wasn't serious; he didn't want to lose his main partner. Perhaps he'd better try and be pleasant.

'Mr Salter, if we take the case, have you thought about how we should deal with the investigation? I can't believe you'd want us questioning staff or campers; it wouldn't be good for business, would it?'

Salter patted his face with a handkerchief again. He looked uncomfortable. 'You're right, it wouldn't. I said that to Stephen. If it gets out girls are disappearing from the camp, people will stop coming to us. I take pride in looking after our customers and making sure they're safe.'

Frank stood up. 'I suggest we have a coffee break, and if you don't mind, Mr Salter, I'd like to talk privately to the rest of the team. I have an idea I'd like to put to them.'

'Why not put it to them now?'

Frank shook his head. 'Bear with me, Mr Salter. I'll take you to the sitting room and we'll bring you some coffee. We'll be as quick as we can. We'll let you know if we'll take the case and if we do, how we'll deal with it, as you have no preference in the matter. Then you can decide if you want us to start working for you.'

Salter looked mutinous, his bottom lip sticking out. 'Very well, but don't take too long. I'm a busy man.'

He noticed, as he led Salter from the room, Laurel was giving Stuart an old-fashioned look, as much as to say: 'Who's being bossy now?'

Laurel finished a slice of Mabel's sponge cake, sliding a finger round the plate to gather up the last crumbs. Stuart Elderkin was doing the same. She'd missed Mabel's cooking last week; she hoped she wouldn't turn into a permanent housewife who devoted herself to making apple pies for Stuart. Not only did she make life easy for the rest of the team by doing all the cooking and housekeeping, but her homely and common-sense presence added a note of realism, which was sometimes needed.

Dorothy piled everything onto a tray. 'Right, Frank let's have your brilliant ideas. We can't keep him waiting too long.'

Frank looked at each of them in turn. 'I'm not completely sure we should take this case on. There's something about Salter I don't trust.' He paused, rubbing his upper lip. 'However, we haven't got a major case at the moment, although there are a few minor things we're working on — '

'I think we should take it,' Laurel said. 'Two women are missing. Suppose another goes missing this summer and we didn't help. I wouldn't be happy about that.'

Stuart was filling his pipe. 'Me, too. Also, it would be profitable; he's not short of money.'

'If we do take it, I think there's only one way we can successfully try and find out what happened to those girls.'

'So, what's your idea, Frank?' Stuart asked.

'I think you, me and Laurel will have to become part of the staff at Sudbourne Camp.'

There was a stunned silence.

Laurel laughed. 'I bet you've got me down as a Stripey coat! I wouldn't mind that — lots of physical activities; I can get really fit!'

'That's a frightening thought,' Frank said.

Stuart looked worried. 'We could be there weeks! Months! I don't think Mabel would be too keen on me being away for such a long time at the moment. After all, we've just come back from our honeymoon.'

Dorothy peered over her glasses. 'What about the rest of the business we've taken on? Who's going to look after that?'

'It's true, Frank. If we became undercover staff we wouldn't be able to come and go as we please. Personally, I wouldn't mind, I haven't got any serious ties,' Laurel said.

So, Oliver Neave wasn't that important. Good. 'I can see your reasoning, Stuart. Perhaps it would be best if Laurel and I take on this case, and leave you,' he nodded to Stuart, 'to carry on with the business at this end.'

Stuart sighed with relief. 'If you don't mind, Frank, that would be helpful.'

'Dorothy?'

She looked not only cross but offended; her arms tight over her chest and her mouth in a straight line.

'Dorothy?'

'I'd like to be considered for a role.'

Miss Piff – secret agent. Frank couldn't stop a laugh bubbling up.

'It's all right you sniggering, Frank Diamond, but I'd like to remind you I served in the war, I'm used to dealing with people and I could work in the camp's office; there's no better place for picking up gossip than the works office. Also, that's where Roberta worked. I'm not afraid of danger, and I'd like to play a more positive role in the agency. I'd like to think I've helped in bringing a murderer to justice, if that's what happened to these poor girls.'

Frank reached out and took her hand. 'Please forgive me, Dorothy, I had a mental picture of you wearing a deerstalker with a bloodhound on a leash.'

She gave a wry smile. 'If that's what I need to do to convince you I'm capable of detective work, I'll buy both immediately.'

'I think you'd be excellent, Dorothy' Laurel said. 'How about a Labrador instead of a bloodhound?'

Frank raised his eyebrows.

Laurel continued, 'However, I wouldn't want you to get into any of the situations I've managed to get myself into during the last two cases. Sometimes things go wrong, and if the girls have been murdered, whoever did it might not worry about adding a third victim to their list, if they thought you were a danger to them.'

Dorothy's chin came up. 'I faced danger during the war, and now, well... there isn't anyone I need to think about. I haven't anyone to be responsible for.' She looked at Laurel. 'I don't mean I'm not fond of all of you, and I'm proud of the work we've done... but you know what I mean.'

Stuart got up and patted her on the back. 'I think you'd be a great asset as an undercover office worker. Mabel and I can look after the business side while you're away sleuthing. Mabel's good with figures and my typing's not so bad. We can keep things ticking over.'

Dorothy looked at Frank. 'Well?'

Frank shook his head. 'It's a stitch up. I agree.'

Dorothy also got up and gave Frank a hearty kiss on the cheek. 'You won't regret it.'

Laurel pointed a finger at Frank. 'So, I'm a Stripey coat, Dorothy's in the office, but what role will you take?'

'Security? Possibly?'

'What do we do now?' Dorothy asked, looking pleased with herself.

'We put this to Mr Salter. He may not go for it, or he may baulk at the cost. Three of us on a permanent basis for possibly several weeks is going to be very expensive. Also, we'll need to be able to have regular meetings to exchange findings. It'll be complicated.'

Dorothy tapped the table with a pencil. 'H'm. We'll have to sleep in the camp, won't we?'

Frank nodded. 'If we don't, the rest of the staff will soon rumble us. I think we'll have to arrive one by one. Too suspicious if we all came together.'

'We mustn't appear to know each other,' Laurel said. 'Also, someone might recognise one of us; we did get a lot of publicity from the last two cases.'

'I'm beginning to think this might not work,' he said.

Dorothy slapped the table with her palm. 'Don't be such a pessimist, Frank. Let's put it to Salter and see what he says.'

He smiled at her. 'You're dying to have a go, aren't you?'

'I certainly am. Shall I get Mr Salter?'

The other three nodded.

Laurel watched Sam Salter's face as Frank told him his thoughts on how they would investigate the case. At first, he frowned, then he nodded knowingly, and when Frank suggested Laurel might be suitable as a Stripey coat, he laughed.

'I shall have to vet your suitability, Miss Bowman.'

'What for? My skills as a detective, or had you something else in mind?'

His face reddened and he pulled at his tie. 'Sorry, out of order.'

'I'll forgive you – just this once.'

'Miss Piff,' Frank said, 'would you like to explain your possible role?'

Dorothy straightened her back. 'If you could find me a job in the main office, Mr Salter, I'm sure I'd be able to hear many matters the secretaries wouldn't perhaps discuss with you. What do you think?'

Salter nodded, sweeping his hand round the room. 'I can see you're a tower of efficiency, you'd be an asset in the office, plus sleuthing at the same time; sounds a bargain to me.'

Dorothy's smile got even broader. 'Thank you. Are there a lot of staff in the office?'

'There are usually four; I've a personal secretary, Miss Tweedie, Belinda Tweedie, she's been with me for several years, and three other girls, two full time and one part time. That's one area I don't move staff round. They deal not only with Sudbourne Camp, but with correspondence between the other camps and my office in London. Stephen, my son, is based there.' His voice rang with pride as he named him.

'Mr Salter, we'll need a list of all the staff who were at the camp both in 1969 and 1970. At this stage I think we'll have to assume holiday makers were not involved in the disappearance of these women. However, if we draw a blank with the staff, would it be possible to have a list of the holiday makers who were in the camp in both 1969 and 1970, on the dates the women disappeared?'

Salter blew out air through pursed lips. 'It's possible.'

'Excellent,' Frank said.

He hadn't used his favourite word all day. His mood must be improving, she thought.

Salter tapped his nose. 'This is opportune, I was going to advertise for a new secretary; one of the girls is leaving soon, going to have a baby. I can speed that up.' He seemed to catch the look on Dorothy's face. 'Don't worry, she won't lose out. I think you could start next week. Is that all right?'

'Excellent,' she said.

Frank bit his lip.

Salter leant forward, rubbing his fingers over his forehead. 'As for you, Miss Bowman, how's your swimming?'

'Pretty good. I've got a life-saving certificate and I took girls for swimming lessons when I was head of PE.'

Salter rubbed his hands. 'This is getting better and better. That'll be your speciality. There's an indoor and an outdoor pool. I'm going to get two for the price of one, even if the one will cost me an arm and a leg. I'll get two days' work out of all of you: a day's detecting and a day in the office or the swimming pool.'

She didn't think this was the right approach. 'You'll need to make sure we have plenty of free time so we can carry out undercover investigations. We won't be able to do much detective work if one of us is slaving over a typewriter all day, and my skin is starting to wrinkle in the swimming pool.'

Salter turned to Frank. 'She's a bit of a tartar is your Miss Bowman. What about you, Mr Diamond? What job do you think you should be pretending to do?'

'I thought you may need some extra security.'

Salter pursed his lips. 'H'm. Not sure that would work. Wouldn't put you in line for much gossip, would it? Have you any other talents, apart from sleuthing?'

'Mr Diamond is an excellent cook,' Laurel chimed in. Frank glared at her.

'That's a great idea! We can always do with an extra hand in the kitchen. Any specialities?'

'He's red hot on omelettes!' Stuart said.

'Really? This could work well. I could bring you in as a speciality chef. Omelettes only, for any camper who didn't like anything on the menu; then you wouldn't have to do any of the mundane work. I often introduce changes many of the staff think are barmy. You could be one of them. Sounds good. What do you say?'

His boyish enthusiasm and the way he'd responded to their suggestions made him seem more likeable, even attractive – especially labelling Frank as a barmy chef.

He didn't look pleased. 'It could work.' He seemed to be musing on the idea. 'I only cook with the best ingredients, and I insist on unsalted butter.'

Salter laughed. 'I think I'll be the first to sample one of your omelettes, Mr Diamond.'

The mood in the room was bordering on jolly. Too jolly, if these girls had been murdered. 'We'll need to have the same day off each week; I presume staff only get a day a week. It means we can meet back here, see what information we've found, and plan our next moves,' Laurel said.

Salter nodded. 'Let's make it Saturdays, it's change-over day. I'll see to that.' He rose as if he thought the meeting was over and everything complete.

'Mr Salter,' Frank said, 'we'll also need to have a safe place we can meet at the camp. We may need to get together, however briefly, if something important turns up. How will you manage that, without making the rest of the staff suspicious?'

Salter sat down, frowning. 'Difficult. I was thinking of putting all three of you in chalets, but if I put you together that wouldn't be right, would it?'

Laurel thought she might feel safer if she knew Frank was next door. However, 'No, this is going to be tricky. I don't think you can do that.'

Salter turned to Dorothy. 'What about you staying in the main house, Miss Piff? No other staff, except Stephen, have a room there. Then Mr Diamond and Miss Bowman can easily come to the house without the rest of the camp staff seeing them.'

Dorothy pursed her lips. 'What excuse would you give for my staying there?'

'I don't need one. I'm the boss.'

Dorothy shook her head. 'That you may be, Mr Salter, but it won't do.'

Salter turned to the others, gazing upwards in frustration.

'One way round it,' Laurel said, 'would be if you said Miss Piff was a relative, a cousin, perhaps, who was helping you out in the office.'

Dorothy nodded in approval.

'Brilliant!' He turned to Dorothy. 'Does that satisfy you?'

'Yes, but you'll have to drop the Miss Piff and call me Dorothy.'

'Of course. Good, then it's all settled. I need to get going. Stephen is going to move from London and stay at the camp for the rest of the season, or until you lot solve the case.' He got up.

'Before you go,' Frank said, 'we need to finalise the days we arrive at the camp and also you need to accept our terms. This is going to be extremely expensive, Mr Salter. Three detectives full time, six days a week and we'll be working on our day off.'

Dorothy's chest puffed out at the three detectives and she gave a beaming smile to everyone.

Salter sat down again with a heavy sigh.

Dorothy moved to her desk. 'I'll type up the details now. Won't take me long.' She lit a cigarette, inhaled deeply and put paper and duplicates into her typewriter.

'Thank you, Cousin Dorothy.' Salter followed Dorothy's example, once more took out his gold cigarette case with the diamond initials and lit up a Woodbine.

Laurel bit her lip and put a hand over her mouth.

'My pleasure, Cousin Sam,' Dorothy replied. 'And don't forget to get those lists to us as soon as possible: all the staff who were in the camp when both those girls went missing. Also, could you get us their schedules for those days, with the times they came on and off duty? We need as much detail as possible, please.'

'Yes,' Frank added, 'and I don't think we should finalise our roles until we know which staff were present when both women disappeared. We need to attach ourselves to likely suspects.'

Salter's shoulders drooped. 'Yes, I can see that.' He smiled at Dorothy as she rattled the keys of her typewriter. 'You'll be all right, Cousin Dorothy; Belinda Tweedie has been with me for years. So, you can start as soon as you're ready. Not that Miss Tweedie could be a suspect.'

'Everyone's a suspect until we find out what happened to these women,' Frank said.

Slater's eyes bulged. 'You'll be saying I'm a suspect next.'

There was an awkward silence. 'You'll need to do the lists yourself, Mr Salter. You mustn't get anyone else involved, even Miss Tweedie,' Frank said.

Salter's face sagged. 'I'll get Stephen to do them, he's excellent at organisation. He's coming down today.' He beamed at them. 'He planned most of Sudbourne Camp, you know. He's full of bright ideas. I'll telephone you when he's finished it.' He looked at his watch. 'It's later than I thought. I need to get back soon,' he said, looking at Dorothy, still tapping the keys of her typewriter.

'Don't go near Aldeburgh,' Stuart said. 'The Music Festival's in full swing; the town will be packed out.'

Salter sighed.

'Would you like some tea while you're waiting?' Laurel asked.

He looked at her with a pitiful expression. 'Got any Scotch?'

Chapter 4

Tuesday, June 8, 1971

Laurel felt lucky as she backed her Ford Cortina into the only parking spaces left in front of the fishermen's huts in Aldeburgh; Stuart was right, the town was busy. She looked at her wristwatch: eleven, she was early. Did she want to read the novel Frank had loaned her? The Spy Who Came In From the Cold? She'd brought it with her, but she was unsettled, unable to read it while she waited for Oliver. She looked out of the car window; the sky was overcast, but at least it wasn't foggy or raining. She decided she needed some fresh air, got out and walked to the centre of the town along the seafront.

Was this the right time to tell Oliver she liked him, liked his company, but probably didn't want to take their relationship to the next level? She blew out her cheeks. It was the evening she'd spent with him last week — it had made her unsure of her feelings for him.

'Would you like to come to dinner tomorrow? I can cook us a meal and there are some good things on the telly,' he'd said.

'Oh, er, yes. That's lovely, Oliver. I didn't know you could cook.'

'I was a boy scout, you have to be resourceful.'

She wondered if Frank had ever belonged; somehow, she didn't think so. 'What are you planning on watching?'

'There's a good film: The Wreck of the Mary Deare, and later there's a programme about James Thurber.'

'I love Thurber.'

'Yes, I know you do. I'm not sure if I get his sense of humour.'

Oliver lived in the higher part of the town, near the library. A well-kept, detached house, built in the 1930s. The home-cooked meal was a meat pie from Smith's bakery, boiled potatoes and frozen peas. Nothing wrong with that, Smith's pies were excellent, but she couldn't help comparing it with the meal Frank had cooked for her on the night she had come to his cottage, her mind scrambled by the discovery of the body of Dr Luxton, the director of Springfield Power Station. She and Oliver had found his body.

Frank's meal had been simple, fillet steak in a delicious sauce, salad and lovely bread. Oliver's cooking couldn't hold a candle to Frank's, and that wasn't the only thing he couldn't hold a candle to. She was being unfair, the bottle of Medoc was delicious, but it was needed to help down the meal. He'd left the pie too long in the oven, it even smelt dry.

After coffee Oliver switched on the television. 'Shall we relax while we watch it?' he asked, as he threw two cushions on the floor, and dragged a reluctant Billy to the kitchen. He was obviously eager to take their love making to the next stage. Was she? They'd got to the French kissing and some breast caressing stage, and she couldn't deny she'd enjoyed the feeling of someone admiring and desiring her. There hadn't been another man since her ex-fiancé, Simon. She'd fancied the pants off him — literally. She still missed his physical closeness and the exciting sex. But she didn't miss him. She'd never forgiven him for labelling her murdered sister Angela a tart and deserving of all she got.

Oliver pulled her gently onto the rug beside him and plumped up the cushions. Was she ready to go further? All the way? She wasn't a teenage virgin, she was thirty and wanted, needed, to be made love to by an attractive man, a man she liked and perhaps could love.

Their bodies fitted well together. His lips were firm and dry. She couldn't stand a sloppy kisser. She opened her mouth for his tongue and he slid his hand under her t-shirt and pulled a bra strap down, caressing her breast. She wriggled under him as he placed a leg between hers. She realised she wanted the sex, but it was sex she wanted, not Oliver. She was using him. As she kissed him, part of her brain said go on any way, but another part said if she did and Oliver was serious, and she thought he was, would she be able to commit herself to him? She wasn't sure.

She pushed him away. 'Sorry, Oliver. Isn't it time for the Thurber programme?'

'Christ, Laurel, what are you playing at?'

He was angry, his normally placid face red and vexed.

'I'm sorry. I panicked; it's a bit too soon.'

'Too soon? How long do you want? Laurel, I'm willing to wait, but I need to know how you feel. I'm crazy about you. If you want to wait for marriage, I don't mind that, as long as it's me you're marrying.'

Tears pricked her eyes. He was a kind, good man, and she liked him enormously.

'That sounds like a proposal.'

'It is.' He got up and gently pulled her into his arms. 'What do you say?'

She kissed him. 'Thank you, Oliver. You've paid me a great compliment.'

'And?'

'I need some time. It's a very serious decision to take. As you know, I love my job; I wouldn't want to give it up.'

He was silent.

'We may have a big case starting soon. Perhaps when that's over...'

He hugged her tight. 'Let's meet next week for lunch. We can talk more then.'

She sighed. She wasn't any clearer in her mind as to what she should, or wanted, to do about Oliver. She turned back towards her car. She chatted to Mr Fryer, the fisherman, in his hut, admiring the acrobatics of the seagulls as they dived to catch the fish skins he threw in the air for them. She saw Oliver, Billy lolloping at his side, walking towards her. She took a deep breath. He was handsome, she did like him and as for Billy... No, she needed to give herself more time.

'Laurel. You look lovely, as always.'

She'd miss the flattery. 'Thank you, Oliver.' She made a fuss of Billy, whose tail was whirring round like an electric whisk.

'Do you fancy a walk to Thorpeness and a quick lunch at the pub there? I've got to get back for a three pm surgery.'

She wasn't keen on that walk as they'd pass the house they had found Dr Luxton's body in, but this wasn't the time to disagree and she'd have to toughen up. At the rate they were finding bodies, in a few years, if she kept on being wimpy, there would be too many places she'd have to avoid.

'Good idea, Oliver. What do you say, Billy?'

Billy wasn't disturbed by dead bodies or anything else. As long as he got his walks, and several meals a day he was in a perpetual good humour. His tail lashed her legs and he pulled on his lead as they headed down the promenade towards Thorpeness.

It was a brisk walk back after a quick lunch at the pub.

They stopped at Laurel's car.

Oliver glanced at his watch. 'Sorry I've got to dash. Are you free Friday evening? We could see a film and have dinner afterwards.'

Now was the time. 'I'm sorry, I won't be able to make Friday. I'll be away on the case I mentioned for several weeks. I'll call you when I get back.'

His smile faded and his expression became like Billy's when he wanted a walk and it wasn't forthcoming. 'Where is this case? I hope it isn't going to be dangerous, like the last one. You could have been...' He stopped. 'Sorry, I know I've no right to say that, but I do care about you, Laurel.'

She felt a heel, and she didn't want to hurt him. 'I'm afraid I can't tell you anything about it.' She swallowed. 'I've been thinking... about us.'

His eyes lit up. 'So have I, Laurel. I think about you constantly.' He frowned. 'There isn't time to talk now. Can't we meet before the case starts?'

Her mouth was dry, her heart was thumping against her ribs. This was worse than dealing with a dead body. 'I think I need some time to myself, Oliver. Being away on this case will give me that.' She turned away and put her car key into the lock; she looked over her shoulder. 'I'll give you a ring in a week or so and let you know I'm all right.' Two pairs of soulful eyes looked at her. She would miss him... and Billy.

Frank and Stuart got out of his Avenger in the car park of the Royal Society for the Protection of Birds (RSPB) at Minsmere. They'd decided to visit the reserve today, before they became totally involved with the Salter case. Stuart had persuaded Frank to join the Society and promised he'd take him round the reserve at the first opportunity. It had to be today or it wouldn't take place in the foreseeable future.

'I feel a bit of a dick-head walking around with a pair of binoculars bouncing on my chest, and wearing this khaki gear,' Frank said. Stuart had persuaded him he needed camouflage clothes; he'd die if he met anyone he knew.

Stuart stopped, frowned, and looked him up and down. 'You make a lovely twitcher, but that colour doesn't do you any favours. Still, I don't think you're going to meet any fair maidens today.' He nudged Frank. 'I don't know, though, here's Miss Trimley, one of the volunteers. She may take a fancy to you.'

Miss Trimley resembled a mole: short, spiky, dark hair, and a pair of horn-rimmed spectacles sitting on the end of a pointed nose. They exchanged pleasantries.

'So, what do you think? She's red hot on different waders,' Stuart said, trying not to smirk.

He gave Stuart an icy stare. 'I thought I'd miss you when we went to Sudbourne, now I'm not so sure.'

'I was only pulling your leg. Actually, there are some really nice girls, well, young women, who are keen on birds. It'd be a good way of meeting a girl. You could chat them up when you sit in a hide together. You can get quite cosy on those wooden benches as you look at some geese.'

He laughed. 'Not everyone can be as lucky in love as you, Stuart. You've had more than your fair share. Two wives and both of them crackers.'

They walked into the main office and shop, signed in, and Stuart handed him a map of the reserve. 'Shall we make for the Scrape? See if we can find some avocets?'

Frank nodded.

As they walked through the car park sand martins whizzed round their heads and dived into holes in the sandy bank, their mouths full of insects. Stuart pointed to a path through a wooded area.

'I wish I was coming with you to Sudbourne; this case is really interesting. I'm looking forward to meeting Salter's son tomorrow and seeing the list of suspects. Perhaps I was a bit rash saying I didn't think I should be involved.'

Frank felt the same. He'd miss Stuart; they'd worked well together when they were policemen and then on their first big case as private detectives. 'I'll miss you too, Stuart, but we'll need you to do background checks on all the suspects as well as keeping tabs on ongoing cases. I'll contact Inspector Revie. We might as well use this special relationship between us; see if the powers that be will keep their word.'

Stuart grimaced. 'I don't think they dare chicken out on that. After all they suggested it to keep us quiet.'

Whenever Frank thought about how they'd been silenced after the David Pemberton case a sour taste invaded his mouth. 'You can use Revie to get background information on all the suspects and Salter himself, and possibly his son, Stephen, if we find out he was around when the girls disappeared.'

'Really? Why would Salter bring this case to us if he was responsible for the missing girls?'

He shrugged. 'After the things we've seen in the last two cases, I... well, I feel I can't trust anyone.'

Stuart shook his head. 'I don't think I feel quite as suspicious as you. Why would he stir up trouble if he'd been responsible for these girls going missing? If he was, he's an idiot, bringing it to our front door.'

He sighed. 'You're probably right, Stuart. I'm getting jaded. How far is the Scrape?'

'Ten minutes. What do you think about Laurel and Dr Neave? Is it serious? He's a good chap and Laurel deserves to have someone she can rely on. That fiancé of hers was a right shit. It must have been tough, him breaking off their engagement because his family were ashamed Laurel's sister was murdered.'

First an inquisition on possible female companions, then this – just what he didn't want to think about: Laurel leaving the firm to shack up with the doc and his Labrador. 'She didn't seem too worried at the thought of several weeks at Sudbourne Camp being a Stripey coat and not seeing Dr Neave.'

Stuart pulled a face. 'True, true, I was a bit surprised. I thought I could see another wedding coming up.'

Frank shuddered. Why was the thought so distasteful?

'Mind you, Mabel didn't think it was on. I said to her, "Why ever not?"' He tittered. 'Know what she said?'

'I'm not a mind reader.'

'Keep your shirt on. She said she didn't think Oliver Neave was exciting enough for Laurel. Felt she needed someone with more passion... she didn't mean in bed, well she did, but she meant passion for life, someone with as much love for danger and justice as Laurel has. She amazes me, my Mabel does, what she comes out with. She clicked with Laurel the first time she met her, when she came into the kitchen of Blackfriars School as Senior Mistress. God, that seems like a lifetime ago, and yet it's not a year since we all met. Changed my life, I can tell you. Has it changed yours, Frank?'

He stopped and looked at Stuart, smiled and gripped his arm. 'It has, and for the better. We've been through some dangerous times: I killed a man, a trained assassin;

Laurel has escaped death twice; Mabel nearly died; Dorothy lost her twin sister and you married your heart's desire. We've formed a detective agency, found a lost boy and now we're starting on another case and who knows what we'll discover? This is what I love: the unknown, the possible crime, the murderer brought to retribution, justice for the victims and their families. To me, the worst thing is not knowing what has really happened; however horrible the real facts are, they can't be any worse than the imaginings of the ones left behind.'

Stuart was looking at him, his brow wrinkled with concern. 'You take it to heart, don't you? I think you need to find some other... interest... you need to meet a few more people who aren't obsessed with crime and death. Get a balance in your life.'

He smiled. 'Perhaps I'll form a relationship with an avocet or even a shag.'

Stuart guffawed. 'Mabel hates me using that word, even for a bird. She says they're all cormorants.'

Wonderful, crystal-ball gazing Mabel. Oliver Neave wasn't exciting enough for Laurel? He hoped she was right.

Chapter 5

Wednesday, June 9, 1971

Laurel went into the garden to look for Dorothy; Stephen Salter was due at eleven and it was already ten thirty. Dorothy would need to get out of her gardening gear into something more suited for the role of chief administrator and soon-to-be undercover detective. The sea-mist had made for a gloomy beginning to the day, but now the sun was shining and the garden was full of bird song and the heady perfume of roses.

Dorothy was kneeling on the grass weeding a border, a rose bush in full bloom above her head. She muttered as she viciously attacked weeds with a hand-fork.

'Dorothy! Time you packed up. Salter junior will be here soon.'

Dorothy tried to get up, but strands of her hair caught in the lower branches of the bush. 'Bugger!'

'Hang on! Let me help you.' Laurel tried to untangle Dorothy's hair; but a thorn jabbed at her finger, bringing blood. 'Bugger!'

They both laughed.

Dorothy scrambled up. 'Love gardens — hate gardening. This was Emily's forte and the roses were her passion. Mind you, I think it was their names that seduced her: Madame Hardy, Maiden's Blush, and this beauty, Madame Isaac Perriere.' She cut a rose from the bush with her secateurs and passed it to Laurel.

She buried her nose in it. The petals felt like silk, the scent overpowering. 'I can understand her addiction.'

Dorothy brushed down her corduroy trousers and started to collect tools, placing them in a hessian bag. 'I think I'll have to get a gardener or the twitch will get completely out of control.'

'Twitch? Sounds like a nervous disease.'

Dorothy pointed at a half-decimated clump of grass. 'That horror. Creeps round all over the place. I hate it.'

'I wouldn't mind helping you, Dorothy, although the garden will be neglected for the next few weeks.'

Dorothy sighed. 'Yes, and I don't think I can ask Stuart or Mabel to start weeding; they'll have enough to do as it is. Right, I'll go and get changed. I've set out the table for the meeting. I wonder what he'll be like, this Stephen Salter; a younger version of his dad?'

Laurel pulled a face. 'One is quite enough!'

Dorothy laughed. 'I know what you mean.'

She watched as Dorothy took her tools to the shed and went into the house. Trousers suited her; she wondered if she could persuade her to buy some for everyday wear. Skirts and minis were great, but for detective work you sometimes needed different clothes and trousers were useful, especially in tight situations. If she'd worn trousers the day she went to lunch at Tucker's she wouldn't have had so much trouble with Hager. Who was she kidding? But he wouldn't have got to her knickers so quickly. She decided she didn't want to think too deeply about their last case. They'd found David Pemberton; better to forget the rest.

Today she'd decided on a sober navy cotton skirt and plain white blouse. Salter Senior was a flirt, and if Salter Junior took after him, she wanted to give him a no-nonsense message. She didn't want any more complications. Poor Oliver, he'd looked shattered when she said she couldn't see him for several weeks. She did like him, he was attractive, good company... and there was Billy. She puffed out her cheeks, trying to lower the tension in her body. When this case was over she'd definitely ask Dorothy if she could have a dog at Greyfriars. And if she said no? Perhaps she'd look for a nearby cottage. She shook her head. She didn't want to leave Dorothy alone; it was too soon after Emily's death, and who would look after her dog when she was on a case?

She strode towards the house.

Frank opened the door of his Avenger and exchanged boots for a pair of black suede shoes. He'd gone for a walk over the heath before driving from his cottage to the meeting. He'd needed a breath of sea-air, as he tried to inject positive vibes into his brain about the new case. He wasn't looking forward to meeting Stephen Salter: he'd instinctively disliked Sam Salter and the thought of a younger version was not enticing.

He wished Stuart was on the detective team at the camp and not Dorothy. He liked and admired her, but Dorothy the detective? She could be blunt at times, and as for subtlety... not one of her strong points. Was he being unfair? Was he a chauvinist? He'd got used to the three of them working on cases: Laurel, Stuart and himself, with Dorothy and Mabel as back-up. If there was something sinister in the disappearance of these girls, it might become dangerous, and if one of them alerted the murderer they were on to him or her, it could prove fatal. Laurel got herself into tight corners, but she was quick-witted, fit, strong and incredibly brave. Suppose Dorothy inadvertently revealed her true purpose to the murderer, if there was one. How would she react in a tight corner? Could, or should, he talk her out of it before it was too late? He bit his lip and looked at his watch. Had he time to talk this over with Laurel before Salter Junior arrived?

He hadn't. When he went into the main office, everything and everyone was ready for the meeting. Dorothy had set out six place settings: writing and blotting paper, pencils and water glasses. He could hear Mabel banging metal in the kitchen, no doubt getting a tray of goodies ready for a coffee break at a suitable moment in the meeting; Stuart was fiddling with his pipe, Laurel straightening the chairs; Dorothy came into the room with a water-jug and began pouring water into the glasses.

The front-door bell pealed. Dorothy put the jug in the centre of the table and made for the front door.

He pointed to one of the side chairs. 'Salter can sit there. It was a mistake to put Salter Senior at the head. It made him feel in charge and, even more important than that, he thought he was.'

Laurel gave him a quizzical look. 'You've taken against them, haven't you?'

He mentally kicked himself. Francis Xavier Diamond, you are pre-judging the man, his mother's voice echoed in his head. 'No, but I don't trust Salter Senior.'

There were murmurings in the hall, then Dorothy opened the door and a young, slight-framed man, dressed in a dark grey suit and white shirt, entered. He was about the same height as Frank himself, five feet eleven, with dark brown hair standing up in a longish crew cut. His blue eyes smiled at them, and he held out his hand, first to Mabel, then Laurel, Stuart and lastly himself.

'Stephen Salter, so pleased to meet you.'

The handshake was firm, the skin dry, his smile lit up his face, changing it from pleasant to handsome. There was no doubt about it, the first impression was of

41

attractiveness and charm and, glancing at his partners, he was sure that was their impression too.

Stephen Salter sat down on the appointed chair and took a wodge of paper from his briefcase. 'This is a most unusual place to have as the headquarters of a detective agency, but it's a beautiful old house. How did you come to choose it?'

Frank nodded to Dorothy, who was smiling benignly at Salter. 'This is my house. When Miss Bowman and Mr Diamond decided to form a detective agency I offered Greyfriars House as the base. It may seem isolated, but so far we haven't been short of work.'

Salter nodded. 'You've built up a formidable reputation in a short time. I'm grateful you've taken on this case. I'm worried about my father, who is concerned another woman might disappear from the camp.'

'I believe you've brought details of the staff who were at the camp when these women went missing,' Frank said.

Salter tapped the papers and passed a single sheet to each of the team. 'I've listed the staff who were present when both women disappeared on this sheet, but I've also further sheets giving you more details on each individual.'

This guy was efficient. Someone he could work with, unless...

'I don't suppose you were at the camp when the women disappeared?' he asked.

Salter flushed. 'What are you implying?'

Was that a guilty reddening of the face? 'We must cover all angles. Would you expect anything less?'

Salter's face was serious. 'I can understand that, but surely if either I, or my father, were implicated we wouldn't have consulted you. Dad was upset when you implied he was also a suspect; he nearly called the whole thing off.'

Laurel leant towards him. 'I'm sure none of us think you or your father are involved, but if you were at the camp you might have some information that would be useful; perhaps some detail you hadn't realised was important. It's surprising how, when you start to talk and think about something in the past, suddenly new facts are remembered.'

Silver-tongued devil. She was good.

Salter's shoulders relaxed. 'Yes, of course. Thank you for explaining that.' He smiled at her, his face once again boyish and charming. 'I was at the camp when both girls went missing.'

'Can I ask why your father decided to continue with the case?' Frank asked.

Salter cast his smile on him. 'I told him if he didn't continue you might assume he'd something to hide; also, he is genuinely worried about what happened to these girls.'

He nodded. 'Fair enough. Shall we look at the list?'

It was brief, with no details of the people, just their names and their roles at the camp.

Charles Frost i/c Entertainments
Eleanor Minnikin i/c Chalets
Gareth Hinney i/c Grounds and gardens
Jim Lovell i/c Maintenance and Security
Belinda Tweedie Personal secretary to Sam Salter
Thomas Coltman Maintenance part-time

'I thought it was easier to keep the list brief so you could decide the undercover roles you will take. Also, today we could decide on when each of you will appear at the camp.' He turned to Dorothy. 'Dad said you'd agreed to take the role of a cousin and base yourself in the house. Is that correct?'

Dorothy, pink-cheeked, beamed at him. 'Yes, Laurel thought of that. So, I'll be your Aunt Dorothy,' she smirked.

'Wonderful! I haven't got any aunts. I hope you're going to spoil me?'

Frank started to feel nauseous. 'Good, that's settled.' He turned to Laurel. 'As Mr Frost is a suspect it looks as though you can take over the swimming pool, Laurel.' She nodded.

Salter looked at him. He was glad he didn't get a smile. 'So, Mr Diamond, what role do you think you should take? Dad said you fancied being part of the catering team, but as you can see, our chef is not a suspect, he's only been with us a year.'

Frank looked at the list again. 'Definitely not a chalet maid. There are two possibilities: maintenance or grounds. As do-it-yourself is not my forte, and I like gardening and have a good knowledge of plants—'

'Frank's got a degree in botany,' Stuart interrupted.

'Really?' Salter asked.

'Really,' he replied.

'I didn't know you liked gardening,' Dorothy interrupted.

'You didn't ask me.'

Dorothy turned to Laurel and made a face.

Salter looked bemused. 'So, that's settled. Miss Bowman will be a Stripey, Miss Piff a secretary... and aunt, and Mr Diamond will assist with the gardens and grounds.' He paused, his forehead furrowing. 'Perhaps it would be better if we said to Hinney we were bringing you in to work on the ornamental gardens of the house, and to assist him in the camp gardens; he's very possessive of his lawns, putting green, and tennis courts. How does that sound?'

Frank nodded. 'Does he know much about plants, or is he more of a machine gardener? Keen on stripes on the lawn and regimental rows of annuals?'

'He was a London parks' gardener before he came to us, so he's well-up with all the machine side, their use and maintenance, but he's a keen vegetable gardener, supplies the kitchen with herbs; he's got his own garden on site, asked if he could use a bit of waste land and seems to spend much of his day off tending that. Busman's holiday, if you ask me. Gives the veg away, mostly to the locals who work on the camp.'

'I think I'll be able to blag my way round any problems,' Frank said.

'Good. Now, let's fix the dates of your arrivals.'

Laurel and Stuart escorted Stephen Salter from the house and watched as he drove away.

'I fancy that car,' Laurel said. 'MGB?' It was a red sports car, with black leather seats.

Stuart blew out a stream of blue smoke into the sunlit air. He pointed the stem of his pipe at the disappearing car. 'MGB Roadster, says he's got a family car too, 1970 Jag, like his old man.'

'A family car?'

'Yes, wife and two kiddies in London. Doesn't look old enough, does he, for such a responsibility.'

She hadn't picked up he was married; she had to admit it wasn't just the car she'd fancied. Just as well he was unavailable, she thought, he was certainly attractive, both in looks and personality. She didn't need any more distractions. 'I didn't hear him mention that.'

'It must have been when you went to the kitchen to help Mabel.' He gave her a long look. 'Disappointed?' he asked. 'Remember your nice Dr Neave will be waiting for you when you get back from Sudbourne. You can't start playing fast and loose.'

She smiled and shrugged her shoulders. She was tempted to tell him about Oliver; Stuart was understanding and sensible. She wondered what his reaction would be. This introspection was getting boring – the sooner she got to Sudbourne and on the case, the better.

They went back to the others, who were all still round the dining table. Dorothy got up and started collecting the blotters. 'Great improvement on his father,' she said.

'I'll reserve judgement,' Frank said.

Laurel sighed. She wished Frank would lighten up a bit; ever since the last case he hadn't been his usual breezy self and she missed the repartee and sense of fun. He'd been soured by the attitude of those on high: preserving the government was more important than justice for the young boys who'd been abused by members of the establishment.

'I thought he was rather dishy,' she said.

Stuart shook his head as though in disapproval. 'Laurel, I told you he's married!'

Dorothy and Mabel stared at her, but Frank looked down at the table.

'What about Oliver? I thought you and he...' Dorothy trailed off.

She took a deep breath; now was the right time. 'Oliver's proposed.'

There was a collective intake of breath.

'Did you accept?' Dorothy asked, her eyes wide behind her spectacles.

'You won't leave us, will you, Laurel?' Mabel asked, looking worried.

'He's a good man, I like him,' Stuart said.

Frank didn't say anything, but he looked at her, his face a blank, showing no emotion.

Laurel sat down at the table. 'I probably shouldn't have said anything. I'm not sure Oliver would want you to know at this stage.'

'This stage?' Dorothy repeated.

'I haven't given him an answer yet. I thought I'd leave it until this case is over. I won't be able to see him for several weeks once we go undercover.'

'You can see him, dear,' Mabel said. 'You'll have Saturdays off; the meetings won't go on all day. There'll be the evening and—'

'The night!' interrupted Stuart, grinning as he started to fill his pipe.

Mabel slapped his hand.

'I don't want to leave the agency,' Laurel said.

'Is Dr Neave happy with that?' Frank asked, his voice clipped and cold.

Her stomach dropped. 'Probably not. He worries about me, especially after the last case.'

'Are you worried?'

'About getting into dangerous situations?'

'Yes.'

'No. I've learnt a lot during the past year. I think I'm more experienced, more able to judge a situation, but I have to admit the dangers I've faced have given me a buzz. I'm not sure if I'm suited to domesticity.' There, she'd said it out loud. It was true, she didn't want to just be a wife and mother, she needed more than that.

Frank didn't make any comment. He got up from the table and stretched. 'I need a walk. Anyone fancy a stroll over the heath to The Eel's Foot?' He looked at her, smiling, his green eyes full of mischief.

She was tempted to shake her head and go upstairs to her room and sulk. 'Yes, I'll get changed. Give me two minutes.'

As she left the room she could see the other three exchanging glances and Frank looking happier than before. She wasn't sure what to make of his change of mood, but she was grateful for it.

Chapter 6

Monday, June 14, 1971

Dorothy sat on the Lutyen-designed bench nursing a cup of tea; it was just gone six on a perfect summer morning. The bench was backed by a high brick wall with swathes of white rambling roses tumbling over the top; on either side of the bench, stone urns were filled with pink patio roses. She hoped Frank was prepared for a great deal of hard physical labour.

She'd arrived at Sudbourne House on Saturday, and as befitting a relative, she'd a weekend to settle in before she started her job in the camp's office today. Both Salters were most solicitous, making sure she was comfortable and had everything she wanted. Her room was spacious with a sofa, arm chair and a small table grouped together near a large window, as well as all the usual bedroom furniture and a luxurious double bed.

She'd free rein of the house and this morning, awake at five, she'd crept downstairs and made herself a pot of tea, drank one cup, and taken the second into the garden.

She got up and walked back across a wide lawn to the house. She wondered what the original Sudbourne Hall had been like; Stephen said it had been built in the seventeenth century, rebuilt in the late eighteenth, then left to go to rack and ruin and finally demolished in 1953.

The new house Sam Salter had built when he bought the estate in the late 1950s was impressive. She wondered if he could have been influenced by Stephen? It seemed restrained for his taste. Like the bench, it was also in the style of Lutyens, constructed of red brick with the edges picked out in white stone; long windows glittered, and tall chimneys towered above the three stories. It was all enchanting and far too relaxing, she thought; she was beginning to feel like a genuine favourite aunt. She'd better sharpen her mind before beginning her first day at the office.

Sam, she'd decided she'd think of him as Sam, held open the passenger door of his Jaguar.

'Hop in, I'll drive you round the camp so you can get your bearings before we go to the office. After all it's what a cousin would do, wouldn't he?'

She was getting tired of his going on about their false relationship. She smiled at him and nodded her head.

'What do you make of this Common Market business?' he asked, as he got behind the wheel. 'French want sterling to end. I don't think we should ditch the pound, do you?'

'I think there's a lot we're not being told,' she replied.

They left the grounds of the house through a brick archway, with a clock tower above and drove a short distance before reaching the entrance of the holiday camp, green-and-white striped flags bearing entwined double Ss, hanging limply in the still air.

'We should be able to drive round without seeing too many campers. Young people, especially honeymooners, like staying in bed,' he sniggered, giving her a suggestive look.

She was glad he wasn't a real relative.

Salter pointed to a low brick building spread out before them. 'Main reception and offices, where you'll be working, public telephone, lost property, and booking for coach trips, tennis courts and horse-riding.' He steered the car right. 'Visitors' car park – most of them come by car. Petrol station – we think of everything.'

'So it seems,' she said.

He turned the car left and pointed to a large building to his right. 'That's the Orford Building, main entertainments, small theatre, discotheque, coffee bar; indoor swimming pool and lots of other amusements for the campers. We show the latest films; got Little Big Man next week. Can't say I care for that Dustin Hoffman, short-arsed Jew if you ask me. Got a shop as well, so if you need anything just ask.'

As well as everything else he was a racist! However, she'd never been in a holiday camp before and had to admit she was snobby about them, but she could see why this kind of holiday would appeal: everything on hand and most things paid for. Very sensible.

To the left were two long rectangular gardens with a path bisecting them, and beyond another large building, a twin to Orford. 'What's in there, that building beyond the gardens?'

'Hold your horses, we'll come to that in a minute.' He pointed to the right. 'Tennis courts, outdoor pool, putting green and you can just about see the stables.'

He turned left along a wide road; on the right side, at the edge of the camp, was a long lake. 'Fishing and boating, and,' he pointed to the other side of the road, 'the chalets.'

Men in boats, despite the early hour, were dangling fishing lines into the water and a few campers were emerging from chalets and making their way to the other building she'd seen.

He slowed down and drove between two rows of chalets until they came to the large building. 'This is Southwold. It's got the main dining hall, kitchens and laundry, then there's a bar and coffee bar on the first floor, the staff canteen is in a separate block behind Southwold, and behind that are the staff chalets.' He turned the car left and they were back at the entrance. 'Well, what do you think?' he asked, as he pulled up in front of reception, a self-satisfied smile on his face.

'It's very well laid out, spacious and extremely well-kept. Congratulations, Mr Salter, I'm most impressed.'

He patted her knee; she steeled herself not to swipe his hand away.

'That's a good beginning, but don't start to enjoy yourself too much, you're here to do a job of work.'

Pompous man. 'In that case let's not waste any more time. Shall we go to the office?'

He scowled at her, turned off the ignition, got out of the car and walked towards the entrance of the reception.

She sniffed. Didn't take long for him to forget his manners, she thought. She opened her door.

He'd stopped at the top of the step, turned, shrugged, and sauntered back. 'Dear me, Cousin Dorothy, you'll have to be a bit quicker; we don't like snails in our office.'

She gritted her teeth. She wanted to tell him she preferred snails to slugs, especially big, slimy blond slugs. 'We can't all be dynamic, Sam. I think we'd better cut the cousin pre-fix, don't you? It doesn't sound natural.'

He grunted and held the door open for her.

There was a young, dark-haired woman behind the polished wooden reception desk.

'Good morning, Mr Salter.' A gleaming smile and then eyes demurely cast down. She knew how to please him.

'Good morning, Sally. Any problems today?'

'No, Mr Salter, everything seems to be going smoothly. No complaints so far.'

'Good, good.' He turned to Dorothy. 'Dorothy, meet Sally who's part of the office team. Everyone takes their turn on the reception desk. Sally, this is my cousin Dorothy, Miss Piff to you. She's going to help out until I can get someone to replace Freda.'

She shook hands with Sally. Did she fit the profile of the missing women? Dark hair but her eyes were brown, not blue. Not that they knew if the similarity between the two missing girls was important.

'Pleased to meet you, Sally. How long have you been working at Sudbourne?'

Sally looked up at the ceiling as though seeking divine help. 'Ooh. I think it's almost a year and a half, isn't it, Mr Salter?'

'If you say so. Let's go in and meet the rest of the team.' He pushed open a door behind the desk and they went into a spacious office with three desks, each equipped with electric typewriters, desk tidies, free-standing five-part file trays, and all the other bits and pieces a secretary needs. Duplicating machines and rows of grey filing cabinets were arranged against the back wall. To the right was an enclosed office, cut off from the main room by a glass partition, with Mr Sam Salter stencilled in gold on the door.

Another young woman was seated at the nearest desk. She stopped typing as they came into the room. 'Dorothy, meet Cindy.' He gave the same introduction as before.

She went to Cindy's desk and shook her hand. Cindy was small, with a frail look to her, but her handshake was firm, and she looked her straight in the eyes. With mouse-brown hair and hazel eyes she didn't match the missing women, but she judged her to be a sensible soul. She hoped she was right. Sally looked a bit of a flibberty-gibbet.

53

'Where's Miss Tweedie?'

'She's in your office, Mr Salter.'

He strode to his office door and opened it. Dorothy was close behind, curious to see what Miss Tweedie was up to. After all she'd been at the camp when both girls went missing.

A well-built woman, about five feet six, was arranging a bowl of roses on an impressive wooden desk. She turned, clutching a long-stemmed red rose to her chest. 'Oh, Mr Salter! You gave me a shock. I wasn't expecting you so early.'

She was attractive, with a tad too much make-up, her blonde hair curling round her face. Her wide shoulders and full bosom were not enhanced by a baby-pink dress, which also clung to her full hips; her legs were slim with fine ankles and small feet. She seemed unsteady on her high heels, and Dorothy worried she might topple over.

Salter again made the introductions. 'Thank you for the flowers, Belinda.' He turned to Dorothy. 'Belinda spoils me, makes sure I want for nothing.'

She wondered how far Belinda went in pandering to his every need; she was certainly gazing at Salter as though he was at least a demi-god, and possibly Zeus himself.

Belinda simpered.

'Right, I'm going back to the house to do some work with Stephen.'

Belinda's face dropped. 'Would you like a cup of coffee before you go, Mr Salter?'

He seemed to hesitate, wrinkling his nose, as though this was a tricky decision. 'Thank you, Belinda, but Stephen is expecting me. I'll be in after lunch; I'll do any signing then.'

Belinda gave the flowers in the vase a final tweak. 'Very well, Mr Salter, everything will be ready for you.'

'Good. I want you to show Miss Piff how the office works, so she can be of use to you. She may see any confidential documents; after all you are family aren't you, Dorothy?'

Dorothy nodded graciously. 'Yes, Sam, always glad to help any of my family out.'

'I'll see you at lunch, Dorothy. Shall I send a car for you?'

'No thank you, Sam, it'll do me good to walk.'

He turned, smiled at Belinda. 'Miss Piff will be working mornings only, unless there's a need for some extra work.'

Belinda blinked and Dorothy couldn't be sure if her expression indicated pleasure she wouldn't be around when Salter came back after lunch or dissatisfaction at the thought Dorothy wouldn't be at her beck and call all day. Unless she was mistaken Miss Tweedie was harbouring lustful thoughts about Sam Salter, but she didn't get the same vibes from him. Was it relevant to the case if Belinda Tweedie had a thing about Salter? Could they, at one time, have been more than boss and secretary? Even if it wasn't relevant it was intriguing. When you thought about it, her blowsiness went quite well with his brashness.

Belinda stood at Salter's office door. 'Shall we start, Miss Piff?'

Time to start being a detective. 'Please call me Dorothy; I've heard so much about you from Sam, er Mr Salter, he doesn't know what he'd do without you, so I always think of you as Belinda.' She wouldn't get information unless she was friendly.

Belinda's face flushed. 'Really? That is nice, I'd do anything for him, you know. He's a wonderful man.' She led the way into the main office. 'Cindy, make two cups of coffee for me and Dorothy.'

Cindy scuttled to a corner of the room where an electric kettle sat on a melamine tray, with a jar of instant coffee and a tea-pot.

Belinda pulled another chair to her desk. 'Come and have a seat, Dorothy, we'll have a little chat before we start work.'

A chat or an interrogation? She'd been warned by Laurel not to plunge straight into questioning any suspects. 'Get them talking about themselves, just sit, nod and smile; you'll be surprised how much information you'll acquire,' she'd said. Right, let's see if it works.

Cindy was dispatched to take over the information desk from Sally, who was due for a break.

'Going to the shop, won't be long,' Sally said, as she popped her head round the door.

'Close the door, Sally, please.' It seemed Belinda didn't want anyone else overhearing their conversation.

Belinda put three spoonfuls of sugar into her coffee, took a tin from a desk drawer and offered Dorothy a coconut macaroon.

'No, thank you, Belinda. I ate an enormous breakfast.'

'Aren't you lucky, staying at Sudbourne? It's a lovely house, isn't it? Have you visited before?'

'Only once, when Mr Salter first moved in.' Must remember to tell him that. 'Have you been inside?' Whoops, there goes Laurel's training.

'Mr Salter had a staff party at the house a few years ago; it's the most beautiful house I've ever been in.'

She wondered if Belinda fancied becoming a permanent fixture at Sudbourne House.

'The gardens are lovely too. I got up early this morning and drank my tea there. Very peaceful,' she said, 'the roses are lovely at the moment. The roses you put on Mr Salter's desk, were they from your garden?'

Belinda stirred her coffee, and devoured a mouthful of coconut macaroon, then swallowed. 'No, Mr Hinney cut them for me from one of the beds in the camp.'

Ah, Mr Hinney, in charge of the grounds. 'Mr Hinney? Does he work here?' She took a sip of the coffee. Too hot.

'Yes, Gareth Hinney, he's been here a few years. He's in charge of the grounds, here and at the house. He's a very capable man, very thoughtful and... helpful.'

So, perhaps there was a rival for Belinda's affections; or perhaps Hinney was just a fill in until Belinda had snaffled Salter. Or perhaps she was getting ahead of herself!

'It's nice to have a man you can trust, isn't it? It's certainly a change for me to live with two men; they make such a fuss of me. I think i'm getting spoilt.'

Belinda's eyes narrowed. 'Are you a close cousin?'

'No, not at all, many times removed, but we've always kept in touch. I'm very fond of Sam... and Stephen of course, he adores me.'

This answer didn't seem to please her as her mouth turned down at the corners. 'It's not any of my business, but... is it right for you to stay with Mr Salter, if you aren't close relatives? After all, some people might think there was something going on between you.'

Dorothy was flattered: Sam Salter's bit on the side, even if he was revolting. Why was Belinda looking peeved? She'd do a bit of embroidery and see where it led.

She tried a simper. 'Well, Sam and I have always been fond of each other, and as we've both got older we seem to have much more in common than we used to. Who knows what will happen?' She put a hand to her mouth. 'Please don't quote me on that. It's early days, but you never know, do you?'

Belinda's cup crashed to the saucer and coffee splashed onto the desk. Blonde curls quivering, she mopped up the mess with a tissue.

My word, that was worth the effort of being a floozy. Belinda Tweedie certainly didn't like the thought of her and Sam being involved with each other.

A cry of pain came from the reception area. Dorothy got up and ran towards it.

Cindy was doubled up behind the reception desk, her right hand clutching her left. Blood oozing from between her fingers.

'Cindy, what's happened?'

Her face was white. 'The scissors slipped, I've cut my hand,' she wailed.

Dorothy turned. 'Miss Tweedie,' she shouted, 'where's the first aid box?' Where was the woman? She grabbed clean blotting paper from the desk and tried to staunch the wound.

Belinda's head poked round the door. She looked at Cindy, her eyes seemed to pop from her head, colour leaving her face like a lift descending at high speed. Her eyes rolled upwards until only the whites showed and she dropped to the floor like a sack of potatoes.

Dorothy rushed to her, Belinda moaned and tried to get up, and Dorothy managed to prop her up on a chair. Bloody hell, she thought, this is all I need. 'I'll be right back, I'll check on Cindy.'

When she returned, Belinda Tweedie was still slumped in the chair in front of her desk, her head resting on folded arms, eyes closed and her face, what Dorothy could see of it, white and sweaty. She went back to the reception area. Cindy, her hand neatly bandaged, was sitting behind the desk, looking green round the gills.

Dorothy dialled Sudbourne House. 'Stephen? Can you come over here quickly, please? Cindy has cut her hand and needs to go to a doctor; she may need stitches and she should have a tetanus jab.'

She nodded at the reply.

'Good, thank you. Also, Belinda fainted at the sight of blood. I think she should go home. See you soon.' She put the receiver down. 'Did you hear that, Cindy?' Cindy nodded. 'I'll see how Miss Tweedie is.'

Belinda moaned, her eyes fluttered and she tried to push herself upright.

Dorothy put a glass of water in front of her. 'Sip this, Belinda. I think it might be better if you went home; you need to lie down.'

Belinda picked up the glass with both hands, Dorothy helped her, and water slopped as she raised it to her lips.

'Do you live on the camp?'

She shook her head. 'In Orford.'

'Did you drive here this morning?'

Belinda nodded.

'I can drive you back, if you'll trust me with your car. I am insured to drive other vehicles. I can get Stephen to pick me up later. Shall we do that?'

Belinda nodded, either unable or unwilling to string a sentence together. There were voices in the reception area. She went out; Sally was back, fussing around Cindy, making baby noises.

'Sally, I'm taking Miss Tweedie home; Mr Stephen Salter will be here shortly to take Cindy to the doctors. Please give Mr Salter Miss Tweedie's address — you do have it? Good. Tell him to pick me up there. You're to hold the fort until I get back. Phone Mr Sam Salter and say I will not be back for lunch. I will stay here to help you until the office closes.'

Sally gawped at her.

'I'll say that again. Make some notes in case you forget anything.' She looked over Sally's shoulder as she wrote on a pad. 'Good, now you had better help me get Miss Tweedie to the car.' She lowered her voice. 'Does she always react like that when she sees blood?'

Sally leant towards her. 'Ooh, she's ever so sensitive; if you even mention the word b-l-o-o-d,' she whispered, 'she starts to wobble, and she can't bear to see anything harmed. I swatted a wasp once, and she went green.'

What a milksop! Probably too young to be involved in the war. No time for sensitive souls then.

'Where is Miss Tweedie's car? I'll drive it to the front of reception.'

Sally took her outside and pointed towards the car park. 'That one there, the pale blue one.'

'The Ford Escort?' Pale blue — well, better than pink. Dorothy returned to Belinda and took the car keys from her handbag. She hurried to the car, but had to adjust the driver's seat, as she didn't quite have Belinda's girth, thank goodness. She found first gear difficult to engage and bumped her way to the front of reception.

'Take Belinda's left arm, Sally.' Luckily, she looked like a strong girl. 'Careful down the steps.' They manoeuvred her into the passenger seat. 'Thank you, Sally. See you later.'

She slid into the driving seat. 'Whereabouts in Orford do you live, Belinda?'

'Daphne Road,' she whispered, her chin resting on her chest.

'Can you give me directions?'

'You know the church?'

'Yes.'

'Go past the church and head for the quay. At the end of Church Street turn left; that's Daphne Road. I'm the last cottage on the left, just before Doctor's Drift.'

'Doctor's Drift?'

'It's a lane, it leads to the river. I'll tell you when we get there.'

Dorothy found first gear more easily this time and, driving carefully, afraid Belinda might keel over, she made their way from the camp and turned right into Ipswich Road, then through Front Street and past the church. She turned when she saw the sign: Daphne Road. The name suited Belinda, a quivering mass of pale pink, like a freshly turned-out blancmange.

Belinda pointed to a semi-detached cottage; there was a small front garden with a standard pink rose surrounded by lavender bushes. The front door was freshly painted, dark blue, thank goodness, with a well-polished brass letter-box and door handle. There was a side path with a tall, wooden gate.

'If you give me your key, Belinda, I'll open the door before you get out of the car. Don't try and move until I come back.' She hoped Belinda didn't collapse again; she didn't fancy heaving that weight round for a second time. The key turned smoothly in the Yale lock; beyond was a small hall with a door on either side and one at the end, to the left of a staircase. Where should she put Belinda? She opened the door to the left, it was a sitting room furnished with a pink velour three-piece suite, sideboard, a television on a stand, and a nest of three tables. She turned back to the car and helped Belinda up the brick path, into the hall, Belinda leaning heavily on her, until she slumped into an armchair.

Belinda leant back, her colour improving, but still breathing rapidly.

'Try to take a few slow, deep breaths, Belinda. You're looking better. My, that was a nasty turn. Would you like me to get you a glass of water? Or shall I make you some tea?' This was an excellent opportunity to have a little snoop, although if Belinda was this squeamish, fainting at the sight of blood, and had the habdabs when a wasp was swatted, she didn't think she was up to doing away with two women. Still, you never know, and it was good practise.

'Tea, please,' Belinda whispered. 'The tea's in—'

'Don't worry, I'll find everything. You just rest, and take some deep, slow breaths. Three sugars?'

Belinda nodded. 'Yes—'

Dorothy scurried to what she presumed was the kitchen, before Belinda could get out another word.

The door to the left of the stairs led into a large, airy kitchen, the width of the house; big enough for a pine table and four chairs as well as all the usual kitchen stuff. The sink was beneath a window, overlooking the back garden. To the right of the sink was an electric kettle and teapot. She found the caddy — tea-bags — she sniffed, filled the kettle, peeped round the door and listened. Belinda was following instructions.

As quietly as possible she began to open cupboards and drawers, looking for anything unusual or suspicious. Everything seemed in order: it was a well-stocked and kept kitchen. Very boring. She made the tea in the pot and opened the fridge, looking for the milk. There was a half-empty bottle of full cream. She pulled a face – not the best for tea. Next to it, in the fridge's door-shelf, were two bottles of wine, both unopened. Was Belinda expecting company? Or was she a secret toper? Bit unfair, she thought, as she, herself, was partial to a gin and tonic before dinner and a glass of red with a good steak. Still?

When she went back Belinda was sitting upright, looking brighter.

'Oh, Dorothy, you've been so kind. I can't thank you enough. What must you think of me? I can't help it. When I saw Cindy...' She started to pale again.

Dorothy pulled out one of the tables from the nest, placed it next to Belinda's chair, and put the cup and saucer down on it. She hoped there wasn't going to be a re-run.

'Now, Belinda, try not to think about it. I'm pleased I could help. Here, drink some tea. Always the best panacea for most troubles, I find.'

Belinda looked at her blankly, took the tea and with her little finger sticking out at an angle, raised the cup to her lips and took small sips, reminding Dorothy of a goldfish.

'Have you a neighbour I could contact, so they could keep an eye on you until you feel better?'

Belinda shook her head. 'The next-door house is a holiday cottage and it's empty at the moment. I feel much better now. I'd rather you didn't tell anyone else. I feel so silly acting like that. You won't tell Mr Salter, will you?'

'I'm afraid he'll know already. Stephen Salter is coming to pick me up soon. I'm sorry, I presumed everyone knew about your...'

Belinda's face flushed, her eyes narrowing. 'Of course, he knows, but I'd have preferred it if you hadn't made such a fuss. I don't want him to think I'm doing this on a regular basis.'

So much for the heart-felt thanks. 'So, if it happens again, you'd prefer to be left on the floor until you come to?' As soon as the sharp words left her lips she knew she'd said the wrong thing. She'd given the kind of reply she'd make to a silly girl in the bread shop who'd whispered a derogatory remark behind a customer's back. All her hard work getting on the right side of Belinda was wasted. Thank goodness Frank wasn't here; she knew he hadn't been convinced of her detecting skills. She'd tell Laurel when she saw her and ask for advice. Laurel was good with people, she'd helped Stuart and Mabel when their romance went through a sticky patch. Better try and put it right, although it went against the grain, as she didn't like the woman.

'Oh, I'm sorry, Belinda, that was most unkind of me. I'll explain to Mr Salter, say you've told me it hasn't happened for years, or something like that. Will that help?'

Belinda's lips quivered.

Was she was upset or angry?

'Very well. Yes, you can say that.'

There was a knock on the front door.

'That's probably Stephen. Shall I bring him in? I'm sure he's concerned for you.'

Belinda shot up from the chair, her eyes bulging. 'No. No. I don't want him to see me like this.'

She did look the worse for wear, with trails of black mascara running from her eyes and her hair flattened.

'Please, just go back with him. I'm perfectly fine now.'

Certainly she was moving normally and seemed agitated at the thought of Stephen seeing her. She could understand if it had been Sam Salter at the door, but why Stephen?

'Very well, Belinda. Will you be in tomorrow?'

Belinda pushed back her shoulders, her ample bosom moving forward in a threatening manner. 'I'll be back at work as soon as I've washed my face and combed my hair.

You won't be there will you? You'll have gone back to lunch at Sudbourne.'

It won't be just a wash and brush up, will it? It'll be the full works: pan-stick make up, rouge and lashings of lipstick. 'No, I'll get Stephen to drop me off at the camp. Sally is on her own at the moment, unless Cindy's recovered. I'll wait until you get back.' She hoped she'd get away before Laurel arrived at the holiday camp; Stephen Salter had arranged she'd come on Monday afternoon, when Dorothy would be back at Sudbourne Hall. Can't be helped, she'd have to try to pretend it was their first meeting.

Belinda's nostrils flared. 'Very well, but tell Mr Salter I wasn't away long, won't you?'

Dorothy simpered at her. 'Of course, my dear. Off I go. See you soon.' She wasn't sure if she was cut out for this undercover detective work.

Chapter 7

Laurel parked her Cortina in the holiday camp's visitors' car park and leant over to look in the passenger mirror. Mm. She'd decided more make-up than usual was required for her new role: blue eyeshadow, two coats of mascara and red lipstick. What would Dorothy and Frank think? She suspected Dorothy would get out her handkerchief, spit on it, and attack her face, like her mother used to when she was a child with a mucky face. Thank goodness she wouldn't see Dorothy today as she was only working mornings in the office.

She slid out of the car and, as she walked to reception, pulled at the hem of her mini-dress. She was pleased she'd practised walking in her new wedge-heeled sandals; they were surprisingly comfortable and gave her another two inches — as if she needed it! She'd enjoyed altering her appearance, and Stuart's wolf-whistle, when she paraded before him and Mabel, had given her confidence she could pull off her undercover role.

'Hello, doll!' said one of two youths, who were lounging outside the reception office, studying a board of staff photographs. Not much over eighteen, she reckoned.

Jolly good, it was working. She smiled at them as they goggled at her legs.

The cheeky one rushed to open the door.

'Thank you.'

'My pleasure, doll. You staying here?'

'It depends.'

He smoothed back his hair. 'On what? I can give you a good time, doll.'

This was becoming tedious; she hoped she wasn't going to spend too much time fending off pimply youths with hair smelling of grease. She drew herself up to her full five feet eleven, plus wedges, looked down at him and gave him her withering teacher's stare. 'I don't think so, sonny. I don't do cradle snatching.'

The youth reddened, tossed his head, let the door close, and swaggered back to his mate. 'Bit past it,' he said.

She didn't know whether to laugh or pick him up by the collar of his jacket and give him a good shake. She did neither, opened the door herself and went into reception. She sniffed — Dettol. Not the best welcoming smell. A young couple were at the desk talking to someone she couldn't see.

'We'd like to book a tennis court for four. Is that all right?' the woman said.

'Let me see. I'm afraid all the courts are booked for four. There is one at four thirty. Would that do?'

No! She wasn't supposed to be here. It was Dorothy's voice. What's happened? Should she leave? Too late, the couple were turning towards her, the man putting his arm round the girl's shoulder.

She moved towards the desk. Dorothy raised a finger to her lips and jerked her head toward an open door behind her. She nodded back.

'Can I help you?'

'I hope so. My name is Laurel Bowman. I've just arrived. I'm a new member of staff. I was told to report to reception and ask for Miss Tweedie. Are you Miss Tweedie?'

Dorothy winked. 'No, I'm Miss Piff. Miss Tweedie has been taken ill, I'm afraid. I've only started work here today, so, I'll ask Sally,' she thumbed towards the office, 'what we should do next. Excuse me.'

There was a muted conversation and Dorothy reappeared. 'Sally is phoning Miss Minnikin; she's in charge of the chalets. She'll be over directly to take you to your chalet and then she'll arrange for you to meet Mr Frost who is charge of entertainments.'

'Thank you, Miss Piff. Will I have a chalet near you?'

Dorothy raised her eyebrows. 'No. I'm a cousin of Mr Salter, the owner of the camp; I'm helping out here,' she waved a hand round reception in a royal gesture, 'until Mr Salter has made a new appointment. I'm staying with him at Sudbourne Hall.'

Laurel pinched her lips together. Dorothy was playing her role to perfection! 'I'm sorry, I didn't realise your position.'

'Quite all right, Miss Bowman. Can I offer you a cup of tea or coffee?'

Laurel refused and sat down on one of the chairs by the wall. Miss Minnikin was one of the suspects, but no one was attached to her, so this would be a good opportunity to make an assessment of her character.

Dorothy ignored her and busied herself at the desk, officiously tidying piles of brochures, rearranging pamphlets and pulling out drawers.

Laurel realised she was hunching her shoulders and tried to relax, taking several deep breaths. The reception door opened and a large figure blocked out the sunlight.

Dorothy looked up. 'Miss Minnikin? Hello, I'm Dorothy Piff, Mr Salter's cousin. Helping out in the office.'

The large woman, with a height that matched Laurel's in her wedges, heavily built, with short, dark hair, reached across the desk and shook Dorothy's hand. 'Pleased to meet you, Miss Piff.'

Miss Minnikin! More like Miss Gigantikin!

Dorothy pointed towards her. 'Miss Bowman is waiting for you.'

Miss Minnikin turned. Her face was as arresting as her body: brown eyes beneath strong eyebrows, a long fleshy nose and thin lips. Laurel decided she'd try and keep on the right side of Miss Minnikin. She stood up.

The handshake was firm, but not fierce and the intimidating face lightened as she smiled warmly at Laurel. 'Pleased to meet you, Miss Bowman. Good to have another tall woman on the staff.'

As they walked towards Laurel's car Miss Minnikin chatted about the lovely weather.

'Have you been at the camp long, Miss Minnikin?'

'Do call me Nellie. My name's Eleanor, but everyone calls me Nellie. I've been here since the camp opened, and I've worked for Sam Salter for a number of years; we go back a long way.'

Interesting. 'Really? Please call me Laurel.' Better not show too much interest straight away, though it was tempting; how far back did their relationship go? To when he was a reckless youth and mixed with criminals?

She drove them to the staff car park and Nellie helped her with her luggage, easily carrying two heavy suitcases as though they were nothing more than two handbags. She stopped before a row of chalets situated behind a large building called Southwold which, she said, housed the main dining hall.

'These are the staff chalets, mostly two staff to a chalet, but I was given instructions you were to have one to yourself. There are only two vacant at the moment.' She pointed to one at the end of the row. 'That's yours, but the fourth one from it is also vacant. Some man's coming later in the week, another gardener I'm told, so if you want to see them both and choose which one you like best, that's fine by me.'

So, Frank was 'some gardener'. She must remember to tell him.

'I'm sure the end one will be OK.'

Nellie produced a key, put it in the Yale lock and opened the door.

'All the chalets, staff ones included, have a bathroom. It's a big selling point.'

It was a good-sized room, with a single bed, wardrobe, dressing table and chair, all in white-painted wood; a small table stood beneath a window and there was an armchair next to it. Nellie opened the door into the bathroom; fresh towels sat on a cork-topped stool, and there was a bath, basin and lavatory.

'This is fine, Nellie. Everywhere looks very clean.'

Nellie sniffed. 'I make sure the chalet maids do a thorough job.'

Laurel believed her. 'So, you're in charge of all the chalets? What happens if the holiday makers break something? Or if something goes wrong, like a broken switch? Do you have to deal with that as well?'

Nellie laughed. 'That's nothing to do with me. I make sure the chalets are clean and the bedding and towels are changed regularly.' She went over to the dressing table and tapped it. 'This will have to double as a desk.' She picked up a notepad. 'If anything is needed, the campers fill in one of these forms and leaves it on the bed. The chalet maid checks each day when she cleans the room and brings any forms to me. I contact Jim Lovell, in charge of maintenance, and he sorts it out. Works well, even though I say it myself.'

70

Mr Lovell, another suspect, but one that no one was attached to, like Nellie.

'Everything seems very well organised.'

Nellie nodded. 'You couldn't have a better run camp. You've got to give it to Sam Salter, he's a good business man.'

'And you've known him a long time? I think I heard he was a bit wild in his youth; is that true?'

Nellie smiled, shaking her head. 'Wild isn't half of it. We were neighbours in the East End; I'm a few years younger than Sam, but my parents were friendly with his.' She stopped. 'Enough of gossiping. You need to meet Charlie Frost and I need to get going. We've got a load of new sheets being delivered later today and I need to be there and check they're up to scratch, or should I say make sure they're good quality. What's your speciality? You're a Stripey, aren't you?'

Pity, the gossip was getting interesting. 'I'll be in charge of the swimming, giving lessons and organising swimming competitions. Where will I find Mr Frost?'

Nellie looked at her watch. 'Hm. Probably on the tennis courts giving some coaching, probably to the girl with the shortest skirt.'

Laurel thought Nellie was giving her a hint.

'Oh, I see.'

Nellie slowly nodded her head. 'Good, you catch on quick. He may be your type, but I don't think so, though lots of the female campers think he's the bee's knees.'

Laurel wondered what Nellie thought her type was. Perhaps a gardener with green eyes; hopefully not well-built chalet organisers! 'I'll let you know.'

'You want me to take you over to him?'

'Thanks, Nellie, just point me in the right direction, I'm sure I'll find him.' She gestured to her suitcases. 'I'll

71

unpack first, won't take me long. Will Mr Frost give me a Stripey jacket?'

Nellie rolled her eyes. 'He'll want to fit it personally.' She gave Laurel directions to the tennis courts. 'Anything you need just let me know. Good luck with the swimming. Hope you enjoy your time with us.' Giving a warm smile she left, and Laurel moved to the window and watched her stride away.

Despite her gargantuan appearance, she'd warmed to Nellie. But she was a suspect, and if she did have lesbian tendencies, then she might have a sexual motive which could be linked to the missing girls. She needed to keep an open mind about Nellie.

Laurel pulled the chalet door closed and walked in the direction Nellie had told her. She'd changed into shorts and t-shirt, white ankle socks and gym shoes, with her hair in a ponytail. She was glad she'd kept up her fitness regime and hoped she looked the part of a Stripey coat who specialised in swimming. She didn't hurry, taking time to get her bearings and to think herself into her new role. It wouldn't be too different to being a PE teacher, except she'd have to treat the campers in a friendlier way, perhaps a much friendlier way. After all they'd paid for a jolly holiday and wouldn't take kindly to an officious manner. She hoped she wouldn't see too much of callow youths, like the one who'd fancied her at Reception. She'd been looking forward to teaching boys for the first time when she took up her appointment at Blackfriars School last September, but murder and mayhem had put a stop to that. She must try to look at this assignment as an opportunity to broaden her skills. She was working undercover and needed to adjust her attitude, especially to pimply youths who thought they were irresistible.

She looked in at the Aldeburgh dining room: a modern spacious hall with rows of regimented plastic tables and chairs; two cleaners were mopping the floor, cigarettes drooping from their lips, but this didn't seem to hinder their chatter. She waved cheerfully to them, and smiled. They looked up, but the languid movements didn't stop and they didn't smile back.

The gardens in the centre of the camp were made up of four spacious rectangular beds with paths in between. There were standard roses in the centre of each bed, each quarter a different colour: red, white, yellow and pink. Beneath them was a riot of colourful annuals. The beds were well looked after – she couldn't see any weeds – but she found it too formal, and the colours brash. What would Frank think? She imagined him dressed as a pre-First World War gardener, with a leather apron and a flat cap, kneeling as he weeded one of the beds. Perhaps she would give him orders to bring cut flowers to Sudbourne House and waylay him in the potting shed. A touch of the Lady Chatterley?

At the end of the path she turned right and walked between the gardens and the campers' chalets. In front of her was the outdoor swimming pool and to its left a bowling green. She paused at the pool; several campers were sitting round it on deckchairs and some were swimming or rather thrashing in the water. A notice warned campers there was no life guard and they entered the water at their own risk.

The plonk, plonk, plonk, of tennis balls being hit guided her to the courts; all were occupied. On one of them a man, wearing a striped blazer and white shorts, was showing a young woman how to serve; the man at the opposite end of the court was chasing the tennis balls and batting them back to her and the other man. He didn't look as though he was enjoying himself.

Charles Frost, she presumed it was him, was behind the girl, a plumpish brunette, one of his hands on her waist, the other guiding her right arm through the arc she needed to make a serve.

'Very good, Mary. I think you've got it now.' He took two balls from his jacket pocket and handed them to her. 'Remember, toss the ball high, keep your eye on it and throw the racket head at it. Remember to keep hold of the handle!' He laughed and she giggled.

'Oh, Charlie! I can't serve proper if you keep making me laugh!'

Charlie was a tall, slim man. Thick, slightly curly dark hair rose from a widow's peak. He moved gracefully over the court, lithe and confident. She had to admit he had good legs. He'd noticed her as she stood at the netting surrounding the court, obviously staring at him.

'Excuse me, Mary. I think someone wants to see me.'

Mary looked mulish. 'I've paid for half-an-hour's coaching. I've only had twenty-five minutes.'

'Be back in a sec. I think this must be our new swimming coach.' As he walked toward her his shoulders went back a few inches, his chest expanded and his gaze moved from her face downwards – and lingered.

She gave him her best smile. 'Mr Frost? I'm Laurel Bowman. Miss Minnikin said you'd be here.'

He came close to the netting; the smell of aftershave was overpowering. 'Very glad to meet you.' He came even closer and whispered. 'Give me five more minutes with this clumsy cow and we'll have a nice little chat. I'll fill you in with all the info,' he said, leering at her. 'Take a seat.' He pointed to a bench on the other side of the court.

His fleshy face with definite eyebrows, straight nose and full lips would be said by some to be handsome, or at least attractive, but the lascivious look in those hazel eyes wasn't appealing. She smiled again and strolled to the bench.

Charlie Frost bowed to Mary as he left the court and she simpered at him. Immediately her partner came up to her and they started rowing as they walked away. Frost strode to Laurel, swinging his racket, looking pleased with himself. He put his left foot on the bench, close to her side and leant over her in a familiar manner. It was tempting to do him some harm. She took a deep breath. 'Please sit down, Mr Frost.' She patted the bench beside her.

He swung round, brushing her knee with his leg. 'Charlie, please.'

'Charlie.' She put out her hand. 'I'm pleased to meet you. I hope we'll work well together.'

He looked a bit taken aback, but quickly took her hand and gave it a squeeze, then held on to it. His palm was hot and sticky with sweat. 'You look every inch a Stripey, can't wait to see you in the pool,' he said, letting his gaze wander over her body.

This was going to be difficult. What she felt like doing was giving him the rough edge of her tongue – not literarily – and making clear to him he was wasting his breath. What she had to do was to make friends with him and find out if he had anything to do with the disappearance of the two women.

'What's your speciality, Charlie?' She thought if he talked about himself he might lose interest in her. He looked like a man who was in love with his image. She mentally ticked herself off. She was making rushed judgements.

He leant back against the bench, stretching out his tanned lags — so she could admire them? 'I'm a performer, an actor, dancer, singer; this job is temporary until the right part comes along.'

'You haven't got a games background?'

He wrinkled his nose. 'Not my forte. I don't mind helping out with tennis, but am I glad you've come to take over the swimming! I can only do breast stroke. I try to do a Johnny Weissmuller sometimes, but I usually end up at the bottom of the pool!' They both laughed. She couldn't see him as Tarzan, in a loin cloth, wrestling a fake crocodile.

She felt herself thawing towards him; he wasn't a complete arse. 'What's your main role? You're in charge of all the entertainments, aren't you?

He straightened up, his face serious. 'Mr Salter gave me the job as he thought I'd be the right person to devise entertainments for a younger age group, the eighteen to thirties. I organise the discos, do some disc jockeying myself, or I hire local DJs, and every Friday night we have a talent show. It's the one night I really enjoy.'

His face was animated, he looked as though he'd forgotten, for the moment, she was another babe, a babe to size up and see if she was worth the effort of seducing. At least that was her summing up of the situation. 'Why is that, Charlie?'

He shifted uneasily on the bench. 'I usually start and end the show, a couple of songs at the beginning and perhaps a bit of dancing. At the end of the show I do requests from the audience. I know most of the popular songs.'

He reminded her of some of the girls she'd taught, mediocre at everything, but when they got parts in a school production they came alive, their confidence grew, and often their academic performance improved as their classmates saw them in a different light and had more respect for them. 'That's wonderful, Charlie. You're keeping your dream alive.'

He turned to look at her and it was if he'd seen her for the first time. His smile was warm, made not just with his lips, but with his eyes. He'd forgotten he was a charmer, and because of that, his relaxed face was handsome and his true charm came through.

'Laurel, I think you're the first person who's understood what I want from life.'

'How long have you been here?'

His lips twisted. 'This is my third year.'

'Do you still try for parts in theatrical productions?'

He sighed. 'Yes, I've got an agent, and I've got an agreement with Mr Salter I can attend auditions; we're not too far from London. I've got a car so I can get there in a couple of hours.'

'But no luck so far?'

He shook his head. 'Thought I was going to get a part in a West End production of Hello Dolly, just before Christmas, got down to the last four, but I wasn't the lucky one.'

This was going well, he was opening up to her. Too early to start probing about the missing girls? Probably, mustn't get ahead of herself.

'Have you tried the smaller theatres? Or some of the touring productions?'

He shrugged his shoulders. 'I keep trying for the London shows, but if nothing happens this year, I'll have to make some decisions. The job here pays well and at least I get to do some proper work once a week; I really enjoy having an audience, getting the rapport going. In the winter I'll have saved up enough money to get by, and

I'll move to London so I can try and get to more auditions. I know I can do it if I'm given a chance. I may have to choose between trying my hand in provincial theatres or making this job my main one. Mr Salter is pleased with how things are going here, and he could move me to one of the larger camps. Some of them have big theatres, and put on proper shows.'

'Don't give up yet, Charlie, although I don't know how good you are.'

He laughed. 'Come and see me on Friday night. Why don't you enter the talent contest? But as you're a Stripey you're not allowed to win. Got a speciality?'

Fighting with mass murderers? She didn't think she'd mention that. 'Throwing the javelin?'

He shook his head, then looked at his watch. He shot up. 'Look at the time! I'll be late for an appointment – got a local band coming in tonight, said I'd meet them and help them set up the sound system. Come on, let's get you a blazer and I'll show you the indoor pool. I've worked out a few schedules: coaching, races etc., but if you don't like them you can change things round.'

'Where's the pool?' she asked as they left the bench and courts.

'In that building in front of you: the Orford building. The pool's on the ground floor, with a coffee bar, shop and the discotheque, and above is the Thorpeness theatre, a hundred-and-fifty-seater, an amusement arcade and a games room: billiards, table tennis and darts.'

'Pretty comprehensive.'

'Mr Salter's thought of everything.'

Had Mr Salter thought it would be clever to bring in a team of detectives to try and find out what had happened to the missing girls, even though he already knew what had happened to them? And Charlie Frost? Did the seduction of young women make up for the disappointments in his career? And had two young women refused his advances and he had taken out his frustrations by murdering them?

Chapter 8

Tuesday, June 15, 1971

There was a clash of cutlery. Frank looked up, put down his biro and pushed his notebook away. 'Something wrong, Mabel?'

She started to lay the dining room table. 'Sorry, was I making a noise?'

'It's a noise that's music to my ears, as it means dinner's on its way.'

Mabel tossed her head, smiling at him. 'Laurel always said you were a silver-tongued devil.' She continued laying the table, but now showed more consideration for the knives and forks.

Frank got up and brought napkins, table mats and a cruet set from the sideboard. He put an arm around Mabel's shoulders. 'You haven't answered my question. Are you all right? You seem on edge.'

Mabel shook her head. 'It's nothing, really. I just don't like it here without Dorothy and Laurel. I know Dorothy's only been gone for a few days, and Laurel, yesterday, but it seems wrong to have a lovely meal without them, especially Dorothy — this is her home. I don't feel right using her kitchen when she isn't here.'

Frank frowned. 'I know what you mean. The house seems half-empty and I miss the sound of Dorothy tapping on her typewriter.' He grinned. 'Hope you'll miss me when I go on Friday.'

Mabel sniffed. 'I might do. I'll let you know.'

'You'll have Stuart all to yourself!'

Mabel's cheeks flushed, as she tried to suppress a smile; she turned and set out side plates and placed the napkins Frank had handed her on them.

Bit too near the bone? He imagined Stuart chasing her round the kitchen next week when they had the house to themselves. He decided to change the subject. 'Is this lovely meal in honour of Inspector Revie?' He'd been invited to dinner so they could ask for help in getting information on some of the suspects at the holiday camp. After the David Pemberton case, there was an unofficial understanding that The Anglian Detective Agency could call on Detective Inspector Revie, the appointed officer, for any help they needed – within reason. This was in exchange for their continued silence about the true happenings of the Pemberton case; they hadn't had any choice, it was silence or be silenced, as the government would fall if the truth was revealed.

'Anything else worrying you, Mabel? You're still frowning.'

'It's my son. He and all the other fishermen in Aldeburgh are really worried about this Fisheries Policy if we join the Common Market. He says it'll ruin the industry. All the other countries will make a beeline for our waters. There won't be enough fish to go around. And they don't know if they'll get the twelve-mile limit. I don't like to see him so upset. He works so hard. It's not an easy life being a fisherman.'

'Your first husband was drowned at sea, wasn't he?'

'Yes, poor soul. He'd have been livid if he knew the way things were going.' She shook her head. 'There, I've had my moan, let's get back to the meal. Stuart said I ought to pull out all the stops; make sure we keep Revie onside.'

'What's the menu?'

'Asparagus, roast leg of Alder Valley lamb, new potatoes, fresh peas and strawberry shortcake.'

His mouth filled with saliva at the thought of fresh mayonnaise with the unique taste of the asparagus. He groaned. 'Why did you marry Stuart? Why didn't we tie the knot?'

She picked up a spoon and rapped his hand. 'One, you didn't ask me, two, if you had I'd have said no, three, I love Stuart and four, we all know you can't bear the thought of being tied down.'

He shook his hand in fake pain. 'Hope you treat the lamb more gently.'

'The lamb can't answer back. Time I put it in the oven.'

He looked at his wrist-watch. 'He'll be here in about an hour and a half. Where's Stuart? I need to go through what we'll ask Revie to investigate.'

Mabel paused on her way to the kitchen. 'He went to the farm shop to get the asparagus; hope they had some, otherwise I'm not sure what I'll do for a first course.' She stopped. 'Here he is; I can hear his car.'

Frank opened the front door as Stuart got out of his Humber Hawk, clutching two brown paper bags from which poked the pointed heads of several bundles of asparagus.

'Mabel will be pleased.'

Stuart slammed the car door shut. 'She won't be when she knows how much I had to pay for them.' He sneezed.

'Bless you.'

'Touch of hay fever. But it's not as bad as yesterday. Worst day of the year so far, the paper said.'

Frank finished making notes as he waited for Stuart to deliver the asparagus to Mabel. 'How much?' Her voice rose as she heard the price. Then silence. Murmurings and Stuart emerged from the kitchen smiling.

Frank looked at him. 'Has she got over the shock?'

'I told her I had to buy the best spears to go with her wonderful homemade mayonnaise.'

'She said I was a silver-tongued devil, but I think I've been up-staged,' Frank said.

Stuart sat down beside him. 'Right.' He pointed to the notebook. 'Let's hear what you've worked out. I wish I was joining you at the camp, feel a bit redundant here.'

Frank tapped his biro on the notes. 'You'll have plenty to do, there's lots of background work on the suspects needed, and when we know how much information Revie can give you, you'll be able to plan your schedule.'

Stuart wrinkled his nose. 'Not like being in the thick of it, is it?'

Frank decided to ignore that. 'I think we should ask Revie to do criminal checks on all the suspects, not just those Laurel, Dorothy and I will be working with. Agreed?'

'Sounds sensible, but it's no good overloading him; perhaps give him the names of the ones you'll be working with first; that way we might get more detailed work.'

'Fair enough. That will be Sam Salter and Belinda Tweedie: Dorothy's suspects; Charles Frost: Laurel's suspect and Gareth Hinney: mine.'

'What about Stephen Salter?'

'Leave him off, for the moment.'

'What do you want me to do?'

'As you've finished off the other work, and thanks for that, I think you should look into the backgrounds of the two missing women. I'm not sure how much involvement the police had, that's something Revie should be able to tell us, but from what Salter said, it wasn't much. I'd like you to visit their parents, talk to their friends, past employers, sniff out what kind of women they were, or are. Had they anything else in common, apart from their looks?'

'Where did they come from?'

'Lucy Milne was local, lived at Sudbourne and Roberta, Bobby Dodd, lived a bit farther away, at Woodbridge.'

'Not too much travelling then, that's good.'

'You could take Mabel with you, it might be useful to have a woman there if things get difficult. She's good with people – as long as she doesn't lose her temper. No doubt everyone, and especially the parents, will be upset as their loss is brought back to them, or they may be pleased someone is searching for an answer to the girls' disappearances. Try not to raise their hopes they'll be found alive. You'll have to make up some excuse as to why you're asking questions, you can't reveal what's really happening.'

Stuart frowned. 'Yes, that could be difficult. If you've got any bright ideas let me know.' His face brightened. 'I think Mabel would like to come with me. I know she wants to be more involved in the cases. I think she's a bit jealous of Dorothy, now she's doing a bit of detecting.'

Frank frowned. 'Let's hope Dorothy's detecting is going smoothly.'

Stuart laughed. 'I can see her now, poking her finger into Sam Salter's chest and saying: "Mr Salter, what have you done with those girls?"'

Frank groaned.

Mabel appeared from the kitchen. 'Stuart, could you be a love and shell these peas for me?'

Stuart got up, patted Frank on the back, and with a broad grin on his face went to the kitchen.

Frank placed his knife and fork together over his clean plate. The smell of roasted lamb lingered in the air. Revie spooned himself a third helping of new potatoes. Stuart looked as though he was counting the spuds on Revie's plate.

'Miss Mabel, I know you're married now, but I always think of you as Miss Mabel, that lamb outshone your bacon butties, and that's saying something.' Revie squinted at Frank. 'You're not trying to butter me up again, are you?' He poured the last of the gravy onto his plate.

'I thought there was no need for that, Nicholas, we've been promised cooperation by the Suffolk police. However, if Mabel's delicious meal puts you in a good mood...'

Revie patted his stomach. 'You should have waited for me, Mabel, not rushed into the arms of old Stuart.'

Mabel got up. 'You're the second man who's said that today.' Stuart glared at Revie. Mabel pointed to Revie's plate. 'You'd better stop talking and eat those up, now you've taken them. I'll get the pudding, then we can get down to business.' She gathered up some of the plates, leaving Revie to gobble up his food.

Frank cleared up the rest of the dishes, including Revie's. 'Stuart, could you give Inspector Revie details about the case? I'll give Mabel a hand.'

Later, in the sitting room, a glass of whisky in one hand, and a list of names Frank had handed to him in the other, Revie pursed his lips. 'Just four? Stuart said there were seven people working in the camp when both girls went missing.'

'That's correct, but we thought we'd give you the people we'll be attached to first.'

'Thought I couldn't cope with all of them at the same time? Or thought I might skimp if there were too many?'

No flies on Revie. 'Would you like the rest of the names?'

'Might as well. Got as much details on them as these?' He tapped the paper. 'Done your homework, which certainly makes my job easier. We'll do a criminal check on all of them first. Let you know straight away if anything comes up.'

Frank went to the office/dining room and collected another list. On returning, he handed it to Revie.

He stared at it. 'Young Salter in the mix, then? Does he take after his father?'

Mabel put down her glass of Tia Maria. 'No, he doesn't. I thought he was a pleasant young man. I must admit I didn't take to Salter Senior.'

'Interesting,' Revie said.

'Stuart's going to do some background work on the missing girls. Could you let us know if the police came up with any hard facts, please?' Frank asked.

Revie nodded. 'Will do.' He continued staring at the second list, then tapped the paper. 'This Thomas Coltman, I think I heard someone at the station talking about him...' He paused, wrinkling his brow, and rubbing his hand over his mouth and jaw as if trying to work the wanted words out of his mouth.

Frank's diaphragm contracted, Stuart's pipe sent out a stream of smoke and Mabel leant forward, her eyes widening.

'That's it.' Revie's raised his fist and pointed a finger upwards, vaguely resembling God on the ceiling of the Sistine Chapel. 'I remember now. It was one of the old-timers having a jaw about famous local murder cases—'

'He's a murderer! Shouldn't he be in gaol?' Mabel interrupted.

Revie laughed. 'My, you do jump to conclusions, Miss Mabel. No, if it's the same chap, it was his wife who was murdered, and his baby boy. Happened during the War, he was overseas somewhere. Man who done it was caught, airman I think. Hanged.'

'Where did this take place?' Frank asked.

A saturnine smile creased Revie's face. 'Where you're about to go – Orford.'

Chapter 9

Friday, June 18, 1971

Frank decided to take the picturesque route to Orford through Tunstall Forest. The road wound between stands of conifers on the right, and sweeping fields, many occupied by pigs, to the left, with sunlight shafting between leafy branches, painting stripes across the tarmac. As he wasn't expected until after lunch, he wanted to look round Orford before going to the camp. He didn't know the village well. He'd been there a few times to eat at the restaurant called the Oysterage when he was a detective inspector based at Ipswich, but apart from a visit to the Norman castle, he hadn't even got as far as the quay on the river Ore, and he wanted to get the lie of the land as he'd researched the history of the village and also the spit of land off its coast, Orford Ness.

He parked in one of the few remaining spaces on Market Hill, a triangular area in front of an antique shop, the Oysterage and the village hall. He thought he'd walk down to the quay and then come back and have lunch in the Oysterage. He might as well have one decent meal before going to the holiday camp; God knows what the food was like there.

He passed a church set high behind a brick wall; it looked interesting, possibly medieval, and worth a visit. Then the road curved, becoming long and straight, with a sign reading Quay Road; he was on the right track.

The brick houses to his left were attractive, with hollyhocks growing from cracks near their walls, and roses trained over door-ways. Further on he passed a large car park; people dressed for sailing were manoeuvring small boats from trailers. Opposite it was the Jolly Sailor pub. He wondered if it sold Adnam's beer; might be a good place to escape to for a quiet pint and a think, if the holiday camp's atmosphere became too frantic. Altogether Orford seemed a busy, vibrant place, hardly a suitable venue for a murder... or two.

A short distance from the pub the road widened into the quay; he hadn't expected it to be so spacious, with a wide jetty butting out into the River Ore. He walked to the edge and peered over the side. There were two sets of iron steps leading down to the river, suitable for embarkation onto motor boats and to the left was a slip-way for smaller vessels. Brick buildings gave way to wooden huts, with boards advertising fresh fish; dinghies were moored in shallow waters, with small sailing boats further on.

The air was buoyant, and the light reflecting off the water dazzling. The Ore ran from north to south, changing its name from the Alde as it flowed from Aldeburgh to Orford. He decided Suffolk folk were possessive, changing the name of the same river as it flowed through different towns. From Orford, the Ore made its way to Shingle Street, an isolated place he'd always wanted to visit; there, it entered the North Sea.

Between the Ore and the sea was the spit of low, flat land he'd read about: Orford Ness. When he had done his National Service at RAF Marsham, Norfolk, he had heard about the Ness, as it was known locally, and from his research he knew it had once been used by the military in the 1950s: testing the components of atomic bombs, and before that for testing bombs and armaments in both World Wars.

The stretch of water between the quay and the Ness was perhaps a mere one hundred yards, making it easy to reach by boat, although the river current looked strong. Swimmable? He thought Laurel wouldn't have too much trouble.

Ministry of Defence notices on the quay made it clear landing on Orford Ness was forbidden, and so it wasn't surprising there was no sign of any activity there, apart from seabirds wheeling over the reeds and scrub. It looked an isolated and forgotten place; who would want to go there when you were likely to tread on a live bomb and be blown to bits?

He squinted against the sun. The only buildings he could see were a white-and-red striped lighthouse and, far to its right, the pagodas; laboratories where the atomic bomb components were tested to destruction. He could see why they were given that name: they stood out against the skyline, grey, squat concrete buildings, with deep oriental roofs supported by strong pillars. He'd read they'd been built to absorb the shock of an accidental explosion.

He imagined the Ness during the last war, busy with technicians and troops. Now it was left to return to how it was a century ago, when it was used for grazing. He turned and looked around the quay; somewhere, not far from here, must be the place where Thomas Coltman's wife had been murdered. Thomas Coltman, a part-time worker at the camp. He'd asked Revie if he could find out more details about the case: exactly when it happened and who was the murderer.

'Why do you want to know that?' Revie asked. 'This is 1971, not 1940 something.'

'Curiosity.'

'You know what happened to the cat, don't you?'

'Hasn't happened so far, touch wood.'

'I think you lost one of your lives not so long ago.'

Revie was right; he didn't fancy another close shave with death.

Frank parked in front of the reception office at the camp, feeling relaxed after a pleasant lunch in Orford. As he walked towards the building he tried to sharpen his mind and get into his role: gardener. Would a gardener be able to afford a meal of smoked fish, oysters and fish patés, half a bottle of Muscadet, followed by rum baba and coffee? He didn't think so. If he was asked what he'd eaten for lunch he'd have to lie.

Behind a desk bristling with leaflets and information was a tall, buxom blonde, a perfect fit for the description Dorothy had given of Belinda Tweedie when they had talked over the telephone earlier in the week.

She brightly smiled. 'Can I help you?'

'Frank Diamond, I was told to report here; I'm a new member of staff.' He held out his hand.

She looked at a piece of paper on the desk. 'Ah yes. A new gardener.' Her eyes widened and she looked as though she was unsure whether to shake his hand or inspect the nails for dirt. She briefly made contact with the tips of her fingers.

'Miss Belinda Tweedie, Mr Salter's personal secretary. Take a seat, I'll see if I can contact Miss Minnikin, who can show you your chalet and take you to meet Mr Hinney, our head gardener.'

'Thank you.' He was wearing jeans and a t-shirt, but now he wished he'd a cloth cap so he could have doffed it to her. She would have appreciated that. Dorothy and Laurel had separately phoned Greyfriars House and reported on all the people they'd met and their feelings about them. Laurel said she was enjoying giving swimming lessons and was feeling fitter by the day, but Dorothy was frustrated because she wasn't in charge of the office. She could see several areas for improvement and didn't like having to do as she was told by Miss Tweedie. Her compensation was staying with the Salters: the house was lovely and the food excellent, much better than the camp.

Belinda Tweedie placed the receiver on the telephone. 'Miss Minnikin asked if you could find your way to the staff chalets, she'll meet you there. She's having a problem with one of the campers; they've asked for another change of bedlinen, third time this week and they're going home tomorrow! Where do they think they are? The Ritz?'

She passed him a map of the camp and circled an area behind a large building. 'She said she'd be there in about five minutes, so you'd better hurry.'

'I'll take my car.'

She looked surprised. Perhaps she thought a gardener shouldn't be able to afford a car. 'Yes, do that. You can't leave it here. The car park is for visitors only.' She bounced her biro off the camp map. 'There's the staff car park. Drive over at once, Miss Minnikin is a busy person, as we all are.' She turned away from him to deal with two campers who had just come into reception. 'May I help you?'

Frank strode out in his effort to keep up with Miss Minnikin. Laurel's description over the phone of Nellie's stature and girth was accurate, but more intriguing was her long relationship with Sam Salter.

'You're a fast walker, Miss Minnikin. Training for a road race?'

She stopped and he nearly collided with her. 'I'm sorry, Mr Diamond, I'm trying to get rid of my temper; some of these campers, especially the ones in this camp, take the biscuit.' She smiled at him. 'I should be pointing out the features, shouldn't I, instead of galloping ahead of you.' She looked him up and down. 'You look fit. Are you?' There was a definite twinkle in her eyes.

He wondered if Laurel's assessment of Minnikin's sexuality was accurate. 'I had a good lunch at Orford. It's a bit too soon to be exercising.'

'At Pinneys?'

'Pinneys?' Blabber mouth – so much for lying.

'Mrs Pinney runs the Oysterage in the Market Place; she's Belgian, you know.'

He stored the name away for later use. 'I thought the place had a continental touch. Yes, that's where I had lunch.'

'Bit too fishy for me, I prefer the Crown, you can rely on their sirloin steaks.'

He imagined her seated in a strongly built chair, with a gargantuan plate in front of her, a fork skewering a fat chip while her knife cut into a large piece of bloody meat. 'You don't sound as though you come from round her, Nellie. Is it OK if I call you Nellie?'

She waved to an empty bench they were approaching. 'Course it is, dear. Let's sit down for a few minutes, give you time to recover from too much food, and me from the cheeky campers. I wouldn't mind but you could tell they were the type who wouldn't change their own sheets more than once a month! These young people nowadays don't know they're born. Spoilt by their parents, and now National Service has ended there's nothing to toughen the boys up.' She let out a long sigh. 'I sound like my old ma, she said the same things about me!' She laughed. 'So where do you think I come from?'

He tried to look as if he was puzzling out the answer, an answer Laurel had already told him. He stroked his upper lip. 'I think I can hear the faint sound of Bow Bells. Am I right?'

Nellie nodded, grinning back at him. 'Very good, Frank. You've got a sharp ear.'

'Didn't Mr Salter come from the East End? I don't suppose you lived near him?' He laughed as though the suggestion was ridiculous.

'Well, you supposed wrong! We lived in the same street; I'm a bit younger than Sam, but my parents were fond of him, even though he was a bit of a rascal in those days.'

He decided to risk it. 'Not one of the Krays' boys, I hope?'

Nellie pulled a face. 'Not far off,' she whispered. 'But he's changed since then. He and his wife, Patsy, moved out of London before the war ended. He kept in touch and I visited them a few times; they'd moved to Essex. He'd changed. Become a real family man. Thinks the world of his son.'

'So, you met Stephen when he was a baby?' God, careless again! He shouldn't have mentioned his name, but Nellie didn't seem to make the connection.

She smiled sweetly, as if remembering the baby in his pram. 'I saw him a few times. They both doted on him.'

He decided a few more general remarks were needed before he asked the vital question. 'He's made a great success of his life and it's nice he's kept in touch with you; he's not turned into a snob, has he?'

She beamed. 'I'm very fond of Sam, and he's been good to me, and to a few of the others he lived near. He likes his flashy cars and expensive suits, but his heart's in the right place.'

Frank leant back. 'His wife died, didn't she? Wonder he never remarried; I heard he was a bit of a ladies' man. Is that right, or is it newspaper gossip?'

Nellie elbowed him in the ribs. 'You're not wrong! Can't do without a woman, can Sam. His wife, Patsy, was a pretty thing. Died a few years after they moved away. Such a pity; never saw the success he made with the camps, although they'd plenty of money. You're right, it's surprising he never remarried.'

'What was she like, Patsy? Blonde or brunette?'

Nellie pursed her lips. 'Patsy was a blonde all the time I knew her, my ma said she was a bottle blonde, but she was a kind person, and was always nice with me, used to give me her old lipsticks. She had a lot to put up with Sam in those days; his eyes would rove every time a skirt went by. But it seemed when Stephen came along, all that stopped and they became closer than ever, or so my ma said. She came with me to see them a couple of times.'

A blonde? When they'd first met Salter at Greyfriars House, he'd shown them photos of the missing girls and he'd said they reminded him of someone. Later when questioned, he'd said the girls reminded him of his late wife, Patsy. But Patsy was blonde and the two women both had dark hair. So, who did they remind him of?

'You've gone quiet, Frank. Hope you're not nodding off! You must have had a good lunch. I better get you to Mr Hinney. He said he'd be working in the flower borders in the centre of the camp.' She got up and he swore the bench groaned in relief. He couldn't wait to tell Laurel and Dorothy about Patsy Salter being a blonde. The three of them were meeting tomorrow afternoon in Dorothy's room at Salter's house. They needed to find out who the woman was who reminded Salter of the missing girls.

Frank and Nellie walked side by side at a leisurely pace as she pointed to various buildings.

'There he is.' A man kneeling on a path in front of a border was weeding between rose bushes; he was wearing corduroy trousers, and a checked shirt.

They stopped near him. 'Mr Hinney, I've brought Frank Diamond, the new gardener, to meet you.'

Gareth Hinney pushed himself up and turned around. He was a strong, muscular man, a little shorter than Frank's five eleven. Knee-pads were tied round his short stocky legs. He wiped his soil-covered hand on his trousers. 'Good to meet you, Mr Diamond.'

The handshake was firm and brief. His face was expressionless, no smile of welcome, or show of disdain. Nothing. Smooth skin was drawn tight over sharp cheek bones, and above a high forehead his greying hair was short; pale blue eyes gave no clue as to whether he was glad or not to see Frank.

'Pleased to meet you, Mr Hinney. I must say the flower beds look good.' Would flattery work?

'I'll be off. Look after yourself, Frank.' Nellie nodded to Hinney and marched off back to her chalets. He'd the impression she wasn't too keen on Hinney, and he'd made no casual remarks to her. This looked like hard work.

Hinney stood looking at him, but there was still no clue as to how he felt about a second gardener being foisted on him. His features were neat: faint eyebrows above a straight nose, and a small, rather feminine mouth. He waited for Hinney to speak.

'I hear you're an experienced gardener,' he said.

'I know a petunia from a Busy Lizzie,' he replied, and pointed to the flower bed. 'Any trouble with slugs and snails?'

Hinney's bow-lips curled. 'I come here at night with a torch, pick them off the plants, put them in a bucket of salt water.' He hesitated. 'Or sometimes I just crush them.'

Sounds as though he hates molluscs. 'Just put the tender annuals out?' That sounded suitably horticultural.

Hinney nodded. 'Never before the end of May.'

Hinney's voice was as flat as his conversation, but he couldn't detect an accent. He nodded in agreement. 'Very wise. A late frost can kill the whole lot off.' Boring. Boring. 'I believe I'm to take over the gardens at the Hall. Is that correct?'

Hinney glowered. 'Yes.'

He doesn't like that. 'I'm only part-time, mornings only, but I'll be able to give you a hand with the borders.'

Hinney looked at his watch. 'I need to get on. You're starting Sunday, I believe.'

Frank nodded. 'I'll visit the house tomorrow and see what needs doing. Shall I report to you on Sunday?'

'No, that's my day off.'

Thank God for that, he wouldn't have to see him until Monday. 'Do you live locally, Mr Hinney?'

Hinney's eyes narrowed. 'No. I live on the camp.'

'What do you do on your day off? More gardening? Or perhaps you like fishing. It's good for crabbing down at Orford, so I hear.' He was desperate to get something from Hinney, to make some kind of contact before he met him again. It was like trying to get hold of an eel.

Hinney stared at him. 'Excuse me, but I need to finish this border, I don't like to leave a job half-done, and I clock off soon.' He turned, knelt down, and with a quick, dexterous movement, picked up a trowel and stabbed at a dandelion.

It was like getting blood from a stone. Or possibly more difficult than that.

Chapter 10

Saturday, June 19, 1971

Dorothy looked up at the afternoon sky from her seat in the garden of Sudbourne Hall; scudding clouds from the North Sea covered the sun, and an easterly breeze raised goose-bumps on her arms. She sighed as she walked back to the Hall. She wasn't feeling herself, she was frustrated and, yes, she had to admit it, lonely. Although she'd seen Laurel, it seemed an age since seeing Frank, Mabel and Stuart. Sam and Stephen Salter had made her welcome, but they were busy running this and their other camps. The season was hotting up, and in a few weeks it would be school holidays and the camps would be bursting. After mornings in the office the afternoons were beginning to drag, and although she'd wandered round the camp and managed to chat to some members of staff, she hadn't learnt anything relevant to the case.

She did miss them, especially Mabel; they'd known each other way before they both became part of The Anglian Detective Agency. Was she still worried about her son? When she'd read about those two sailors dying on the Plymouth to Fowey race, she knew Mabel would be upset. Since her husband drowned at sea she dreaded her son might meet the same death. Dorothy wished she was there to comfort her.

In her room she glanced at her watch: sixteen twenty-five, they should be here soon. When she had first arrived at Sudbourne Hall, she'd been impressed by the architecture, and the spaciousness of the rooms, but it hadn't taken long for her to find the elegant spaces and grand features cold and unfriendly, and she wished she was back in her Tudor house in Dunwich, with its low ceilings and cosy nooks and crannies. She sighed. She did miss the companionship of the team... and Mabel's cooking. Staff came to the house in the morning to clean and cook. She was in the office so she rarely saw them and prepared meals were left to be reheated for dinner. Here there was a sanitised, too clean, no dust smell; at home, there were the aromas of Mabel's cooking, Stuart's pipe and her favourite furniture polish: beeswax and lavender. Here there was no clattering of pans, sound of Laurel's steps as she ran downstairs, or Frank's car skidding to a halt on the old tarmac drive. It was too quiet.

The front door bell peeled. She rushed downstairs and pulled back the heavy oak door. 'My word, I'm glad to see you two. It seems I've been here on my own for an age.'

'Tired of sleuthing already, Dorothy?' Frank said, giving her a hug.

She laughed, not caring if he did think she wasn't cut out to be a detective. She was coming to that conclusion herself. 'Laurel.' They clung to each other.

'Are you all right, Dorothy? I have missed you – and Stuart and Mabel. It's strange working on your own, isn't it?'

Dear Laurel, she was always understanding. 'It's been difficult in the office, holding myself back when I can see something going wrong. I'm not good at pretending.'

'I thought you were brilliant when I arrived. Don't pay any attention to Frank. After all he's only the gardener – the under-gardener.'

It was Frank who wasn't paying attention; he was looking round the hall. 'Wow! What a pad. Better than my chalet, although I have a lovely neighbour, a tall, blonde bombshell.'

Laurel shook her head. 'Hope you know your trowel from your fork.'

'Glad to hear you two haven't stopped bickering.' She pointed up the curved stairway. 'We'll go to my room. There aren't any staff here at the moment, but we'd be better talking in complete privacy.' She led them up shallow stone steps, a wrought-iron balustrade on one side. The staircase led to a wide corridor with cast-iron radiators. The sunlight shone through a series of small, latticed windows, set deep in stone walls; its light played on pictures and furniture, and a red carpet stretched out down the centre.

'This place must have cost a fortune. You could fit your cottage into just this corridor, Frank,' Laurel said.

'I must say I'm surprised; from what I've seen so far, this house doesn't reflect Salter's personality,' he replied.

'My thoughts exactly.' She opened a door. 'My room.'

'You clicked lucky, it's lovely,' Laurel said.

Dorothy sat down on the armchair and pointed to the sofa. 'I think I'd rather be in the camp with you two; once I've done my stint in the office, there isn't a lot to do here, and Salter and son are usually somewhere else. I'm not doing much detecting.'

Frank sat down next to Laurel. 'Don't worry, Dorothy, you've settled in and once we've worked out what each of us needs to do, I'm sure you'll get more involved.'

They spent the next hour talking about the suspects they'd met, answering each other's questions, and throwing out ideas. Dorothy made notes as they chatted.

Frank got up and walked round the room, stopping to look out of the window. 'Let's sum up. What do we know that may be useful about each of the suspects we've met?' He sat down. 'Dorothy, you start. Belinda Tweedie: could she be responsible for the girls going missing?'

Dorothy put down her notepad and pencil. 'Her possible motive could be jealousy. I think she's besotted with Sam Salter. It's not only my opinion, but when I've chatted to the other girls in the office, they hint at the same thing. Sally, she's the most indiscreet of the two, she said she thinks Sam and Belinda may have had a fling a few years ago. She doesn't know that for sure, it's gossip from before she started working at the camp.'

Frank nodded. 'Do you think Belinda's capable of committing murder?'

Dorothy shook her head. 'I'm afraid not.' She told them about Belinda's squeamishness, her fainting at the sight of blood. 'She's big enough, and strong enough, to overcome a smaller woman, but I can't see it. She's a real wimp!'

'Unless she killed them by remote control,' Laurel said.

Frank stared at her. 'Method?'

'Poison?'

'There's a thought,' Dorothy said. 'But what would she do with the body? No. I can't see it.'

'Let's move on. Laurel, what about Charles Frost, do you see him as a likely candidate?'

She frowned. 'I changed my mind about him as we talked. At first, I thought he was just a lecherous young man, but when he revealed the other side of his character and his love of all things theatrical I must admit I did warm to him.'

'Is he good-looking?' Dorothy asked, leaning forward.

'Very, dark haired and spectacular legs.'

'Ladies, control your hormones. Could he be the murderer? If there is one.'

'Having doubts, Frank?' Laurel asked.

'We've no bodies. Let's hope Stuart finds something relevant when he talks to the girls' families. Come on, Laurel, stop salivating over Charles Frost, and try and be professional. Do you fancy him as a murderer?'

'I'm not sure. He certainly is lecherous. When I saw him on the tennis courts he was getting far too familiar with a girl he was coaching – her boyfriend was furious. Both the missing girls were attractive. We need to find out if he was involved with either or both of them. Nellie Minnikin certainly gave me a coded warning about him.'

He seemed much more interesting than Belinda Tweedie, Dorothy thought. 'What about Nellie? Could she be the one?' she asked.

Laurel shook her head. 'She's certainly strong enough to murder anyone, man, woman or elephant, but I thought she was a pleasant person. But then I've met two villainous people who seemed nice to begin with, so maybe I'm not the best judge of character. I thought she might be a lesbian, so she could have lusted after the girls and murdered them when they rejected her and said they were going to report her to Salter.'

They sat in silence. They didn't seem to have made much progress, Dorothy thought. She looked at Frank, hoping he'd come up with a positive suggestion. 'What do you think, Frank? Could the murderer be Nellie?'

'I've met her and I agree with you, Laurel. I liked her.' He raised a hand. 'This is nothing to do with her as a suspect, but she told me something important.'

She sat up, relief loosening her shoulders. Good old Frank.

He told them about Sam's blonde wife, Patsy.

'That's something you can work on, Dorothy. Try and find out who was the woman who reminded him of the girls,' Frank said.

She beamed at him. 'I'll do my best. What about you, have you met Hinney?'

Frank pulled a face. 'Briefly, yesterday. The man is as forthcoming as a block of wood. A cold fish. Can't see him getting worked up enough to chat a girl up. The only time he looked slightly animated was when he talked about squashing slugs who'd attacked his petunias.' He blew out a frustrated stream of air. 'I'm going to try and meet Jim Lovell tonight, maintenance and security, he's the only one we've not made contact with, apart from Coltman, his part-time worker —'

Dorothy interrupted. 'Sorry, just remembered something; Stuart rang. Revie contacted him with some information.'

'Hope it's interesting,' Frank said. 'I'll just fill you in on this, then you can tell us what Revie said. Going back to Jim, he lives in Orford and goes to the Jolly Sailor when he's not on duty, so I'll drive down tonight and see if I can have a chat with him.' He turned to Dorothy. 'What's Stuart got to say? And how's Mabel?'

'Mabel's fine, but Stuart says she's missing us.'

'Just returned from her honeymoon and she wants company? I better have a word with Mr Elderkin when I next see him,' Frank said.

'Since when were you a marriage guidance counsellor?' Laurel replied.

Dorothy had missed them, too. 'Quiet!' She took a deep breath, and flicked back the pages of her notebook until she came to the notes she'd taken down when Stuart phoned her. 'Revie phoned back with details of the murder of Thomas Coltman's wife and son. Audrey and John.'

'Does it have any relevance to our case?' Laurel asked.

She frowned. 'Not that I can see. It's a very sad story, and although I haven't met him, I feel very sorry for Mr Coltman. Have you two seen him at all?'

They shook their heads.

'Tell us about it,' Frank said.

Dorothy glanced at her notes. 'Mr Coltman was an RAF pilot in the war, he was posted to Java. The family lived in London, where he worked as an architect, but when the bombing started, Audrey, his wife, John, their son, and Mr Coltman's mother, moved to a cottage they owned in Orford. Audrey was originally a local Orford girl from a good family, and she and Thomas, I'll call him that, met as teenagers when the Coltman family regularly came to Orford for holidays.'

'Is that where Thomas Coltman lives now?' Frank asked. 'In the holiday cottage?'

'I don't know,' Dorothy said. 'Revie didn't say, but I suppose it's likely. Shall I go on?'

Frank nodded.

'Thomas was captured by the Japanese and Revie said he was badly tortured. While this was going on, and obviously unbeknown to him, his wife was murdered. One afternoon she'd taken John out for a walk in his pram. Old Mrs Coltman was out for the day, and didn't get back until late. She raised the alarm when she found the house empty and no sign of, or note from, Audrey. The police and several local people searched the area by torch light, but no one was sure where she'd gone. The police started a major search the next day. They brought in some of the men from the RAF camp to help.'

Laurel put her hand to her throat. 'How awful, the poor man wouldn't know his wife and son were dead.'

Dorothy blinked. 'Yes, truly awful.' She sniffed. 'They found her in a field near the River Ore.' She stopped and gulped. 'Dear me, you'd think I'd be used to terrible things happening, wouldn't you, after all we've seen over the past year?'

'When you don't get upset for victims of crime, that's the time to quit searching for the criminals,' Frank said. 'Go on, Dorothy.'

'The poor woman had been raped, strangled and her underwear ... her knickers were missing.' She was unable to continue. She swallowed hard and blew into her handkerchief.

'What about John? How could anyone kill a little child?' Laurel asked.

'They never found his body. They thought he'd been taken away by foxes, or thrown into the River Ore. They dragged the river, but he might have been swept out to sea. His grandmother never got over losing her daughter-in-law and her grandson; neighbours said she roamed the fields, walking by the river, staring into it, trying to find the boy's body. She passed away two years after the murders.'

Laurel shuddered.

'Revie said they found the murderer. Who was it?' Frank asked.

Dorothy pushed her glasses back up the bridge of her nose. 'It was an airman based at Orford Ness where there was a small barracks. The police acted on an anonymous tip-off. Someone saw the killer that afternoon, near where the body was found.' She consulted her notes. 'His name was Adrian Hovell. He'd been seen in the vicinity of where Audrey was found. He was a bird-watcher when not on duty, and other people had seen him talking to Audrey on several other occasions.' She paused. 'Sorry for the jargon, it's as Revie dictated it to me. It seems so cold and heartless to talk about it in this way.'

'We understand,' Laurel said. 'I know it happened thirty years ago, but somehow, being so near to where Audrey and John were murdered, makes it seem closer in time.'

Frank grimaced and shuffled in his seat. 'It's the thought that while Coltman was incarcerated by the Japanese he must have been glad his wife and child were safe in Orford, away from the bombing in London; that must have kept him going through years of hell. He imagined them waiting for him, if and when he got home. From what I've read about the lives of prisoners of war, deep ties at home sustained them through the darkest times. Imagine what he felt when he managed to survive, and then finds his wife and child have been murdered.'

'Revie said old Mrs Coltman was also dead by the time he got back; his father died before the war started. All he had were their graves in St Bartholomew's Church yard, and the terrible absence of John's body. Was he a heap of bones in a fox's den, or at the bottom of the sea?' Dorothy took off her glasses and wiped tears from her cheeks.

They sat in silence.

'Did Revie say what happened to the murderer? There must have been more proof than just a sighting of him near to where Audrey was murdered,' Frank asked.

She shook herself and glanced once again at her notebook. 'Yes, there was conclusive proof. The police searched the barracks and they found a pair of woman's knickers, stained with blood in Hovell's locker. The blood group was AB. Audrey's blood group was also AB.' She straightened her shoulders. Come on, pull yourself together, she thought, you're part of a team of detectives. 'Revie said the attack was brutal, she suffered deep injuries, and old Mrs Coltman identified the knickers as Audrey's; she'd trimmed them with lace for her.'

'So, no doubt of his guilt. What happened to him?' Frank asked.

'Hanged.'

Laurel shuddered, 'What he did was awful and he deserved to be punished, but I'm glad we've abolished the death penalty. There's always the chance of a wrong verdict, although that can't be true in this case.'

A deep rage welled up in her chest. 'I disagree, Laurel. I wish it was still in place. I'd have been pleased if Emily's killer, that wretched man, Nicholson, had been hung by the neck. I fact I'd have offered to pull the lever myself.'

Laurel looked shocked.

Dorothy glared at her. 'What about your sister? Didn't you feel the same? If they'd found the man who killed her, wouldn't you want him dead?'

Laurel's face drained of colour and she slumped back in her seat. Frank placed a hand over hers, and frowned at Dorothy.

Oh no! What had she said? Laurel looked devastated. She shouldn't have mentioned her sister – her murderer was never found. It must be dreadful to think he was still free, unpunished, and might kill again. 'Laurel, I'm so sorry. Please forgive me. You know I wouldn't hurt you for the world.' She tried to stop tears flowing again.

Laurel's colour was coming back. She held out her hand. 'I know, Dorothy. I'm not sure why I...'

Dorothy moved to the settee and hugged Laurel. 'I'm a silly old fool. I think I ought to pack this detecting in and get back to my typewriter.'

Laurel shook her head. 'We both got a bit worked up over poor Mr Coltman.' She turned and looked at Frank. 'What is it you usually say, Frank? Women, heh!'

Frank got up and looked down at them. 'I could think of something a bit stronger, but as I'm a gentleman I'll restrain myself. Dorothy, back to your notes. Did Revie give you any more details about, what was his name, Hovell?'

She scrambled back to her seat and picked up the notebook. 'No. No details. But surely that couldn't be relevant to this case, could it?'

Frank grimaced. 'No... I suppose not, but could you contact Stuart and ask him, if he's got the time, to see if he can dig up any facts about Hovell's family, where they live.' He shook his head. 'Tell him it isn't a priority, it's more important he finds out details of the missing women.'

'Right.' She jotted down some shorthand, then looked at Frank. 'Anything else to discuss? Shall I make some tea?'

'No thanks, Dorothy.' He picked up the Daily Telegraph, lying on the table. 'Oh, go on then.' He jabbed at the paper. 'There's a Sutton's advert for a new plant food. I'll gen up on this, impress Hinney when I next see him.' He looked at her. 'No, second thoughts, I'll skip the tea. I need to get back to the camp and then I'll see if I can contact Lovell at the Jolly Sailor tonight.'

Dorothy looked at Laurel, dreading her answer. She didn't want her to leave without making sure she'd forgiven her for her crass remark about her sister.

'Yes, I'd love a cup, and it's best if I'm not seen leaving with Frank.'

She uttered a sigh of relief. 'Right, see you in a week, Frank. We'll be going back to Greyfriars House next Saturday for a meeting, won't we?'

Frank nodded. 'Hope Mabel will have a slap-up meal for us.'

At seven o clock, when Frank arrived in the municipal carpark, the weather had turned wet and windy. He ran across the road to the Jolly Sailor, a low, red-brick building with large, many-paned windows, giving it a pleasing look. Even more pleasing was a sign for Adnam's ale. How had he missed that when he passed it before? His observational skills were slipping.

He sheltered under the tiled porch which protected two doors. He chose the door to the right, signed Tap Room. There were two old men having a game of dominoes, and three callow youths he was sure he'd seen mooching round the holiday camp. No one looked like a maintenance man. He nodded to them and retreated into the rain. The other door was signed Lounge Bar.

This room smelt of polish, fresh flowers and best of all, hops. Sitting at one of the pine trestle tables were two men, a dog at the feet of the smaller man and behind the mahogany bar, with its gleaming taps and pumps was, he presumed, the landlady. She was leaning towards a middle-aged, fair-haired woman, on the other side of the bar, both obviously enjoying their conversation.

He looked around in approval; the walls were rough un-plastered brick, and the tables, their white tops grooved by scrubbing, were surrounded by wheel-backed Windsor chairs. In the hearth of an inglenook fireplace was a blue-and-white jug filled with roses. It was a proper old-fashioned pub; he hoped the ale lived up to its surroundings.

The landlady stopped chatting and moved towards him. 'Yes, my dear, what can I get you?'

'A pint of Adnam's bitter would be great.'

'Ordinary or best?'

'Ordinary.'

'Jug or straight?'

'Straight, please.'

'Not seen you before, my dear. Visiting us, are you?' The ale swished into the glass as she bent a plump arm.

He held the glass up to the light. 'Clear as a bell.' He swallowed – it was smooth and hoppy, with just the right hint of caramel. So smooth, you'd be half-way down your glass before you realised it. 'Excellent. Congratulations. You keep a good cellar.'

The landlady flushed, smiled and, turning to the other woman, pulled a knowing face.

'To answer your question, I've just started work at the holiday camp, but I thought I'd sample the local beer.'

Her face expressed surprise. 'That's a coincidence, Mr Lovell, over there,' she pointed to the two men who were in a deep conversation at a table near the fireplace, 'he works at the camp. Jim!' The taller man looked up.

'Jim, here's someone who's just started work at the camp.' She turned to Frank. 'What's your name, my dear?'

'Frank Diamond.'

'Jim, meet Frank Diamond.'

Jim got up, a friendly grin on a somewhat gormless face. 'Nice to meet you, Frank. What do you do?' he asked, his voice loud and penetrating.

'I'm a gardener.'

Jim hooted with laughter. 'Have you met Gareth Hinney?'

Frank took another pull at his pint. 'Yes, we met yesterday.'

'Say much, did he?'

'Not a lot.'

'It's like talking to a brick-wall. But he's a good gardener, worked in one of the parks in London before he

111

came here. Never mind, you can always come and have a cuppa and a fag with me in my workshop, if you need a bit of company.'

'That's kind of you, Jim. Cuppas would be welcome but I don't smoke.'

Jim raised his eyebrows, then nodded towards Frank's glass. 'See you like your beer, though.'

Frank nodded, then swallowed another mouthful. This was working out well and Jim Lovell seemed a nice chap, certainly brighter than his features suggested, and a bit of a gossiper, which was helpful. Though he'd need earplugs if he worked with him.

'I need to finish talking with Bert.' He nodded to the chap with the dog and leant nearer to Frank. 'He's in a bit of a state, but I can't make out what he's worried about,' he whispered. He turned to the fair-haired woman. 'Joan, meet Frank, he's working at the camp. Joan's my missus.'

She smiled and patted the stool next to hers. 'Come and have a chat with us, Frank.'

Jim went back to Bert and his dog.

'That's Albert Wiles talking to my husband,' she hissed. 'I wish Jim wouldn't have anything to do with him, but Jim's too nice, he'll talk to anyone.'

Even me, Frank thought. He moved closer to the two women. 'What's Bert been up to? Not smuggling, I hope?'

The two women looked at each other. 'I wouldn't go as far as to say that,' Joan said.

'I wouldn't be surprised,' the landlady chipped in.

'He's a poacher,' Joan hissed. 'Got caught last year pinching oysters from Pinney's oyster beds. Him and that Basil – '

'Basil?' Frank interrupted.

Joan sniggered. 'His little terrier. Awful dog it is, as randy as its master. Basil wraps himself round yur leg, while Bert attacks other areas!' The two women dissolved into peals of laughter.

Joan wiped her eyes. 'Nothing like a good laugh!'

'Do you want me to rescue Jim?' Frank asked. He wanted to talk to him, especially as he wasn't above dishing the dirt on people.

'Oh, would you, dear? I am grateful. Would you like another pint?' She eyed his empty glass and the landlady ogled him.

Frank smiled and nodded. He was glad Laurel wasn't here; he'd get no end of teasing.

As he got close to the men he heard Bert say: 'Something's wrong, Jim. I don't like it. I blame myself.' It was difficult to be sure he'd heard correctly as his Suffolk accent was as thick as treacle.

'I'm not sure what you mean, Bert. Who're you talking about?'

Bert looked up and glared at Frank. He was slightly built with a craggy face, his forehead deeply lined and there were grooves on each side of his mouth.

'Bert, this is Frank, he's working at the camp.'

Bert made a quick nod of his head, but ignored Frank's offered hand and Basil acknowledged Frank's presence by curling his top lip and snarling. Bert raised his glass and downed what was left of his drink. 'Got to go. See you, Jim.' He prodded Basil with his boot and the dog followed his master out of the door.

'Sorry,' Frank said, sitting down, 'I seem to have interrupted something important.'

Joan brought his refilled glass and her own drink to the table. 'What was all that about, Jim? He's in a worse mood than usual, and that's saying something.'

Jim shook his head. 'As far as I can make out, he's worried about someone, thinks something bad's happened, thinks it's his fault. Says he doesn't want to go to gaol again.'

Joan sipped her sherry. 'Not like him to be worried about someone else. Always put himself first for as long as I can remember.' The landlady joined them and the conversation flowed.

'Does he just poach oysters? I'd have thought there was a limited number of customers for them,' Frank asked.

'No, he'll take anything that's not tied down. He's got a boat and lobster and crab pots are one of his favourites to steal from,' the landlady said.

'He'll drown one of these days; the waters sea-side of the Ness are dangerous, strong currents and deep waters,' Joan said.

Jim leant forward. 'I heard he lands on the Ness, puts out traps for rabbits.'

'If he does, he's a fool. He'll get blown to bits,' the landlady said.

Jim's lower lip turned down. 'He's no fool, he must know which areas have been cleared. But I've never known him like this. He's really worried, even scared, I'd say.'

Frank bought the next round of drinks. Later he risked a few questions. 'Perhaps you ought to find out what's worrying Bert,' he said to Jim. Joan pulled a face. 'Sorry, Joan, but it might be important. Where does Bert live?'

'Burnt Lane, not far from us; we live in Daphne Road. Do you know where that is?'

He did. Dorothy had told him Belinda Tweedie lived in Daphne Road. And he'd noted the road sign as he'd walked to the quay on Friday morning. 'Yes, seems a nice quiet place, I don't suppose you get many visitors down there.'

'Only walkers,' Jim replied. 'I'll think about what you've said; I must admit I've never seen old Bert so agitated. Do you think he's worried about someone I know? Someone at the camp? Is that why he tried to tell me?'

He thought Jim might be right. 'That's a shrewd guess, Jim. Any idea who it might be?'

Jim gazed into his beer. 'Must be someone Bert knows.'

'Belinda Tweedie lives near us in Daphne Road, do you think it could be her, Jim?' Joan asked.

Jim pursed his lips. 'Not in a million years! She won't speak to him. Bit of a snob is our Belinda.'

The two women nodded in agreement.

'What about Tommy Coltman? He's always wandering round at night, so I've been told,' the landlady said.

'Who's Tommy Coltman?' Frank asked. He'd struck lucky tonight. Coltman was another suspect. He'd already put Jim Lovell at the bottom of his list; he couldn't see Joan letting him off the leash to chase dark-haired girls.

'He's my assistant at the camp; I'm in charge of maintenance, Tommy's part-time, mornings only. He wouldn't hurt a fly, poor chap. He lives near us too, Doctor's Lane, and he does know Bert, but I can't see him being the reason Bert's worried.'

Joan tapped her finger on the table. 'But supposing he saw Mr Coltman doing something wrong, something really bad, when he was out at night poaching? We know Mr Coltman goes out at night, people have seen him.'

'He can't sleep, Joan, he's told me that. Poor bugger, he was tortured in a Jap camp during the war and came back to find his wife and baby murdered. He was a wreck, still is. Sam Salter took pity on him and gave him his job. Gives him something to live for, I suppose.'

'Still, he's weird, I wouldn't like to meet him at night down a dark alley,' the landlady said, shivering in mock horror.

It was late when Frank got back to the camp. There was a light in Laurel's chalet. He thought of visiting her, hoping they might mull over his findings with a glass or two of malt whisky. He shook his head. Too risky, someone might see him going in, and make the wrong assumptions. He didn't want to ruin her reputation. Not just yet.

Chapter 11

Monday, June 21, 1971

Laurel sat down on one of the chairs arranged round several tables grouped to form a rectangle in the staff canteen. The seat felt sticky against the tops of her legs and she wished she'd worn jeans instead of shorts. The weekly staff meeting was due to start at seven thirty; she glanced at her watch, ten minutes to go, she was early. Did she have time to go back to her chalet and change? She was afraid she'd stick to the seat and leave a strip of skin behind when the meeting ended.

Too late! The door to the kitchen swung open and Nellie Minnikin, carrying a loaded tray, came in.

'Laurel! You're prompt. Could you give me a hand?'

'Morning, Nellie.' She peeled her legs from the seat, wincing.

Nellie laughed, put down the tray and threw her a towel from a pile on a counter. 'Sit on that. We need new chairs, I must tell Sam, see if he's prepared to shell out.'

Laurel helped her to unload mugs, a large jug of coffee, a smaller one of milk and a plate heaped with buttered toast. As they were doing this, other members of staff drifted in, exchanging good mornings, hellos and nods of the head. Laurel sat down next to Nellie and Charlie Frost made a bee-line and sat on her other side. Frank came in, ignored her and sat down between two men. On Frank's right was Gareth Hinney, and on his left a man she didn't know, but she heard Frank call him Jim. He must be Jim Lovell, in charge of maintenance. Frank must have met up with him on Saturday night as Lovell was chattering away as though they were old mates. Hinney was staring in front of him, talking to no one.

Jim lit up a cigarette.

'No smoking in the canteen,' Nellie said.

'Soon I won't be able to smoke anywhere, if everyone follows them Glasgow councillors' lead,' he replied.

'What's that?' Charlie asked.

'They're talking about banning it on the underground, and buses and not giving away free cigarettes at council functions,' Jim said, giving Nellie a withering look.

'That's the Jocks for you. We wouldn't stand for that here,' Charlie said.

Belinda Tweedie, in a baby-blue dress, sailed in, carrying a wire-tray full of office paraphernalia, followed by Dorothy, looking as though she'd smelt something nasty.

Belinda walked to the head of the table and pointed to the spaces in front of two chairs.

'Set two places here, Miss Piff,' Belinda commanded. She turned to Gareth Hinney. 'Mr Hinney, could you ask Mr Lovell to move down two places. I need to sit next to Mr Salter, and Miss Piff must sit next to me.' She gave him a winsome smile. He nodded, got up and they all shuffled down.

'Someone should tell Belinda pastels don't do anything for the fuller figure,' Nellie whispered.

Laurel put her hand over her mouth to deaden the snort.

Nellie passed round the coffee and milk. 'I thought everyone could do with something in their stomachs as it'll be ages before we get our proper breakfasts.' It was true, she wouldn't get anything to eat until the campers had finished their breakfasts, but she wasn't tempted: the coffee smelt like Camp and milk was in short supply. The toast was also unappetising: white, sliced bread with a thin coat of margarine.

She thought of Frank grinding coffee beans, the plop, plop of his percolator, and the taste of his coffee: rich and smooth. The coffee's smell wasn't even strong enough to mask the lingering greasy odour of last night's food. 'Not hungry?' Charlie Frost asked as he clamped his dazzling teeth round a piece of toast.

She shook her head and smiled, not replying; she didn't want to get into a conversation with him. She wasn't in a detecting mood. She should be chatting to both Nellie and Charlie; that was what she was paid for. Frank was in conversation with Jim Lovell, extolling the quality of the beer at the Jolly Sailor.

'You can rely on the beer there, I've never had a bad pint,' Jim boomed.

God, he'd double as a ship's fog horn!

Dorothy was trying to get a conversation going with Hinney. 'Mr Hinney, I believe. I'm Dorothy Piff, I work in the office.'

He turned to face her. She held out her hand, then winced as he shook it. 'Goodness, you've a grip like a vice, Mr Hinney. I don't think I'll be able to type for the rest of the day,' she simpered.

Laurel caught the look on Frank's face and quickly looked away.

Belinda nudged Dorothy. 'You've forgotten the blotters. You'd better get them, be as quick as you can, it's nearly half-past.'

Dorothy's face flushed and her mouth tightened as she got up.

'Oh, for goodness' sake, sit down,' Belinda countermanded, 'there isn't time. Try to be more careful next time.' She looked round shaking her head and rolling her eyes.

If Belinda Tweedie was found murdered tomorrow Laurel thought she'd know who the murderer would be.

Frank said something to Jim Lovell, but she couldn't hear what.

Then Jim turned to the rest of the staff. 'Frank, here, was asking me about Bert Wiles. He met him at the Jolly Sailor last night. Old Bert was in a right funny mood, but I don't know what's the matter with him, he buggered off before he told me,' Jim said.

Belinda glared at him.

'Sorry, Miss Tweedie, beg your pardon, ladies. Anyone know what's the matter with him? Something's bothering him. You know Bert, don't you, Miss Tweedie? Has he said anything to you?'

Belinda sniffed. 'I know of him, I do not know him.'

'What about you, Tommy? He lives near you. Do you ever see him when you're out at night?'

So that was Thomas Coltman, the poor man who'd lost his wife and son. He'd slipped into the room and taken a seat at the far end of the table.

Coltman looked embarrassed; it was unnecessary for Lovell to mention his nocturnal walks, though that was interesting. 'I see him, but we don't speak,' he muttered.

Lovell shrugged. 'I'll have to see if I can talk to him soon. It wasn't like him, he seemed worried about something, said something bad's happened and it's his fault. Not his usual line, I can tell you—'

Miss Tweedie rapped on the table and pointed. Sam and Stephen Salter were standing in the doorway; Laurel wasn't sure how long they'd been there, she'd been so interested in what Lovell was saying and also noting the faces of the rest of the staff as he spoke. Some looked vaguely interested, some bored, but Belinda Tweedie's lips trembled: in anger? fear? disgust? Frank and Dorothy were also clocking the expressions of the people round the table.

Sam and Stephen Salter took up their positions; Sam pulled a face and waved away the jug of coffee, but Stephen smiled at Nellie and politely refused.

'Right, I'll keep this short and sweet today,' Sam said as he glanced at Belinda whose pencil was poised over her notebook; Dorothy was in the same position.

'No need for you to take notes, Miss Piff,' Belinda hissed.

Dorothy looked at her over her glasses. 'I need to keep up my shorthand speed, and you might miss something. Belts and braces, you know.'

Belinda's pencil squiggled over the page. She tore it off and smoothed a fresh sheet.

Dorothy wasn't being diplomatic; she wouldn't get much information from Belinda Tweedie at this rate. It was difficult when you instinctively took a dislike to a person to pretend all was well, but it did pay off. She'd learnt more about Charlie Frost once she'd got him to talk about himself. However, she wasn't doing too well today and as soon as Salter finished the meeting she must try and be more sociable.

'First, bookings for the end of July and August have gone up in the past week, so that's good news.' He turned towards Stephen. 'Mr Salter Junior must take credit for that: the television adverts, although expensive, have paid off and it looks as though we'll be at full capacity for August.'

There were murmurs of congratulations, but a few groans as well. Salter glowered at them.

'I thought the advertisements were very clever, Mr Salter,' Belinda said. 'It's such an innovative idea, a holiday camp for the over eighteens, and the one about the honeymoon couple was so romantic.' She fluttered her eyelashes at Sam.

'Thank you, Miss Tweedie,' Stephen responded.

'That's the good news,' Sam said, 'but you can't rest on your laurels, especially not hers.' He pointed to Laurel, laughing so much at his own joke, his face reddened. Most of the staff joined in.

She bit back what she wanted to say.

'Now for the bad news. We've had some complaints and Stephen will see those members of staff concerned when the meeting is over. I don't like complaints, I like happy, satisfied campers. Campers who'll come back next year and hopefully bring some friends with them. Now the floor's open to you. Any questions?'

There were a few tentative raised hands.

'Yes, Miss Minnikin?'

'Mr Salter, I'd like to draw your attention to the state of the chairs in this dining room. I had to get Miss Bowman a towel to sit on, the surface was taking the skin off her legs.'

Why did she have to bring that up? Everyone was looking at her and one of Frank's eyebrows was raised, as though saying: 'Poor lamb!'

Salter stared at her. 'We can't have our lovely swimming coach appearing with rough skin, can we? The campers might think she's got a disease.' Everyone laughed. Laurel could feel her face heating up.

Charlie dug an elbow into her ribs. 'I'll volunteer to rub some cream in.' He leered.

She took a deep breath and tried to smile.

'Contact our suppliers, Miss Minnikin and give me some costings. We'll see what we can do.'

Nellie smiled broadly. 'Thank you, Mr Salter.' She turned to Laurel. 'You'd better watch it, Belinda's glaring at you,' she whispered.

She looked up and indeed Belinda's nostrils were stretched wide and her lips puckering into a sphincter. She'd enjoy telling Frank which sphincter it reminded her of. God, the woman looked as though she'd be happy to see her dead. Ridiculous. What was that saying? 'Envy feeds on the living; it ceases when they are dead.' She glanced again at Belinda. She was looking down at her writing pad, stabbing at the paper with her pencil. She looked up, her blue eyes cold and calculating. Ice slid down Laurel's bones, slowing her heart, knotting her guts. Had Belinda been jealous of the two missing girls? Jealous enough to kill them? But if so, she hadn't achieved her goal: she didn't have Sam Salter's heart. Belinda Tweedie had ceased to be a fat, silly woman with a crush on her boss.

There were a few more questions and then Salter called the meeting to a close, reminding everyone to be here next Monday morning at the same time. He marched out followed closely by Stephen, then Belinda with Dorothy bringing up the rear.

Frank was talking to Hinney. 'What do you want to me to do this morning, Mr Hinney?'

'Before breakfast you can weed the top right-hand bed in the centre of the camp. You know which one I mean?'

Frank nodded.

'There's some couch grass between the standard roses; get out as much as you can. I'm going to mow the bowling green before the campers get to it. After breakfast you can concentrate on watering the flowering baskets near the office and tidying up the flower beds near there. Any questions? You know where the tools are.'

'Where are the compost heaps, and what do I do with the couch grass? You won't want that to get put in with the rest of the compost.'

Well done, Frank. He sounded as though he'd been gardening all his life.

'I'll show you. It's an area tucked away so the campers can't see it.' He turned, expecting Frank to follow him, but before he left Frank looked at Laurel and pulled his right ear lobe. It was a sign they'd worked out when they needed to talk to each other. She resisted winking at him. How would they manage to meet without arousing suspicion? And why did Frank need to see her? What had he discovered? Was it about Belinda Tweedie? Would her gut feelings about the woman be justified? Bubbles of excitement fizzed round her brain. Was this a break-through?

Frank pulled the black polo-necked jumper over his head and pulled it down over dark jeans. Should he black his face as well? After all he was going past three chalets to get to Laurel's. He was sure she'd seen the sign, and hopefully would be expecting a visit. He glanced at his watch; the luminous figures showed ten minutes past midnight. He grasped his torch and carefully opened the door, pausing on the threshold, listening, watching. The night breeze sighed over the chalet roofs and moved a discarded cigarette packet a few inches over the tarmac path in front of the chalets. He stepped out slowly, closing the door behind him. There were no lights in any of the staff chalets, including Laurel's. He leant back against the door, waiting. In the distance voices, laughter: probably campers on the way back from the disco or the pub. They faded away to nothing. He moved his head from side to side, letting his eyes become accustomed to the darkness: the sky was cloudy, the moon and stars hidden. He flinched as the cigarette packet galloped a few more feet, scraping the ground as it was pushed by a gust of wind. The difference between solid objects and the night sky increased and moving over the grass verge he crept towards Laurel's chalet.

He leant on the door, listening. Each door had a quartered square of glass in the top half, giving the impression of a window. He scraped against it with a fingernail, and pressed his ear against the door. Nothing. He'd presumed she'd be in, but perhaps she was out sleuthing, or possibly carousing with Charlie Frost, perhaps his legs were irresistible. He tried again. The sound of a key turning and the door opened a few inches.

'It's me.'

She opened the door wider and he slid into the chalet. The air was fragrant with a familiar scent of lemon soap; he breathed deeply. She silently closed the door behind him.

'What would you have done if it was someone else?'

There was a giggle. 'Depends on who it was,' she whispered.

'Tart!'

'Yes, please, but I'd prefer crisps.'

There was a tang of whisky on her breath. 'You've started without me. How cut are you? Half-cut, quarter-cut?'

Another giggle. 'Only one shot. I got bored waiting for you.'

'Have you got something to cover up the door? I've brought a torch.'

125

She placed something over the square of glass and the blackness of the room increased. He switched on the torch, focussing the beam at the floor. There was the scrape of a match and a sulphurous flame revealed Laurel, in blue pyjamas, lighting a night-light in a saucer on a bedside table.

'More romantic, don't you think?' She grinned at him.

He'd missed her. Although he'd seen her around the camp, his inability to talk to her had been frustrating; they worked so much better when they were sparking off each other, bickering and joshing. His shoulders relaxed. 'May I?' He pointed to the bed.

Her eyes widened and the corners of her mouth turned up. She nodded and sat down in the only chair in the room. 'Would you like a tot?'

'Several, please.'

She went into the bathroom and came back with another glass, a third full. He stared at her and then the glass.

'You did say several.' She picked up her glass next to the night-light and they carefully chinked glasses. She looked him up and down. 'Haven't you forgotten something?'

What was she on about? He didn't remember her ever being in a mood like this, slightly fey, devil-may-care, almost flirty. Was this the whisky speaking? He didn't think so. 'What do you mean?'

She gesticulated with her hand, sweeping it from his head to his feet. 'The chocolates, where are the chocolates?'

Light dawned, the man in black in the TV advert. 'I didn't know you liked Cadbury's chocolates and I certainly can't see any ladies in this room.'

The giggle again, then her expression changed, and in the flickering light her face became serious. 'Why the meeting, Frank? Have you found out something?'

He leant towards her. 'I think somehow we need to contact Bert Wiles.'

'The poacher? You think whatever he was worried about might have something to do with the missing girls?'

'I'm not sure, but it's the only unusual happening we've come across. I met Bert, very briefly, at the Jolly Sailor. He seems a tough little man; if he's worried about something and he needs to tell someone about it, I think it's worth looking into. He may have seen something, although it's nearly a year since the last girl went missing. I can't see why he'd begin to worry now, if that was the case. It must be something that's happened recently, unless his conscience has a slow fuse.'

'How do we find him?'

'I went back to the Jolly Sailor this evening; Jim Lovell and his missus were there, but no sight of Bert. I remarked on this, but Jim said he sometimes doesn't come in for a few nights, has other fish to fry, or poached game to sell. Are you free tomorrow afternoon?'

Laurel frowned. 'I think I've a swimming lesson booked for two, but after that I'm free. What do you want me to do?'

Frank took a deep swallow, letting the scotch trickle down his throat. 'Could you give his house a look over? See if you think he's there.'

'Do you want me to talk to him?'

Frank grimaced. 'Not sure. I don't think he's dangerous, although I suppose he might be a possible suspect, but I doubt it.'

'How could he be? He's no connections with the camp, apart from knowing Jim Lovell.'

'And Belinda Tweedie,' Frank said.

Yes, Belinda Tweedie. I want to talk about her, but first let's finish off Bert.'

Frank described him and his dog. 'Bert's small, but wiry and he's probably strong for his size, but you shouldn't have any problem with him if he turns nasty. I'll leave it to you as to whether or not you decide to talk to him.' He passed her a piece of paper with Bert's address on it.

'I'll take the car and park nearby. I could knock and ask for directions, pretend I'm looking for Belinda.'

'How would you explain that to her?'

Laurel shrugged. 'It doesn't sound as though they're buddies, so she might never hear about it.'

'Excellent. Let me know if you've made contact.'

'How will I do that?'

'When you come back, leave your car windscreen wipers to the right if you've seen him, to the left if not.'

She raised her eyebrows. 'Not only the man in black, now it's Mr James Bond.'

He grinned at her. 'Fun though. If you haven't got anything I'll go back to the Jolly Sailor tomorrow night.'

She sniffed. 'That will be a sacrifice, having to down pints of beer.'

'You wanted to talk about Belinda Tweedie.'

Laurel reached for the bottle of scotch. Frank held out his glass and she poured in a good measure. 'I think we ought to take Tweedie more seriously. Dorothy said she's squeamish, but the way she glared at me when Salter made that comment, made my flesh creep. It wasn't even as if it was a flirty remark, but she can't stand any other female coming between her and her boss. She's extremely jealous.' She gave herself another top up.

Frank sipped his drink. Women. Dangerous women. Women in love. After his brief and disastrous infatuation with Carol Pemberton earlier in the year, an infatuation which could have resulted in them being removed from the case, he'd resisted any entanglements and concentrated on work. He wouldn't make the same mistake again: involvement with a client. He glanced up; Laurel was studying him quizzically. Shadows moved over her face from the flickering flame of the night-light; one second her mouth hidden in shadow, then revealed, her lips curved in a smile; her loose hair dark, then golden.

'How's Oliver?' He wasn't sure why he'd asked that question. He didn't really want to know the answer.

Laurel leant back, the smile fading. 'Fine, as far as I know. I rang him a few days ago, we're meeting next Saturday, after our business meeting, time permitting.'

'And Billy?'

The smile reappeared. 'On top form. Chased a few cats and nearly caught a rabbit.'

Frank shook his head. 'You love that dog, don't you?'

Laurel sighed. 'I adore him, he's so much fun.'

'Feel the same way about the owner?'

Laurel looked at him and took a long swallow.

'Sorry, none of my business.'

'Correct. Let's get back to the case. How are you getting on with Hinney? He looks a cold fish to me. I should think he's boring you to death.'

'I can't get a handle on him, he's so uncommunicative. He believes no sentence should stretch beyond five words and as for body language, he hasn't got any.' He paused. 'There's no doubt he's a good gardener. He's got an area under cultivation where he raises ornamental plants for the camp's flower beds, it's where the compost heaps are.'

'Where's that?'

'You know the staff car park?' She nodded. 'It's behind there. You can't see it because of the high fence.'

'You sound impressed.'

'There's a large heated greenhouse, several cold frames, and besides bedding plants and the perennials he propagates, he also works a vegetable bed.'

'Why? He lives on the camp. He can't do any cooking.' Frank did look grumpy.

'Seems he gives them away to local staff. He's got some unusual plants growing in the greenhouse and outside. Can't see the use he has for some of them.'

'Did you ask him?'

Frank shook his head. 'No. I didn't want to reveal my erudition.'

Laurel snorted. 'Not like you.'

'Tut, tut, Miss Bowman. I didn't think spouting Latin names would fit into my role as second gardener.'

'Touché. Frank, I think it's time you—' There was a scraping sound from outside, close to the door. She put a hand over her mouth. Frank sprang up and pinched out the flame of the night-light.

Tap, tap, tap on the door.

Laurel reached for Frank's hand.

The situation reminded him of the time when a teacher had found him and Janet Brooks in the stationery cupboard. If only he'd had another ten minutes he wouldn't have had to wait eighteen months to lose his virginity.

Tap, tap, tap.

Laurel's shoulders were shaking. He squeezed her hand hard. The shaking increased.

Tap, tap, tap. 'Laurel, I know you're in there. I heard you talking. Who's in there with you?' The voice was male – a drunken male.

Laurel pressed her mouth close to his ear. 'It's Charlie Frost.' Her lips were soft and warm. The ear was an erotic area, and memories of the stationery cupboard became sharper.

'Laurel.' His voice was getting louder; soon other members of staff would be woken up.

Frank turned his head and whispered into her ear, deliberately pressing close, tempted for a moment to brush his tongue over her ear lobe. 'You'll have to get rid of him.'

She shuddered and pulled away from him. He got up and moved into the bathroom, keeping the door ajar.

Tap, tap tap. 'Laurel, open the door. I want to talk to you. I need your help. I don't know what to do.'

Frank tensed.

'Charlie, please be quiet. You'll have everyone up soon,' she hissed. 'Go away. If you don't I'll scream and say you were trying to break the door down. I'll report you to Mr Salter.'

She'd give him detention soon.

There was silence.

'I thought you liked me. We get on so well together. Please let me in, Laurel,' Charlie pleaded.

There was an exhalation of impatient breath. 'Sod off, Charlie. I'll not tell you again. If you go now I promise to see you tomorrow morning and I'll help you if I can. I need to get some sleep, even if you don't.'

After what seemed like an interminable time, there was the sound of shuffling footsteps slowly fading away, then silence.

Frank came out of the bathroom. Laurel removed the material covering the glass in the door and peered out into the night. He moved next to her. 'Has he gone?'

'I'm not sure, he could be hiding round a corner, waiting to see if any one comes out. Wouldn't put it past him.'

'He sounded pretty drunk to me. More likely he's fallen down in a stupor.'

They bumped into each other. Laurel laughed. 'I nearly exploded. I felt like a teenager caught snogging my boyfriend on the sofa.'

He didn't tell her what the situation reminded him of. 'Any idea what he was going on about?'

'No. Another one who doesn't know what to do. Do you think it could be important?'

He decided he needed to get out of the chalet: the darkness, the nearness of Laurel, the whisky roaring through his veins, it all spelt disaster if he didn't get out soon. 'I'm off, let's hope Frost has hit the hay in his chalet. Which one is it?'

'I'm not sure, I've not noticed him going in or out of any of them, and I certainly didn't ask.'

'You'll try and see Bert tomorrow?'

'I said I would.' She hesitated. 'I don't think it's a good idea to meet like this, Frank. It's too risky.'

She was right there.

'We need to have some way of communicating; a weekly meeting back at Greyfriars isn't going to work. Perhaps we could arrange to meet regularly in Dorothy's room. As long as we're careful, make sure we arrive at different times. What do you think?' he asked.

'Yes. We could try and meet tomorrow night, then I can tell you if I had any luck with Bert.'

'Watch out for him: Jim Lovell's wife said he was a randy old man.'

'Not another!'

He hoped she wasn't referring to him. He opened the door, waited, then slipped back to his chalet.

Chapter 12

Tuesday, June 22, 1971

Sam's Jaguar pulled up in front of the camp's office. Dorothy started to open the passenger door, but Sam placed a hand on her arm.

'You wait there, Dorothy.' He jumped out and opened her door.

This was a change. Why the sudden concern for her? 'Thank you, Sam.'

'My pleasure, Dorothy.'

As they walked towards the entrance, Belinda Tweedie, who was standing in the doorway, probably waiting to chastise her for being late, swivelled on her heels, and disappeared.

'I've been very impressed by your grasp of what's needed to make the camp's administration run more smoothly,' Sam said.

The previous evening they'd watched the end of an exciting match at Wimbledon; she and Sam rooted for the veteran Gonzales, who beat the whipper-snapper Orantes, supported by Stephen, in five sets. After, over dinner, she'd enjoyed telling them the changes she'd thought would make improvements to the camp's administration, and as they'd talked about various aspects, new ideas came to both Sam and Stephen. Stephen made notes and he and his father decided to try out one or two ideas immediately. They'd ended the evening with a few drinks. Even if she wasn't discovering anything new about the disappearance of the two women, she was pleased they'd appreciated her organisational skills.

Sam ushered her into the office. 'Good morning, Sally. Any problems today?'

'Not so far, Mr Salter.'

'That's what I like to hear. Where's Miss Tweedie?'

'In your office, Mr Salter.'

Dorothy moved towards her desk.

Sam held up his hand. 'Come with me, Dorothy. I need you to explain to Miss Tweedie your ideas for improving the booking system for the tennis courts, horse-riding and mini-golf course. I'm not sure I can remember all the details.'

She moved closer to him. 'Do you think that's wise? Miss Tweedie might be upset if you started implementing my ideas. Perhaps I should have discussed them with her first. She might see it as me going behind her back.'

Sam shrugged. 'Diplomacy was never my strong point. My motto is get things done fast. If you see a better, more economical way of doing something, get on with it.'

Butterflies fluttered in her chest. 'Perhaps you could tell her it was your idea, not involve me. Remember why I'm here,' she whispered.

He shook his head, ignoring the hint. 'You're too modest, Dorothy.' He opened his office door. 'I can't say that's a quality you find in many women nowadays. But I like it!' He beamed at her and placing his hand in the small of her back, gently pushed her into the room.

Belinda was rearranging the telephone, blotter and other bits and pieces on Sam's desk, a duster in one hand and a tin of furniture polish in the other.

'Good morning, Mr Salter.' She promptly finished her polishing and moved away from the desk, allowing Sam to sit down.

'Good morning, Belinda.'

She turned to Dorothy and tapped her watch. 'You're late, Miss Piff. There's a pile of letters on your desk. Make sure replies are completed for the mid-day post.'

Dorothy started to move towards the door.

'That can wait, Miss Tweedie. Dorothy, please sit down.' He pointed to the chair Belinda normally sat in when she was taking dictation or instructions from him. 'You can sit down as well, Miss Tweedie and take notes. Dorothy will explain to you how we can improve the booking system for the tennis courts etc.' He smiled at Dorothy. 'Dorothy's got lots of good ideas for improving many of the systems we use. I want this one put into operation as soon as possible.'

Belinda flopped onto the chair, her face set in stone, a stone with a red flush.

Dorothy's butterflies turned into birds, birds batting their wings against her rib cage. She'd never ingratiate her way into Belinda's good books now. There would never be a tête-à-tête, she would never discover any of Belinda's secrets. Oh well, she might as well enjoy her little triumph. She'd have to concentrate on delving into Sam's secrets, being as she was the flavour of the month. No, she'd have one last try to save the situation.

'I'm sorry, Belinda. I think you run the office very efficiently. These ideas came up over dinner last night. I would have preferred to have discussed them with you, but Sam, Mr Salter, like all business moguls, is an impatient man.'

Sam chuckled. He obviously liked being described as a mogul. 'You do have a way with words, Dorothy. I like a sassy woman.'

Belinda looked ready to burst into tears. 'What about the letters, Mr Salter? If they don't get typed we'll miss the post.'

'Get Sally to phone Cindy, see if she can come in straight away. You can give them a hand when we've finished here. I want Dorothy to get on with changing the system. I'm putting her in charge of it. She can drive it through.' He pointed at the door. 'See Sally now.'

Belinda clutched her pad and pencil to her bosom, took a deep breath, her nostrils expanding, and opened the door. At the desk talking to Sally was Gareth Hinney with a bunch of long-stemmed red roses.

'Hello, Gareth,' Sam shouted. 'Those flowers for me?'

'Yes, Mr Salter.'

Sam got up and went to him, bending over to smell the flowers. 'Lovely, thanks, Gareth.' He took one of the roses and gave the rest to Sally. 'Put them in a vase and bring them straight in.'

He walked back into his office and gave the rose to Dorothy. 'A beautiful flower for a very clever lady.'

He was enjoying upsetting Belinda Tweedie; he must know how she felt about him. She didn't like being used in this way, but what could she do? 'Thank you, Sam.' She didn't need to look at Belinda to know what her expression would be like. However, it was a new role for her: the other woman.

Laurel, freshly showered after giving her swimming lesson and dressed in jeans and a t-shirt, manoeuvred her car out of the staff car park and set off for Orford on her mission to try and contact Bert Wiles. As she drove through the camp gates a sense of relief came over her. The camp did seem like a prison at times. If she didn't find Bert at home, and she was hoping he wouldn't be there, she decided she'd drive to Woodbridge and explore the town, rather than go back to the camp straight away.

She parked in the municipal car park near the quay and walked back to Bert's house. It was such a pretty village, the gardens were well-tended, the passers-by friendly, nodding and smiling, everyone enjoying a pleasant summer's day. Murder belonged in the harsh streets of cities, desolate moors, or by litter-filled canals. Not here. But murder could happen anywhere: the school on the sandy cliffs of Dunwich, the Edwardian house in Aldeburgh, the beach house on the shore at Thorpeness. She'd seen those dead bodies herself in the last two cases. So, why not here? She shuddered; it was as though someone had slid the point of a sharp knife down her backbone. She slowed down. Was Bert Wiles dangerous? Frank said he was a small man, she shouldn't have any trouble dealing with him if he became violent, but did she want to deal with him if he got nasty? Was he responsible for the disappearance of the two girls? They'd decided to concentrate on members of the camp staff as the main suspects, but what if they were wrong and it was someone outside the camp who was responsible? Wasn't it foolish to go to his house on her own? But she and Frank couldn't go together; they mustn't be seen to know each other. She gnawed at her top lip.

She turned around and marched back to her car, opened the boot and removed a tennis racket from its metal press. Frank had delivered a fatal blow with a cricket bat, so why not a tennis racket as a weapon? She slammed down the boot lid, clenched her jaw and strode back towards Bert's house. Thank goodness Frank couldn't see her! But having something she could use as a weapon gave her confidence. She smiled. Perhaps if she saw Bert, she could say she was looking for her tennis ball. Tell him she hit it over his hedge when she was bouncing the ball in the lane.

She turned right into Daphne Road, home of the dreaded Belinda, and then left into Burnt Street. It was a short, rough lane. At the end, on the right-hand side, was a derelict cottage, with one window only on both the lower and upper floors. The bedroom window was small, under a sharply angled roof. On the gate, half-hanging off its hinges, a wooden sign had Willow Cottage burnt into the wood. Bert's house.

It was hard to imagine the house was lived in: it looked neglected, its garden overgrown with weeds, the windows filthy and no sign of life. She pushed open the gate, lifting it so it didn't completely lose its connection with the flaking brick wall. The hinges screeched and she left it open in case she needed to make a sudden retreat. The brick path, once possibly red, was slippery with mosses and liverworts. The beds on either side were lush with prize-winning nettles and docks, laced-over with a net of goosegrass and convolvulus.

She hesitated before the front door. It looked as though it hadn't been open for years; a sudden breeze flailed brambles against the peeling panels, and a spider's web masked the keyhole. No good knocking. The path veered to the left under the downstairs window. Flattened weeds, bent and broken, showed it was in regular use. Clenching the tennis racket, she followed it, looked in at the window, but filthy panes and ragged lace curtains obscured her view.

The path went down the side of the house, shrubs forming a tunnel; an acrid smell came from an elder bush as she brushed against it. She peered round the wall into the back garden. The weeds had recently been scythed down round a whirly line, its plastic ropes sagging under the weight of a few garments: a shirt, two tea-towels and a pair of underpants, all in different shades of grey. She walked over and felt them: they were stiff and dry, as though they'd been hanging there for days. Near the base of the whirly-line was a rubber ball and a plastic bone. Her heart softened: Basil's toys; perhaps Bert wasn't that bad if he played with his dog.

Built onto the back of the house was a brick lean-to, the windows relatively clean. There was a window to the right of the lean-to; she glanced up, but there were no windows on the upper floor at the back. There was probably only one room upstairs with a solitary window looking out at the front. Still no sign of anyone and she was sure if Bert was at home, Basil would have started barking. Her shoulders unknotted. She could leave. Frank could make contact with him tonight at the Jolly Sailor.

Should she look into the lean-to before leaving? It was surprisingly tidy; she wrinkled her nose as she saw stacked up against the walls the tools of Bert's trade: traps, some looked illegal, but there were catch-them-alive traps, some large enough for rabbits or squirrels, as well as fishing rods, lines with bait-hooks, lobster and crab pots and several wicker baskets. Well-kept tools hung from the walls. The back door leading into the house was ajar. Was the lean-to door locked? She turned the brass handle and it swung open. Should she go in? What if Bert came back and found her? What excuse could she make? She thought she saw someone suspicious going into the house: a masked man with a bag over his shoulder marked swag? She heard a cry and thought someone was injured? That was better. Not much better, but if she tried to find a stronger excuse for trespassing she'd be standing here for hours.

The back door creaked as she pushed it wide open. She clapped a hand over her nose: the kitchen smelt of rotten food. A chipped butler's sink contained a washing-up bowl piled with dirty dishes, there was a grey dishcloth draped over a tap, water dribbling down it onto the plates. Plop, plop, plop. She wrenched the tap handle, it continued to drip. Dead flies lined the window sill and she waved the tennis racquet at live ones buzzing round her head. There was a single ladder-backed chair at the wooden table, wall cupboards, and on the floor two bowls, one containing water, the other licked clean with a few flies crawling inside it.

The door from the kitchen led to the front room. It didn't look as if it was used much, although there was a television to the right of a tiled fireplace. Everywhere was coated with dust and even the spiders' webs looked neglected. A sagging two-seater sofa and matching armchair were the only furniture. On the right narrow stairs must lead to the single bedroom. She hesitated. She'd seen enough. But had she? Had her disgust at the state of the house stopped her from looking at it from the perspective of a detective? A detective searching for any evidence that two women might have been held here? She should be searching for clues: hairclips, underwear, stockings. Sometimes trophies were taken from victims. She shuddered, remembering the locks of hair Philip Nicholson had cut from the victims he'd raped and murdered. She should be examining cupboards, drawers, looking for loose boards or locked boxes. Was she a detective, or wasn't she?

She tightened her jaw. God, she wished Frank was here, or Stuart Elderkin or Dorothy or even Mabel. She'd start in the bedroom and work her way down, that was the correct way to search a house, or so Frank said. She wished she had someone to watch her back and hoped Bert wasn't light on his feet. Hopefully, if he came back while she was searching, Basil would bark and warn her.

The staircase was steep, with narrow, uncarpeted steps, a pale centre between stained sides, showing there had once been a carpet runner. The banister was greasy and coated in grime. On the seventh step she stopped – grimacing, pinching her nose. A terrible smell was gravitating towards her. Bile rose in her throat. She gripped the banister with her right hand, put down the tennis racquet, and fumbled in her jeans pocket for a handkerchief, which she pressed over her nose. It was a ghastly smell: rotten flesh, dissolving fat, decaying faeces and stale urine. She spat bile into the handkerchief before she choked. She tried to calm her mind; she didn't know there was a body up there, and even if there was, it might not be a human body. God knows what Wiles got up to. It might be some animal he'd caught. Get real, she told herself. Who slaughters an animal in a bedroom?

Climbing those last steps, she'd feel like a mountaineer climbing a sheer cliff face who was suddenly frozen with fear. She picked up the tennis racquet, pressed the handkerchief more tightly to her nose, and forced herself up the remaining steps.

Think. Think. Get a grip. She could either go down and call the police or face what was upstairs and then decide what to do. She shouldn't be here. How would she explain that? She should act like the detective she was supposed to be. Would Frank or Stuart even think twice about going up those last few stairs and facing whatever was there? No. Would Dorothy? She imagined her, squaring her shoulders, shaking her head and marching upwards.

A door was at the head of the stairs and it was open a few inches. The foul smell gained strength as she got nearer. She pushed back the door with her racquet. The room was small with a low ceiling, a single window covered with dirty lace curtains faced the front garden. The light was poor, and at first she wasn't sure what she was seeing. A single brass bed sat in the centre of the room. If there was any other furniture she didn't see it, for what she saw made her flesh contract in horror.

A body appeared to be floating over the bed. Its arms and legs were tied by ropes to the corners of the bed, pulled so tight the body was suspended several inches above the blood-soaked mattress. Blood, brown and dried, covered by gorging flies. She pressed the handkerchief tight against her face, her stomach heaving. Red bubbles of rage effervesced through her. This wasn't just murder, it was savage torture. She imagined the agony of stretched limbs, the pulling of bones from sockets. She moved nearer to the body. It was a man, a small man – it must be Bert Wiles. He'd been cut to death. So many wounds, it was impossible to calculate their number. The flesh was peeling away, furling back from the black cuts. There was a gag in his mouth, and black dried blood masked his face, making him unrecognisable.

Why had he been killed? Because he knew who had murdered the girls? Or because of what he'd seen? He'd wanted to tell Jim Lovell. Or was this nothing to do with the case they were investigating; perhaps something to do with poaching gangs, or even the smuggling of contraband? But why torture him? To get some information from him? There was a chair at the foot of the bed, facing the body, as if someone had sat there watching him die.

She must act. Contact Frank. No, she couldn't do that. The police. Revie. That's who she must get hold of. She looked round the room again. A battered chest of drawers and an iron chest were the only other furniture. She swallowed hard, and used her handkerchief to open the drawers and search through rumpled underclothes, socks and jumpers. A strong smell of moth balls was all she found. The chest contained several pairs of boots, and an old black suit wrapped in a plastic bag. She'd done what she could, now she must get out and raise the alarm. How she would explain all this at the camp? She shuddered. Her brain wasn't capable of concocting a lie at the moment.

She turned away from the bed, fighting down an urge to cover the body with one of the discarded bedclothes that lay in a heap under the window. No one should die like that. The murderer was a vicious, perverted beast.

Supposing the same person kidnapped the two women? Had their deaths been as cruel as Bert's? This murderer was a sadist who enjoyed not only killing, but watching someone die in agony.

As she staggered down the stairs another thought hit her. Where was the dog? Where was Basil?

Chapter 13

Saturday, June 26, 1971

Frank looked at their faces as they sat round the dining table, ready to start the meeting. Their expressions varied between worried and puzzled, but all looked determined.

'We've got a lot to get through before Revie arrives for lunch,' he said.

'He rang up just before you got here, said he was bringing Mr Ansell with him, if that was all right,' Mabel said.

Ansell was the pathologist whose evidence had been crucial in the conviction of Nicholson for the murder of Dorothy's sister, Emily, and several other women and girls.

'Excellent! He'll be able to give us details of the post-mortem.'

'I'm not sure I want to hear them,' Laurel said. 'I can't get the sight of his body out of my mind.'

Frank nodded. 'Understandable. Is it OK if we start with you, Laurel? Could you tell us exactly what happened last Tuesday, what you observed and how you managed to convince Revie to keep you out of the investigation?'

Stuart nudged her. 'What did you promise him?'

She gave him a school-mistress look.

'Stuart,' Mabel chided. 'Laurel's had a terrible time, no need for remarks like that.'

'Sorry, Laurel.'

'That's OK, Stuart. If you must know, I promised Revie Mabel would cook him a slap-up meal if he kept me out of it.'

Mabel simpered and pulled a face at Stuart, who glowered, took a pipe from his pocket and started to stuff it with shag tobacco.

Frank rapped on the table. 'Come on, folks. Let Laurel tell us what happened.'

Dorothy flicked open her notebook and looked at him.

'Yes please, Dorothy, we need details noted. They could be important, and we may need to go over them at a later date. Especially if the case gets stuck.'

'I think it's stuck already,' Stuart said.

Frank nodded to Laurel.

Hesitating between sentences, she told them about going into the cottage, finding Bert's body and then phoning Revie from a telephone box in the village. 'He asked me to wait in the garden. It was the longest half-hour in my life. He knew if I became involved in the case it would blow my cover at the camp. He's putting it out that a holiday maker, a passer-by, thought he heard someone screaming and went to investigate. He says if and when the case comes to court, then I'd have to give evidence if necessary, but he wants us all to remain in our roles. He can't see how this murder could be connected to the missing girls, but he thinks we're more useful undercover at the camp.'

'How was he?' Frank asked.

Laurel smiled. 'He was very kind. He brought a flask of coffee with an added shot of rum. "Not again!" he said. "You seem to home-in on dead bodies like a blue-bottle."'

Mabel tutted.

'I reminded him I was with you, Frank, when we found the Harrops, and with Oliver when we discovered the body of Dr Luxton.'

Dorothy tapped the table with her biro. 'But you found Felicity's bones, and Emily, so he does have a point.'

Frank studied Dorothy, who hadn't flinched when she mentioned Emily. Soon it would be the first anniversary of her death. Dorothy visited her grave every week before the Sunday service, taking flowers from the garden. Afterwards she was always quiet and reflective.

'Revie has brought in extra police and they're doing house-to house, talking to all the villagers and holiday makers, getting names and addresses. He said they'll check alibis when Ansell has nailed down the time of death.'

'Thanks, Laurel.' He turned to Stuart. 'Have you had any joy with the parents and friends of the missing girls?'

Stuart sucked on his pipe, then sent a stream of grey smoke over the table.

Laurel coughed.

'Sorry.' He passed a sheet of typed A4 paper to each of them. 'Here's my notes. Thought it would save time my telling you I discovered SFA,' he said.

'SFA?' Mabel asked.

'Sweet Fanny Adams. Absolutely bloody nothing.'

'Nothing?' Frank asked, frowning.

'Only things we knew already. Both girls acted out of character, no one seemed to have a bad word to say about them. The parents cried, the relatives wept and the friends howled. There's been no communication from either of them, and I wouldn't like to repeat what they think of the police.'

'You found nothing at all?'

'Look, Frank, I've just said so. Read what I've written. If you can see anything interesting, let me know.'

'It's time for coffee,' Mabel said. 'You can read Stuart's notes while you drink it.' She turned to Frank. 'He's been working all hours seeing these people. He's very frustrated.'

He thought of making a ribald comment about frustration, newly married couples and conjugal rights, but he settled for: 'I'm sure you did a thorough job, Stuart.'

Laurel caught his eye. She was beginning to read his mind.

'I'll tackle the other matter next week,' Stuart said.

'What's that, love?' Mabel asked, half-way to the kitchen.

'I'll see what I can find out about the young airman who was hanged for Mrs Coltman's murder. Can't see how it can be connected, but you never know.'

Frank sipped the last of his coffee. 'You're right, Stuart.' He tapped the sheet of notes, 'There's nothing to help us in here, but you did an excellent job.'

Stuart, finishing off his second doughnut, looked mollified.

'Dorothy, anything to tell us?'

She wiped away traces of sugar from round her mouth with a napkin. 'There is something, but it doesn't make sense.' She told them about how Sam Salter had been taken with some of her ideas for increasing efficiency in the office and Belinda's jealous reaction when he'd showed her too much attention.

Stuart chortled. 'A red rose! I didn't have him down as a romantic chap.'

Mabel glared at him. 'A woman likes flowers, or have you forgotten already?'

Everyone laughed and Mabel gathered up the cups and plates and whisked them to the kitchen.

Frank waited until she returned. 'So, what followed, Dorothy?'

She leant forward. 'The next few days were difficult in the office, the atmosphere, well, you could cut it with a knife. Then, yesterday, Belinda is as nice as pie, compliments me on my hair-do, and says she agrees with the changes I suggested. She's invited me to visit her next week for supper.' She looked at them over her spectacles. 'What do you make of that?'

There was silence.

'It could be genuine, she might be feeling bad about how she's treated you, she might be hoping to get back into Sam's good books via you,' Laurel said.

'Are you going to accept the invitation?' Frank asked.

'What do you think? I might as well; I might learn something.'

'Is the date fixed?'

'No, I said I'd let her know on Monday.'

'We need to meet in your room, Dorothy, on Monday night, then you can tell us when you're going,' he said. 'Let's say eight.' Laurel nodded.

Dorothy stared at him. 'Why? You can't think she'd do me any harm. She's as soft as a brush; faints if you mention the word blood.'

Laurel placed a hand over her arm. 'Be careful. Look what happened to me, I thought I was having lunch with a cuddly old art dealer and nearly got killed.'

'I can look after myself; remember I saw out the war, more than you lot did,' she said, putting her nose in the air.

'You didn't see Bert Wiles' body. There's someone out there who enjoys inflicting pain. Be careful,' Laurel said.

Dorothy shrugged and lit up a cigarette.

'What about you, Frank? Have you got anything to report? Though if you had, you'd have told us by now,' Stuart said.

He pulled a face and slowly shook his head. 'The only piece of information I can tell you is that Bert's dog, Basil, turned up at the Jolly Sailor Thursday night. He was in a bad state, whining at the door, hungry and with some deep cuts on one of his legs.'

Laurel gasped. 'Do you think he was attacked as well as Bert?'

'Hard to say. The landlady's taken him in, took him to the vet straight away and he's been stitched up and given a few jabs. Jim Lovell told me Friday morning. He and his wife were at the Jolly Sailor when Basil appeared. They thought he must have been caught by barbed-wire. The details of Bert's death haven't been released, so they didn't make the connection.'

Laurel looked stunned. He thought she was imagining the little dog escaping from the murderer's grasp, running away, yelping, in pain, deserting his master.

Frank carried the tray of coffee and several spirit bottles into the garden and placed it on a table under an old apple tree where Laurel, Stuart, Revie and Ansell were sitting.

He remembered the first time he'd seen Ansell; he'd impressed him with his knowledge and expertise, and he certainly hadn't fitted the description Stuart had given him: a bungler who had got the time of death of Susan Nicholson completely wrong. Vindicated by outstanding work on that case and the one following, he was now held in high regard, not just by The Anglian Detective Agency, but also by Revie and the Suffolk Police force.

Mabel was behind him with a tray of cups and saucers and glasses. 'Come on, Frank, you're holding me up. This tray's heavy.'

'Sorry, day dreaming.'

'Is she beautiful?'

'I was thinking about Martin Ansell,' he whispered.

She snorted.

Martin looked tense, although he'd eaten well, tackling the lobster salad, lamb cutlets and raspberry ice cream, with relish. His long body looked uncomfortable in the wicker basket chair, and his gaze moved from one face to the next; however, he seemed to spend more time looking at Laurel than anyone else.

Revie patted his gut. 'Once again, Miss Mabel, you've cooked a wonderful meal. Why don't you divorce that old fart,' he pointed to Stuart Elderkin, 'and marry me?'

Mabel, coffee pot hovering over a cup, looked at him. 'Because your love would be cupboard love, and nothing else. Whereas,' she smiled at Stuart, 'Stuart loves me not only for my apple pie,' she winked at him, 'but for my other attributes.'

Good God. Mabel had made a double entendre.

Stuart blushed. 'Steady on, Mabel!'

Revie's eyebrows were raised. 'Worth a try. What do you think, Ansell? That was a superb meal, wasn't it?'

Ansell's long legs were knotted together, his floppy brown hair hiding his face. 'Lovely.' He looked at the lawn as though something interesting might crawl out of it,

Revie looked at Frank and pulled a face. 'Right, enough of the jollity, let's get down to business.' He turned to Laurel. 'How are you? That was a nasty scene. How've you been?'

Laurel smiled at him. 'OK, Nick. Thanks for being so kind.'

So, it's Nick, is it? The bastard did have a heart.

'You've got a good girl here,' Revie said to Frank. 'Brave as a lion, she is.'

'Don't you mean a lioness?' he retorted.

'Could be,' Revie replied. 'I believe the female lion is deadlier than the male.'

'That goes for most animals,' Stuart muttered, glancing at Mabel.

'Shall we get on with it, Nick?' Laurel asked, her face flushed.

Frank couldn't tell whether it was with embarrassment or pleasure.

'Right. I think you'd better go first, Martin. What you have to say is very worrying,' Revie said.

Martin Ansell put his cup on the table. 'I examined the body in situ and then in more detail at the post mortem. I can give you the scientific details, or I can also give you my impressions of what I think happened. My suppositions wouldn't stand up in a court of law, even if I was asked by the prosecution for them; the defence would jump on me like a ton of bricks.'

Stuart lit up his pipe, sucking at the stem, until there was a satisfactory glow in the bowl. Dorothy took out her cigarette case and Stuart leant towards her with a lighted match.

Smoke drifted through the garden. Frank allowed himself a few seconds of secondary smoking. He still fancied a cigarette, especially after a good meal and with a cup of coffee.

Ansell's body unwound itself and he metamorphosed into the assured pathologist. 'Wiles bled to death. Death by a thousand cuts. Not quite that many, but nearly a hundred.'

Dorothy shivered.

'There was bruising on the back of the head, so I think he was knocked unconscious and then tied to the bed. He was suspended, no part of his body was in contact with the bed, apart from his hands and feet, which were tied to the bed posts. The poor chap must have been in considerable agony when he came round, even before the torture started.'

There was silence round the table; they couldn't meet each other's gaze.

'Were all the wounds made before death?' Frank asked.

Ansell nodded. 'I'm afraid so. They were gratuitous wounds.'

'What do you mean?' Laurel asked.

'They were not made to kill Mr Wiles, or even to do him serious harm, they were made, in my opinion, to inflict pain. Some of them were tentative, these were probably the first ones made, and then others were deeper, but not deep enough to penetrate arteries. Some of the minor veins were cut, and the man slowly bled to death. I can't think of a more agonising, or terrifying, way to die, unless we look at mediaeval torture machines.'

'We're dealing with a brutal sadist,' snapped Revie. 'We've got to find him quickly. If and when details of how Wiles died get out, and they will, they always do, we'll have a right pandemonium on our hands. Press, TV crews, locals having hysterics, I can see it now. We've got to find him before he does it again.'

Frank looked at Revie. 'I presume you haven't found the weapon?'

Revie glowered back at him. 'No.'

'I'm pretty sure it was a cut-throat razor,' Ansell said.

'You mean like Jack the Ripper?' Mabel gasped, her eyes wide with horror.

'The Ripper used other instruments as well,' Ansell said, 'some of the kidneys had—'

'Never mind him, tell us why you're so sure it was a cut-throat,' Revie said.

Ansell gave him a school-masterly look. 'Since I last saw you I've carried out some experiments on a pig—'

Dorothy gasped, coughed and waved her cigarette at him. 'How could you? That's disgusting!'

Ansell shook his head. 'Really, Miss Piff! The pig was dead. I acquired it from a butcher.'

'Sorry,' Dorothy mumbled, glaring at Stuart and Mabel, who were sniggering.

'I purchased a cut-throat razor from an Ipswich barber, and the cuts I made were identical with the cuts on Mr Wiles.'

'Would you say a cut-throat was a good weapon, Martin?' Revie asked.

He shook his head. 'No, not for an initial attack, although I know they are used for slashing people. It's more of a tool than a weapon. It's not very sturdy, and usually the grip is poor, especially if it becomes slippery with blood.'

Laurel pulled a face.

'Sorry, Laurel, but Revie did ask.'

Frank was right, Ansell did have a soft spot for her.

'That's OK, Martin, please go on. It's really interesting, if gruesome.'

Ansell's chest expanded slightly. 'The grip could be improved, but the blade could easily break if any force was used. So, no I don't see it as an initial weapon.' He looked round the group.

'How long do you think it took him to die?' Frank asked.

'I'm not sure, hopefully he might have passed out with the pain. It was a long, slow death.'

'And the time of death?'

'He was well dead when Laurel found him. I believe he was killed on Monday night, sometime between ten in the evening, and two in the morning, I can't be more accurate than that.'

Frank turned to Revie. 'At the staff meeting at the camp on Monday morning Jim Lovell told everyone, in a loud voice, Bert was worried about something, not only worried, but scared.'

'Who was there?' Revie asked.

'Everyone, all the suspects we've been investigating over the disappearance of the girls.'

'What about Salter? Was he there?'

'I'm not sure if he was there when Jim started speaking as we were all focussed on him, but when I turned round, both he and his son, Stephen, were in the doorway. They could have heard everything, Jim has a penetrating voice.'

'And the same night Bert Wiles is murdered. Could be a coincidence, but I don't believe in them,' Revie mused.

Ansell wriggled impatiently. 'There's another piece of information.' Their gaze turned to him. 'It wasn't clear at first, and I only realised it after you left, Inspector Revie.'

'What?' Revie shouted. 'You should have contacted me straight away.'

'I wasn't sure, it seemed so unlikely.'

They all shuffled to the edge of their chairs.

'There was a pattern, the cuts had a pattern; not all of them. I've made a sketch, it's easier than me trying to explain.' He reached into his briefcase and took out a sheet of paper and a black-and-white photograph. He placed them in the centre of the table. The photograph was of Bert Wiles' body, cleansed of blood; a shot taken from above. The cuts were clear to see. The drawing showed an outline of the body and a pattern of marks.

Frank pointed to the paper. 'I don't understand. What are these marks representing?'

Ansell pointed at the photograph with a pencil. 'I didn't see it at first, there were so many wounds, but as I looked at the photograph some patterns emerged.'

'In your head, I think! I can't see any patterns!' Revie grumbled.

Ansell looked at him. 'Neither did I to begin with, Inspector Revie. I believe these cuts were made at the end of the... er... process, for want of a better term. They were superimposed over the other cuts.'

'When he was dead?' Laurel asked hopefully.

'I'm not sure. It must have been difficult for him to see what he was doing, there must have been so much blood.'

Mabel gripped Stuart's arm. 'I need to lie down. I can't look at this.'

He put an arm round her waist. 'I'll take you back to the house.' They made an unsteady retreat.

Ansell looked round. 'Everyone else OK?'

He glanced at Laurel and Dorothy. Despite their white faces they nodded.

Ansell once more placed his pencil over the photograph. 'Follow the point of my pencil.' He moved it over the right side of the body. Starting above the right nipple and curving inwards he traced a line which then curved outwards over the abdomen and then moved inwards once more to finish above the right testicle. He looked up 'Can you see that?'

Laurel was frowning, but nodding slightly, as though she could just about make out the curving line. Dorothy was inhaling deeply on a cigarette and shaking her head.

'Yes, I can see it,' Frank said.

Stuart came back. 'She's having a lie down in the sitting room. I've given her a small brandy.'

'You should have given us all one,' Dorothy said, pointing to the tray. Stuart dispensed the drinks.

Ansell repeated the demonstration for Stuart.

'Why?' he asked. 'Why did he do that?'

Ansell didn't answer, but placed his pencil once more on the photograph. 'Look on the other side of the body.' He moved the point from above the left nipple, this time curving outwards towards the left armpit, then moving inwards to near the navel, then curving out to end above the left testicle. He then turned to the paper. 'I think these marks were made deliberately; the murderer was sending us a hidden message, perhaps one he thought we wouldn't see.'

'He's playing games,' Frank said.

'SS, do you think there could be a Nazi connection?' Stuart asked.

He shook his head. 'Possibly, but SS could stand for Sam Salter.'

Dorothy gasped.

'Or Stephen Salter,' Laurel added.

Revie puffed out his cheeks. 'And it could mean a steamship or a saint. Very interesting Ansell, but not much use in catching the murderer, as far as I can see.'

Ansell's shoulders drooped.

'I disagree, Nick,' Frank said, 'this murder tells us quite a bit about him or her.' Revie glared at him. 'The person is a sadist, he's committed one of the most awful murders I've seen. I believe he sat in a chair at the end of the bed watching poor Bert bleed to death and delighted in the pain he'd caused. The letters carved on his body could be a subliminal warning to the Salters, or it could be a calling card of a super-inflated ego, one boasting of his murdering prowess, and sure he will not be caught. Whoever he is, he's as dangerous as any of the villains we've met recently and we all need to be suspicious of all our suspects, and possibly someone who isn't yet on our radar.'

'Any idea who it is?' Revie asked.

'I haven't got a clue,' Frank replied.

Chapter 14

Sunday, June 27, 1971

Laurel stepped from the warmth of the late afternoon sun into the cool interior of St Bartholomew's church in Orford. It was deserted: the quiet between the morning and evening services. The inside was a square space, more like a great medieval hall than the inside of a church; beautiful stained-glass windows shed their coloured lights over the stone floor and brass figures were dotted about the church. She wandered down the wide aisles, looking at inscriptions on windows and the carved scenes on a stone font, but nothing was registering.

She sat down on a pew, clasped her hands together, rested them on the shelf in front of her, and lowered her head. She desperately needed peace and quiet after the recent horrifying revelations, and hoped she'd find it here. She wanted to expunge the memories of Bert's body suspended above the bed, the blood and the lingering smells of decay and death.

After the last swimming session of the afternoon she had had to get away from the camp. Having to be jolly, shout encouragement to swimmers, award prizes, with the assistance of Charlie Frost, who was at his obnoxious best, had driven her to the edge of her patience. She had reminded him of his late night visit to her chalet, and asked him if he still needed her help, he'd grunted and said he'd sorted it out himself. That was something to be thankful for.

The silence and isolation weren't working. When she closed her eyes, the images and smells she wanted to forget climbed once more into her brain. Blood, torn flesh. flies, dust, dirt, shit and piss. Her pulse racing, she tried to take some deep, slow breaths, fighting the oncoming panic attack. Get a grip. She placed her hand over her diaphragm, feeling her abdomen rise and fall. Slowly the smells of wax candles, damp stone, musty cassocks and hymn books replaced that of death. Her pulse slowed.

With a calm mind, neurones falling into order, she tried to make sense of what had happened. They had to find out why Bert Wiles had been scared. It must be something to do with his job, if you can call poaching, or smuggling, a job, but she couldn't see how his murder could be connected to the missing girls. It was a brutal murder. Did Bert do something so awful it was a revenge killing? Perhaps they shouldn't get involved in this case; the police were in charge of Bert's death. They should concentrate on what Sam Salter was paying them for.

Sam Salter – SS. Was there a connection? It could have been a random swipe of the razor. Two random swipes? A threat or a signature? Sam wasn't her favourite person – but was he a sadistic killer?

She shivered. She needed fresh air, so got up and stepped out of the south porch into the warmth of the sun. She wandered through the graveyard, stopping to look at the inscriptions on gravestones. On the east side of the church were ruins of an earlier building, the original Norman church, stone pillars and arches standing alone on well-kept grass.

She meandered towards the newer part of the graveyard and came to a sudden halt. Kneeling in front of a grey marble headstone, head bowed, was Thomas

Coltman, the handyman at the camp, the man whose wife and child had been murdered when he was a prisoner of war in Java. There were fresh flowers, pink roses and gypsophilia, in a grey marble urn, and the grass covering the grave was neatly clipped. Coltman, his back to her, looked a picture of extreme misery: head bowed, shoulders sagging. Her heart clenched tight for him. After all these years he was still bereft. To his right was a discarded bunch of dead flowers, withered delphiniums and white roses, their browned petals scattered over the grass; and beside them were a pair of grass-clippers.

What should she do? Leave him in peace? Leave him in despair? Should she take this opportunity to make contact with him? Neither Frank nor Dorothy had managed to do that.

She didn't have to make her mind up. He must have heard her feet on the gravel path, as he turned, grasping the clippers, as though to protect himself. Or attack?

'Hello. Is it Mr Coltman? I've seen you at the camp, but we haven't had a chance to meet properly.' She spoke slowly, clearly and in a tone she'd used as a teacher talking to a pupil who was unsure of themselves.

He got up, and stared at her with frightened eyes, the clippers shaking in his hands. He didn't speak.

She knelt down in front of him and looked at the gravestone.

In memory of Audrey Coltman, beloved wife of Thomas
Taylor Coltman
Cruelly taken from me
And my son, John. Taken and never returned.
We will all meet on some distant shore.

The words, etched in gold on the cold grey surface, were personal and different to the usual epitaphs. Her heart ached for him. He must have erected this stone after he came back from the war, for by then his wife had been buried for several years. She wondered where his mother was buried.

She looked up at him. The clippers dangled from his hands; his gaze moved from the words on the gravestone to her face.

'Thank you.'

She understood what he meant. She shared, for a moment, his grief and he'd seen that on her face. 'It's hard to stop grieving when someone is taken unnaturally.'

He knelt down beside her, his hand resting on the edge of the gravestone. 'You understand?'

'I do, but your loss is enormous, your wife and child.'

'And yours?

'My sister, Angela, was murdered a few years ago.' As she said those words, her own grief welled up, as raw as ever. Tears, sharp as acid, pricked her eyes and she blinked.

He tentatively placed a hand over hers, his fingers trembling, as though he wasn't used to having contact with another person. 'I'm truly sorry. I don't want anyone to feel what I have felt.' His voice was low, pleasant, cultivated, unlike his careworn appearance. 'What's your name?' he asked. 'I've seen you round the camp. You're a Stripey coat, aren't you?'

She smiled at him and clasped his hand. 'I'm Laurel Bowman. I'm helping with the sports, mainly swimming.'

They both got up, still clasping hands. He was a little taller than her, but thin and stooped; his clothes, clean but worn, hanging from his spare frame. He reluctantly released her hand. 'I used to love swimming when I was younger.'

'You don't swim now?'

'The sea is too cold for me.'

'Why don't you use the pools, they're heated. Staff can use them when the campers are having their meals.'

He looked horrified. 'I hate swimming pools. They smell of chlorine.'

She would have liked to know more about his wife. Was this the right time? Was she abusing the bond they'd just formed? She decided to risk it.

She placed a hand on the gravestone, and hoped she wouldn't offend him. 'Someone at the camp said you didn't know Audrey and John were dead when you were a prisoner of war. It must have been a terrible shock when you came back, especially if you'd been traumatised from your experiences.'

His face paled, he gulped, his Adam's apple moving up and down his throat, and the clippers were again tightly gripped. She'd gone too far, too soon.

'Is that what they say? What do they know? They treat me as though I'm an idiot. Sam Salter gave me a token job. I do it because I need the money. I need to buy Audrey flowers and it gives me the time to walk the fields at night, looking for my little John and to find...'

He was in extreme distress. 'Was your wife, Audrey, beautiful?'

The name seemed to distract him, his anger died, and a faint smile curved his lips. 'She was very beautiful, everyone thought so. Even my mother, who was not given to making compliments, said she was one of the most beautiful girls she'd seen.'

'How did you meet her?'

The smile broadened 'Here, in Orford. Where I live now, the cottage, was our family holiday home; we lived in London, but came to Orford whenever we could. She was a local girl; she could swim like a fish, and we both loved boating. We were childhood sweethearts. We never wanted anyone else.'

'She sounds a wonderful person. I wish I could see a picture of her.'

His back straightened. 'Would you like to see her?'

For a moment she thought he was offering to dig her up. 'Yes, I would.'

He gripped her arm. 'Come with me. We can go to my cottage. I'll show you Audrey's photograph, and you can see how beautiful she was.' He pulled her towards the lych gate, and she reluctantly followed.

He stopped and released her arm. 'Are you sure you want to come? I can make some tea for you,' he said, his voice once more tentative and unsure.

What had Frank said: 'We mustn't take risks, there's a sadistic murderer out there.' If she went with Coltman no one would know where she was. Could he be the murderer? Crazed by the loss of his wife and child, taking revenge on anyone who he came across? Had he met Bert on one of his night walks? Had Bert upset him in some way and he'd overpowered him and taken him back to Bert's cottage and killed him in a most horrific manner?

She looked into his pleading eyes. He wanted someone to share his love and grief. Someone who understood what it was like to have a loved one murdered.

'Yes, I'll come with you, and I'd love a cup of tea.'

It was a short walk to Daphne Road, and as they passed the entrance of Burnt Lane there were two police cars parked outside Bert's cottage. Her throat contracted and foul smells invaded her brain. She swallowed hard. She mustn't let this opportunity pass.

'What's going on there?' she asked him.

He shook his head. 'That's where Bert Wiles lives. Perhaps he's been arrested again. He's a poacher.'

He didn't know about the murder, or was he pretending he didn't? How was it possible for him not to know?

'They said at the camp there'd been a murder in Orford. Do you think those police have anything to do with that?'

He turned into Doctor's Lane. 'Murder? That's terrible. Was Bert murdered?'

'I think his name was mentioned.'

He stopped outside a cottage, his shoulders hunched. 'Why would anyone murder Bert Wiles?'

'I don't know. I've never met him. Do you know him? I suppose you must, you live near each other.'

He beckoned her to follow him up a brick path leading to a cottage. Surely he wouldn't attack her, if he was the murderer, with police close by?

He walked round to the back of the house and she followed him. The garden was well-tended, not like Bert's scrubby patch. He bent down near the back door and took a key from a plant pot behind a rosemary bush.

He turned the key and stepped back. As she passed into the house it was a relief to find a spartan kitchen, clean and orderly, contrasting with Bert's hovel. A pine table stood in the centre of the room, a chipped but clean butler's sink underneath a window, plus a tall pine cupboard, a gas oven and sitting on top of a worktop, a kettle and an electric toaster.

He pointed to the only chair in the room. 'Please sit down, I'll make some tea.' When was the last time another person had come and shared a meal with him? Or even a cup of tea or coffee? Should she feel honoured he'd asked her, or worried? She wasn't sure, but he didn't seem threatening. However, he hadn't answered her question about Bert.

'Did you say you knew Mr Wiles?'

As he was filling the kettle, his back stiffened. He snapped the lid shut and switched it on. He opened the cupboard, and she craned her head, but couldn't see inside. He took some cups and saucers to the sink, rinsed and dried them, then placed them on the table; they were fine bone china, patterned with daffodils.

'Yes, I've known Bert for many years. If he has been murdered I'm very sorry, but we weren't friends, just neighbours. We have nothing in common, apart from both of us leading solitary lives.' He carefully poured boiling water into a teapot and placed it on a stand on the table.

'Excuse me.' He left the kitchen and came back carrying a dining room chair. 'Would you prefer to sit on this? It's probably more comfortable than that.' He pointed to the kitchen chair.

'I'm fine. That's a beautiful set of china, such a lovely pattern.'

He smiled, pouring tea into the cups and passing her one. 'Milk? I'm sorry I don't have any lemon. The china's my mother's. I haven't used it in a long time. She'd be pleased to see it having an airing.'

She was able to glimpse something of the man he must have been. Cultured, well spoken, courteous, charming even, and she thought he was enjoying having someone to talk to and to share a cup of tea with. Her former feelings for him, empathy and sorrow for the loss of his wife and child, returned.

'I'm sorry I can't offer you some cake or a biscuit. I'm afraid I don't buy them.'

She sipped the tea. It was strong and malty. 'Just as well, I need to keep my weight down. The tea's excellent.'

He smiled shyly. 'Audrey said I always made a good cup of tea. I haven't many domestic accomplishments, I'm afraid, but my mother insisted I learn to make decent tea. She said a drink of tea was the basis for an ordered existence. I never followed her logic there.'

They both laughed.

He hadn't said much about Wiles. 'What was Mr Wiles like? Can you think of any reason someone would kill him?'

He looked puzzled. 'Why do you want to know? You said you'd never met him.'

She'd have to tread carefully. 'I suppose I've become more interested in murder cases since…'

He placed his cup on the saucer. 'Of course, stupid of me. I'm afraid it had the opposite effect on me. I can't bear to read about such things.'

'I think it helps to talk about it, somehow it makes the tragedy shrink, gives more room in your mind for other things. Otherwise the thoughts of how it happened and how much my sister suffered are overwhelming and you can't think of anything else.'

He stared at her. 'You're very brave to face up to your sister's death. I don't think I've ever done that. All I think of is how she died, and that I wasn't here to protect her.' He paused, sipping his tea again. 'What happened to the man who did it? Did he get a sufficiently long sentence?'

She looked at the table, not trusting the expression on her face. 'No one was ever arrested for her murder.' That was true. He, Vernon Deller, did get a death sentence, but not through the courts. That was her secret, one she'd shared with Frank; if he had turned her in for her part in Deller's death, she'd be in gaol. She could never repay him for that.

His cup rattled against the saucer. 'Really? That's awful! Never to know who did such an awful crime. That must be difficult to bear. I'm sorry, Miss Bowman.'

'The police did their best.' That was a lie. The police thought Angela was a flighty girl who got what she deserved. 'What happened to the man who killed your wife? They did find him, I hope?'

His smile had disappeared. 'Yes. He was a young airman, based at a camp on the Ness.'

'The Ness?'

'Orford Ness. The stretch of land you can see from the quay. He was hanged.'

'How did you feel about that?'

His eyes were full of pain. Should she be prying into his life? It must be a rare occurrence for him to reveal his feelings. She hoped Thomas Coltman was not the one responsible for the missing girls, or for the terrible murder committed nearby.

'I don't believe in the death penalty; I was glad when they abolished it. I wish the man, his name was Hovell, had been alive when I came back. I hated him, despised him, and if I'd been there on the day he attacked her, I would have killed him to save her and John, but I don't believe in a State taking a person's life. Also, sometimes the wrong person is hanged. At least, if a person is gaoled but they're innocent, there's always the possibility they may be released if the real murderer is discovered.'

'You don't think there was any doubt it was Hovell?'

He shook his head. 'The evidence was overwhelming. I wish they hadn't hanged him. I would have liked to see him, to ask him why he did it, to let him know what a truly lovely person Audrey was and to find out what he'd done with my boy's body. I need to find him and place him with Audrey. Can she ever rest in peace without our son beside her?'

'He never confessed to where he'd put John?'

'No. In fact, he professed his innocence to the end, even as they took him to the gallows, so I was told. I tried to find out more about him, but when I went to his family's address in London, they'd moved away and I couldn't trace them.'

'It's understandable; their life must have been wrecked as well. Imagine having a child who grows up to be a murderer.'

He nodded slowly. 'Yes, I hadn't thought of that. And for him to be hanged. No wonder they moved away. They must have felt tainted, unable to meet the eyes of their neighbours and friends.' He got up. 'I'll fetch a photo of Audrey. You said you would like to see her?'

'Thank you, Mr Coltman, it's good of you to show me.'

She quickly looked around as he left the room. How much time did she have? Not much. She opened the drawer in the table and looked inside. She'd been expecting to see nothing more interesting than knives and forks, or cooking utensils. On the right were three scalpels, of different sizes, fitted with removable blades. Could the wounds on Bert's body have been made with these and not a cut-throat razor? Her heart was pounding against her ribs. She gulped and tried to take in the other contents of the drawer. There was a brown unsealed envelope. It contained short pieces of fine wire. There was a pile of paper: pages cut from magazines, photographs, or drawings of pretty girls, some obviously adverts. She closed the drawer. Should she leave now? Was this enough evidence for Revie to make an arrest?

The door opened and Coltman came through holding two framed photographs. He didn't seem to notice her agitation. She swallowed hard and tried to look interested.

He handed her one of the photographs. 'This is John. My mother took him to Ipswich to have this taken.'

It was a formal studio photograph of a baby; he looked happy, with a sunny smile, dark hair and blue eyes.

'Mother wanted me to be able to see him at different ages when I got back.'

'He's a lovely boy. He looks very bright and aware.'

His finger traced the boy's outline. 'I never knew him, or he me.'

She was torn between getting out quickly and trying to help him. Perhaps he used the scalpels for some kind of handicraft, and there was no crime in collecting pictures of pretty girls.

He passed her the second photograph. 'This is Audrey. Wasn't she beautiful?'

As she looked at the face in the frame an icy chill grasped her throat, making her unable to speak. The woman in the frame was indeed beautiful; she had dark hair falling about an oval face, a pale, smooth complexion, a small straight nose and almond-shaped eyes. The photograph had been tinted and her eyes were a clear blue. The resemblance to the photographs Sam Salter had shown them of the missing girls, Lucy Milne and Roberta Dodd, was so strong, she could have been their mother.

Chapter 15

Tuesday, June 29, 1971

Laurel sat on the edge of her chalet bed, not looking forward to the task ahead. Frank had decided they needed to search the chalets of the main suspects for evidence. Searching a dead person's room, although not pleasant, was interesting and revealing, but searching a room when the occupant was alive and might return to find you with your hands in their underwear drawer, was a different matter. The thought was making her jittery.

When she, Frank and Dorothy had met last night in Dorothy's room at Sudbourne Hall, she'd told them about her meeting with Coltman and the discovery of the scalpels and pictures of pretty girls in the table drawer, and even more worrying, the close resemblance his late wife had to the missing girls.

'Excellent. Well done,' Frank said. 'Mr Coltman goes to the top of the list of suspects. I'll phone Revie and see if he thinks that's enough evidence to bring him in for questioning.'

'Goodness,' Dorothy said. 'Weren't you scared, Laurel?'

She nodded vigorously. 'I was. All I wanted to do was up sticks and get out of that house as soon as I could.'

'Do you think he suspected your feelings?' Frank asked.

She bit her lip. 'No, I'm sure he didn't. When I said I needed to get back to the camp, he thanked me for having tea with him. He said he felt much better having talked about Audrey and John, and he thought, for once, he might sleep that night. It seems he gets these awful dreams and walks the night away instead of going to bed.'

Frank leant forward. 'Did he tell you what he dreamed about?'

'No, and I didn't want to know. I wanted to get away, although afterwards I wished I'd asked him. But I still can't believe he's capable of torturing and killing Wiles.' She hesitated. 'However, I'm not so sure about the missing girls – their resemblance to his wife is incriminating.'

Dorothy tapped her biro against her notepad. 'We don't know if the two things are connected. He might be responsible for the girls disappearing but have nothing to do with Bert's murder.'

'What about the scalpels?' Laurel asked. 'They could have been used to cut Bert Wiles and not a cut-throat razor.'

Frank leant back against his chair and Dorothy lit up a cigarette.

There was a long silence.

Frank straightened up. 'You did well, Laurel. You've formed a relationship with Coltman and even though you couldn't do much searching, what you found is important.' He frowned. 'This shows me what we need to do next.'

'Yes?' she asked.

'We need to search the chalets of Minnikin, Hinney and Frost. See if any incriminating articles are in their chalets. This will help us to move them up or down our list of suspects.'

'Isn't that risky? If we're caught it will blow our cover,' Dorothy said.

Frank's jaw was set. 'We need to check on these people. What Laurel found is significant, and it's shown me how we can progress. We're undercover, we can't ask direct questions, but if we can give Revie something to persuade him there is a sinister side to the missing girls, he will want to get his team involved.'

She looked at Dorothy who was nodding her head. 'How will we go about it?'

'Can you get a master key for the chalets from Salter?' he asked Dorothy.

'I can ask him. He and Stephen should be back in half an hour.'

'Excellent.' He turned to Laurel. 'I'll search Hinney and Frost's chalets and you can do Minnikin's. I'll act as lookout for you, and vice-versa.'

'When will we do this?'

'Tomorrow, if possible.'

'I'll check their rotas tomorrow morning,' Dorothy said, 'and somehow get in touch with one of you during my coffee break.'

'Excellent.' He turned to Laurel. 'We'll meet up after lunch and try and search the chalets tomorrow afternoon.'

Laurel looked at her watch, took a deep breath and picked up the master key from the table. She opened the chalet door. Frank was lounging against the wall of the chalet opposite, pretending to read a newspaper. He had a clear view of anyone approaching; they'd arranged if the suspect came back the watcher would bang on the chalet door, and hopefully they'd get out before it was too late. He looked up and nodded.

She ran to Nellie's chalet, her heart beat rising with each stride. She fumbled the key as she tried to put it into the lock and it jumped out of her hand, making a metallic sound as it bounced on the path. Bugger! She could almost hear Frank laughing behind his newspaper. She snatched it up, shoved it into the lock, turned it and pulled open the door, slamming it behind her. What a detective!

She leant against the door, looking round the room; the layout was similar to hers. Where to start? Don't think – do it! The bathroom didn't reveal much, a bottle of Milk of Magnesia and one of Steradent, suggesting Nellie had a problem with her digestive system and false teeth.

On the bedside table were several books; the top one was a Barbara Cartland, the next The Price of Salt by Claire Morgan. She picked it up, frowning. Wasn't this book written by a well-known author using a pseudonym? She wasn't sure. Underneath it was Therese and Isabelle by Violette de Duc and lastly a pulp fiction novel, the cover showing two women, one blonde, the other brunette, in their undies, the blonde in black and the brunette in pink. Spring Fire by Vin Pecker. Frank and Dorothy would have a laugh at that name. Obviously, another pseudonym. She flicked through a few pages. Soft-core lesbian.

This seemed to corroborate her suspicions about Nellie. But was she active? One capable of murderous rage if her advances were rejected? One capable of kidnapping a desirable young woman to satisfy her sexual needs? She remembered Nancy Whintle asking her if she knew any homosexuals, when Nancy's homosexual brother was murdered, and how she'd calmed her, saying she knew several homosexuals, men and women, and they were all good people, no different from the rest of humanity, except for their sexual orientation. Being a lesbian didn't make you a murderer. However, Nellie's interest in women had to be noted.

She opened the wardrobe. Smells of mothballs and lavender competed for dominance – camphor won. She searched all the pockets of coats, jackets and overalls, looked in shoes, but found nothing.

This was frustrating. She turned to the chest-of-drawers. Goodness, Nellie had an exotic taste in knickers. Would she be able to look her in the eye again without thinking of pink silk and cream lace? As she carefully lifted a pile of vests she found a small framed photograph. She picked it up and took it to the window. Probably it had originally been a black-and-white snap, but had faded to brown and sepia. Two girls, hair blowing sideways by a sea breeze, walked down a beach-side promenade. The girl on the right was a teenage Nellie, the smaller girl was blonde, pretty, smiling up at Nellie, whose arm was round the other girl's shoulders; Nellie's expression was one of love and admiration.

She gulped and placed it back underneath the vests, feeling guilty at uncovering such an intimate, long-ago secret. Where was the other girl now? Were they still friends? Or had Nellie lost her early love to another woman, or possibly a man? She sighed. Since the recent change in the law, it wasn't a crime to love someone of the same sex, but the majority of people didn't approve. Finding love was difficult enough if you were heterosexual, and sometimes when you thought you'd found it, it didn't last. Her fiancé had dropped her when her sister was murdered, and his family were horrified by the scandal. She shuddered. Poor Nellie. She hoped she'd found someone to love and be loved back. She'd like to find someone herself. Was that someone Oliver?

Annoyed with herself for wasting time she started a quick search through the rest of the drawers, but found nothing. She looked around the room, making sure it looked undisturbed, opened the door and peeped out. Frank gave her the thumbs up and she strode towards him, and exchanged the key for the newspaper.

Frank decided to search Hinney's chalet first. He knew he was safely mowing the grass between the borders. He wondered if Laurel had found anything of value in Nellie's chalet? She hadn't said anything; her expression was one of relief at having completed her work undetected.

He scanned the bathroom, very neat and tidy; there was nothing of interest in the medicine cabinet: toothpaste, plasters, a bottle of Dettol, scissors, aspirin and an eye-bath. He moved into the main room. The most interesting things were in the bookcase to the left of the bed. He squatted down and looked at the books. Most were horticultural. He nodded approvingly. Two of his favourite writers were there: Vita Sackville-West's Garden Book; he leafed through it. It was a compilation of her gardening articles from the Observer. Also, Hardy Perennials by Christopher Lloyd; Hinney went up in his estimation. Four volumes of Bean's Trees and Shrubs Hardy in the British Isles, took up most of one shelf, together with a Ministry of Agriculture, Fisheries and Food book on British Poisonous Plants. Tomes on pruning fruit trees, vegetable gardening and growing flowers for decoration and many other books on horticulture filled the shelves. He shook his head. Hinney was much more erudite than he'd given him credit for. He was annoyed with himself – he hadn't read Hinney correctly. He'd a real interest and love for his subject. Anyone who liked Christopher Lloyd's writing couldn't be all bad. His search of cupboards, drawers and wardrobes yielded nothing suspicious. You couldn't arrest someone because they had a boring line in clothes.

He peered out of the window; Laurel looked engrossed in the newspaper; then she glanced up, looking down the road to see if anyone was approaching. He slid out of the door, locked it and raised a hand. She saluted back and he moved towards Frost's chalet.

He wrinkled his nose as he entered it. The air was redolent with a mixture of Old Spice aftershave, suntan oil and cigarettes. The bathroom cupboard was crammed with toiletries; not only Old Spice and the suntan oil, but Brylcream for his hair, Nivea for his skin and several packets of condoms; at least he showed some sense of responsibility. The shelf was a mess of several combs, brushes, safety razors, blades, tweezers and small scissors. For nasal hairs? No sign of a cut-throat razor. Not a well organised man, but one who spent a deal of time and money on his appearance.

He moved to the main room and started on the chest-of-drawers. There was more organization here; all the contents were expensive: crisp cotton handkerchiefs with the woven initials CS, racy underpants, a few vests and in the drawer beneath, several fine wool sweaters in the same V-necked pattern in blue, cream and pale green. The last drawer contained folded shirts and more jumpers, thicker and chunkier. He felt underneath them. His fingers slid over glossy paper. Magazines. He carefully folded the clothes back and laid the magazines on the bed.

Pornography. He looked at them in turn, making sure he kept them in the right order. It was a mixture of different levels, from top-of-the-shelf stuff, to hardcore, sadomasochistic porn. He flicked through them. What would Laurel think if she saw these? Her sympathetic feelings towards Frost might take a dive. He looked closer. The wanker, and he thought that was no exaggeration, had given each of the girls a mark out of ten. He wasn't sure how his marking scheme was devised, but it certainly wasn't for fashion sense. After a few pages, he flicked back. Frost definitely preferred brunettes. Hard luck, Laurel.

The last magazine was truly disgusting: young girls and women tortured, strung up, handcuffed, beaten, throttled by muscular men in masks. Close ups of breasts and vaginas being cut, invaded... A bitter taste filled his mouth. He went back into the bathroom and spat into the basin, turning the tap on to wash away his bile and disgust. He placed the magazines back in the drawer and carefully placed the clothes over them. He wanted to ring up Revie and tell him to arrest Frost, but he knew the possession of filth didn't mean you were a murderer. However, Frost had a prurient interest in torture and the degradation of women, and so he became of greater interest.

The wardrobe was full of blazers, smart trousers and two suits as well as a well-stocked tie and belt rack. On its floor were several pairs of leather shoes, all with shoe-trees. Charlie Frost didn't stint himself. He pulled out a plastic bag tucked into a corner of the wardrobe, and there was a metallic clink as he turned its contents onto the bed. A pair of handcuffs, a leather gag and a knuckle duster fell onto the bedspread. He wondered when these had last been used. Or was Frost a fantasist? Had the handcuffs clamped wrists? The gag pushed between soft lips? The knuckle-duster smacked against cringing flesh?

Charlie Frost moved up the list of suspects.

Dorothy sat in her room waiting for Frank and Laurel. She sighed deeply. This wasn't what she'd imagined when she'd insisted she wanted to play a more active role in the detective agency. She'd thought she would be able to uncover clues leading to the discovery of what had happened to the two girls, but she'd made a poor contribution. Laurel and Frank had uncovered several interesting facts, especially Laurel, and tonight they'd tell her what they'd found in the suspects' chalets. When she'd offered to search Sam Salter's private rooms, Frank had vetoed the idea and Laurel had backed him up.

'Much too dangerous, Dorothy,' she'd said.

She was sure they didn't want her to search his rooms, not because it was dangerous, but because they didn't trust her to do a competent job. They were afraid Salter would find out she'd been snooping and cancel the agency's involvement in the search for the girls.

When she heard the front door bell, she went downstairs. She shook her shoulders and tried to put on an animated expression. She hoped the case would soon be solved and she could return to Dunwich and her role as agency administrator.

Laurel and Frank bundled into her room, laughing as they both tried to get into it at the same time.

'Laurel's shoulders are getting broader each time I see her,' Frank said.

'And your hands are getting rougher — look at your finger nails! Disgraceful!' Laurel pointed at Frank's hands.

Frank inspected the offending articles. He shook his head. 'No matter how often you scrub them, somehow the dirt creeps back.'

Dorothy sat down. 'Shall we get down to business?'

They both looked at her.

Laurel sat down beside her on the settee. 'Are you all right, Dorothy?'

'Fine, couldn't be better.' She edged away from Laurel. 'We need to get on. Did you find anything in the chalets?' She brandished her notebook and biro.

Laurel and Frank exchanged another look.

She glared at them. 'You go first, Laurel.'

She told them about Nellie's choice in literature and the photograph.

'Not a very productive search,' Dorothy said.

'I disagree,' Frank said, 'it confirms Laurel's initial suspicion — Nellie is a lesbian, and that gives her a possible motive. She moves up a notch in the suspects list.'

Laurel looked grateful.

Guilt pinched at Dorothy's conscious. 'True,' she managed to utter.

Frank told them what he'd found in Hinney's chalet. 'Nothing incriminating there, as far as I could see, but it's a different matter as far as Frost is concerned.' He didn't spare them any details.

She felt her face flush, not with embarrassment, but with anger and disgust.

Laurel looked as though she'd chewed on a slug. 'How am I going to work with him without looking disgusted?' she asked.

'As a professional detective, you'll have to hide your feelings,' Frank said.

Dorothy rapped the biro against her notebook, wishing it was a stick to beat Frost. 'This certainly makes him a stronger suspect than anyone else.'

'Apart from Coltman. Although I feel deeply sorry for the man and the terrible life he's had, the scalpels and the pictures of the girls made my flesh creep,' Laurel said.

'We haven't got enough to pin this onto anyone at the moment, although Revie might be persuaded to bring Coltman in for questioning.' He turned to her. 'Have you got anything of interest to report, Dorothy?'

She felt her face grow hot once more, this time for a different reason. 'Being as I wasn't allowed to do any searching, the only thing I can tell you is that I've accepted Belinda Tweedie's invitation to her house in Orford for a drink and a chat tomorrow night. I don't suppose I'll learn anything new, but she continues to be suspiciously nice to me, and as I haven't got anything to do, I thought I might as well go.' She got up and thumped her notebook down on the table. 'Anyone like a drink?'

Laurel got up and took her arm. 'Are you sure you want us to stay, Dorothy? I'd love a scotch, but not if you're going to be grumpy.'

Frank raised his eyebrows. 'You're living dangerously, Miss Bowman!'

Dorothy looked at them over the rim of her glasses. She was letting this get on top of her. She remembered how supportive they'd been, as well as Stuart and Mabel, when her twin sister Emily was murdered; how her involvement in the agency had given her an anchor, so she didn't drift off into a sea of misery.

'I want you both to stay. I'm sorry I've been so ratty, it's because I think I'm achieving so little. It would have been better if I'd stayed in Dunwich.'

Laurel hugged her. 'I need you here, and so does Frank. It's given us a base, and talking through all the points with you puts a clear perspective on the case.'

She hugged Laurel back. 'Scotch?'

'Make it a double, Dorothy,' Frank said. 'You never know, Buxom Belinda might confess to the crimes.'

She sniffed as she poured whisky into a cut-glass tumbler. 'She'd faint if you put tomato ketchup on your chips!'

Laurel shook her head. 'I've told you before, Dorothy, you can't judge a book by its cover. I've been fooled too often in the last year by seemingly innocent or harmless people.' She turned to Frank. 'I think we ought to be nearby when Dorothy goes to see Belinda.'

Frank nodded. 'Agreed.'

She tried to suppress a smile of pleasure. It was good when people cared about you, especially people dear to your heart. 'Nonsense! Does anyone want their drinks cut with water? Thought not.' She passed them round. 'Anyone want to stay and watch Wimbledon, Match of the Day?'

Laurel looked at Frank. He nodded. 'Good idea. We all need a break from this case.'

Chapter 16

Wednesday, June 30, 1971

As Dorothy drove to Belinda Tweedie's house the low rays of the evening sun dazzled her, making her nauseous; she was still feeling the results of drinking too many whiskies the night before. However, her hangover was worth it as she'd enjoyed her evening with Laurel and Frank; it had been like old times. She snorted. Old times! A year ago, she hadn't met either of them. What a year – from school secretary, to sacked school secretary, to administrator of a detective agency and now, undercover detective. She shook her muzzy head, trying to clear it. Her present role was not a success, although both Laurel and Frank assured her she was playing an important part in the investigation. She didn't believe them but was pleased they'd said so. Thank goodness she'd persuaded them not to come with her to Belinda's, promising she'd return by nine o'clock and would let one of them see her.

As she pulled up outside Belinda's house she resolved to try and be pleasant towards her. The poor woman obviously saw her as a rival for Sam Salter's affections. She must reassure her that wasn't the case, but it wouldn't be fair to encourage Belinda to believe Sam was keen on her. It would be better if she could accept that Sam would never look at her in that way, whatever had happened in the past.

The difficulties of being in love. She pulled on the handbrake, and through the open window listened to the lush evening bird song. She put a hand to her throat.

She'd been in love once, it seemed a lifetime ago, at least half a life time, nearly thirty years. If she didn't have his photograph on her bedside table, she doubted she'd be able to clearly recall him. She hadn't brought it with her and she missed seeing his dear face. She had loved him for his passion for life, his sense of humour, his willingness to have a go at anything and not mind if he made a fool of himself. What would her life have been like if he'd survived the war? Would they have had children? Where would they have lived? She couldn't imagine not living at Greyfriars House with Emily, but now Emily was dead.

Thank God for Laurel, Mabel, Frank and Stuart, and her friends in the village. They'd helped her, and were still helping her through a difficult time. To be in love. There was no feeling like it. She was lucky, she'd loved and been loved back. For Belinda, there was only disappointment and jealousy as she thought Sam Salter was falling for someone else. Dorothy snorted. How could Belinda believe Sam was interested in her? Ridiculous! She mentally slapped her hand; she'd been naughty encouraging the notion; she must lay that one to rest this evening.

The front door opened and Belinda burst out and rushed down the path. She'd obviously been waiting for her by the window. She wore a cream dress with puff sleeves, a low neckline and a skirt several inches above her knees. Dorothy's magnanimous feelings started to fade. She mentally told herself to behave. Probably Belinda thought she looked a frump in her cotton skirt and sensible blouse. To each his own.

She got out of the car, picked up her handbag and walked towards Belinda, not bothering to lock the car; who was going to pinch an old Morris Traveller?

Belinda hugged her. 'I thought you weren't coming. Do come in,' she gushed, pushing her up the path and through the open front door.

What was the hurry?

Belinda turned and looked down the road. 'Go in. Go in.' Once they were inside and the door closed, she relaxed. 'I'm so pleased you came, we can have a nice drink and a chat.' She beamed at her and opened the door to the sitting room.

What a peculiar welcome. First nervous and twitchy, then rather too warm and effusive. Why the sudden change? Had she decided she wasn't a rival for Sam's affections?

'Do have a seat.' Belinda pointed to the pink settee.

Its velour was harsh and rough against Dorothy's skin, like the coat of a short-haired terrier, and the perfume drifting from a bowl of pink roses was overpowering. Why hadn't Belinda opened a window? It was a warm, pleasant evening. She couldn't breathe properly.

'You must have a drink,' Belinda said. 'A glass of wine? I've red or white.'

This was the last thing she wanted, but she didn't want to seem rude, and she'd promised herself to be nice to Belinda. 'Thank you, but could I have a glass of water first, and perhaps a glass of wine later?'

Belinda looked hurt. 'But you will have some wine, won't you?'

Oh, dear. Then she remembered the wine bottles in the fridge when she'd snooped in the kitchen when Belinda was unwell. Perhaps she badly needed a glass and doesn't want to look as though she's desperate. 'Yes, I'd love some, but a glass of water first, please, as I do feel thirsty. Then I can enjoy the wine. It's very kind of you to entertain me like this, Belinda.'

Belinda bustled out and quickly returned with a silver tray, on which was a glass of water, another of red wine and a lazy Susan, its compartments filled with crisps, peanuts and horrible Twiglets; vile things, coated with blobs of salty brown stuff.

'Oh, lovely,' she said. You hypocrite, Dorothy Piff. If Emily had been here she would have given her an old-fashioned look, and they would have corpsed and ruined the occasion.

Belinda passed her a miniscule napkin and pointed to the Lazy Susan; she took a few crisps and some peanuts. Belinda handed her the glass of water and for a few embarrassing seconds she juggled everything before managing to put the glass down on a side table.

'Drink up, Dorothy, then you can have some wine.'

Was she trying to get her squiffy then interrogate her on her relationship with Sam Salter? She smiled back and sipped the water.

Belinda tipped back a third of her glass, a few drops of wine escaping, gliding down her chin. She dabbed at them with her napkin. 'Have you settled in at Sudbourne Hall?'

Dorothy swallowed a crisp, coughed and had a drink of water. 'Yes, it's a lovely place. I do like the way the house has been built, it's so spacious.'

Belinda wriggled against the plush of her seat, her nyloned legs scratching against the velour. 'Do you think your move will be permanent? You won't want to go home, will you, after living in such luxury?' She smiled, but couldn't hide the note of envy in her voice.

Dorothy wasn't sure which way to play it. If she told Belinda she wouldn't be staying at the camp long, she might be so pleased to hear about her departure, she wouldn't reveal much. She decided on an enigmatic smile and no answer.

Belinda's nostrils flared.

She changed the topic of conversation, hoping she might learn something new. 'Sally was telling me about the two girls who disappeared, one last year and one the year before. She said one worked in the office. Is that right?'

Belinda's wine glass wobbled; she grasped the stem with both hands. 'Why do you want to know about her?'

'Sally said she'd heard she was nice, and very pretty, and Mr Salter was paying her attention and had taken her out a few times. Sally imagined what it would be like to be Mrs Sam Salter, the second, with all that money and posh cars.'

Belinda lower lip protruded, as though she was about to have a tantrum; she looked like an elderly baby in her cream dress. 'That's disgusting. I'll have a word with that Sally. It's rubbish. Mr Salter wasn't interested in that girl. He was just being kind. She was a silly, stupid girl.'

'Was? You think she's dead?'

Belinda placed her wine glass on the table. 'No, of course not. She hasn't been seen for ages, that's all.'

'Perhaps she went back to her parents. Have any of you heard from them?'

Belinda blinked hard, as though there was something in her eye. 'No,' she whispered. She turned her head towards the kitchen, as though listening for something, then turned back. 'I'll fetch you a glass of wine. Red or white?'

She still didn't want any, but as this conversation was getting interesting, at least Belinda's reactions were, it meant she would have something to report back to Laurel and Frank. She nodded. 'That would be lovely, white please.'

Belinda took the tray and her own glass to the kitchen and returned with a wine glass two-thirds full of white wine and her own brimming with red.

She hadn't put her down as a lush, but she certainly seemed to need the prop of alcohol tonight. 'What was the name of the girl who worked in the office?'

Belinda took a long swallow. 'Roberta Dodd,' she spat. 'She had loose morals. Went off with some married man, I expect.'

'Really? Sally said she was a nice girl, came from a respectable home. That isn't in character.'

Belinda's pale face contorted. 'What does she know?' She glared at Dorothy. 'Don't you like the wine? You haven't drunk any yet.'

She took a small sip. It tasted awful, it might be good wine but last night's session had left her mouth in a foul state. She quickly chewed at a crisp. 'Lovely, but could I have some more water?' She passed Belinda her empty water glass. 'I'm afraid I drank too much whisky last night.'

Belinda's eye narrowed. 'With Mr Salter?'

Damn. Shouldn't have said that. 'Er, yes. We had quite a session.' Well, she couldn't tell her who'd she really been drinking with. She should have kept her mouth shut.

'Drink the wine up, I'll get you some water.' She went to the kitchen.

She had to get rid of it, but she'd offended Belinda enough as it was. She got up and poured most of the wine into the vase of pink roses until it was almost full. She grabbed her handbag and took out a bottle of aspirin. She unscrewed it, pulled out the plug of cotton wool, tipped the tablets into her handbag and poured the rest of the wine into it. She hoped it wouldn't leak out and spoil the lining of her bag. At least it was white wine and wouldn't show.

Belinda returned with the glass of water. She stopped when she saw Dorothy's empty wineglass. 'You've drunk it all?'

What was the woman playing at? First, she wanted her to drink the wine, now she seemed upset because she'd drunk it too quickly. 'Yes, it was delicious. Very greedy of me.'

Belinda handed her the water; looking relieved. 'Oh, not at all. I'll get you some more.'

'Thank you, Belinda, but no more for me, I'm driving. I'll sip the water; you sit down and relax, you haven't finished your own wine.'

Belinda flopped down and stared at her.

Was there something wrong? Had she smeared lipstick all over her face? 'Are you all right, Belinda?'

She jumped at her words. 'Yes, yes, of course. Are you all right?'

Good Lord, what a silly conversation. 'Yes, I'm fine.' She couldn't stand this, she'd make her move in a few minutes, invent some excuse to get away. 'That was dreadful, wasn't it? The murder of that man. He lived near here, didn't he? Aren't you scared? I think I would be, if a murder had been committed so near to my home.'

Belinda's mouth opened, then shut. She looked like a landed fish.

'Sorry, I shouldn't have mentioned it. I'd forgotten how sensitive you are about things like that.'

Belinda took a handkerchief from the pocket of her dress and dabbed at her top lip. 'Terrible, terrible.' Her eyes were bulging and she looked terrified.

She hoped Belinda wasn't going to have one of her turns; then she'd never get away.

'Make sure you lock and bolt your doors, back and front tonight, but I'm sure you're safe, there are lots of police about at the moment.'

This reassurance didn't seem to work as Belinda became more agitated, her right hand clasping the base of her neck. 'How are you?' she asked, standing up and moving towards her. 'Do you feel woozy?'

What was the matter with the woman? Was she drunk?

'Would you like to lie down?' Belinda asked, her voice trembling, pleading.

It was the last thing she wanted to do.

There was a noise from somewhere in the house – like breaking glass. Was it from the kitchen?

Belinda put a hand to her mouth.

'What's that? Is there someone else in the house?'

'No. No. It's that cat. It must have knocked something over.'

There'd been no sign of a cat when she was last here. No food bowl and Belinda didn't seem to like animals. She felt as though an earwig had wriggled its way under her clothes and was crawling down her spine. Panic bubbled up from her stomach. She knew she must get away from this house and from this woman. She didn't know why.

She sprang up, grabbed her handbag, and pushed past the startled Belinda. 'Sorry, must go. Just remembered something I have to do.' She ran down the hall and pulled at the front door handle.

'No, you mustn't go,' Belinda was behind her, panting, grabbing her arm.

She pushed her off, fumbling with the Yale lock.

'You must stay. Please stay!'

The woman was desperate, but so was she.

The knob turned and she pulled the door open, knocking Belinda backwards. 'Sorry, Belinda. See you in the morning. Thank you for the wine and nibbles.'

Belinda followed her to the car, wringing her hands. 'I didn't mean it to go this far. Please help me.'

For a moment she was tempted to stop and try to find out what Belinda was going on about, but that earwig was still crawling around and all she wanted was to get as far away from Belinda and her oppressive house as quickly as possible.

Thank goodness she hadn't locked her car; she jumped in, turned on the ignition, slammed into first gear, stamped on the accelerator and kangarooed away.

She looked in her rear mirror. Belinda was standing on the pavement, looking not at her, but back, towards her house.

Chapter 17

Thursday, July 1, 1971

Frank pushed the wheelbarrow containing his fork, hand-tools and a couple of buckets, towards the reception area. His morning's instructions from Hinney were to work on the flower beds near the camp's entrance, and those in the visitors' car park. He was to weed, remove any dying plants and replace them with others from the nursery garden. Hinney was his usual dour self: uncommunicative and surly. It was a good job he had little contact with the campers.

Frank liked the gardening, especially on what promised to be a lovely, sunny day. It was relaxing, as when he was concentrating on digging up weeds he forgot the frustrations of the investigation, and the regret they'd decided to go undercover. They weren't making much progress and the murder of Bert Wiles had clouded the issue. A few hours of weeding might free his mind, let his subconscious take over the problem of the girls' disappearance, and present him with a new line of investigation. What he needed was a session in his cottage, with paper and a biro, drawing spider diagrams, and trying to make connections. Plus, a good bottle of wine and a decent meal. The food at the camp was wholesome, plentiful, but boring. Perhaps next Saturday he'd spend some time with a frying pan, a Dover sole and a bottle of Muscadet. He sighed, that would be good. Mabel's cooking was superb, but he needed the thinking time.

As he pushed the barrow in front of the reception office, Dorothy came hurtling through the door, looking fraught. She waved and ran towards him.

'Mr, er, Gardener, sorry I've forgotten your name.'

Excellent, Dorothy, ten out of ten. 'Frank Diamond, madam. How can I help you?'

'I need a man to come with me.'

The others would like this one. Then he saw how agitated she was. What was the matter? Was Laurel in trouble? 'Of course. Where to?'

'It's Miss Tweedie. She hasn't come into work. She may have had one of her turns.'

'Can someone in the office tell Mr Hinney where I've gone? I don't want to get into trouble.'

'Yes, you tell them, I'll get my car.'

Frank waited until they were clear of the camp. 'What's up, Dorothy? Why are you so worried? I thought you looked flustered when we saw you in the camp last night.'

She ground into fourth gear. 'As you know I went there last night to have a drink with her.' She explained everything she could remember. 'I was going to tell you and Laurel tonight. She was so keen for me to drink the wine, but when she thought I'd had a glass she kept staring at me, as though she thought something was going to happen.'

'You think it was drugged?'

Dorothy nodded, turning the car into Daphne Road.

'I was scared, Frank. There was something evil in that house. Not just her, but I think there was someone else there, hiding in the kitchen. Waiting for me to fall down in a stupor. I had to get out. She was terribly distressed herself. I think she was as frightened as I was, but for a different reason. I should have done something straight away, but I'd have felt a fool, as there wasn't anything I could call the police about.'

She pulled up in front of Belinda's house.

Her hands were gripping the steering wheel as though she didn't want to let go, didn't want to find out what had happened. He placed a hand over hers. 'You did the right thing. We all trust your judgement. Hopefully, she's not feeling too good – from what you've said she'd a skin full of wine.'

Dorothy gulped. 'Let's hope that's it.'

The curtains at the windows of both up and downstairs rooms were drawn. He knocked on the front door. They waited. He knocked again, louder.

'This looks bad, Frank.'

'She could be in bed with a blinding headache and doesn't want to see anyone.'

Dorothy was getting more agitated by the second. 'What shall we do?'

'Do you think any of the neighbours would have a spare key?'

She looked doubtful. 'I could ask.'

'Do that, I'll go round the back. If needed, I'll break in.'

'Wait until I get back. I'll try the houses on each side, but I think one is a holiday home, and no one's there. I don't think she's the kind of person who doles out keys to her house.'

'I'll explore. There's a side path to the right. Come down that, I'll wait at the back. Let's hope you can find a key. Wish I'd brought some tools with me. What have you got in the car?'

She shook her head impatiently. 'I'll look if we need to break in.' She raced off to the next-door house.

There was a gate at the entrance to the back of the house. He tried to unlatch it, but it wouldn't budge. Felt like a bolt. He puffed out his cheeks. Up and over. He wished he wasn't wearing gardening boots, the steel toe-caps were fine for protecting tootsies from spades, and a wonder for firming in plants, but not flexible enough for scaling gates. He got a good grip on the top of the gate and pulled himself up. Leg over and a swing of the hips and he was safely down. All the recent physical activity was paying off. There was a single bolt near the top, it moved smoothly and he left the gate open for Dorothy, using a loose brick to keep it ajar.

A narrow red brick path ran down the side of the house. The only window was on the second floor. At the rear of the house a stone step led to the back door. It was locked. He peered into a window to the right of it – the kitchen – net curtains partly obscured his view, but as far as he could see there was no one there. It seemed tidy, no chairs tipped over, or dishes on the floor.

He turned and looked at the garden. It was neat with another brick path running down the centre, flower beds on either side, full of rose bushes, the blooms past their best, the edges of the petals browning. He walked down the path towards a shed on the right-hand side. He grimaced. Padlocked. Pity, it probably held some useful tools.

The sound of running feet. 'Frank?' Dorothy came puffing round the corner of the house. 'No luck. There was a neighbour in. She said she was sure no one had a key to the house, and Belinda isn't close to anyone. So, I didn't waste any more time looking for a key.' She waved a tyre-lever at him. 'Found this in the car. Any use?'

He took it from her and smacked it against his palm. 'Should do the job. I'll break the back window and climb in. I had to climb the gate, that was bolted.' He waited a second, expecting at least a nod of approval for his feat.

'Well, get on with it,' Dorothy said.

He should have known better. He took of his t-shirt and wrapped it round his fist, and grasped the tyre-lever. 'Step back, Dorothy.' Putting his other arm up to shield his eyes, he smashed the glass near the handle.

'Crikey!' Dorothy said. 'That'll have the neighbours worried. I explained to the neighbour we were concerned about Miss Tweedie and we might have to beak in; she just shrugged.'

He found a bucket, upturned it and placed it below the window. 'Could you give me a bit of support, Dorothy, this bucket's a bit wobbly.'

She placed two hands on his back. 'Naked flesh! Aren't I a lucky old lady!'

Frank snorted. 'You might not think so in a minute.'

'Too true. Sorry.'

He knocked out jutting pieces of glass which fell inwards, splintering into the sink below. He gingerly put his hand through the hole and eased the handle of the window open; more glass tinkled. He took a deep breath. In the last case they'd had to break into two houses, first he and Laurel and then Laurel and Oliver; both times it hadn't been good news. He had a feeling it was third time unlucky.

'Give us a push up.'

Dorothy's hands moved to his bum, propelling him upwards through the open window. He grasped a tap over the sink. Luckily the sink was empty, and there were no dishes on the drainboard. His steel toe-caps clanked against the sink. Then he was on the tiled floor. The key was in the back door, he opened it.

'Well done. Goodness, it smells of bleach in here.' She looked around. 'Perhaps she's in bed. The kitchen's tidy, she must have washed up the glasses and plates last night.' She grimaced. 'She'll be furious if we find her with her hair in curlers.'

He hoped that was what they would find. Better a furious woman than...

They opened the kitchen door and moved into the hall. His nostrils dilated with disgust and he searched his pockets for a handkerchief. Dorothy clamped a hand over her nose and mouth. He put out an arm. 'Stay here.'

'Wait a minute.' She went back to the kitchen and came back with two tea-towels soaked in water. She handed him one and he placed it over his mouth and nose. She'd mixed washing-up liquid with the water; he was grateful for the lemony smell. 'Good thinking,' he muttered.

'Picked that up from a crime novel.'

It was pointless trying to hold her back. 'Ready?'

She nodded, grim but determined.

Another tough woman.

The door to the lounge was ajar and as he pushed it wide open the stench of death grew stronger, even though he had the towel pressed close to his face. He turned to her. 'I need another tea-towel. Mustn't smudge any finger prints.'

She nodded, turned and came back and handed him a third tea-towel. He used it to turn on the light, holding out his other arm to prevent her from going past him.

There was a sharp intake of breath behind him.

Belinda Tweedie lay on her front across the shag-pile rug. She was wearing a cream dress, parts of it stained dark red. The back of her head was a misshapen mass of blood, splinters of white bone, and sodden hair. A few blonde patches showed between the blood-soaked brown. Belinda and the carpet were covered in jagged shards of glass, splinters of glass glinting in her hair and withered pink roses scattered over the body and rug. A funeral homage. There was a poker on the carpet, its end coated in black blood.

He moved to the window and using the tea-towel, pulled back the curtains. Sunlight peeled into the room making the details vivid.

'Don't touch anything, Dorothy.'

She was silent, eyes wide behind her spectacles.

He went to the body. Pointless feeling for a pulse. No one can exist without a brain. He got hold of a shoulder and partly turned her over so he could look at her face. Christ, the murderer had smashed her face in as well. The whole head was just a bloody mass of torn muscle, smashed bone, scattered teeth.

'Absolutely sickening,' Dorothy fumed. 'He's a vicious beast.'

'Can you think of any reason someone would want to kill her?'

She was breathing heavily. With anger?

'There was something going on last night. I'm sure someone else was in the house. That someone has to be the murderer. She was supposed to drug me, that's what I think. Then perhaps when I'd conked out, he, the person in the kitchen, would have...' She shivered.

'Disposed of you?' She nodded.

'Let's see if we can find what's left of the wine in the kitchen. There are no bottles or glasses in here.'

He was grateful to get away from the corpse and the coppery smell of blood, together with other disgusting smells: death had voided the body of Belinda Tweedie.

In the kitchen, using the towel, he searched the fridge, and waste bin – there were no wine bottles, full or empty. In a cupboard was a row of sparkling glasses.

'Damn. The murderer's cleaned up. If we'd had a sample of the wine we could have asked Revie to have it analysed. The kind of drug, if there was one, might have given us a clue to the murderer.'

Dorothy inhaled sharply, then grasped his arm. 'We have got one.' She explained about putting some in the aspirin bottle.

'Excellent. We'd better get on to Revie straight away. Drive to the village hall, that's where Revie is setting up a control centre. Will he be pleased to see you! Get him here as soon as possible and then get that aspirin bottle.'

He heard her drive away. He took a deep breath and went back to have another look at the crime scene before the plod arrived.

Frank decided to be diplomatic and keep quiet as he sat in the back of the police car, next to a young PC he hadn't met before. If he made any quips Revie was likely to change his mind and throw him out. Then, not only would he have to walk back to the camp, but he'd miss out on the search of Thomas Coltman's house.

On Revie's arrival at Belinda Tweedie's house, after viewing the body, setting up the forensic team and contacting the pathologist, Ansell, he told Frank he'd considered what Laurel had discovered at Coltman's house: the scalpels and the resemblance of Coltman's late wife to the missing girls and he'd obtained a search warrant. He was about to go there when Dorothy arrived with news of another murder. Frank had little difficulty in persuading him to let him join in the search.

'He should be home by now,' Revie said. He turned to the driver. 'What time did he clock off, Cottam?'

Detective Constable Johnny Cottam had previously been a member of Frank's team when Frank had been a detective inspector on the Susan Nicholson case. Frank was pleased he'd been promoted to the plain clothes force as he not only liked the lad, but he was a good officer.

'Finished at noon, sir.'

Revie turned and stared at Frank. 'You do realise this could blow your cover?'

'It'll last as long as you've got hold of Coltman. If I'm found out, Laurel and Dorothy can still operate as camp employees.' He sighed. 'Frankly, I'm not sure going undercover has worked out as well as I'd planned. I don't think I'd do it again in a hurry.'

Revie sniffed.

They pulled up in front of Coltman's cottage.

'Mr Diamond,' Revie grunted, 'remember you're not a copper any more. Keep quiet, but keep your eyes and ears open; you can tell me anything you think is important after we do the search. Everyone ready?' There were nods from Cottam and the PC.

'Right, let's see what we can find. Some blood-stained clothing would be handy, or a diary noting down when and where he killed his victims. I could do with an early night.'

He looked at the front door. 'That's not been open in a while. Round the back.'

Coltman was in the back garden hanging out some washing on his whirly-line. He froze, a peg in his mouth, a shirt hanging by its sleeve from the line. He stepped back, his eyes wide.

'Mr Thomas Coltman?' Revie bawled.

Coltman's arms dropped to his side, the peg tumbled from his mouth.

'Yes. What is it? What's happened?'

'I'm Detective Inspector Revie. I have a warrant to search your house and any outbuildings. Please accompany me inside.'

Coltman shook his head. 'No, you can't do that. Why? What do you think I've done?'

'Come along, sir,' Cottam said, moving to his side and placing a hand on his arm. Coltman flinched and jerked his arm away.

Revie turned to the PC. 'Bag the washing.'

'All of it, sir?'

'Yes, pegs as well.'

Coltman pointed at Frank. 'What's he doing here? He works at the camp, I've seen him. He's a gardener.'

'Mr Diamond is helping us with our enquiries,' Revie prevaricated. 'Come along, Mr Coltman, do as you're told, or I'll have to arrest you.'

'Arrest me? Why? What's this about?'

The man was agitated, body quivering, skin glistening with sweat, and his face as pale as the underbelly of a fish. His shoulders slumped and he allowed himself to be taken towards his house by Cottam. Could this be the man who'd abducted two girls? Possibly the killer of Bert Wiles and Belinda Tweedie? It was hard to imagine. Frank followed them into the house.

'Sit down.' Revie pointed to a solitary kitchen chair.

Coltman slumped into it, put his elbows on the table and buried his head in his hands.

Revie looked at Frank, a questioning look, as though to say, 'Really? I don't think so.'

'Mr Coltman, where were you last night, between seven and midnight?'

Coltman slowly raised his head and stared at Revie. His lips moved but no words were spoken.

Revie pointed to the cupboard. 'Cottam, search in there.' He put on cotton gloves and pulled the table drawer open, obviously wanting to be the one who found the scalpels, if they were still there. Revie smiled. They were. He removed them and laid them out on the table top. 'Mr Coltman, are these yours?'

Coltman looked at him, his eyes full of pain. He stared at the scalpels and looked up at Revie again. 'Yes, of course they're mine, whose else could they be?'

Good question. Revie glowered at him; he didn't seem to like the answer.

'Just answer the question, Mr Coltman, I'll do the asking. What do you use them for?'

Coltman shiftily glanced from side to side.

Revie leant towards him, obviously scenting blood. 'Scalpels are used for cutting, Mr Coltman. Who or what did you cut with these scalpels?'

Frank had never seen Revie at work on a suspect before – he was good, certainly frightening; he wouldn't want to be on the receiving end.

'What do you mean who did I cut?' Coltman shrilled. 'I only use them for cutting holes in cardboard, for cutting out pictures. What are you suggesting? Are you saying I killed Bert Wiles?'

Revie screwed up his face so all his features seemed to coalesce. 'Why do you say that, Mr Coltman. Are you saying Mr Wiles was cut up?'

Coltman was becoming hysterical. 'It's gossip. Someone at the camp said he'd been sliced up, like the Teddy boys used to slash people.'

'Who was that?'

'I don't know, I can't remember.'

Revie removed an envelope from the drawer, opened it and tipped its contents onto the table. 'What are all these pieces of wire for, Mr Coltman. What did you do with them?'

Coltman looked at Cottam, who was waving a hand, trying to get Revie's attention. When he saw what Cottam was holding, he sprang up from the chair and darted towards him. 'Put that down. Don't touch her. She isn't finished.'

Revie grabbed him and forced him back into his seat. 'Sit still or I'll put you in handcuffs.'

Coltman's body went rigid. 'No, don't do that. Don't tie me up.'

Revie turned to Cottam. 'What is it? What doesn't Mr Coltman want us to see?'

Cottam placed it on the table out of Coltman's reach. It was the bottom half of a cardboard box. Revie's eyebrows shot up and he swiftly turned his glance to Coltman, as though he couldn't believe what he was seeing.

Frank moved forwards so he could see what was inside the box. The interior was intricate, created with care and some artistry. In the centre was a picture of a pretty dark-haired girl, who smiled knowingly. It looked like part of an advert for something feminine: shampoo, lipstick or possibly underwear, as she was scantily clad in a pink slip. Round her, glued to the box were seemingly hundreds of tiny snail sea-shells, the grey outer covering removed or worn away by the sea, revealing pearl-like nacre. They formed whirls and loops, leaves and flowers. It resembled the boxes fishermen used to make for their sweethearts as love tokens. Round the edge of the box neat holes had been cut, ready to receive something.

'You two,' Revie pointed to Cottam and the PC, 'search the rest of the house. If you find anything of interest, leave it there, and come back and report to me. In the meantime, perhaps Mr Coltman would like to tell me about this.' He tapped the box. 'Who's this pretty woman supposed to be?'

'You wouldn't understand,' Coltman wailed. 'I wanted to make her safe. That's all I wanted to do, make her safe.' He buried his head in his hands, sobs racking his body. He sounded as though his guts were being twisted into knots, his cries wretched and full of despair.

'Sir!' Cottam called.

'What is it?'

'Photograph.'

'Bring it here.'

Cottam returned and passed it to Revie. 'It was in the front room.'

Revie flashed it at Frank and nodded. It was as Laurel described, a photo of Audrey Coltman; the resemblance to the missing girls was obvious.

Revie looked at Frank, put an index finger on his temple and whirled it round several times. He had to agree, Coltman was seriously disturbed. Did the picture of the girl in the box have anything to do with the missing women? Was Coltman acting out a scenario of taking a girl and putting her somewhere?

'Sir! I think you ought to look at these.' It was Cottam's voice from upstairs.

Coltman didn't look up, his grief was not lessening.

'Come on down.'

Feet clattered on the staircase.

'Watch him.' He pointed to Coltman. 'Where is it?'

'Front bedroom, sir.'

Revie jerked his thumb at Frank. 'You, come with me.'

Where they going to find more bodies? From Cottam's face he didn't think so, but his eyes were sparkling, it must be a significant find.

It was a steep flight of stairs, covered with a red runner held down with brass stair rods; the carpet looked and probably was, pre-war. The constable was waiting for them at the top and pointed towards the bedroom at the front of the house. Frank remembered when he'd joined the police, the excitement of his first serious crime scene, and the elation when praised by the detective in charge for his observations; it had made him determined to become a detective. He hoped whatever he was going to see would help to solve the case of the missing girls.

The bedroom was spacious, running the length of the house, the furniture old and dark, but clean; a half-open window brought in smells of the sea. The constable moved to a large mahogany wardrobe, its doors open; he was almost quivering with excitement, like a greyhound waiting to come out of the traps. The right hand-side of the wardrobe was full of hanging clothes, from which came a smell of mothballs. He pointed to the left side of the wardrobe where there were a series of shelves. The shelves were stacked with boxes of various sizes.

'Detective Cottam took one down to look at, sir, but he used gloves and put it back where it came from.'

'Did he now?' Revie carefully took a box from the top of a pile and moved to the window to get a clearer look. 'Bloody hell, Diamond, look at this.'

He was right behind Revie, and had a good view of what was in the box. Like the one downstairs, it was the bottom part of a cardboard box, it looked like half of a chocolate box you bought a girlfriend, in exchange, you hoped, for a passionate evening.

Revie tilted the box and he got a view of the contents. The top was covered with a grill of fine wires, like the wires in the envelope downstairs, and below this another picture of a beautiful girl smiled up at him, surrounded not by shells, but crushed coloured foil, probably from sweet wrappers; they formed a kaleidoscope of jewel colours shimmering in the sunlight.

Revie laid the box on the sagging bed and turned back to the wardrobe. He took down another box: much the same as the first, this time she was surrounded by silver paper cut into tiny flowers, each with a boss of golden stamens. The work must have taken hours. Again, she was caged. To keep her safe? To stop her escaping?

After the fifth box Revie turned to him. 'I'm not removing any more, I've seen enough. I need to get the photographers and the finger print squad here. This house needs a thorough going over. We need to see if we can find any clues, any sign those girls were here. We may need to rip up a few floorboards, you never know, their bodies might be hidden in the house – or buried in the garden.' He grimaced. 'Any ideas how he could be connected with Wiles and Tweedie's murders? If he's as barmy as he looks, he may have been on a killing spree.'

Frank picked up one of the boxes with his gloved hands. 'It doesn't add up. The only reason for killing Wiles and Tweedie, if the murderer is sane, is they were a danger to him. They knew or suspected what he'd done. He realised that and he had to get rid of them. The most worrying thing about the two murders is the extreme sadism shown in the killing of Wiles and violence and anger in the murder of Tweedie. I think they were murders of convenience, and they showed us the character of the murderer: a violent and sadistic killer.'

Revie pursed his lips. 'Do you think Coltman is the murderer?'

'I'm not sure. You certainly can't ignore the scalpels and those weird boxes. Also, he's a loner and his internment and torture as a POW, coupled with the murder of his wife and son, may have warped his mind and turned him into a killer.'

The PC's head was moving back and forth as they spoke, his eyes round, his mouth slightly open. Frank turned to him. 'What do you think, Constable? You said you were a local lad. Do you know Coltman? Have you ever had dealings with him before?'

There was an intake of breath from Revie. Had he overstepped his brief?

The constable looked at Revie.

'Go on, lad. If you have something to say spit it out.'

The PC squared his shoulders. 'I do know Mr Coltman slightly, and I've heard quite a bit about him, sir.'

'Yes?'

'Apart from the facts everyone knows, I think you may find what happened last year interesting.'

Revie pulled a face at Frank.

'A little girl, on holiday with her parents, went missing. After they and local people had searched and couldn't find her, the landlady of the Jolly Sailor rang us. I came down with my sergeant. I'd only been in the force a few months. As we were getting out of the car we heard cheering. It was Mr Coltman, he'd found the girl in his back garden making mud pies and he'd brought her back. They seemed to have got on very well. Her parents were grateful, they wanted to give him a reward, but he wouldn't take it. He was overcome with all the fuss and made off as soon as he could.'

Frank smiled. 'That's a lovely story.'

'Doesn't prove anything,' Revie harrumphed.

'I've not heard anything bad about Mr Coltman, sir. He's a bit strange, but when you think about what he went through it's not surprising.'

'You don't think he's our murderer?'

'I'm not experienced enough to judge, Inspector Revie. I'm still learning.'

Frank smiled. The lad would go far. Diplomatic enough to make chief inspector?

'Don't you brown-nose me, sonny. You'd better join Cottam downstairs.' The reply was harsh, but he detected a note of admiration in Revie's voice.

When the constable had clattered down the stairs Revie pointed to the pile of boxes in the wardrobe. 'Young Jack-the-Lad might be right, Coltman may be nothing but a poor old codger, crippled by his past, but we haven't got any other suspects, unless you can tell me different, so I'm taking him to Ipswich for questioning and we'll give this house a proper going over.'

Frank nodded. 'You can't do anything else. Does this mean I can stay undercover? Will Coltman be safely locked up for a few days?'

'Yes, he won't be going anywhere until he's eliminated, if he ever is. If we've got the wrong man, the real murderer might feel safe if we have Coltman at the station; he might make a mistake. You, Laurel and Dorothy might pick up gossip at the camp. How's Dorothy getting on? Is she detective material?'

Frank pulled a face. 'She's beginning to doubt herself, but her sixth sense certainly got her away from a dangerous situation last night.'

'She's certainly a whiz in the office; she ought to stick to that. I've sent off her aspirin bottle and contents. We should have the results in a few days. My, her face will be red if all it contains is cheap white wine.'

'Somehow, I doubt it,' Frank said.

I only planned to take one. One was all I needed. It was a hard decision to make, to take a life. No, I'm lying, it wasn't hard at all. What was the life of a silly girl compared to my loss? I enjoyed the planning and the thought of what I would achieve. At last, after so many years, I would have satisfaction.

I needed an accomplice. That would increase the risk of getting caught, but it would put another layer between me and the police. I decided to sound out Belinda Tweedie.

I flattered her, made false compliments, deceiving her into believing her own attractiveness. Eventually she invited me to her cottage; we agreed on a secret meeting as she didn't want anyone to think there was something going on between us. I made sure no one saw me enter or leave her home.

I listened to her and her worries about her rival. I drip-fed the idea we could make her disappear.

'She won't suffer, will she? You won't harm her? I can't stand the thought of you hurting her.'

'No, she will wake up in another country. She'll even have all her own clothes. The drug will erase her memory. She'll be well looked after.'

Belinda was a silly, squeamish woman, who was overjoyed the rival would disappear. Whether she believed my lies, or talked herself into believing them, I'm not sure. I didn't ask. After Bert Wiles death, she became a bag of nerves, although I assured her his death had nothing to do with me, and he'd been smuggling drugs and it was gang related.

I planned to make her the last victim; she couldn't be left behind when, after finishing my work, I escaped and made a new life for myself. I didn't plan to kill her in that manner. His cousin, Miss Piff, was to die before her. I was looking forward to that. She prides herself on being tough and efficient; I wanted to see how she'd react to the razor. She escaped me. She was too sharp for that stupid bitch, Belinda.

The first one worked perfectly, but I hadn't known how I'd feel when she woke up and realised what had happened. Her eyes were full of fear, her body shook, her skin went a pale green and she urinated, the liquid gushing down her legs and puddling on the floor; the acrid smell was disgusting.

If she hadn't done that perhaps I would have finished her quickly, but the sight and smell offended me and I wanted to punish her. I hit her - her head snapped back and she thrashed at her bonds, muted screams behind the gag.

I relished it. I hit her again. Harder. I'd never had this feeling before. No, another lie. When I was in the forces I had a fore-taste, but nowhere as intense. I went drinking with some friends and we got into an argument with some local yobbos. We bumped into one on our way home to barracks. We beat him up in an alley. I did most of it, the other two held him down. As I punched his head and kicked him in the balls I got surges of pleasure and excitement I'd never felt before, much more than when I'd shagged a girl. It was his cries of pain and pleading for us to stop, that sent waves of pleasure through my body.

'That's enough,' my mate said. 'You'll kill him.' He gripped my arms and tried to pull me off.

'I swear you're getting a hard on,' the other one said. He wasn't wrong.

When I'd finished with the first girl, I could have stopped and completed the plan. I'd stolen *the object to put near the body; it would lead the police to him. I didn't need more than one, but a worm in my mind burrowed away at me.*

'It would be better with two. Two would make the case stronger. Wait until the summer and take another one.' The thought of having another girl to play with made my juices run. I would have time to plan, to think up different ways to hurt her. A second one - I would make her last longer, I would refine my techniques. Inch by inch she would approach death. There would be many nights of pleasure.

When another rival appeared, Belinda needed little persuasion to repeat the process.

Chapter 18

Friday, July 2, 1971

Dorothy was driven to the camp's office by Stephen Salter; his father had gone ahead, unable to sleep after hearing of Belinda Tweedie's murder. He'd given up his office to the police as they started to interview the camp staff. She supposed the police would ask what they knew about Belinda and would check alibis for Wednesday evening.

'Are you sure you feel able to work today, Dorothy?' Stephen asked, as they turned into the camp site. 'I'm sure I could fill in for you, although...'

She glanced at his profile. He looked sombre, but composed, the opposite of his father, who was becoming increasingly agitated as the hours went by. She'd found Sam's behaviour disturbing. Was it worry the murders would be bad for business? Was he genuinely upset by Belinda's death? Was the rumour he and Belinda had been more than boss and secretary in the past, true? She'd certainly been besotted with him.

'I'll manage, Stephen. We're one short as it is. Sorry, that's a callous way of putting it, but I think Cindy and Sally, judging from their reactions yesterday on hearing of Belinda's murder, will need as much support as possible. I wouldn't be surprised if one, or both, don't turn up for work today.'

Stephen glanced at her. 'I think they'll be in. I rang them last night to see how they were. I know Belinda was a bit of a tyrant in the office, but they're the ones who knew her best. They both said they'd be in. I'll help as much as I can today. We'll get hold of an office girl from one of the other camps as soon as we can, but it might not be before Monday.'

She nodded approvingly. He was a quiet, steady man. Good in a crisis, and this was definitely one of those. 'Your father seems very agitated, Stephen. He's known Belinda a long time, hasn't he?'

Stephen smoothly parked in one of the spaces marked Staff, next to the camp's office, where there were also two police cars parked. 'Yes, I'm worried about him. First the missing girls, then Bert Wiles' death and now Belinda's. He's acting as though it's all his fault. I've tried to persuade him to see a doctor, to get some sleeping tablets, but he won't hear of it.' He turned off the ignition and pulled on the handbrake. 'Perhaps you could have a word with him, Dorothy. I know you're only a pretend relative, but he admires you and he's been impressed by your ideas on making the office more efficient.'

She bit her lip. Sam feels responsible? Was he responsible? She didn't want to believe that, to think she was living under the same roof as a mass murderer. But something stank. 'Why would your father feel he was responsible? How could he be linked to these awful events?'

Stephen turned to her. 'I really don't know. He's got very emotional lately, which is not like him. Perhaps he believes all this will put people off coming to the camp; it was his pet idea, a camp for young people.'

'Do you think that's the reason?'

'If it is, then I think he's over-reacting. People's lives are more important than a successful business. I think there's something else.' His eyes widened. 'You mustn't think I'm worried my father had anything directly to do with the murders. I hope I haven't given you that impression.'

She put a hand on his arm. 'No, of course, not, Stephen,' she lied.

A sign was fixed to the reception door:

CAMPERS. RECEPTION CLOSED UNTIL FURTHER NOTICE. IF URGENT CONTACT MISS MINNIKIN IN STAFF CANTEEN.

Sam Salter sat behind the reception desk, his face pale and sweaty. Sally was passing him a mug of coffee.

'You're here at last,' he said. 'Cindy's over helping Nellie Minnikin, but the phone's not stopped ringing since I got here. It's in the papers, and on the television this morning. People are ringing up wanting to know if we'll be open next week, or asking if they can cancel. They say they don't want to come to a place where there's been two murders. What shall we do, Stephen?' His usual brash and buoyant self had vanished and he sounded at the end of his tether.

Stephen went over to him and placed a hand on his shoulder. Sam grasped it. 'My boy, I don't know what I'd do without you.'

'Try not to worry, Dad. I'm sure we'll get through this. The main thing is to help the police catch whoever's responsible for these awful murders. As soon as he's caught, then we can try to get back to normal.'

Sam Salter looked up at his son with teary eyes, seemingly too overcome to speak.

Dorothy went up to them. 'I'll take over the telephone and try to reassure people; after all, the murders didn't take place in the camp, we're a few miles from Orford. I'll stress security is tight.' She paused, and looked at Stephen. 'Is it?'

Stephen shrugged. 'Jim Lovell is in charge of security, checking fences, and staff are on a rota for walking round the camp at midnight to check for anyone who's the worse for wear, or intruders. We've not had any problems so far, but I'm afraid I can't guarantee it's watertight. I think it may be better not to mention it, unless they ask you.' He smiled at her. 'I'm pleased you've offered to take over, Dorothy; you've an authoritative voice, I'm sure it will help.' He turned to his father. 'If people want to cancel I think we should let them and refund their money; we can't afford to have any more bad publicity. Do you think that's the best way, Dad?'

Sam was still holding his son's hand. 'Anything you say, Stephen.'

Goodness this wasn't like Sam Salter.

The door to the staff offices opened and Revie barged into reception. He stared at them. She hoped he'd remembered she was undercover and didn't say anything while Sally was around.

'This you son, Salter?'

Sam let go of Stephen's hand, stood up, smoothed down his jacket, as though trying to gain control of himself. Probably didn't want Revie to think he was a wimp. 'Yes, this is Stephen, and my cousin Dorothy Piff, who's helping out in the office.'

Revie grunted and nodded to them. 'Right. I want you to organise a rota of all the staff. Start with the most senior, I'll interview them and the junior ones will be seen by DC Cottam. Space them out, say fifteen minutes each, if we need to talk to them in more depth, we'll see them again.' He looked at his watch. 'First one in twenty minutes.' He turned towards Salter's office, then spun round. 'What's your name?' He pointed at Sally.

'Sally,' she gasped, her face reddening. 'I didn't do anything, Inspector Revie.'

He laughed. 'Well you can do something now. Two coffees, milk and sugar, and sandwiches. Ask the canteen to rustle up bacon butties. I know they won't be as good as my favourite cook's,' he sent a knowing look to Dorothy, 'but my stomach thinks my throat's been cut.'

Sally was rooted to the spot.

'See what you can do, Sally, please,' Stephen said.

Dorothy felt her blood pressure rising. Revie's manners were atrocious and his choice of words hardly appropriate for the situation. She glared at him, but all she got was a wink and a cheeky grin as he went back into the staff office.

Laurel, standing by the outdoor swimming pool, blew her whistle and the final of the medley race began. Spectators lining the sides of the pool raucously cheered on their friends. She was pleased she'd managed to persuade so many of the campers to take part: four teams of four swimmers, each doing a length of the pool, crawl, breast stroke, back stroke and a last length whatever they wanted. Water shot out, drenching the spectators, adding to the hysteria. She shouted encouragement, even though she knew the swimmers couldn't hear her.

The race over, swimmers shivering under towels, she handed over the proceedings to Charlie Frost to present the prizes. As swimmers and supporters left, they shouted thanks to her for organizing the competition. She was glad she hadn't needed to jump in the water and rescue anyone. Now she was cold, hungry and wanted her lunch.

Charlie ambled towards her. 'Heard the latest?'

She hoped it wasn't an off-colour joke. 'No, and I need to get back to my chalet and change, I'm freezing.' She started to walk away.

'There's been another murder!'

She halted. 'A murder? Who?'

'You know Miss Piff? She's Salter's cousin and has been working in the office—'

Her legs buckled.

'Hey, hold on!' Charlie leapt to her side and put an arm round her waist.

'Miss Piff's been murdered?' she gasped.

Charlie's hands tightened and he pulled her close. 'No. It's Miss Tweedie who's copped it. Miss Piff and that new gardener, Spade, or Diamond, found her dead at her home yesterday. I say, Spade's a good name for a gardener, isn't it?' He squeezed her tighter and rubbed his cheek against hers.

Relief and joy ran through her, followed by anger. She levered his hand off her waist and pushed him away. 'Stop that!'

'I was only trying to help; you looked as though you were going to faint.'

He was right, she was being unfair. 'Sorry, Charlie, it was the shock of hearing of another murder. When did it happen? I haven't heard anything.'

He still looked ruffled. 'Seems Miss Piff went over to Belinda's house when she didn't turn up for work yesterday morning. Not sure why she took the gardener, mind you he looks as though he'd be handy in a fight.'

He didn't know how right he was.

She wanted to rush round to Dorothy to see how she was, then to collar Frank to find out details of the murder. It happened yesterday? Why hadn't one of them told her? 'I didn't hear anything. When did you find out?'

Charlie shrugged. 'Police kept it quiet, but it's in the papers this morning – not much detail. Jim Lovell told me after breakfast.'

That follows, she thought, Jim always seemed to be the one with hot news.

'Police are here, interviewing everyone. You'll get a call soon, I expect. Hope you've got an alibi.'

'When was the murder?'

'Must have been Wednesday night. I'll give you an alibi, if you like. You can say we spent the night together,' he said, leering at her. 'Save a lot of bother if you were by yourself.'

She stared at him. 'That would mean I'd give you an alibi, Charlie. Do you need one?'

'Me?' he blustered. 'They won't be interested in me.'

'In that case, why would they be interested in me?'

His face reddened. 'Well, if you're going to be like that, forget it!' He marched off.

No hope of that, Charlie. Your lack of an alibi is noted. Tonight, she'd visit Dorothy and hope Frank would be there too.

As Frank made his way to the plant nursery, he thought he'd better see Hinney as soon as possible and make sure he understood why he'd disappeared from his work yesterday. Hinney was in the greenhouse, potting on plants.

'Morning, Mr Hinney. Sorry I didn't finish my work yesterday, but you've probably heard what happened.'

Hinney stared at him, his hands deep in a pile of potting compost. He firmed a plant into its new pot, watered it and placed it to one side to drain. 'Yes, I got a message from the office, but I didn't expect you to be gone all day. What happened?'

It was the first time Hinney had asked him a question that wasn't to do with plants or gardening. 'What did you hear?' This should be interesting; he might get Hinney to put a few sentences together.

Hinney frowned. 'Why ask me? Have you forgotten what you saw already?'

Frank bit his lip. What a wanker! 'The police asked me not to discuss the case. I just thought if you told me what you'd heard I could confirm if it was true or not. That's all. I'm not being awkward, just doing as I'm told.'

Hinney grunted, and prised another plant from the tray of seedlings.

End of sparkling conversation.

'Shall I carry on with what I was going to do yesterday?'

Hinney potted another seedling. 'You may as well. Let's hope you don't have to do any more police work, hey?' He looked up and stared at him.

Had Hinney rumbled him? He was in a foul mood, and he looked as though he'd like to do him an injury, but at least he'd got some reaction out of the man.

'You know it was Miss Tweedie who was murdered?'

Hinney's face looked like thunder. 'Yes, that's what I heard.'

'Did you know her? I don't suppose you came across her very often.'

'What's it to you? The police will be asking the questions. Or do you want to do their job for them?'

He decided to shut up; it was getting too near the bone. 'No reason, it must be upsetting for the staff who knew her well, like the girls who work in the office.'

Hinney grunted.

He decided to change the topic. 'You've got some interesting plants in the greenhouse and nursery. What

219

are those?' He pointed to the newly potted seedlings. 'I don't know them.'

Hinney looked up, his eyes narrowing. 'Streptocarpus,' he said. 'Good for indoor decoration.'

'Interesting. Well, I'll be off, let's hope it's a quiet day!' If they were streptocarpus, he was a rotten detective. He grimaced, but then, that could be true. He needed a morale booster, and hoped Laurel would make her way to Dorothy's room tonight.

Laurel was seething with unanswered questions as she made her way to her chalet. Belinda Tweedie murdered and Dorothy and Frank had discovered the body! Why were they together? She felt jealous. Finding bodies was her speciality. It should have been her and Frank, not Dorothy and Frank. She mentally slapped herself for being childish and insensitive, but over the last year she'd been the one discovering bodies: the suitcase containing the bones of a young girl, the body of Dorothy's twin sister, Emily, the bodies of the Harrops, and lastly, with Oliver, the body of the director of the Easterbrook power station, Dr Luxton. She shook her head. She was becoming addicted to murder.

'Laurel!'

Nellie Minnikin waved to her. 'Have you heard? Isn't it dreadful?'

Her face was strained, and the rims of her eyes red.

'Yes, Charlie Frost told me.'

'You look frozen. It's not shorts weather today.'

Laurel nodded. 'I've just finished by the pool.'

'Come into my chalet, and I'll make you a hot drink.'

She wanted to go to her chalet and have a bath, but detectives didn't turn down chances to snoop, and Nellie might have more news. 'Thanks, Nellie, a cup of tea would be good.'

In the chalet Nellie offered her the only chair and fussed round as she made the tea. 'I can't believe it. Who would have wanted to murder Belinda Tweedie? There's a rumour going round that the police have arrested Tommy Coltman.' She looked at Laurel. 'You know, he's a part-timer, helps Jim Lovell with the maintenance.'

She felt sick. If it was true, she'd had tea with a murderer, been alone with him in his house, felt sorry for him. She remembered the scalpels and the photograph of his wife, her blue eyes and her dark hair matching those of the missing girls. 'Who told you that?'

'One of the girls in the canteen; she's a friend of Sally, in the office, who overheard a policeman.'

'The police?'

'They've taken over Sam Salter's office, started questioning the staff. I've just been there. An Inspector Revie questioned me, wanted to know where I was on Wednesday evening and night, and what I knew about Belinda. Dare say they'll get round to you soon, although as you haven't been here five minutes, I don't suppose you'll be a suspect.'

Revie was here. That was good news. 'Did you have an alibi, Nellie? Charlie wanted me to give him one, he didn't care if he ruined my reputation by saying we spent the night together!' They both laughed.

Nellie shook her head. 'I've not got one either; perhaps you'd prefer to give me the alibi, instead of Charlie?' She gave her a knowing look.

She felt her face redden.

Nellie laughed. 'Sorry, dear, I know you're not inclined that way.'

Laurel's stomach twisted. She'd searched this room and found the photograph of Nellie and her friend. 'How are the girls in the office coping?'

'Miss Piff seems to be holding the fort; she's made of strong stuff, finding the body and all.'

She was right there. Dorothy Piff had seen war service, lost her fiancé in the war, and suffered the murder of her sister, but she didn't make that an excuse for weakness.

'Sam Salter is taking it hard. I had a chat with him. I don't know what he'd do if he didn't have Stephen. He's a lovely young man, calm as anything, helping Miss Piff with the telephone calls and trying to cheer up his father.'

He's not going to pieces like Sam. 'Is Stephen more like his mother? Was she a steady woman?'

Nellie pulled a face then frowned. 'It's a long time since I saw her. She was a lovely girl, but not one for reading and writing. He got his brains from his dad and his nature from Mum, I think.'

'Sam Salter must be bright to have built up such a successful business,' she said, hoping Nellie would tell her more.

Nellie nodded. 'Want another?' She peered into Laurel's cup. 'You've not drunk that! Come on, it'll get cold.'

She obediently sipped; it was lukewarm.

Nellie poured herself one. 'We were all surprised when they had Stephen.'

'Why was that?' She held up her cup for a refill.

'Sam had mumps in his late teens; you know what that does!' She made an obscene gesture, opening her legs and pretending to hold two large balls with her hands.

'Gosh, I hope they shrank.'

Nellie roared with laughter. 'You'll have to ask him. I'm sure he'll put your mind at rest.'

'No fear!'

'Anyway, it's a good job he's got Stephen, he's leaning on him now.'

'What about Mr Coltman? Do you think he killed Belinda?'

Nellie shook her head. 'Hard to believe, he seems a quiet chap. I don't know why Sam gave him a job, he's a bundle of nerves, doesn't talk to anyone. That's a bit mean of me, he's had a rough life. You know about his wife and everything?'

'Yes, someone told me.'

Nellie placed her cup on the saucer. 'Makes your blood run cold, doesn't it? But if it was Tommy Coltman, then we can rest easy in our beds tonight. There won't be any more murders.'

Laurel wasn't so sure.

Laurel, Frank, and Dorothy sat huddled together, drinking whisky, in Dorothy's bedroom at Sudbourne Hall.

Laurel told them about Frost and Minnikin not having alibis for the time of Belinda's murder, and how they'd both propositioned her, and that she preferred Nellie's offer to Charlie's.

Frank raised his eyebrows. 'Everyone's after your body!'

She shrugged her shoulders. 'Can you blame them? I've never been so toned. With all this swimming and the tasteless food, my muscles are like steel and I've lost half a stone.'

Dorothy patted her stomach. 'Wish I could say the same. I think your half-stone has settled round my middle.'

'Anything else to report?' Frank asked her.

She scrunched her face. 'Nothing really, except Charlie Frost has fallen from my favour yet again; he seems to have more hands than an octopus. I chatted with Nellie; Sam seems to be breaking up, according to her.'

'I'll agree with that,' Dorothy said. 'I think his reactions to the deaths of Bert and Belinda are highly suspicious. He could be involved in some way, although I can't imagine how.'

'What about you, Frank? Heard anything interesting?' Laurel asked.

'No, Hinney was in a foul mood, cross because a certain lady,' he winked at Dorothy, 'asked for my assistance, and took me away from my work. He's a most objectionable man. I'll certainly not miss him when all this is over.'

'Has he got an alibi for Wednesday?' Laurel asked.

'I don't know, I didn't dare ask him. I think he may have rumbled my cover.'

'Really? What did he say?'

'Something about doing the police's work for them and asking too many questions.'

She pulled a face. 'You could be right. Why would he react like that if he's not involved?'

'Because he's a sour, miserable sod, who doesn't like anyone, including himself.'

Dorothy sipped her whisky. 'I must say, this,' she raised her glass, 'is making me feel much better.'

'Ditto,' Laurel said.

'I suppose the only good thing about Mr Hinney is he's an excellent gardener; the flower beds are a treat,' Dorothy said. 'Came from one of the London parks, is that right?'

Frank nodded. 'Yes, and before today I couldn't fault him.'

Laurel tilted her head. 'What happened to make you change your mind?'

'He was potting up plants in the greenhouse this morning and I asked him what they were, he said they were streptocarpus.'

'You've lost me, sounds like a deadly bacterium,' Laurel said.

'Is their common name Cape Primrose?' Dorothy asked. 'Don't they come from South Africa?'

'Dorothy, go to the top of the class. You,' he pointed to Laurel, 'must stay after school and write streptocarpus three thousand times.'

'It wasn't a streptocarpus?' Dorothy asked.

'No, it wasn't. I'm not sure what they are, think I've seen them before, but not for years. My botany's getting rusty.'

'If you don't use it, you lose it,' Dorothy said, peering at him over her spectacles; she sighed. 'I won't be able to take the day off tomorrow and drive back to Greyfriars; I couldn't leave the Salters and the office girls to cope by themselves.'

Laurel nodded. 'It's a pity, but I think you're right.' She turned to Frank. 'Do you think it would be better if we stayed here as well?'

'Possibly, but we do need to meet and share information with Stuart and Mabel. Hopefully Stuart will have found out something about the missing girls; also, he may have discovered details of the family of the murderer of Mrs Coltman.'

'I can't see how that would help us,' Dorothy said.

'It might shed some light on Coltman's possible motives for these murders if he's guilty, or possibly give us a clue as to where the girls might be.'

Laurel took a sip of her drink. 'You mean where the bodies might be, don't you? I can't imagine they're still alive, not after everything that's happened in the past week.'

Frank leant back against the settee and drained his glass. 'No, I'm sure they're dead. They bore a strong resemblance to Coltman's wife, so suspicion falls on him, but unless Revie can find evidence in Coltman's house linking him either to the missing girls, or to Tweedie's and Wiles' murders, he'll have to let him go.'

Dorothy got up, fetched a bottle of Glenlivet, and did refills. They half-heartedly chinked glasses; no one offered a toast. She looked at her wrist watch. 'Anyone feel like watching Wimbledon? Find out who won the women's final?'

They both shook their heads.

She sighed.

'What about those boxes Coltman made, pictures of pretty dark-haired, blue-eyed girls imprisoned in boxes? And the scalpels? All this is seriously weird,' Laurel said, hitching her cardigan more tightly round her shoulders.

'Why did he make things like that?' Dorothy asked.

'What do we know about Coltman? About his life before he went to Java?' Frank asked.

Laurel went over the details Coltman had told her when she had tea with him, and the information from Stuart and Revie.

Frank rubbed his chin. 'Married a childhood sweetheart, thought she was safe with his mother away from London, had a promising career as an architect cut short by the war,' he mused.

'Captured by the Japs, interred and tortured,' Dorothy chimed in.

'Returns to find his wife and son murdered and the killer hanged,' Frank repeated.

'His son's body never found,' finished Dorothy.

'And his life since?' Frank asked.

'A shattered man, he roams the fields at night, he has a boat and obviously, from all the shells used in the boxes, rows to beaches and collects shells and any other things he can use as decoration,' Laurel said.

'I wonder where he goes for the shells; I suppose any beach round here would do,' he said.

'Where is his boat kept?' Dorothy asked.

'I don't know, but he'd have to row a fair distance, down the Ore, before he came to any beaches. I suppose Shingle Street is the nearest point, but the waters round there are treacherous,' Laurel replied.

'Unless he rows across the river to Orford Ness. If he did that he could walk to the beaches.'

'But wouldn't that be dangerous? All the unexploded bombs and armaments?' Laurel asked.

'Not if he knew which areas had been cleared. Perhaps he doesn't care very much if he does blow himself up; he seems an unhappy man, with nothing to live for except to try and find the body of his dead son, and to make boxes to imprison paper girls.'

Laurel straightened. 'Perhaps he wasn't trying to imprison them, perhaps he was trying to keep them safe, to put them behind the wire so no harm could come to them. He wasn't able to protect his wife. Perhaps he feels guilty he wasn't there to protect her.'

Frank made a circle with his thumb and forefinger. 'That's what I call lateral thinking, and it ties in with what Coltman said: "I only want to make her safe."'

Chapter 19

Saturday, July 3, 1971

Back in his cottage, with the sound of waves beating against the pebble beach below the sandy cliffs, the tension in Frank's shoulders eased as he started to prepare lunch. He'd missed that sound.

The previous evening as he and Laurel were leaving, Dorothy called them back. 'Stuart's on the phone.'

'Sorry, Frank. I won't make the meeting until after four. I'm following up a lead.'

'Want to tell me about it?'

'No, it may come to nothing. See you tomorrow.'

'We can have the morning off,' Laurel said. 'I can meet Oliver.'

'I'll go to the cottage and have a think,' he'd replied.

'And a cook?' she'd asked.

He nodded.

On his way back from the camp, he'd picked up a freshly cooked lobster in Aldeburgh from Mr Fryer, the fisherman, who'd broken the claws and split the body for him. Now, he put it on a wooden board, gave the good-sized claws a few more cracks and eased out the pink meat, then removed the white flesh from the tail and cut it into thick slices. Usually with a fresh lobster he'd settle for some mayonnaise and a green salad, but today he wanted to cook; he wanted to concentrate on something apart from murder. He'd chosen a fiddly recipe: Lobster à L'Americaine. He chopped up carrots, onions, a shallot and a clove of garlic, and sighed deeply as he breathed in the smell of the vegetables sweating in butter.

Later, he wiped a piece of bread round the plate, soaking up the last of the rich sauce, and chewing it slowly, savouring the different flavours. He got a bottle from the fridge and poured the last of the Chablis into his wine glass. He carried it to the sitting room and settled back into the sagging settee, closing his eyes, appreciating the lingering taste in his mouth, but also the calm and quiet of the cottage.

He wasn't cut out for life in a holiday camp with the perpetual presence of too many people. Being undercover was not his bag, and he hated being bossed around by the grumpy and unpleasant Hinney. He opened his eyes, drank the last of the wine and decided it was time to put his brain into gear and try to work out who was responsible for the murders of Wiles and Tweedie, and, if possible, to find a link between these crimes and the missing girls. First coffee.

Back in the kitchen, he put on the percolator and settled down at the table with an A4 pad of lined paper and a biro.

Suspects
Sam Salter
Stephen Salter
Charles Frost
Nellie Minnikin
Thomas Coltman
Gareth Hinney

Did any of these people fit the bill? Coltman looked the most likely, the most believable. If his face appeared in newspapers with details of his midnight wanderings and obsessive behaviour, people would nod their heads in agreement. It must be him, they'd think. He's a weirdo.

The rest? No one jumped out at him, although there were disturbing facts about all of them, apart from Stephen Salter. Hinney wasn't a strong suspect either; he didn't appear to like anyone, wasn't interested in women, but those facts didn't add up to making him a murderer.

He decided to add another name to the list.

Person unknown.

He was looking for a sadist, a person who showed no humanity, had no feeling for anyone. A sadist who took pleasure in watching his victims suffer. He started to analyse the personalities of the list of suspects.

Laurel opened the door of the Cross Keys pub and walked into the bar. Oliver was sitting by the fireplace with Billy under the table beside him. As she moved towards them, Billy pulled on his lead, shaking the table, making Oliver's beer slop over the rim of the pint glass.

Oliver laughed, pulling the dog back by his collar.

She bent down and rubbed her face against Billy's head. The smell of his fur was delicious, and his rough tongue curled round one of her ears, his hot breath engulfing her face.

'I hope I'm going to get an equally warm welcome,' Oliver said, pushing Billy back under the table.

She wiped her face with the back of her hand, and kissed him on the cheek. 'Don't think your tongue can match his,' she whispered.

He looked shocked.

'Sorry, it's the company I've been keeping.'

When he was at the bar ordering her drink, she once more resumed her love affair with Billy. She bit her lip. How would Oliver feel if he knew when she came into the pub, it was the sight of the black Labrador that made her heart race and not him? This wasn't a basis for a lasting relationship, was it? You couldn't marry a man because he owned the most delicious dog in the world.

She was being silly. It was the effect of being enclosed in that wretched campsite, discovering the body of Bert Wiles and hearing of the murder of Belinda Tweedie, no wonder her mind was in turmoil. She liked Oliver, he was good company, but did she fancy the pants off him? Did she lust after him as she'd once lusted after her fiancé, Simon? Did she want to take the final step, to commit herself to him, body and soul? If they married would she have to give up being part of The Anglian Detective Agency? If she did, what would she do? Just be a doctor's wife? Looking after the office? Booking appointments? Become a stalwart of the Mothers' Union? She could go back to teaching. Did she want to do that? No. She wanted to remain a detective. She wanted to keep the close relationships she had with Frank, Dorothy, Stuart and Mabel, but especially Frank. Would Oliver be happy with a different kind of relationship? They could be friends and lovers, with no serious commitment. God, she was starting to sound like Frank.

She pushed Billy back under the table as Oliver returned with a half of Adnams. 'Lovely, thank you.' It tasted clean and hoppy.

Oliver took a sip from his pint glass. He frowned at her. 'I've been worried about you, Laurel. These murders in Orford, are they anything to do with the case you're working on?'

She spluttered, the beer going up her nose. She coughed, pulled out a handkerchief from a pocket and wiped her face. 'I hope you're not accusing me of murder?'

'You know what I mean,' he said.

'Really, Oliver, you know I can't talk about cases we're still working on.'

'You're at that campsite, aren't you? And Diamond is with you, isn't he? Also, Dorothy Piff's absence has been noted.' He paused, his face flushing. 'I think you owe me an explanation. When people ask me where you are, I don't know what to say. You know what it's like round here, everyone knows everyone else's business.'

Did she owe him that? Was everyone assuming they were a pair? Did they see her as the future doctor's wife? Booking medical appointments, raising a family, becoming part of the town's establishment and a regular churchgoer? Did she see herself in that role?

She looked into her glass as though the future might reveal itself in the frothy beer. She looked up at him; his expression changing from angry to dismayed.

'I'm sorry, Oliver, if you're upset, but my first allegiance is to my partners and the client whose case we're working on.'

His nostrils dilated. 'I see.'

This was ridiculous, she only had a few hours before the meeting, she didn't want to waste this precious time quarrelling. She wanted and needed some light-hearted banter, a good meal, and a walk with Billy. They could sort out their relationship when this case was over and she was back at Greyfriars House.

'Please, Oliver, let's not fall out. I haven't much time left before I have to go back. I'm quite safe, honestly. We can talk about all this when things are back to normal.'

The expression on his face didn't change. 'Normal? Your life hasn't been normal since you came to this part of Suffolk, has it? As long as you're a member of that detective agency you'll always be in danger, and what with the crazy hours you work, and my doctor's rota, we hardly see anything of each other.'

Her throat tightened, and bubbles of anger started to fizz though her brain. Diplomacy wasn't working. She'd been looking forward to seeing Oliver and Billy, casting off her Stripey blazer and not having to perpetually smile at the campers.

'I refuse to discuss this anymore today. If you can't forget it for a few hours so we can have a pleasant lunch, then I think it's better if we go our own ways.'

His jaw dropped and he grabbed her hand. 'You're not giving me the brush-off, are you? Please, Laurel. I'm sorry, but I've not been able to sleep properly since I heard about the first murder, and then when the news came about the camp secretary...'

She inwardly sighed. Now she knew what it must be like for men who had truly dangerous jobs, like soldiers, fishermen, the lifeboat crew, and the police; how some of their wives couldn't understand how much their jobs, however dangerous, meant to them, and how when they were asked to give those jobs up, the marriage sometimes fell apart, either because they refused to do that, or they gave in, and were unhappy and resentful afterwards. If Oliver did ask her to marry him, then before and if she said, yes, there would have to be a lot of negotiations.

'No, I'm not, Oliver. I just meant for this afternoon. Look, let's have some lunch. I'm starving. Can we eat here and then take Billy for a walk towards Thorpeness?'

He looked relieved. 'We could go back to my place, I can rustle up something.'

And what would that lead to? Sex? More quarrelling? 'Thank you, Oliver, perhaps next time. I need to get back by four.' Not strictly true, but she hoped she'd have time for a chat with Mabel before the meeting started; she'd missed her.

'Oh, OK. I'll get a menu. Like another drink?'

She hadn't drunk much of her half pint, but she needed an alcohol boost. Could she ask for a whisky? Better not, or Oliver would think she was a real toper. She smiled, imagining his face if she asked for a double Bell's. 'Another half would be lovely, Oliver.'

Frank gave Mabel a tight hug. 'God, I've missed you, Mabel.'

She hugged him back. 'You mean you've missed my cooking.'

'That as well. But I have missed the gang. It's so much better when we're working together and able to constantly exchange information. I've missed everyone's company; although Laurel and Dorothy are at the camp, and we manage to get together now and then, it hasn't been the same.'

Mabel opened a cake tin and took out a spectacular sponge cake. 'We can have a slice of this and a cuppa while we're waiting for Laurel and Stuart. I'm sorry Dorothy can't make it; I do miss her.'

'When will Stuart be back? What's he been up to?'

She switched on the kettle. 'He said not before four. He's following up on the family of the boy who was hanged. Seemed quite excited about it. Don't know any more than that.'

Stuart excited? 'That sounds promising.'

Mabel cocked her head. 'Laurel's here.'

All three were round the kitchen table gossiping, when the noise of Stuart's Humber Hawk silenced them. Frank looked at his watch. 'Four thirty, bit late, but we'll let him off.'

Stuart marched into the kitchen, a big smile creasing his tired face. 'Laurel!' Followed by a bear hug. 'Frank.' Hearty hand-shakes. He turned to Mabel, nodding to what was left of the sponge cake. 'See you've left me a few crumbs.'

She shook her fist at him.

'Glad to see you're both still madly in love,' Frank said

Grinning, Stuart and Mabel hugged each other. 'We have missed you, it hasn't been the same,' Stuart said.

Stuart nodded. 'Where's Dorothy?'

Laurel explained.

'Right, let's move to the dining room and start the meeting,' Frank said.

'Don't I get any tea and cake?' Stuart moaned.

'You go ahead, I'll bring it in,' Mabel said.

'Who's going to take the minutes as Dorothy's not here?' Stuart asked, as he sat down at the dining room table.

'Thank you for volunteering, Stuart. Try not to get too many crumbs in the typewriter when you type them up,' Frank said, winking at Laurel.

Stuart blew out his cheeks. 'I've changed my mind, it was better without you.'

'I'll do the minutes; Stuart needs to drink his tea and I think he's got something important to tell us,' Laurel said.

Stuart Elderkin's grin reappeared. 'I have. Don't know what it means, but it must mean something.'

Tea drunk, cake eaten, pipe lit, Stuart took his notebook from a briefcase and flicked through the pages. 'As you know I interviewed the families and friends of the two missing girls and there is absolutely nothing new to report, except their disappearances are out of character – both of them. After they joined the camp staff they didn't come home very often, and the visits became less and less. They both told their parents and friends how much they enjoyed their jobs and Roberta did mention Sam Salter had taken her out a few times and she really liked him, even though he was older than her.' He paused to take a deep suck on the briar pipe, and then blew out a stream of smoke.

'Thanks for doing all that leg work, Stuart. Sorry you didn't get the reward you deserved,' Frank said.

'That's detective work for you,' Stuart said. 'It has to be done, you can't leave anything unexplored; you don't strike gold very often ...'

'I'm sure you were thorough, and...' Stuart was smirking. Frank groaned. 'Come on then, tell us what you have found.'

Stuart leant forward. 'We agreed I'd look into the family of the man who was hanged for the murder of Mrs Coltman and her son, John. I must say I couldn't see how it could be connected to the missing girls, and I'm still not sure what the connection is, but there must be one.'

Frank tapped his fingers on the table and Laurel wriggled impatiently.

'I traced the family back to their original address, but they'd moved soon after their son was hanged. I managed to find a few neighbours who remembered them and the murder case. They said the family — Mum, Dad, and a younger brother — were devastated. They wouldn't believe he was guilty, even when the damning evidence against Adrian Hovell was presented in court. The newspapers were full of it, and one old man I spoke to said people turned against the family when he was sentenced to death, and they learned he'd raped the mother and killed her baby. It was especially hard on the young brother; he was picked on at school and the teachers didn't do anything to stop the bullying.'

Laurel looked up from her notes. 'Children can be cruel, it must have been hell for him, and his mum and dad.'

'Were any of the people who remembered Adrian surprised he was a murderer?' Frank asked.

Stuart gave a last puff and knocked out the pipe on an ashtray. 'The old man said he only started to believe the charges when he read the evidence in the News of the World. Said Adrian was quiet, read a lot, liked bird-watching, and the last time he'd spoken to him, when he was home on leave, Adrian had said he didn't like being in the Forces; he found some of the men crude; all they were interested in was boozing, smoking and chasing skirts. Couldn't wait for the war to be over.'

'It's the quiet ones you have to be careful of,' Mabel said, looking at Stuart.

Frank leant back against his chair. 'Is that it?' he asked, disappointment rising from his guts.

Stuart shook his head. 'That's just for starters. After a lot of digging – I nearly gave up at one point – I managed to find out where the family moved to. They'd changed their name, but both parents died recently, within a year of each other, and the younger son, now a man, has moved away.' He stopped and looked at them, grinning.

'Come on spit it out, Stuart!' Frank snapped.

'Don't deny me my moment in the limelight! The boy's Christian name was… is Gareth.'

Frank's stomach clenched. Was his analysis of the suspects right? Was this the murderer?

Stuart sat up straight. 'The family changed their name from Hovell to… Hinney. I believe Gareth Hinney, who's the head gardener at Salter's camp, is none other than Gareth Hovell, the young brother of Adrian Hovell who was hanged for the murder of Audrey Coltman and her son, John.'

There was silence. Frank looked at Laurel.

'Could it be coincidence?' she asked.

Frank shook his head. 'No. I don't know how this ties up with the disappearance of the girls, and the murders of Bert Wiles and Belinda Tweedie, but this morning after a good lunch and several glasses of wine, I went through the case and I kept coming back to Gareth Hinney.'

'Why?' Laurel asked.

'We have absolutely no clues, or even half-clues, pointing to Hinney. There's more evidence pointing to Coltman being the murderer. I based my reasoning purely on an analysis of the characters of the suspects. He, Hinney, is the one person who shows no humanity, no feelings at all for others; all he shows is contempt, and I suspect hatred. The only other pointer to him is the plants he's growing in the camp's nursery.'

'The ones he said were streptocarpus?' Laurel asked.

'Yes. I remembered what they were at the end of my lunch; it must have been the Chablis oiling my memory. I'm sure those plants weren't streptocarpus but mandrake, Mandragora officinarum, which is full of alkaloids, poisons and, as I remember, was used as an anaesthetic in surgery in ancient times. Also, he's growing henbane in an outside nursery bed.'

'The wine?' Stuart asked.

He held up his hand. 'We don't know what happened to the girls, we suspect they've been murdered, we don't know how they died, but whoever murdered Bert Wiles is a sadistic sod, who enjoyed torturing the poor man. Belinda Tweedie had to be killed quickly; she was connected to the murderer in some way. Revie, hopefully, will soon get the results of the analysis of the wine that was meant to drug or kill Dorothy. If Tweedie had been successful, I think we'd be in the terrible position of looking for the murderer of Dorothy, as well as the others.'

'No!' Mabel's strangled cry made the hairs on the back of his arms stand to attention.

'Stuart, we ought to get Dorothy out of that holiday camp NOW!'

Stuart's eyes bulged. 'Calm yourself, Mabel. Dorothy can look after herself, she showed good sense getting out of that woman's house. You know what she's like, she wouldn't thank you if you start to make a fuss.'

Mabel's body quivered as she turned to Laurel. 'And, I don't think you ought to go back.'

'What about me, Mabel,' Frank asked. 'Don't I count?'

She pushed out her lower lip, looking like a middle-aged rebellious teenager. 'You're all right, you're a man.'

Laurel snorted.

There was silence.

Mabel, her breasts heaving, looked down at the table. Gradually pink came back into her cheeks. 'Sorry, I overreacted. It was the thought Dorothy could have been drugged and murdered.'

Laurel went to her and put an arm round her shoulders. 'I felt the same way. I thought at one point she was the murder victim; my legs turned to jelly and unfortunately Charlie Frost was on hand to give me support.'

Frank smiled as he imagined how Charlie's actions were received. 'Let's get back to Hinney. We need to find a connection between him and Belinda Tweedie. Laurel, any ideas?'

'I've never seen them together.' Laurel paused, her forehead wrinkling. 'But, Dorothy did mention Hinney brought flowers for Belinda, to put in Sam Salter's office.'

Stuart nodded knowingly. 'That's a connection.'

The phone rang. Frank picked it up. He listened, then mouthed to the others, 'It's Revie.' He switched the phone to conference so they could all hear.

'I've got two pieces of information for you, one you're not going to like, not sure I like it either. I've had to let Coltman go. We found no evidence he'd been in either Bert Wiles' cottage or Belinda Tweedie's house, and there were no signs in his cottage to connect him to the missing girls. However, we're keeping him under covert observation; bit difficult in Orford, but I've put my two best men on to it.'

'I'm glad,' whispered Laurel, 'I don't want it to be him. He's had such a rotten life.'

'Women,' Stuart whispered back.

'Who can I hear talking in the background? Is it the lovely Miss Mabel? Tell her the camp's bacon butties were a pale shadow compared to hers.'

Mabel fluttered her lashes at Stuart, who sighed.

'We're all here except Dorothy, who's stayed at the camp to help out,' Frank said.

There was silence for a few seconds. 'Your Dorothy had a close call with death, no doubt about that. Thank God she's got a nose for danger.'

There was an intake of breaths, and the temperature of the dining room seemed to drop several degrees.

'You've had the results of the analysis of the wine?' Frank asked.

'I have. It's not complete, they need to do further tests, but they've found something called alkaloids in it, they think they're plant alkaloids. Don't understand the chemistry, but the boffins say they need time to work out which plants they came from.'

Frank's vertebrae clicked together and air hissed from his throat. 'Revie, write this down. Get on to whoever's working on this. Tell them the plants are probably mandrake and henbane.' He spelt out the Latin names. 'Mandragora officinarm, and Hyoscanmus niger.'

There was silence. He imagined Revie writing on his pad and staring at the names. He waited for the riposte.

'Come on, Diamond. How do you know that?'

'Because I've seen both those plants growing in the holiday camp's nursery gardens, grown by Gareth Hinney. The mandrake plants were in the greenhouse. He lied to me when I asked him what they were. He said they were streptocarpus.'

'Strepto what? Is that a poisonous plant?'

'No.'

'So how do you know so much about deadly plants?'

'Don't know if I ever told you, but I've got a degree in botany.'

There was a snort. 'Didn't have you down as a pansy lover, still, well-spotted.'

'Revie, I think you ought to bring Hinney in. I think he's your man.' The other three moved closer to him, the air tense with excitement, Laurel's sweet breath caressing his cheek.

The long silence that followed knotted Frank's stomach. He wanted to shout down the phone for Revie to get his finger out and get hold of Hinney before anyone else was harmed.

A dry cough. 'Have you got anything else on him? Anyone could have taken those plants from his garden. It's probably not illegal to grow them. I can find that out, but it's not enough to make a case.'

Laurel dug him in the ribs. 'Tell him about who he really is.'

'I'm passing you over to Stuart Elderkin, who can tell you what he's discovered about Hinney. I don't know how it all ties up, but there must be something we're not seeing.'

Stuart, looking pleased, explained his findings to Revie.

'Well, that's a facer,' Revie said. 'I'll bring him in straight away, see what explanations he gives for growing strange plants and why he's come back to the area where his brother committed a terrible murder.'

Frank's shoulders relaxed. 'Thanks, Revie. I'll sleep easier tonight knowing he's in your tender care.'

There was a wheezy laugh. 'When are you and Laurel coming back to the camp?'

'We were going to sleep here and leave early in the morning.'

Another wheezy laugh. 'In separate beds, I hope.'

Laurel leant closer. 'No. We're having a foursome with Mabel and Stuart. Pity you can't come, we could make a fivesome!'

Frank glared at her. Stuart sniggered and Mabel's face coloured up.

'I thought you were a nice girl, Miss Bowman. I think I'd better arrest you as well, I'm not sure that's legal!'

Laurel mouthed 'Sorry,' to the other three.

'Sleep well, pets. You've deserved it. Let's hope Hinney feels like having a little chat. See you tomorrow.' The phone went dead.

Hinney chatting? He didn't think it would be that easy. Frank turned off the phone and turned to the other three. 'Let's hope I'm right and Hinney is the murderer, otherwise there could be more mayhem.'

'I could do with a drink. Anyone else?' Laurel asked.

'A small brandy would be nice,' Mabel said.

Stuart got up. 'I'll get them. Whisky?' Laurel and Frank nodded.

Laurel looked at him. 'That was brilliant, Frank. Recognising those plants and immediately correlating them to the drugged wine.'

The genuine warmth and admiration in her voice gave him a good feeling.

Stuart came back with two bottles, a jug of water and four glasses.

They saluted each other.

'Here's to crime,' Stuart said.

'Here's to solving crime,' Laurel said.

As Frank raised his glass to his lips the phone shrilled out again. 'Must be Revie again, asking for more advice!'

The phone was still on conference mode. Dorothy's voice, shrill and taught filled the room. 'It's Dorothy! Who's speaking?'

They put their glasses down, leaning forward. Frank's throat tightened. Something was wrong. 'Dorothy, it's Frank. We're all here. What's the matter? Are you all right?'

'Yes. Yes. I'm all right. It's Stephen and Sam. Sam's going mad, someone's taken Stephen.'

She was gabbling, not making sense. 'Dorothy, try and calm down. Start from the beginning, take it slowly.'

Her breathing was rapid, she gulped and it seemed an age before she spoke again. 'Right, yes, just let me think for a moment. Sorry, but I'm sure they'll both be killed.' Her voice rose again. There were swallowings and coughs.

Laurel was white-faced, Mabel horror struck and Stuart picked up his glass and knocked back its contents in one go.

A final cough. 'I'm OK now. I'll try and remain calm. Sorry. Someone take notes.'

That was better. Miss Bossy Boots.

'I was coming down the stairs at Sudbourne Hall, when I heard a shout, and a terrible moan. I hurried down to find Sam Salter holding a letter, the envelope on the carpet. He turned to me, his face grey, horror-struck, his hands trembling. "He's got Stephen. He's going to torture him, kill him." I went up to him and tried to take the letter from his hands, but he knocked me away.'

'Who's got Stephen?'

'Sam said, "It's Hinney and he'll kill Stephen unless I follow his instructions. I've got to try and save him." He was wild; he's not thinking straight.'

Frank broke in and told her about Hinney.

'My God, I can't make sense of this.'

'What happened next?' Frank asked. The tension round him was electric.

'I said he should call the police immediately. He replied if he did Hinney would kill Stephen. He must meet Hinney and try to rescue Stephen. He had to go to Orford quay.'

'He's gone?'

'Yes. He made me swear I wouldn't call the police. I haven't, I called you. You can get hold of Revie.'

'Did he take anything with him?'

'I'm not sure. He went into the kitchen, so he may have taken a knife.'

'Do we know if Stephen has been taken? Hinney might have set a trap for Sam. Stephen may be safe.'

Another gulp. 'Sorry I should have told you. Sam did show some common sense, he checked. Stephen was supposed to be going to London to see his family, but Sam found his car in the garage. One of the doors was open and there was blood on the garage floor.'

'Did Sam leave the letter?'

'No, he took it with him.'

'No clues as to where Stephen is being kept?'

'No, but if they're meeting at the quay, then...'

A picture shot into his mind. The view from the quay. The mysterious spit of land called Orford Ness; forbidden territory, riddled with unexploded armaments. Bert Wiles had a boat and may have poached on Orford Ness, may have seen something there which scared him, and that may have been the reason he was killed. What about Thomas Coltman? Did he collect his shells from the Ness's beaches? Has he seen anything?

'Dorothy, Laurel and I will drive back to Orford now. Stuart will contact Revie. He's out looking for Hinney. I'm sure he's the murderer; I'll give you details later. The police will be with you shortly, but the priority is to find Sam and Stephen.'

'Right. What are you two going to do?' Her voice was full of trepidation.

'We need to get on to Orford Ness. I have a feeling that's where Hinney has taken Sam, and I think we'll need the help of Thomas Coltman. Let's hope he'll help us after all he's been through.'

Chapter 20

Laurel's boot studs clattered against the hall floor. She carried a parka and an extra jumper and hoped it would fit Frank.

Frank was waiting at the front door, his body tense and impatient. She threw him the jumper. 'Thanks. Ready?' he asked.

She pointed to his feet. 'Hadn't you better get your boots?'

'No time. It'll have to do.'

She didn't think jeans and trainers were going to cut it through water and mud.

'Here, borrow my waterproof,' Stuart said. 'Bit big for you, but it'll keep you dry.'

'Thanks, Stuart. We'll take my car, I'll drive.'

Her stomach clenched.

Mabel rushed out of the kitchen and thrust a plastic bag into Laurel's hand. 'Few things to keep you going.'

She hugged her.

'Come on, we need to shift,' Frank said.

'Will we go to Dorothy first, before we see Coltman?'

Frank frowned. 'No. We might miss him if he goes out on one of his walks.' He turned to Stuart. 'Revie might be out looking for Hinney. When you contact him, tell him where we're going and ask him to get the Ordnance squad. Then phone Dorothy and make sure she's all right.'

Stuart, his face serious and taut, nodded. 'I'll drive over to Dorothy as soon as I've done that.'

'Good idea.' Frank said.

'I'll come with you,' Mabel said. 'I'm not staying here by myself, worrying about all of you.'

Frank grabbed her arm. 'Come on, Laurel. Let's go.'

They rushed to the Avenger, she threw the bag on the back seat, and before she could close her door, the ignition fired, the car's lights came on, Frank slammed the car into first gear and they accelerated out of the drive of Greyfriars House. There would be skid marks.

'Which way are you going?' she asked, as they tore down the narrow road to Westleton.

'I'll make for the A12, then go to Snape and through Tunstall Forest.' He changed down gears as he came to the turning for Westleton village.

'OK.' She gripped the door handle and steeled herself.

Frank turned right in front of Scarletts garage and drove like a mad man down the narrow road to the A12. She admired his skill; using the width of the road he slid the car round bends, changing gears to slow down for possible oncoming traffic. Thankfully there wasn't much of that. After a few hair-raising minutes, adrenalin kicked in and her body became one with the car as she swayed into bends, her right foot wanting to press down on an accelerator.

Frank shot her a quick glance. 'This is almost as good as when Stuart and I raced along the beach to rescue you from the evil Nicholson.'

She snorted. 'You were a bit late... as usual.'

They reached the A12 and Frank put his foot down, the needle on the speedo jumping upwards.

'You know where Coltman lives?'

'Yes. How should we tackle this? He probably despises me – he must know it was me who told Revie about the scalpels. What if he won't help us?'

Frank's knuckles showed white as he gripped the wheel, swerving round a red Mini. 'I really don't know. We need to get on the Ness; it could be hours before Revie and the squad arrive. It's Saturday night, can't see that they're sitting at home waiting for an emergency.'

She gnawed at her lip. 'I'll be straight with Coltman. Tell him I was the one who told the police. Apologise. Then I'll plead with him to help us. I'm sure if we explain Stephen Salter's life is in danger, and possibly Sam's, he'll forgive me and help us. After all Sam gave him a job; not many people would have risked employing such an eccentric man.'

'Sounds good; you can charm anyone if you put your mind to it.'

'Even you?'

'Especially me.'

That was good to hear. 'Are we going to tell him about Hinney?'

He slowed the car as they drove through Snape village. 'Damn!' Traffic was turning out of the Maltings; it must be the end of a concert. He slowed to a crawl. 'Difficult one. What will he think when he knows Hinney is really Gareth Hovell, the brother of the man who murdered his wife and child?'

She looked at him, his green eyes staring at the road, face pale and tense, a muscle twitching at the corner of his mouth as he pulled on the steering wheel, accelerating as he turned the car towards Tunstall Forest and Orford. 'I don't think we should tell him, Frank. If he does help us we need him to be calm; if we mention the murder of his wife and child he may go to pieces. He's a bundle of nerves at the best of times.'

He overtook a blue VW campervan. 'Always fancied one of those.'

'Frank, you haven't answered me.'

'Sorry, concentrating on getting to Coltman in one piece. I'm not sure, let's play that one by ear.'

She was silent until they roared through Sudbourne village. 'There must be a connection between Hinney or Hovell, his brother hanged for murder and Thomas Coltman, the husband and father of the victims. But what has Stephen Salter and Sam Salter got to do with it? What's the connection there?'

Frank frowned. 'I don't know. There must be a link between the missing girls and the murders of Bert Wiles and Belinda Tweedie. I can see Hovell's connection with Wiles. Wiles knew the landscape round Orford intimately from his poaching, and that probably includes Orford Ness. Perhaps Hovell deliberately became friendly with Wiles and gained knowledge from him, especially of the Ness and the areas that were safe, those cleared of bombs.'

Realization dawned. 'Yes, I'm sure you're right. Bert Wiles became worried as he suspected Hovell was doing something on the Ness, something so dangerous, or wrong, he became frightened and tried to talk to Jim Lovell.'

Frank banged his hand on the steering wheel. 'Then blabber-mouth Lovell told everyone at the staff meeting about Bert being nervous and worried about something.'

'So Hovell killed him. But why torture him?' Bile rose to her mouth as she remembered Bert suspended over the bed, his body ripped and torn, the gag in his mouth, silencing nothing. How he must have suffered. 'We could do with some sort of weapons, Frank. Hovell is a maniac.'

'Sorry, haven't got my cricket bat with me today.' He slowed as they came into Orford, changing gear as they rounded the tight bend near the church, 'But you're right. Let's see if Coltman's got anything.'

She pulled at his sleeve. 'Turn left here into Daphne Road.'

They passed Belinda Tweedie's house. 'Left here.' He slowed the car to a crawl. 'There's his cottage. There's a light on. Thank God, he's in.'

Laurel went up the narrow path to the back of the house, Frank following her. 'Let's hope he opens the door.'

She knocked.

'Bit harder, Laurel. He'll think it's a branch blown by the wind.'

She glared at him. 'You do it, then.'

He leant across her and thumped on the door with his fist. The light went out.

'He probably thinks we're the police and he's going to be arrested again,' Laurel moaned.

Frank put his face close to the edge of the door. 'Mr Coltman,' he shouted, 'it's Frank Diamond, the gardener from the camp. I need your help. It's urgent, please open the door.'

Someone was moving towards them, there was a thud as something hit the floor. The light didn't come on. Had he fallen?

She took a deep breath, 'Please, Mr Coltman. It's Laurel Bowman, as well. The police aren't here, it's just the two of us. We know you didn't have anything to do with the murders of Mr Wiles and Miss Tweedie. We need your help. Mr Salter and his son Stephen are in danger. We believe the murderer is Gareth Hinney. We need your help to find them,' she shouted.

'Not lost your teacher's voice,' Frank whispered.

She didn't reply.

The light came on, a chain rattled, and a key turned. The door opened and a wild-haired Thomas Coltman stared at them.

'What are you talking about? Mr Hinney is the murderer? I can't believe it. You say Mr Salter and Stephen are in danger?'

Frank shepherded him back into the kitchen, where the solitary chair was on its side on the floor. He righted it. 'Please sit down, Mr Coltman, we'll try and explain. You'll have to trust us. We need your help.'

Coltman looked at Laurel, his eyes sad and unsure.

She gulped. 'Mr Coltman, I must apologise to you. When I came back for tea the day I met you in the graveyard, I opened that drawer.' She pointed to it. 'I saw the scalpels. I thought of Bert Wiles' body and I was afraid it might have been you.'

His back straightened and his eyes widened. 'Me? How could you think that? I wouldn't murder anyone. I wouldn't harm a dumb animal. I hate all killing. I saw too much of murder and torture during the war. My darling Audrey and John were murdered. Why would I want anyone to suffer as I've suffered?'

Laurel hung her head. The pain in his voice stabbed at her heart. 'I'm truly sorry. Can you forgive me?' She looked up. He was looking at her; there was heart-breaking loneliness and suffering in his eyes. She tentatively reached out a hand. 'Please help us to save them.'

He grasped her hand. 'Of course I will. What do you want me to do?'

Frank leant over the table towards him and succinctly told him as much as they knew, but he didn't tell him Hinney was the brother of Adrian Hovell, who had murdered his wife and child.

As the story progressed Coltman's shoulders lost their hunched appearance, his eyes brightened as he became caught up in the narrative. He released Laurel's hand. 'It's incredible. I know Hinney's got a boat, a small motorboat. I know where he keeps it.'

'Down by the quay?' Frank asked.

'Yes, and he took over one of the fisherman's huts as well. I'm not sure what he uses it for.'

'Should we go there first?' Laurel asked Frank.

'Yes.'

She turned to Coltman. 'You also have a boat, Mr Coltman?'

He looked puzzled. 'Yes.'

'Is your boat big enough to take three people?'

He frowned. 'At a push, I suppose. Why?'

'We think Hinney may have taken Stephen to Orford Ness. Could you take us there?'

'Why me?'

'I believe you may know which parts of the Ness are safe. We think you may have landed there.'

Coltman hesitated, looking from one to the other.

'Your shell boxes – we guessed you picked up the shells on the beaches of Orford Ness. Is that right?' she asked.

He looked at them. 'Why are a gardener and a Stripey coat involved in this affair? Shouldn't you have told the police?'

Damn! They should have explained at the beginning. She glanced at Frank.

'Mr Coltman, the police are being informed, someone is contacting Inspector Revie, who you know,' Frank said.

The name didn't seem to inspire confidence.

Frank continued, 'Frank Diamond and Laurel Bowman are our real names, but we're private detectives, hired by

Mr Salter to try and find out what happened to two women who went missing from the holiday camp.'

Coltman's shoulders slumped, and his eyes dulled. He turned to Laurel. 'You came back to have tea with me because you wanted to spy, didn't you? That's why you started snooping when I left this room. You opened the drawer on purpose.'

This was awful. He once more felt betrayed. What could she say to reassure him she was interested and cared for him as a person?

'Mr Coltman, I can understand you being upset; you've every right to be, but you must put your own feelings aside. We need to try and save lives, and we need your help. Sam Salter may lose his son. You've lost your son; do you want him to suffer the same tragedy?'

He straightened his back. 'No. I don't want him to suffer as I've suffered. No one should lose a child.'

'Will you help us?' Frank asked, his voice strong and firm.

'Yes. We'll go to his hut first, but I think I know where he's taken Stephen. I could be wrong, but I think we should look there first.'

Ripples of excitement played down her spine. 'Where?'

'Over the past few years, when I've been on the Ness, I've sometimes seen a light, from a torch I think, and always in the same place. I've never investigated it, I was afraid to go there, so I can't be sure.'

'Where?' demanded Frank.

'In one of the... pagodas.' As he whispered the word pagoda fear showed in his eyes, his body seemed to shrink as he reverted to the unstable man who had opened the door to them minutes ago.

Chapter 21

Frank drove them to Orford quay. He glanced at Coltman, who was in the front passenger seat; he seemed to have recovered from his terror at the thought of going to a pagoda, and before setting off he'd shown resourcefulness, thinking of things they might need. He'd led them to a garden shed and flashed torch-light over an array of tools. 'Do you think any of these might be useful?'

'Excellent!'

'Help yourselves. I've got two more torches — it would be better if we each had one in case we get separated.'

Frank chose a crowbar and Laurel picked up a hand-scythe. Coltman shuddered.

The quay was deserted. The murders had cleared the streets, the locals preferring to be at home as daylight started to fade. Coltman walked to the left of the jetty, away from the river to a line of fisherman's huts, some with blackboards advertising fresh fish and lobsters, others, trips to Shingle Street, or Havergate Island. Frank, armed with his crowbar and torch, followed Coltman, Laurel behind him.

Coltman pointed to the last in the line of huts. 'That's his,' he whispered.

Laurel pointed to a padlock and put her ear to the door. 'I can't hear anything. He can't be here.'

'I think we should break in,' Frank said. 'There might be a clue as to where he is, or what he's up to.'

Laurel nodded.

Coltman fixed the beam of his torch on the padlock.

Frank levered the crowbar between the hasp and padlock and applied as much force as he could. There was a splitting of wood as the hasp came away from the door frame. He pulled on the door until it gaped open, hanging lop-sided on its hinges.

Coltman moved the beam over the interior of the hut. Frank grabbed his arm. 'Stop!' The beam's light was reflected from glass and metal.

'What is it?' Laurel asked, peering over Frank's shoulder.

'It's a still,' Coltman replied. 'Whatever does he want with that? Has he been selling boot-leg spirits?'

Frank flicked on his torch and went into the shed. He stopped, looked down at the bench on which the still rested, and picked something up. He turned to them and thrust out his hand, palm open. On it were dried leaves.

'This is how he makes the drug to knock out people.' He rubbed the leaves and sniffed them. Laurel and Coltman did the same.

'What are they?' Coltman asked.

'I think they're dried mandrake or henbane leaves. He probably soaked them in alcohol and then distilled the mixture to get a liquor laced with the poisons. In some countries it was the method used for an anaesthetic before chloroform.'

'I wonder if the missing women were drugged?' Laurel asked.

'It's possible, look what nearly happened to Dorothy. I think Belinda Tweedie lured them to her house, offered them wine and then when they were unconscious—'

'Hinney came and took them away,' Laurel gasped.

'Why? Why has he done such things? Why has he taken Stephen Salter? Is the man mad?' Coltman asked.

An idea was beginning to ferment in Frank's mind. Was it preposterous? No time to think it over. They needed to get to Orford Ness and find Stephen and Sam Salter. If they were on the Ness... If they weren't he didn't know where they would be. Already they could be too late.

'Mr Coltman, we need to get to the Ness urgently. Where's your boat?'

'It's in an inlet not far from here. Mr Diamond, come with me.' He pulled on Frank's sleeve. 'Miss Bowman, make to the left of the quay, we'll pick you up there.'

'No fear, I'm coming with you. I think we'll need all the man-power we can get. I'm not risking being left behind.'

Frank laughed.

'I'm sure Mr Diamond and I can—'

'Don't waste your breath. She won't be left behind; if we dumped her she'd swim across the river. And call us Frank and Laurel, please.'

'You're a brave woman... Laurel. Please call me Thomas. Or Tommy.'

'Tommy, I think,' she said.

'Lead the way, Tommy,' Frank said. If lives weren't at risk he'd be enjoying the adventure.

Tommy led them over grass and scrub. He halted and pointed to the river. 'Hinney's boat isn't there. That's where he moors.' They followed him, their clothing swishing against the grass and bushes, the sounds mixing with the swirling river as it washed against the banks.

Tommy shone his torch on a small rowing boat. 'Just about room for all of us.' He stepped into shallow water which lapped round his Wellingtons, and held out a hand to Laurel. Clutching the scythe and the plastic bag Mabel had given her, she stepped in, the boat rocking. 'Move to the front... Laurel. I'll take the oars, I'm used to rowing.' He helped Frank into the boat. 'Sit next to Laurel, keep your weights evenly balanced.' He moved to the stern and pushed the boat into deeper waters. He clambered in. 'Not as young as I used to be,' he said, his voice boyish and full of energy, but he winced as he sat down. This is bringing him back to life, Frank thought.

Tommy took the oars, put them in the rowlocks and with short, brisk strokes, avoiding the banks in the narrow inlet, propelled them forward into the River Ore. As soon as they entered the river the flow sent them downstream, and Tommy eased off rowing and used the oars to guide them to the middle of the river.

'We'll land south-west of the pagodas, on the edge of the Stoney Ditch, opposite Havergate Island. That part of the Ness is shingle. All the AWRE work, Atomic Weapons Research Establishment, was there. We'll have to go carefully, there's lots of debris and some unexploded ordnance, but if we keep to the roads we should be safe. We'll land near a clump of trees and shrubs. They'll give us some cover.'

Although there wasn't much light, Frank could see that Laurel was smiling and Tommy had cast off his obsessive misery. The man who loved boats, rivers and the sea had reappeared. He had a purpose, a reason for living: to save a life, perhaps two lives. For his sake, as well as the Salters', he hoped there would be a good ending. The three of them, although he wasn't sure how much use Tommy would be in a fight, should be enough to overcome Hinney. But he'd killed at least two people, possibly four, and he enjoyed torturing and killing. A formidable opponent.

But he'd also killed someone, and not long ago. Could he kill again? If needed, he knew he was up to it, although it wasn't something he looked forward to. The best scenario would be to disable Hinney and hand him over to the law for trial. Damn! They should have brought some rope.

'Tommy, have you got any rope on board?' he asked.

Tommy shipped the oars, letting the current carry the boat downstream. 'Yes, I see what you mean. I think there's some just behind you.'

He understood.

'What do we need rope for?' Laurel asked.

'To tie Hinney up when we overpower him.'

'We should have thought of that,' she said.

'We'll knock him unconscious, and then tie him up,' Tommy said.

Frank revalued his opinion of Tommy's usefulness in a fight. 'Are you volunteering?'

'I'll be right behind you!' Tommy laughed, a strangled sound as though his vocal cords were rusty. He pulled at the oars again.

'Tommy, I know you haven't been to the pagodas, but do you know anything about them? Anything that could help us?' he asked.

'I have some idea what they're like inside. Jim Lovell talked about them, along with everything else. He said they were built to test the explosive mechanisms of atomic bombs, the high explosive charge that detonates the atomic bomb.'

'Why were the pagodas built with the roof on pillars?' Laurel asked.

'In case the worse happened and the charge exploded. The idea was if there was an explosion, the roof would collapse, and bury the chamber, stopping the debris spreading. The charges were enormous, an accident would have caused terrible damage to Orford as well as the Ness.'

'Any idea what the inside is like?' Frank asked.

'I believe there's a pit, the size and shape of an aircraft bomb bay, that's where they tested the bomb. Everything inside, all the machinery, was removed after they stopped testing. There were hydraulic lifts to drop the bombs from different heights, things like that. I'm not sure of the details.'

'Jim certainly knew a great deal about them,' Laurel said.

'Jim's a local, lived in Orford all his life. He's interested in the history of the area. I didn't want to hear about the pagodas, but I must admit it was fascinating learning about what went on there in the 1950s.'

The current speeded up, along with the wind. Beside him, Laurel was fiddling with her hair, tucking the end of her pony tail into an elastic band. Getting ready for action.

'Here's where we land. There's Havergate island to the left,' Tommy said.

Frank could just make out low land through the fading light; the sound of the river had changed, its water slapping into the banks of the island and the Ness.

'I'll beach the boat. I've been here once before, years ago. I usually row to Shingle Street and back up the coast before I land. Hold tight, it may be bumpy.' He pulled on the oars and they edged towards the bank.

'Can you shine a torch? I'll pick the best spot,' Tommy said.

Torch light showed branches of shrubs, and stunted trees leaning over the water. Tommy manoeuvred the boat nearer to the bank.

'Look! A boat! Is it Hinney's?' Frank asked.

A dark-coloured motor-boat, half-hidden by the overhanging branches, was moored to a tree.

'He's here,' Tommy said. 'If he can moor here, we should be able to as well.' He skilfully manoeuvred the boat so it nudged Hinney's. 'Can you jump out, Frank and I'll throw you the painter.'

Frank passed his torch to Laurel who played the beam onto the bank. There was a clear patch of muddy sand and he placed one foot on the rim of the boat and hurled himself towards it. He landed with a thud, his feet sinking into mud. Phew! Not disgraced himself.

Tommy threw him the rope and he clambered up a short, steep bank, found a stout tree and passed the rope twice round its trunk. Tommy could check it when he was on dry land. 'Shall I bring whatever Mabel gave us?' Laurel asked.

'No, we haven't time for a picnic.'

Laurel jumped onto the bank, then offered Tommy a hand.

'Take these.' He passed her the torches, tools, and a length of rope. He jumped, missed the bank and splashed ashore. He laughed. The laugh came easily. 'Well done,' he said, 'we've made it.' He shone a torch into the trees and pointed to a pathway. 'It looks as though Hinney regularly uses this spot.'

Branches were chopped back, the cut ends shining white in the torch light. On each side of a two-foot-wide path debris had been pushed into the overhanging shrubs.

'This is mainly Holm oak,' Frank said, flashing a beam over stunted trees.

'There's a belt of them at Blackfriars School,' Laurel said, frowning.

'Don't think about it, Laurel,' Frank said.

No reply.

'Why's this the only shrubby part of Orford Ness?' he asked Tommy.

'Another Jim lecture: in the 1930s, a family called the Ropes had a summer house here and they planted these trees for shelter.'

Not a place he'd choose to sunbathe.

'We'll follow the path. We'll use one torch, save on the batteries,' Frank decided. 'No more talking, we're well away from the pagodas, but just in case.' He turned to Tommy, 'or laughing,' he said, smiling at him.

'Ay, ay, Captain,' Tommy said.

'Remember Hinney is a killer,' Laurel said.

He couldn't see the disapproving expression, but he knew it was there. Tommy dug him in the ribs.

Single-file they slowly advanced

'Keep to clear ground, if you can. The sounds of breaking twigs will carry,' Frank ordered.

They were making good progress when he suddenly halted. Laurel bumped into him. 'My God!' He pointed into a small clearing.

Nailed into the trunk of a sturdy Holm oak were metal frames, hung with chains, two at shoulder height, the others near the ground. At the end of each chain was a heavy metal handcuff. The area nearby was flattened, the earth scuffed and grooved, as if prisoners had kicked out, trying to free themselves.

His stomach clenched as his imagination took over. Who had been held here? Stephen Salter? Lucy and Roberta? Images flashed through his mind. He thought of how they must have felt when they came round from their drugged sleep: fear, anger, then incomprehension. Why was this happening to them? Who had done this? The waiting for something to happen. The fear they had been left to die. The terror when they heard footsteps. Then dreadful understanding. He took a deep breath.

They stood silently, looking at the handcuffs, and then each other. It was difficult to read Laurel's and Tommy's faces in the diffused light, but Laurel's jaw was tight, and Tommy's eyes wide with shock.

'What's this about?' he asked. 'People have been held here. Handcuffed. Why?'

'I think it was a holding spot. Hinney brought a drugged girl over by boat at night. If you're right, Tommy, and it is the pagoda he's using, he'd have to carry her to it if she was still drugged. If he left her in handcuffs overnight, then the next night, when the drug had worn off, he could come back and make her walk to the pagoda,' Laurel said, her voice icy.

'Wouldn't they shout out? Surely someone would hear them; there's quite a lot of river traffic, especially in the summer,' Tommy said.

'Not if they're gagged. It's a good hypothesis, Laurel, I'd go along with it,' Frank said.

Tommy's breathing was rapid. Was this bringing back his own terrible war-time experiences? They'd have to try and calm him down. They couldn't risk him going off half-cocked tonight. Sometimes the best way is to confront your fears. He nudged Laurel and nodded towards Tommy. She was better at this than he was.

'This must remind you of your sufferings in the prisoner of war camp, Tommy. Were you ever chained up like this?' Laurel asked.

Tommy's body jerked, as though he'd been pulled back to the present. He stood in silence. Was he going to answer?

He nodded. 'Yes, they put me in a cage, a bamboo cage. It was so small I couldn't stretch out my legs, I was perpetually hunched. Every day I expected them to take me out and behead me, or torture me. All that kept me going was the thought of Audrey and John waiting for me when I got... if I got, home.'

He turned and looked into Frank's face. 'The nights were worse than the days. Although the sun baked my body and brain, at night the mosquitos came, whining round my head, landing on my face and body, the bites itching and swelling. It drove me mad. I scratched where I could reach, but I was confined, like some creature in a mediaeval torture chamber.'

Laurel tentatively put a hand on his arm. He placed his hand over it.

He hung his head. 'Nearby there were three pagodas. When they took me out of the cage to... question me, they dragged me into one of them. I knew what they would do to me in there. It seemed an abomination – a holy place being used for torture and murder. They made me watch other people being tortured: their fear, their pain.' He stopped, his breathing rapid. 'They executed my friends in front of me. It was terrible to see the terror and anguish on their faces, the moment they gave up hope, when light died in their eyes. Worse of all was my shame. I was glad it wasn't me being tortured, glad it wasn't me being beheaded. Although I knew my turn was coming soon, at that moment, I was thankful it was him and not me. It was sheer luck I wasn't killed as well.'

Frank was shocked. The awfulness of Tommy's experiences, the raw pain and self-loathing in his voice, made a meaningful reply impossible.

Laurel moved closer to Tommy. 'I'm truly sorry, Tommy. This has brought all those terrible memories back. We didn't want this.'

He lifted his head and looked at her. 'Yes. It has. The cruelty. The lack of human feeling. Thank you. I could have done with your comfort all those years ago.' He stood silent for a few minutes. 'I've never spoken of this before. I couldn't bear to put it into words. I never sleep at night, I'm afraid of the nightmares sleep brings. I sleep during the day, always with the curtains open so when I wake it will be light.'

He paused, straightened his shoulders and gave them a weak smile. 'I think we'd better make a move.' He pointed ahead. 'The safest way is to follow the path Hinney's made. When we get clear of these shrubs, we must go slowly and follow the man-made roads if possible, but there'll be a stretch of shingle to navigate before we reach a road. That will be the most dangerous stretch. I suggest we keep well apart. Then, if the worst happens...'

Frank's chest tightened. 'Good thinking, Tommy. Are you sure you want to go on? Laurel and I can manage.'

'Yes. I want to help. It's a relief to talk about what happened. I'm alright now.'

'Good. I'll take the lead. You go behind me, Tommy, and Laurel, you bring up the rear.'

They followed the path Hinney had chopped through the trees and came into the open. The sound of the sea beating against the shingle beach was loud and steady, and the salt-laden wind straight off the North Sea stung his face.

He shone the beam of the torch in a low semi-circle. There were shingle ridges, clumps of plants growing in the grooves. Ahead were the outlines of the pagodas, black against the night sky, with lighter gaps between the pillars supporting the roofs. They sat solid and menacing, and now he was nearer he realised their immenseness as they squatted on the horizon like medieval Japanese fortresses.

'Look!' Tommy gripped his arm and forced the beam onto the shingle. 'There.' Some of the stones had white spots. 'He's marked out a path so he can get safely to the pagoda.'

Frank's stomach sagged with relief. He didn't have to be a hero leading the way through a minefield. They could get to Hinney without being blown up. The stones with their blobs of white paint were about a yard apart, leading to the farthest pagoda.

There was a sigh of relief behind him. 'Thank goodness for that. I didn't fancy scraping you up off the shingle. Very messy,' Laurel said.

Was there a touch of hysteria in her voice? Understandable.

'I'll lead the way,' Tommy said. 'I'm used to walking on the shingle. I think we ought to each use a torch and shine them at our feet. Some of the stones are boulder-size, no good risking a sprained ankle. Keep the beams low. Let's hope he's too busy to see the lights.'

Laurel moaned.

'Sorry,' Tommy apologised.

Busy? Busy doing what? Frank hoped they weren't too late. They couldn't afford to rush and injure themselves. This must be where he'd taken Stephen. If Hinney ran true to form, then he wouldn't give him or Sam a swift death. He'd want to linger, taking sadistic pleasure in their suffering. Was he right? Had Hinney kidnapped Stephen to lure Sam into his hands? What was there in Sam's past they didn't know about? When he was a young man, he'd mixed with East End gangsters. Where was he during the war?

'Everyone ready?' Tommy whispered. 'Switch on your torches and follow me. I'll go carefully, just in case Hinney's laid a booby trap.'

'Perhaps I should lead,' Frank said.

'No,' Tommy said. 'I want to do this.' He readjusted the coil of rope over his shoulder and started to walk towards the pagoda.

Tommy was acting as Frank imagined he had when he was in the RAF, before he was captured, when he was in charge of a group of men. He hoped the change would be permanent. It lifted his heart to see and hear him becoming confident, less tortured by his own demons. If they got out of this mess he'd try and help him. He deserved a better end to his life; he'd spent too many years guiltily mourning for his wife and child and reliving his imprisonment and torture in Java.

It was hard work trudging through the shingle, the uneven stones making balancing difficult, and trying to walk silently was impossible. Plants hid dips and crevasses in the shingle. The spent flower heads of sea-thrift showed brown in the torch light, and clumps of sea-poppy, and tree-lupins masked hollows. Laurel slipped, sending stones clattering down a steep ridge. They froze, looking towards the pagoda, waiting for a sound they didn't want to hear. There was only the cry of a startled gull, wind soughing through sea-cabbage and waves pounding the shore. They moved forwards.

Tommy stopped and raised his hand. Frank edged towards him, Laurel's body close to his. He looked up. The pagoda was before him. He'd been so intent on where he was placing his feet, he hadn't realised how close they were to it. It rose, black and solid from the shingle beach, like something from another world. The castle of a black wizard, a place to be feared and avoided.

'We need to get to the wall of the pagoda and then edge our way round until we find a door,' Frank said.

'Any plans?' Laurel whispered.

'No, we'll make it up as usual.'

Tommy shook his head.

'We know Hinney favours a knife, or some sort of blade, and also probably a blackjack: Bert was hit with something like that. We'll attack together to overcome him. There are three of us, so we should be able to manage.'

'Unless he has a gun,' Tommy said.

'Frank grimaced. 'Haven't got my cricket bat with me, unfortunately.'

'What?' Tommy said.

Laurel pinched his arm. 'Look!' she hissed, pointing back across the Ness to Orford. There was activity on the quay. The lights of several cars criss-crossed the black sky. Then there was the sound of a motor boat engine revving up.

'Sounds like Revie is on his way. Let's hope Hinney doesn't hear them,' Frank said.

'The pagoda walls are thick; they used tons of concrete to make them and reinforced it with shingle from the beach,' Tommy said.

Frank bit his lip. Supposing his deduction as to why Hinney had kidnapped Stephen was right? If it was, and this came out when they were inside the pagoda, how would Tommy react? It would be a terrible shock. He might go berserk. He couldn't take the risk. It would be too dangerous, not only for Stephen and Salter, but for the three of them as well. He mustn't let Tommy go into the pagoda. He should have thought of that before. He and Laurel would have to deal with Hinney.

He gripped Laurel's hand and squeezed it tightly, hoping she'd catch on and go along with what he was going to say.

She squeezed back.

'Tommy, the police are on their way. Could you meet them at the quay? You must tell them what we think is happening and show them the way to the pagoda. Warn them to make as little noise as possible, but to get to us as soon as they can.'

Tommy drew back. 'I don't think that's a good idea. I think it would be better for Laurel to go,' he said, his voice full of doubt.

'Frank's right, Tommy. You know the way, you'd be quicker. I'd be afraid of going off course and stepping on a bomb,' Laurel said.

'I don't like to leave you two to tackle Hinney. It doesn't seem right.'

'I assure you, Tommy, Laurel has fought tougher men than Hinney. I don't have any worries about her. We'll be able to disarm him.'

Tommy looked at Laurel and shook his head.

'You must go now. We need to get to Stephen and Sam.' Frank knew he sounded like some squadron major giving drill instructions.

Tommy straightened up. He passed the coil of rope to him. 'Right. I'll cut across the ditch near the old headquarters, that's the nearest way to the jetty. That's where they'll land. See you later. Take care.' He turned and walked away, the disc of light from his torch gradually becoming smaller and dimmer.

'Why did you want to get rid of him? He seemed well in control of himself,' she whispered.

'No time to tell you now. Let's get to the wall and make our way round. Hopefully there's an open door. If we can't get in, we're fucked!'

The dank, cold walls of the pagoda were built of pale bricks, which time had patched with moss and lichen, their surfaces stained black where rivulets of water trickled down their sides. They crept round the perimeter, Frank wincing as their feet crunched on the uneven pebbles. The pagoda was intimidating, built like a mausoleum, or an Egyptian pyramid, impossible to get in or out of. A place to house the dead.

They inched forward round abrupt corners, and an incline, angling down from the roof pillars like a ski-slope. They came to the end of a wall. As he edged round the corner he grabbed Laurel's arm.

'Turn off your torch,' he whispered, as he switched off his and tucked it into his belt.

There were three doors set in the wall. The farthest showed a rim of light.

He put his mouth over her ear. 'We'll go in. Let's hope he doesn't see us first; we can suss out where everyone is. Don't do anything until I give the word.'

'OK. What's the signal?'

'Go.'

He inched towards the door, Laurel close behind him. They mustn't rush in. They needed to find out if Stephen and Sam were still alive. He prayed they weren't too late. He moved the carjack to his left hand, took a deep breath, put his hand on the edge of the door, and started to push it inwards.

Chapter 22

Laurel gripped the handle of the scythe. She didn't know why she'd chosen it and doubted if she'd have the guts to use it. Frank slowly opened the door wide enough for them to slide in. The main part of the building was hidden; there was a flickering yellow glow coming from around a corner. Mixed with the blood-chilling cold were foul odours of decay and death. Does evil have a smell?

Frank edged to the corner of the wall. She pressed close to him and looked over his shoulder. The space was immense, like a ruined and despoiled church. Several guttering oil lamps cast moving shadows over the concrete walls. Frank's face was tense, body rigid. In front of an iron handrail was a rectangular, dark hole, from which came another yellow glow – the pit. Handcuffed to the rail by chains, staring down into the pit, his body rigid, his face white, was Sam Salter. To his right, a small table and chair.

Frank edged nearer, keeping close to the wall, out of Salter's view. She followed him. This must be the pit Tommy had talked about, the size of an aeroplane's bomb bay. The light suggested someone was down there. Hinney? The closer they got to the pit the stronger was the smell of dank decay; it crept into her nose and coated her mouth and throat. She glanced at Frank. The horror of the place was etched on his face, but his eyes seemed to burn with rage.

On the wall behind Sam were three horizontal metal bars, with a cross cut out at each end, and a wide groove running between the two crosses. They must have been used to fit hoists for dropping bombs from different heights. The crosses lent a grim ecclesiastical touch to the horror inside the pagoda.

'Salter.' A voice came from the pit. Hinney's voice.

Salter's shoulders hunched and he leant as far forward as the handcuffs would let him.

Was Stephen down there with Hinney?

'I've waited long enough. I know what you did, but I want to hear it from your lips. Answer my questions or you'll see your son cut to ribbons. Do you want to hear his screams? Do you want him to plead to you? To say "For God's sake tell him!" I'm going to bring him round, it's time for you to tell him and me the truth.'

Stephen was alive. Thank God! She looked at Frank. He nodded.

There was the sound of liquid being splashed about, as though Hinney had thrown a bucket of water over Stephen. Feeble groans came from the pit. Her stomach clenched and Frank's body, close to hers, stiffened, his muscles as hard as the wall they leant against.

'You bastard, Hinney. Leave him alone. Come up here and settle this like a man. Stephen's never hurt anyone. Let him go,' Salter shouted.

A laugh. The laugh of someone enjoying themselves, glorying in his power. 'He'll live if you tell the truth.'

Salter strained at his handcuffs, rattling the chains against the bar. 'Bastard. Bastard.' He was trying to get over the rail, ready to leap into the pit. He shook his imprisoned hands in frustration.

They must do something. They couldn't let this go on. She started forward. Frank clamped a hand on her wrist. He shook his head. He tapped his ear and pointed to the pit. They needed to listen. She understood his reasoning, but it was unbearable.

Slap. Slap. Slap. The sounds of hand meeting flesh.

'Hinney! Stop it. Leave him alone.'

The laugh again. 'Just bringing him round. I want him to hear what you say.'

Louder groans. More slapping.

'Stephen! Son! I'm here. I'll get you out.' His voice was desperate.

'Dad? What's happened? Dad?' Stephen's voice was weak, bewildered, frightened. There was a pause. 'Hinney, is that you? What are you doing? Where am I?' His voice seemed to gather strength, some control. He didn't yet realise what was happening and the danger he and his father were in. 'Dad? What are you doing up there? Please come down. Hinney's tied me up.'

A stinging slap echoed round the chamber.

A roar of anger from Salter.

She grabbed Frank's sleeve with her free hand. He put an arm round her and held her tight.

'Shut up and listen to him, Stephen Salter. Your father is about to make a confession. If he doesn't tell the truth, and I know what the truth is, you'll pay. He'll watch you being cut into pieces. With this!'

'Dad, he's mad. He's got a razor and a knife. Help me!'

Sam screamed with rage and fear, once more impotently shaking the rails, his face reddening, saliva bursting from his mouth as he screamed at Hinney.

'Right, Salter, let's start with something easy, shall we?' Hinney said. 'Is it true you were in the RAF, stationed here, on Orford Ness during the war?'

There was no reply from Salter.

A scream came from the pit.

'Stop it. Stop it! Yes, yes, I was here.'

'That's better. It's only a small cut, but if you mess me around, the next one will be deeper.'

'Dad, don't tell him anything. Let him do his worse. Someone will come soon—'

His words were cut off by a scream of pain.

'Shut up! Salter, did you know a man called Adrian Hovell? Answer NOW!'

'Yes. I knew him,' Sam spluttered. 'I didn't know him well; he was a bit of a loner.'

'Did you know Audrey Coltman?'

Sam's back went rigid. 'Who? No, I don't think so.'

There was a scream from the pit.

'For God's sake leave him alone. Yes, yes, I knew her. I spoke to her a couple of times.'

'Was she beautiful?'

There was a pause. 'Yes, she was beautiful.' It was difficult to hear his words.

'Speak up, Salter. What was she like? What colour was her hair?'

Sam's shoulders slumped. 'Dark, she had dark hair and blue eyes.' His voice seemed resigned, as though he knew where this was leading. The fight was slipping from him.

'Dad, why is he asking you these questions?' Stephen cried.

'Shut up, I'm in control here – not you. I want you to tell me, Salter, about the last time you saw Audrey Coltman. It was near Doctor's Drift, wasn't it? She had her son, John, with her, didn't she?'

Salter hung his head.

'Didn't she?' Hinney screamed. 'Answer me or your son will start to lose more of his skin.'

'Yes. That's the last time I saw her.' His voice was a whisper. Laurel strained to hear his words.

'She was sitting in a field; the baby was in a pram. The sun was shining, it was a lovely day. She looked beautiful.' He spoke like an automaton.

'Dad! What's this about? Are you talking about Mr Coltman's wife? The one who was murdered?' Stephen's voice was hysterical.

'Yes, that's who he's talking about. You didn't know about him being there when it happened, did you, Stephen?'

There was no reply.

'Go on, Salter. Tell us what happened next. Remember, the truth, or your son loses another piece of flesh.'

Sam grasped the handrail, his knuckle-bones shining through the skin, his chest heaving. 'I... I went to her. I'd talked to her before. She'd always been pleasant, friendly, smiling, happy. I could see she was a good mother. The little boy was quiet. I think he was asleep,' he said, sobs punctuating his words.

'And then? What did you do then?' Hinney hissed.

Frank's grip on her shoulder tightened.

'I didn't mean to harm her.' He choked, then coughs racked his chest. He bent his head so he could wipe away tears and snot with a hand.

'Go on. Spit it out, or my hand will slip.'

'I wanted to kiss her. I thought she'd like to have a man's arms round her. Her husband was abroad, she couldn't have had sex for some time, unless she'd taken a lover, like most women do.'

Laurel's throat tightened.

'I sat down beside her. I could see she didn't like that and she tried to get up.'

A hissing sound came from the pit.

What had Salter done? The foul air seemed to thicken and she couldn't swallow — she was afraid she'd choke. She wanted to put her hands over her ears, not to hear what was coming. Now she knew why Frank had wanted

Tommy out of the way. She took a deep breath, trying to control herself. What was Stephen feeling as he heard his father's confession?

'Go on,' said the voice from the pit.

Salter sagged over the rail. 'I grabbed her, tried to kiss her, but she struggled, pushing me away. She slapped me across the face. Said she'd report me. Her voice was cold, haughty, but mad with rage. I was angry. No one treats me like that.' There was a pause. 'I didn't want to have her like that. I didn't want to hurt her. I didn't mean to… but she fought me. She made me…'

A terrible groan from the pit. 'No. Dad! Dad! No. Please say it isn't true.'

'Yes, it's true, Stephen Salter. Your father raped and strangled Audrey Coltman. Deny it, Salter. You can't, can you?' Hinney's voice was triumphant.

Salter remained slumped over the rail. Silent.

Heart-rending sobs came from the pit. 'Dad, what happened to the baby? To John Coltman? What happened to him?'

She strained to hear the answer.

'I threw him in the river,' he whispered.

A cry of anguish.

'Shut up, Stephen. I've not finished yet.'

Salter straightened up, gripping the rail. 'What more do you want?' he shouted. 'You've ruined my life. You've made my son hate me. Whatever happens now I don't care what you do to me. Let him go. He's innocent. He's done nothing wrong. I'm the guilty one.'

'Do you think I care if your son hates you? This isn't the end of the story, is it? I've not finished with either of you yet. Let's go back to Adrian Hovell. You saw him that day, didn't you?' There was silence. 'Didn't you?' Hinney screamed. He was losing control, his voice full of venom, hysterically high. She imagined him shaking with rage and hate, the razor in his clenched hand.

Frank's grip on her arm tightened; she turned – he shook his head. No, not yet.

They must save Stephen. He was worth saving. She didn't want to risk her life for Salter: a rapist and murderer, a man who'd thrown a child into a river. He hadn't needed to do that; the baby was too young to recognise him. Her blood was boiling, frustration mounting. They must wait until Hinney came up from the pit. Unless he attacked Stephen again. Then they'd have to jump down on him. Risky. For Stephen, for themselves. The top of a ladder protruded a foot above the rim of the pit. One of them could jump down onto Hinney, and the other go down by the ladder. Better if she jumped. She'd have to do it before Frank realised.

Salter shoulders were heaving. He mumbled something.

'What did you say, Salter? Speak up or your son gets another cut.'

'Yes, I saw him.'

'When?'

'Before I saw Audrey Coltman. He was walking towards the river, and stopped and looked at some birds through his binoculars.'

'Did he see you?'

'I don't know. He may have done.'

'You took something from Audrey after you strangled her, didn't you?'

'I don't remember—'

A terrible scream came from the pit. 'Help me, please help me. I'm bleeding. It won't stop!' Stephen's terrified voice was full of pain.

Salter's chains rattled against the rails. 'Don't hurt my boy. For God's sake stop cutting him.' He clasped the rails and shook them, as though trying to loosen them from their concrete sockets. 'I took her knickers, I wiped them between her legs. I put them in Hovell's locker.'

Laurel squeezed her eyes tight, sickened, furious. He'd deliberately sent Hovell to his death. He'd put the vital evidence into Hovell's locker. He'd let him hang.

A great roar of rage bellowed from the pit. 'Murderer! You murdered my brother!' There was the sound of metal against concrete. Had he thrown away the razor, or the knife?

Salter's body collapsed and he dropped to his knees, his chained hands above his head as though he was a supplicant at the altar asking forgiveness

There was a clanking of metal, the top of the ladder vibrating against the wall of the pit. Hinney was coming up. Frank pulled her back into deeper shadows. He placed his mouth over her ear. 'Wait for the word.' She nodded.

Hinney's head appeared above the rim, and he clambered out and rushed towards Salter, a knife in his hand, its long narrow blade glinting in the light of the oil lamps.

Hinney kicked Salter in the side. 'Bastard. Bastard.' He spat on him. 'Filthy, lying murderer.' He turned away from him and pulled the table and the chair towards Salter, hauled him to his feet and shoved him onto the chair. He pointed at the top of the desk. On it were paper and a biro.

'You're going to write down everything you've confessed to. You are going to clear my brother's name. The world will know you are the man who killed Audrey Coltman and her son, that you are the man who framed my brother and sent him to the gallows to have his neck broken. You are the man who condemned my parents to the agony of losing their oldest son in the worst way possible. Each day they went to his trial, and on the last day had to watch the judge place the black cap on his wig and sentence Adrian to death. He waited in a cell for the hangman to come and weigh and measure him, to tell him he'd try to give him a quick death. You sentenced them to grief and despair. You sentenced me to the loss of my brother's love and kindness. You made me the man I am today.'

Salter slumped over the table, like an old scarecrow, full of rotten straw. A defeated man.

Hinney kicked him again. 'Everyone hated us. Most of my friends deserted me, their parents wouldn't let them see me. I was bullied and beaten up at school. Mum and Dad said we had to move away. I didn't want to go. Why should we give in to them? Adrian was innocent. I knew he was. If we left we'd be admitting his guilt. Mum couldn't stand it: the neighbours' looks, the silence when she went into a shop, the bruises she found on my legs and arms. We moved. I had to leave my school and the few friends I had, those who'd stuck with me. He'd been found guilty, but I never believed it. He wasn't interested in girls. I'm sure he was a virgin when he died. I loved him. He was always kind to me, looked out for me, helped me with school work, he loved me,' Hinney said, his voice thick with emotion.

Salter was a murderer, a rapist, but Hinney was using this as an excuse for his appalling crimes. They were both vile, but Hinney was unhinged, a dangerous sadist.

Salter didn't move.

There were faint groans from the pit. She looked at Frank. His eyes were narrow, nostrils wide, jaw clenched.

He shook his head. They must do something. Stephen could bleed to death.

Hinney poked Salter in the ribs with his knife. 'Wake up, you bastard. Listen to my story. You wrote this story when you framed my brother, you cowardly piece of shit.'

Salter lifted his head. 'Please help Stephen. I've told you everything. He'll bleed to death if you don't get help for him.'

'He'll get help when you've listened to me. I want you to realise what you've done to me. My father died ten years ago, and my mother followed six years later. I went home to clear out the house. I found letters from Adrian, written from his prison cell.' Hinney reached inside his jacket and pulled out a sheet of paper.

'This is the last letter he wrote. The prison chaplain brought it to them. He'd written to my parents before he came to see them, he thought basically Adrian was a good man, but it was a great pity he never confessed and saved his soul. Idiot! Want to hear it, Salter?' His voice had risen to a scream, the paper quivering in his clenched fist.

Salter's didn't move.

Hinney prodded him with the knife. 'Want me to go down the pit again? Do a bit more damage?'

Salter's head shot up. 'No. No. Let him go. He needs a doctor.'

'He'll be all right. If you want him alive do as I tell you.' He waved the letter in front of Salter's nose. 'Shall I read what Adrian wrote to my mum and dad? They never showed me his letters. But, if they didn't want me to read them, why didn't they burn them? They knew when I saw what he'd written I'd do something about it. They knew I'd get Adrian justice, whatever the cost, whatever the method.'

He held up the yellowing sheet of paper; so thin it looked as though it might disintegrate into the freezing air. 'After you've listened to this you're going to write your confession. You'll write down everything you've told me. When you've done that I'll help your son, Stephen. The sooner you listen and then write, the sooner I'll stop his bleeding.'

'"Dear Mum and Dad."' His voice was raw, he held the letter with both hands, but his right hand was still holding the dagger.

Laurel gripped Frank's arm. He frowned and shook his head again.

'"This will be the last letter I will write to you. Tomorrow I will die. When you read this, it will all be over. The past few months have been horrible I am glad the time has come, although I'm scared of what's going to happen."'

As Hinney read his brother's last words his voice cracked and heaving sobs shook his stocky frame. Salter turned his head, staring at him as though he saw him for the first time, as though this was a stranger he'd never seen before. Was he realizing the consequences of his actions?

'"I tell you again, I did not kill Audrey Coltman and her child. I knew her and her son John. I met her several times when I went bird-watching near the river. We spoke. Not for long, but she was a nice woman. She'd ask me about the birds I'd seen and she told me how worried she was about her husband; he's called Thomas, he's away in the Far East somewhere. John was a lovely baby, always smiling and she was a good mother, she loved that baby."'

Salter's head drooped.

She wasn't sure who'd she rather use the scythe on, Hinney or Salter.

Hinney took a deep breath. '"That afternoon, before she and the baby were murdered, I spoke to her. She was sitting in a field, and John was crawling in the grass. She was trying to stop him putting flowers into his mouth. I stayed with her for a few minutes and we talked about the war. I told her I didn't like being part of it and I wasn't sure if I'd ever have enough courage to kill someone, even if they were a German. She smiled at me and said, "I'm sure you'd protect me and John if you saw a German attacking us." Suddenly I knew I could do it, she made me feel proud. She was sure I'd be brave enough."'

Hinney turned on Salter. 'How ironic is that? If he'd been there when you attacked her, he'd have had a go, even though you were bigger and stronger than he was.'

There was a weak moan from the pit. 'Please help me.'

Salter straightened up. 'Get on with it, Hinney, or whatever your name is. Get it over and let my son go.'

'My name is Gareth Hovell, and if you don't do as I tell you, I'll go down into that pit, I'll pick up my razor, and your son will be a few pounds lighter, and I don't mean money,' he sneered. 'One more paragraph for you to hear.'

He refocussed on the letter. '"She put the baby in the pram, he was tired and fell asleep almost at once. He was a lovely child. I said goodbye to her and John and walked away. She was alive when I left her, but I never saw her again. I walked down to the Ore and then back along the shore to the barracks. I did see one person. After I left her and John, I stopped to watch some gulls – little terns – I followed their flight path back the way I'd come. I saw him, Sam Salter, he was walking towards where I'd left Mrs Coltman. Salter's married but he's well known for liking the ladies and some of the boys say he likes a bit on the side. Sorry, that's the words they used. I believe he killed her and the baby and I think he put her blood-stained underwear in my locker. I told the police all this. They checked up on him, but he said he had two days furlough and he'd driven to London to see his wife. The police picked on me because they'd had an anonymous telephone tip off, saying I was sweet on Mrs Coltman and I'd pestered her. When they found the underwear in my locker, I'd had it. No matter what I said it made no difference. With the war on, they wanted a quick trial and someone punished for the horrible murder of a mother and child.

Don't let Gareth think I'm a murderer. Show him this letter. Tell him I love him and I promise I will look down from Heaven and watch over him. I know I'll go to Heaven because God knows everything, and He knows I am innocent.

My love to both of you and to Gareth

Your son

Adrian."'

Laurel put her hand to her throat and pressed to stop cries of pain and anger spilling from her.

Gareth Hinney

At last I have him, the murdering bastard, who took three lives and never paid the price. Adrian paid that for him. It is nearly over. I'm still undecided if I should leave Salter alive or dead. It would have been good to read in the newspapers of his humiliation and court case, but could I be sure he wouldn't wriggle out of it? I'll leave his son alive and hope he survives long enough to confirm his father's confession. I want to kill Salter; I want to see him in pain, to plead for his life. He deserves to die rather than to spend the rest of his life in prison. Adrian didn't have that luxury. Perhaps if he'd been given a life sentence he might have been reprieved. I would have done everything I could to prove his innocence.

Have I time to give Salter a slow and painful death? Unfortunately, not. However, half an hour, or even a few minutes, can be an eternity if you are tied up, helpless and someone is cutting you to pieces with a razor.

It will be the second quick and unsatisfactory death. It was a pity about Belinda. She would have made a perfect victim. I planned to kill her, I thought I could make her Salter's final victim. It was a good plan: to murder young girls who resembled Audrey Coltman, and to lay the blame on him. What I hadn't anticipated was the pleasure the torture and humiliation of the first girl gave me. There had to be a second. Then stupid Bert Wiles. I was surprised how good a death that was. Seeing that dirty old man suffer was just as exciting and arousing as the two girls.

When I've finished in the pagoda, I'm ready to leave. It should go smoothly, everything is planned. A new name - I've had two already, a change of appearance, nothing drastic, perhaps I'll grow a beard and dye my hair. Another job. I can turn my hand to a few trades. Then I'll start again. This time just for me. Not for Adrian. Each one will be carefully planned, victims wisely chosen, and a suitable killing area found. I can live my life to the full.

Time to deal with Salter. First the written confession, then a brief period of seeing and hearing him suffer before killing him.

Chapter 23

Frank glanced at Laurel. She was breathing rapidly, staring at Hinney, her body tense, leaning forward, ready to charge him. He dug his fingers into her arm and when she looked at him, he mouthed, 'Knife, too close.' They couldn't act while Hinney's knife was at Salter's throat. If Hinney wanted Salter to write a confession he'd have to release his hands. That would be the time to attack.

Hinney lowered the knife. 'I'm going to take off the handcuffs. Don't try anything. If you do I'll kill you.' He took a key from a trouser pocket. 'Then I'll kick your body into the pit, so he can get one last look at his murdering father before he bleeds to death. Will he cry for you? Or is he so disgusted by what you've done he'll be glad you're dead?'

Salter slumped from the chair onto his knees, his arms above his bowed head and said, 'I'll do what you want. Please hurry.' He raised his head. 'Stephen. Stephen,' he shouted, his voice desperate. 'Can you hear me? Are you all right?'

Hinney laughed. 'What a fucking stupid question. Of course, he's not all right. His chest's slashed and he's losing blood. Probably unconscious by now.'

Salter groaned. 'Stephen, Stephen,' he shouted hysterically.

A feeble moan came from the pit.

'Still alive then.' He inserted a key into the padlock imprisoning Salter's right hand. Salter slumped, groaning, as the handcuff swung loose, the chain clanking against the rail. Hinney opened the left handcuff and Salter completely collapsed into a ball, crying out in pain. He rubbed his wrists, continuing to moan.

'Get up, you piece of shit.' Hinney put the knife to Salter's throat and heaved him up towards the table. He pushed him onto the chair.

Salter continued to moan and rub his wrists. 'I can't feel anything.'

'Pick up the biro.'

'I can't. Give me time. My fingers won't work.' He started flexing them, his face screwing up with pain.

Hinney dug the knife deeper into Salter's neck.

Salter screamed, blood trickling from the wound. Hinney pulled the knife away a few inches and looped his left arm under Salter's armpit. He shook him, as though he was a naughty child who wouldn't obey his father. 'Pick it up. Write what I say. Try any funny business and I'll knife you, then I'll go down into the pit and cut up your boy until the floor is awash with his blood.'

Slater groaned. 'Please don't harm him again. He's not part of this. I'll do as you ask.'

'Write. Write what I tell you,' Hinney said, holding the knife against Salter's throat.

Frank put his mouth over Laurel's ear. 'I'll knock the knife out of his hand. You get down the ladder and protect Stephen.'

She nodded, her face white, eyes narrowed, muscles contracted ready to leap forward. Ready to face another killer.

Salter picked up the biro, his hand shaking, probably from a mixture of fear and cramp.

'Write down what I tell you,' Hinney said, pressing the knife against Salter's neck. 'Put down the date. July 3rd, 1971.' He leant over Salter whose shaking hand scrawled words over the paper.

'I am Samuel Salter, and this is my confession,' Hinney intoned.

Salter's hand moved over the paper.

'I raped and strangled— '

'Go!' whispered Frank. He raced across to Hinney, the crowbar held high.

The sound of their feet on the concrete floor made Hinney swing round, scraping the blade over Salter's neck. Salter shot to his feet screaming, his hand grasping his neck, blood seeping from between the fingers.

Frank smashed the crowbar across Hinney's wrist and the knife shot from his hand, cartwheeling through the air, clattering and bouncing off the floor, spinning out of Hinney's reach. Hinney screamed with pain, his face a rictus of shock and fear. Frank raised the bar again, but before he could deal a knock-out blow, Salter lunged at Hinney and Frank pulled his arm back, in case he hit Salter.

Hinney, on his knees, scrambled towards the door holding his right arm.

Frank started after him.

'Let him go!' Laurel shouted. 'Let the police get him!'

Frank juddered to a halt. She was right. He couldn't get away.

Salter, red-faced, froth forming round his mouth, blood running down his neck started after Hinney. 'The bastard. He's ruined my fucking life. He's killed my boy.'

Frank tried to grab his arm, but Salter escaped his grasp, picked up the knife and ran out of the pagoda shouting, 'I'll fucking kill him!'

Frank started to follow.

'Don't go, Frank. The mines. You'll be blown up.'

'So will they.'

'They both deserve it.'

It was true. What was the point of risking his own life for a pair of murderers? They couldn't escape. Revie and the rest of the police would be close. But Hinney might get to his boat. He'd have to try and stop him escaping. He wanted to see him in court. He wanted justice for the missing girls. He needed to see Salter in court as well, for the sake of Thomas Coltman, for him to finally know what had happened to his wife and son and to see the man who killed them sentenced and imprisoned. Perhaps then he would find some peace.

'See to Stephen. I'll be careful.' Still holding the crowbar, he took the torch from his belt and raced after them.

Chapter 24

Laurel wanted to run after Frank, grab hold of him and stop him following Salter and Hinney. They could all be blown up. She didn't care if the two murderers were killed, but the thought of Frank being torn to pieces was terrible. Damn the man.

Stephen. She must get to him. She raced to the edge of the pit and grasping the top of the aluminium ladder she clattered down into the semi-darkness. The drop was deep, about fourteen feet. The smell she'd detected as they came into the pagoda intensified as she reached the bottom of the ladder. A musty, rank, putrid smell, mixing with the coppery reek of fresh blood. The foul smell came from a pile of old clothing heaped in a corner to her right. She flinched as a rat jumped from the pile and scampered to the far end of the pit. Her throat constricted – there was a jumble of white things mixed with the shreds of fabric: bones.

She forced her gaze towards Stephen and gasped as she saw him stretched out against the far wall. A flickering oil lamp on the floor to his right played a yellow light over his naked body. She pushed away the images of the bones and rags, and what they meant, and ran to him. He was tied to the wall, his body forming a T, arms outstretched, each wrist roped to a steel bolt concreted into the wall, his feet tied together and tethered to another bolt, his head hanging, a Christ-like figure. Rivulets of blood ran down from wounds on his chest, forming patterns on his abdomen and legs, and making pools around his feet.

She stood still for a few seconds assessing the situation. The wounds looked shallow, and although he appeared to have lost a great deal of blood, she knew this could be deceptive. The blood seemed to be congealing. The greatest concern was shock, from not only the terrible wounds and frightening situation, but the harrowing realization his father was a rapist and murderer.

Laurel cupped his face in her hands. He was cold, his face so white it was almost blue.

'Stephen. Stephen. You're safe. Hinney's gone. I'm Laurel Bowman. The detective. You're safe, Stephen. A doctor and the police and will be here soon. Stephen, can you hear me?'

She raised his head slightly. His eyes were closed, his bloodless lips hanging loose. She placed an ear close to his mouth and sighed with relief as she felt a whisper of breath against her cheek. 'Stephen. Open your eyes. Look at me. I'm Laurel. You know me. You're safe, but you must try and do as I say.' She gently patted his cheek. No response. She had to make him wake up, to make him realise he was safe. She needed to get him down from this crucified position, then she could use her own clothes to try and warm him.

'Stephen. Wake up please.' Where was Revie? He should have been here by now. Or had he been diverted by the escaping murderers? Stephen needed urgent medical attention. She knew shock could kill. If only she had a blanket. Her stomach was churning and the mixture of awful smells, topped with the greasy stench of the oil lamp, was sickening.

She needed a knife to cut him loose. There was the scythe. Then she remembered the metallic noise as Hinney threw something down before he emerged from the pit, knife in hand. Stephen had cried he had a knife and a razor. The razor must be down here. She gently removed her hands from Stephen's face and scanned the floor of the pit. What had happened to her torch? It must be with the scythe. No time to climb the ladder and search for them. She picked up the oil-lamp by its handle and raising it high searched the area to Stephen's left. Nothing. She bit her lip and turned to the right, moving towards the heap of cloth and bones.

Something glinted as she moved the lamp backwards and forwards. Gold and sparkling stones. Not the razor. Trying not to breathe in she went towards it. The flickering light showed remnants of soiled and stained fabric; she could make out two patterns, one blue with what had probably been white stripes and the other a pink material with a flowery pattern. Summer dresses. There were scraps of other cloth: underwear? And bones. Eaten clean. Ribs, long limb bones, delicate finger bones. She moved some of the cloth. There was a skull, hanks of dark hair still attached to its surface. Was it Lucy or Bobby? She'd found the lost girls, sure both their remains lay in this fetid heap as there were too many bones for one body. She shivered as she remembered finding the skeleton of Felicity in the suitcase on Minsmere beach. There was the razor close to the pile of cloth, and near it a gold cigarette case with the initials SS picked out in diamonds. Sam Salter's, the one he had had to replace. Stolen by Hinney to incriminate him. Had Hinney killed the girls to lay the blame on Salter? Innocent women used for revenge? Rage ran through her. She was determined he wasn't having another victim.

She knelt down and started sawing at the ropes tying Stephen's feet to the steel spike. The blade was sharp, but she sawed carefully, not wanting to blunt it. As his feet became free there was a sigh from above, then cries of pain as he stretched out his toes. She rubbed his calves, chafing them, ignoring the blood. This kind of pain was good. It was bringing him back to consciousness. She stood up and started on the ropes round his right wrist. He groaned. She moved the razor away. He was looking at her unfocussed, blinking.

'Stephen. I'm cutting the ropes. Try to take your weight. Can you do that?'

His pupils were enormous, his mouth was moving, but no words came, just a low moan.

The last threads of the rope gave and she tried to support his body as it slumped to the right, his feet folding under the weight. She held him tight, jostling him upright as you might treat a child who is tired and wants to go to bed.

'Stephen. Try to take some of your weight so I can free your other arm. Then you can lie down. Help will soon be here.' Where were they? What had happened to Frank?

He moved, trying to grip her with his freed hand.

'Good. Hold tight, I'll cut the rope.' She supported his body with her shoulder and managed to reach out and start sawing.

'Where am I?'

Thank God. He was making sense. 'We're on Orford Ness, in one of the buildings, a pagoda.' She sawed more rapidly and as the rope parted she threw down the razor and wrapped her arms round his collapsing body, slowly lowering him to the floor. She propped him up against the wall and took off her jacket, laid it on the floor and heaved him on to it. Next, she pulled her jumper over her head and wrapped it over his abdomen. She looked around for something she could put his feet on so she could elevate his legs and get blood to return to his brain.

There was nothing but the pile of rags and bones, and a metal bucket, on its side. She wasn't using them. She lay beside him, pushed her legs under his and raised her knees. That would have to do. Then she took him into her arms, as a mother would, pressing herself close, hoping the warmth of her body would seep into his.

He raised his head from her shoulder and looked at her. 'Did you hear what my father said?' he whispered.

'Yes, I did.'

'Is it true?'

She hesitated. What was the use of lying? 'Yes, I believe what he said is true.'

A great shudder went through him, and he buried his head into her body, anguished sobs tearing at her heart.

Chapter 25

Frank burst into the night, holding the torch in his right hand and the crowbar in his left. The sweet, salt-laden air was welcome after the foul stinks of the pagoda. He stopped, took in several deep breaths as he looked around. Salter's voice echoed back over the beach, cursing and shouting. Frank directed the torch's beam towards it. Salter was chasing Hinney over the shingle ridges. It looked as though Hinney was heading for his boat, but was he on the right path? Was he following the white markings? He must make sure he did; he shone the beam on the ground in front of him, looking for a white-spotted stone. It wasn't worth risking his life trying to stop them escaping. The light reflected back off a spot of paint. He moved as quickly as he could, making sure he followed the white dots.

To the right was the light of several torches, their beams focussed on the ground, silently moving closer. 'Over here,' he shouted. The beams froze. Then their shafts criss-crossed the black sky. 'Hinney's escaped. Salter's after him. Help needed urgently in pagoda — Stephen Salter wounded.'

Silence was broken. Orders were shouted. Was that Revie's voice? The beams of light diverged, some pointing in his direction, some towards the pagoda. Thank God. He hoped Stephen was alive.

Feet clattered over the shingle towards him. 'Follow the white-painted stones,' he shouted. 'Tommy knows the way.' Coltman would be with them, he knew the safe path. He didn't wait for them, but ran on, flicking the beam from the white markings to the two figures stumbling over the shingle ridges.

Salter was closing in on Hinney, both of them tripping and scrambling over industrial debris scattered over the ground. The ridges became deeper, made treacherous by the dense growth of plants in them. He lost the markers, stopped and shone the light round, mounting frustration making his temper rise. There was one! He continued running.

'Stop, you bastard and fight,' Salter screeched, holding up a clenched fist like some old-time boxer, energised as he sought revenge. Did he still have the knife? Hinney scrambled away, hampered by his injured arm, seemingly not looking for a fight.

'I'll fucking kill you, you bloody murderer!' Salter screamed.

Frank puffed his cheeks. That's rich. They're both pieces of shit. If they killed each other it'd be rough justice. What am I doing here, he thought. Risking my life for these two. He shook his head. If they died it would be rough justice, but it wouldn't be true justice. He increased his pace, targeting them with the beam of his torch.

Salter was getting closer to Hinney. Why wasn't Hinney turning to fight? This could be his last chance to take his revenge for the murder of his brother. Was he only brave when the dice were loaded in his favour? When he'd a drugged young woman or an old poacher at his mercy? Did he need a razor or a knife in his hand to be brave? Did his victims have to be tied up and immobile before he'd the courage to kill them?

Salter's legs became tangled in a ridge's plant growth, and he cried out as he slipped and landed heavily.

Hinney glanced round, his left hand on the ground to steady himself. His face gaunt, terrified. He turned and ran on, increasing his pace, pebbles flying up from his pounding feet. He caught his foot on something, and his momentum shot him into the air, and he landed, shrieking with frustration.

Instantaneously there was a huge explosion which sent shock waves through the air. Frank threw himself to the ground, clasping his hands to his ears, folding his body into a ball. Pebbles and debris rained from the sky, pelting his head and body. There was a second loud explosion. Through his fingers the sky was lit up by a dazzling white starburst, as if a giant firework had been set off, the shimmering silver stripes zipping up into the black sky. He couldn't see Salter or Hinney as clouds of white smoke erupted from the area where they'd been. The smoke billowed towards him.

He froze. It was a WP. A white phosphorus bomb. A Willie Pete. Already he felt the increasing heat, could taste the acrid fumes. He blinked as his eyes started to hurt. He turned and dashed back in the direction he'd come from. He knew the damage WPs could do. He wasn't staying to see theory become reality. He stopped when he thought he was safe and looked round.

Out of the white smoke a figure staggered, a figure alight from head to foot, shrieking with pain, its arms raised, a human candelabra. There was a final guttural cry and the man, either Salter or Hinney, concertinaed to the ground, the flames subsiding, flickering, sputtering and then dying.

Chapter 26

Laurel rested her head on Stephen's as she held him to her, his blood seeping through her clothes. He was still sobbing quietly, as though he couldn't accept the terrible facts he'd heard from his father's lips: his father was the murderer of a young woman and her son. He must know Tommy Coltman, even though he only worked part-time in the camp; it must make the dreadful truth worse. A connection from the present to the past. He probably knew Tommy's story, everyone in Orford seemed to, how the murder of his wife and son, plus his treatment at the hands of the Japanese, had left him a shell of his former self. Before the war he had been an architect with a bright future and a young family he loved. Now he was a social misfit and recluse, mistrusted by some people, a figure of fun to others. Stephen's father had given him a job. To ease his conscious? Salter was despicable.

'Stephen? Hold on, someone will be here soon. Try and calm down, preserve your strength.' She stroked his matted hair from his forehead. 'You've had a dreadful ordeal, but you've come through. Think of your wife and children. Hold on to that.'

He looked up at her, his eyes red-rimmed, full of pain and grief, his skin pale, skimmed with a cold sweat. 'What will Mr Coltman think when he finds out…?'

She shook her head. 'I don't know. He's on the Ness, he brought us across in his boat.'

'Where is he now?'

'He went to meet the police and bring them to the pagoda.' It was good he was talking, showing he needed to know what had happened.

'Where's my father?'

She told him about Frank, Hinney and Salter.

He shuddered. Perhaps she should have lied. It could all be too much for him.

'Mr Diamond is chasing them?'

She nodded.

'Yes, I told him not to, but— '

There was a muffled explosion. Her blood froze and she gripped Stephen to her. He moaned with pain. 'Sorry.' She loosened her hold.

'What was that?'

She gulped. Terrible thoughts raced through her brain. Images of bodies thrown up into the black sky, disintegrating into dismembered arms and legs landing randomly over the shingle. Frank. Frank. She wanted to rush from this hell pit, up the ladder and out into the night to search for him – to find him alive.

'It sounded like an explosion.' Her voice sounded remarkably calm.

Stephen stiffened. 'They've set off a mine, haven't they?'

'Yes.'

'I pray Mr Diamond's alright.' No mention of his father.

Life without Frank would be unbearable. She couldn't imagine it.

The clattering of boots on concrete, then beams of torch light shone above their heads.

'Miss Bowman. Laurel? Stephen? Where are you?'

It was Revie's Birmingham twang. Tonight, she loved his accent.

'Down here, in the pit. There's a ladder. Stephen needs urgent medical attention.'

He nimbly climbed down, the beam from his torch swinging wildly in the air. 'Bloody hell! What's that pong?' He shone the torch onto the pile of bones and clothing and made a noise in the back of his throat of disgust and anger. He shone the beam onto her and Stephen and stopped, his face shocked and concerned. 'God Almighty!' He turned and looked up towards the faces peering over the edge of the pit. 'Quick, Doctor, get down here.'

He sat down beside her. 'My word, this is a right to-do. How is he?'

'I've never been so pleased to see you. Stephen's in shock, he's got several cuts on his chest.' She eased Stephen's body from hers so Revie could see his injuries. 'Stephen. Inspector Revie is here.'

A man climbed down the ladder, holding a black medical bag. 'Here's the doctor, Stephen. He'll be able to help you.'

Stephen raised his head and looked at Revie. He didn't say anything. Revie patted his shoulder. 'You'll be looked after. We'll get you to hospital as soon as we can.'

The doctor, a middle-aged man, stared at them. 'My God, what's happened?'

'Stephen's in shock, not only from his wounds, but from what he's heard while he was tied to the wall.' She pointed to the sawed-off ropes dangling from the steel pegs concreted into the wall.

The doctor shook his head 'This is terrible. I'm not sure I understand, but if you'd move away from Stephen I'll examine him. I think an injection or two is needed. Do you know what kind of instrument inflicted the wounds?'

She pointed to where she'd flung down the razor. 'There it is. I used it to cut him free.'

The doctor pulled a face. 'Tetanus jab needed, but that can wait till we get to Ipswich.'

She gently extricated herself from Stephen. Revie helped her up and they moved a few paces away from the patient and doctor. He took off his jacket and handed it to her.

'Was there an explosion? Is Frank all right?' she asked, her stomach in knots.

Revie gripped her arm. 'Yes. Two. First one set of the other. A white phosphorus bomb. Still had a good kick after sitting there all these years. RAF used those to "fire storm" Dresden in World War 2. Sorry, don't know about Frank. I came straight here. The ordnance experts are searching for survivors, but the bloody smoke's making it difficult.' He studied her face. 'He'll be all right. Fill me in as to what's been going on.'

She pulled away from him. 'That can wait. I'm going to find Frank.'

Revie raised his eyebrows. 'In that case I'll have a shufti at that pile of old rags in the corner. Is it what I think it is?'

She turned, half-way up the ladder. 'I think it's the remains of Lucy and Bobby, killed by Hinney. God knows why.'

She pulled herself over the edge of the pit.

'Miss Bowman! Are you OK?' It was Johnny Cottam. From his horrified expression she realised she must look as though she'd committed a murder; Stephen's blood was all over her.

'I'm fine. Have you seen Frank?'

'Inspector, oh, sorry, Mr Diamond?' Cottam was Frank's number one fan. 'No. He wasn't out there was he?' His voice was riddled with concern.

'Yes. He went after Sam Salter, who was chasing Hinney. I'm going to look for him.'

'I'll come with you. I've got a torch.'

She wasn't sure what had happened to hers.

Several people were milling about, more coming into the pagoda, including two men carrying a stretcher. It would be a difficult journey for Stephen: carried to a boat, a short crossing to Orford and then the ride to Ipswich. 'Come on, let's go,' she said to Cottam, as she ran from the pagoda.

In the doorway she almost collided with a tall thin man, supporting another. It was Tommy Coltman holding Frank, whose eyes were swollen and red,

Relief, joy and then concern, shot through her. 'Frank. Thank God. I thought you'd been blown up.' She hugged him as best she could and kissed his cheek. He coughed and spluttered, unable to reply.

'Laurel! What happened? Are you injured?' Tommy asked, his eyes like saucers.

'No, this isn't my blood, it's Stephen Salter's. He's alive, the doctor's with him. I'll explain later. I need to get the doctor to see Frank.'

Frank wriggled free. 'No. I'll be all right,' he whispered, his voice as rough as sandpaper.

'The medics irrigated his eyes with water, but he'll need to be checked out at hospital. He wouldn't go to the boat until he knew you were safe and Stephen was alive,' Tommy said.

A warm glow filled her chest. 'I'm fine, Frank. Stephen's in a bad way, but I don't think his life is in danger.'

'Good,' Frank wheezed.

'Glad to see you're in one piece, sir,' Johnny Cottam said.

Frank raised a thumb and tried to smile.

'I'll get back inside if you don't need me.'

Frank nodded.

'What about Hinney and Salter? Are they both dead?' she asked.

'Hinney's dead — went up like a fireball — terrible way to die,' Frank whispered.

She shuddered. Retribution? She didn't want to think about it. 'And Salter?'

'Alive, just. Badly burnt. They've already moved him, given him morphine. I'll be surprised if he's alive when they get him to hospital. Poor man,' Tommy said. 'Whatever was this about? What was Hinney trying to achieve?'

She glanced at Frank who gave a miniscule shake of the head. 'It's complicated, Tommy. Would you mind if I had a word privately with Frank? I need to ask him something.'

'No, please, go ahead. I'll see if I can be of use.' He moved into the pagoda. He seemed to have lost his fear of the place.

'Frank, we need to tell him, before someone else does. Revie may have worked it out.'

Frank nodded. 'You'll have to do it, I can't talk.'

His voice was awful; she hoped there wasn't permanent damage. 'Shall I bring him back? Let's go outside to tell him. Will you stay? You ought to get to hospital as soon as possible.'

'Get him. We'll sit on the beach. The wind's coming off the sea, it'll have blown the smoke away.'

'Should Revie be there?'

'Good idea. Tell him to shut up and listen.'

Laurel thought she'd better phrase it more diplomatically.

The four of them sat on up-turned oil-drums she'd found on the beach. They were silent, the sound of the waves scraping the shingle the only sound.

She straightened her back and took a deep breath. 'Tommy, I've something important to tell you. Tonight, when Frank and I were hiding in the pagoda, we heard Hinney force a confession from Sam Salter,' Laurel said.

'A confession? You don't mean Salter killed those poor girls?' Tommy asked.

'No. We believe Hinney did that, with the help of Belinda Tweedie. He also murdered her and Bert.'

'My God, this is unbelievable. Then what did Mr Salter confess to?'

She tried to keep a calm voice. 'Sam Salter confessed to murdering your wife and child, all those years ago,'

Tommy half-rose from the ground, his face white in the moonlight, his eyes black holes of horror. 'But Adrian Hovell was found guilty and hanged! Was he innocent? No. This is terrible.'

Laurel reached out and took his hand; he collapsed beside her.

'John? Did he say what happened to John?'

Laurel gulped. 'He said he threw him into the river.'

Tommy threw back his head and howled. 'I saw him lying on the shingle, badly burned, I cried for him and for the terrible pain he was in. My God, if I'd known I'd have finished him off with a rock and be damned to the consequences. That man gave me a job. I thought he was a kind, generous person, giving me a chance to earn a few pounds, when no one else would lift a finger to help me. Was he salving his conscious? How could he live with himself after killing my Audrey and John? May he rot in hell.' He was quivering with rage and hate.

Laurel waited until he seemed to have gained control of himself. 'Do you want to know exactly what happened? I'll try and remember everything. Or would you rather wait?'

He sighed, his shoulders sagging, chest caving in, reverting to the disturbed man they'd met at the beginning of their journey to Orford Ness. 'Tell me now.' But his voice was strong, determined.

She started from the moment they'd gone into the pagoda and seen Salter chained to the rail and heard Hinney speaking from the pit.

Chapter 27

Sunday, July 4, 1971

Frank finished his last telephone call and went into the garden of Greyfriars House.

He wrapped his hand round a cool glass of beer, the beads of condensation trickling between his fingers. He raised it and took a long, slow drink, the bitter taste of hops, contrasting with the smooth malty flavour. Heaven in a glass. He sighed.

'That's the first time you've looked relaxed for ages,' Laurel said.

He smiled at her and took another mouthful.

It was the evening of a warm, sunny day; Frank, Laurel and Stuart were drinking beer, Dorothy a gin and tonic and Mabel was sipping a Babycham. The mood was sombre.

'I should have stayed at the camp to help,' Dorothy said. 'I wanted to get away, back to my house. I didn't think about how they were going to manage, especially in the office.'

'You're better here, among friends. You've all been through enough; I can't believe everything you've told me,' Mabel said.

Frank smiled at Dorothy. 'Try not to worry, I've just talked with Nellie Minnikin – she's holding it all together. She say's Stephen's wife, Eve, has turned up, and she's helping out between hospital visits. Her mum's looking after their two boys. Also, the extra office help Stephen arranged has arrived.'

Dorothy emitted a sigh of relief. 'Thanks for that news, Frank.'

Stuart lit his pipe and as Dorothy took a cigarette from her case he bent towards her and lit it with the same match.

'Any other news?' Laurel asked.

'Jim Lovell is keeping an eye on Tommy, making sure he doesn't do anything rash.'

'I'm glad about that. I want to see Tommy again, perhaps we can help him,' Laurel said.

'And Salter is still alive,' Frank said.

Mabel shook her head. No one looked pleased.

Laurel gave him a long look. 'You sound relieved?'

Frank nodded and took another pull on his pint.

'Anyone want a nibble?' Mabel asked passing round bowls of crisps and peanuts. There were no takers. 'I could do a proper meal if anyone wants one,' she said half-heartedly, looking at Stuart.

Stuart blew a stream of blue smoke into the air. 'Not for me, love. This is one murder case that hasn't given me an appetite.' He shook his head. 'It's not been very satisfactory, has it?'

'You shouldn't put yourself and the others down,' Mabel said, 'you found out what happened to those poor girls, the murderer's dead, and it won't be long before that Salter joins him, I hope. Fancy him coming here, as bold as brass, asking us to find the girls, and all the time he was a murderer too.'

'I know what Frank means,' Laurel said, 'we needed Hinney to stand trial, to give satisfaction to the girls' families.'

'At least they've got some bones to bury; I think that's the only positive thing I can think of,' Dorothy said.

Frank studied her. Tough cookie.

'I don't understand why Hinney killed those girls. What was his motivation? Obviously, something to do with Salter. Was he trying to pin their murders onto him? In that case why kill two; one would have done if he'd managed to incriminate Salter,' Stuart ruminated.

Mabel passed the eats round again. They started nibbling.

'You could have been blown to smithereens, Frank. Your eyes still don't look right. Have you remembered to put those eye drops in?' Mabel nagged.

Frank sighed and drained his glass. 'Top up, anyone?'

Laurel and Stuart drained their glasses and passed them to him.

'Bring the gin bottle and there's another tonic and one of Babycham in the fridge,' Dorothy said.

As he set up the drinks on a tray in the kitchen he decided to tell them his suspicions and what he thought they should do. He could be wrong, but as there was little time left, if he didn't do it he would spend the rest of his life wondering if he'd been right or wrong.

Birds were signalling the end of the day and the light off-shore breeze carried with it scents of heather and bracken. For once he didn't find this soothing. What would they think? That he was mad? He hoped not. He studied their faces as he carried the tray towards the table. Everyone looked subdued, wrapped in their own thoughts.

Once they were sipping their drinks he said, 'I don't think this case is finished.'

Laurel stiffened. 'Not finished? There's nothing more to be done, not by us. Hinney is dead, he murdered the girls, Bert and Belinda Tweedie. End of that story and Salter confessed to the murder of Audrey and John Coltman. Are you thinking of a pardon for Adrian Hovell?

That isn't in our power to grant. I can't think of anything else.'

The others remained silent, but leant towards him, looking intrigued, waiting for him to speak.

'We need to talk to Sam Salter, before he dies.'

'Why?' Dorothy asked. 'I shouldn't think you'll get much out of him, he'll be drugged to the eyeballs. Will the doctors let you do that?'

'I spoke to Revie. He said he's semi-conscious and might be able to speak if the medics cooperate. I think we need to try, and we need to do it soon.'

He told them what he thought had happened.

'It could be true, it's a possibility. Yes, we must try,' Laurel said.

Frank reached out and took her hand. 'I think you're the best person to talk to Salter. Will you do it?'

She inhaled deeply. 'Yes.'

Chapter 28

Monday, July 5, 1971

Laurel remained silent as Frank talked to the doctor. It was seven in the morning, the hospital quiet, apart from the chinking of crockery as a tea-trolley was pushed past them. They were outside Sam Salter's room, along with Inspector Revie and Detective Constable Johnny Cottam.

'Are you sure, this is necessary, Mr Diamond? I can't see what more you can hope to achieve by interviewing Mr Salter. I know he committed dreadful crimes, but we must show humanity, even to a murderer. Let him die in peace.'

'It's essential we talk to him,' butted in Revie. 'If we don't, vital information will be lost forever.'

'You do realise the extent of his injuries?' the doctor asked.

Revie shrugged. 'We know he's badly burnt; we saw it happen.'

The doctor sniffed and twiddled with his stethoscope. 'His hypermetabolic state is—'

'What's that when it's at home?' snarled Revie. 'We're wasting time.'

The doctor reddened. 'I think you should understand the condition of the patient.'

Frank shook his head at Revie. 'If you could explain briefly, Doctor, then I think we need to talk to Mr Salter. Miss Bowman will conduct the interview. She has an excellent bedside manner.' His tone implied hers might be better than the doctor's.

'I'm sure I could learn by watching you, Doctor, but unfortunately there isn't time,' she said, giving him her best smile.

Revie grimaced and made a I'm going to be sick face behind the doctor's back.

'What we mean by a hypermetabolic response is the patient with severe burns will have an increased metabolic rate, multi-organ dysfunction, muscle protein degradation and increased risk of infection.'

'Does all this matter? He's going to die, anyway, isn't he?' Revie asked.

The doctor looked offended. 'That may be so, but we are doing everything we can to save his life. Would you expect anything else?'

'No, of course not,' Frank said, 'but can we go in now?'

The doctor nodded. 'The nurse knows of your request and will stay with you. If she's at all concerned she will immediately send for me.' He indicated a middle-aged, plump woman, who looked sensible and not in awe of the doctor.

'Please follow me,' she said opening the door of Salter's room.

It was cool and dark, the blinds drawn, but the smell of disinfectant couldn't disguise the stink coming from Salter's bed. Laurel swallowed hard and tried to control the urge to cough. Salter lay unmoving on his bed, liquid from several drip bottles feeding into his veins. There was an oxygen cylinder to the right of the bed, a mask hanging nearby.

One chair was close to the bed, and others to the side, probably out of Salter's view, presuming he could still see; the doctor hadn't given them much useful information about his actual state.

The nurse ushered them into a corner. 'He should be able to talk to you, presuming he cooperates. I lowered the morphine dose as soon as I heard you were coming to talk to him; he won't be too drowsy, but you won't have long before I need to give him another dose. Phosphorus burns are awful, very deep and painful. One area of his left leg was burnt to the bone. I doubt if he'll last another night, whatever the doctor says; phosphorus has been absorbed into the body through the burned areas, it will have damaged his heart, liver and kidneys.' She pointed to the seat by the bed. 'Who's going to talk to him?"

Laurel moved towards Salter, and the others, including the nurse, sat on the group of seats. Cottam took out a notebook and biro from his jacket pocket, flicked back the cover, and stared at the bed.

Laurel sat down and looked at Salter. His face was haggard, but unmarked, although there was redness round his eyes and nostrils. His body was protected by a wire cage, keeping the sheet from touching his skin. His cheeks seemed to have collapsed, the skin hanging down in folds, his lips shiny, covered in some sort of cream.

'Mr Salter, can you hear me? It's Laurel Bowman, one of the detectives you hired to find the missing girls.'

His eyelids flickered.

'Mr Salter, I need you to talk to me. It's really important. I need to know what really happened the day you saw Audrey Coltman in the field. The day you say you murdered her.'

His eyes half-opened and he turned his head slightly so he was looking at her. His eyeballs were blood-shot, the edge of the eyelids rimed with sores. He blinked, grimacing.

'Mr Salter can you remember what happened that day?'

The figure by his bedside came in and out of focus. He squinted, trying to see her clearly. Laurel Bowman. The tall one. Not his type. Blonde hair, shoulders too wide. Not like Audrey. The most beautiful woman he'd ever seen. Whenever he saw her in the village, the baby in a pushchair, or in the little shop near the church, she was more beautiful than before, and each time his desire grew. He even started to go to church on a Sunday so he could see her; she sang in the choir along with her mother-in-law. She was all he thought about.

He day-dreamed they'd become lovers; her husband would die abroad and he'd get a divorce from Patsy. They'd marry. He'd change for her. If he had her he'd never want any other woman. He imagined kissing her; she would be shy at first, but as she was aroused she'd kiss him back, opening her mouth so their tongues would join. Whenever he got to this point, his cock would harden and the blood would surge through his body. He wanted her so much his breathing was raw and every muscle screamed for release.

At night, as he lay on his bed in the barracks, he imagined making love to her. She would lie naked on a feather bed covered in a satin sheet, her hair spread out on the white pillow like the darkest silk. She opened her arms to him and they would melt together, his blond head above hers, her face full of love for him. Sometimes he would groan out load when he climaxed.

'Dreaming of your wife again, Sam,' some wag would shout.

His wife: Patsy. He'd see her this weekend, he'd furlough for three days. She wasn't happy. Missed all her old friends from the East End. Said she didn't know anyone where they'd moved to. Little blonde Patsy. He's fancied her rotten, so much he'd married her when she wouldn't come across until she had a ring on her finger. What would happen to her, if Audrey fell for him? He didn't care, but he'd make sure she was alright; she could go back to the East End. He'd give Audrey a splendid home, and the boy as well. He'd planned what he would do after the war, supposing it went the Allies' way. If it didn't, well, there was always a way to make money. He'd quit his ties with the East End mob; he'd enjoyed it, frightening people, making them cough up protection money. He'd a tidy sum in the bank. Got a nice car for a good price, only a few years old; they were leaning on the car dealer, so he had to play ball. He hated the thought he might have to leave it at home soon: rumour had it there'd be no more petrol coupons for private use. The price for black market 'motor spirit' coupons, as the old fogies in the government called them, was rocketing. Would they ever win this war with that lot in charge?

He liked the envy in the other airmen's eyes when he offered to take them to Ipswich in his SS Jag. He had a better car than any of the officers. He might only be a mechanic but one day he'd be a millionaire. He wanted a wife to match his ambitions. He wanted Audrey.

The morning he drove off from the barracks on his three days' leave he couldn't get Audrey out of his mind. He had to see her. He parked the car near her house and waited. She came out, the baby in a pushchair, and headed down Doctor's Drift; he'd seen her there before and chatted to her. She was polite, smiled nicely, but usually turned back home saying John needed his bottle, or changing. When she talked to her son, her voice was warm, full of love. He wanted that voice – for himself.

He waited so she'd be well away from the village when he met her, then drove the car a short way down the lane. He needed to make her realise he wasn't just any Tom, Dick or Harry. If she saw the car she'd realise he was someone; perhaps she'd come with him for a drive. Wish she didn't have the baby; he took up too much of her attention.

As he walked down the lane he saw Hovell, the Nancy boy, on the skyline, looking through his binoculars. What a pansy! He smoothed down his jacket and tightened his tie; he wished he was wearing his new suit, tailored by the Jew with the big nose and a good sense of self-preservation. Thirty bob he'd paid him, the material must have cost all of ten quid. He'd miss some of the perks of being part of a gang, but soon he'd be able to go to Savile Row and get as many suits as he liked, and all legit.

She was sitting in a field. She'd laid out a rug, probably for the baby. He was in his pram, asleep. He hoped he didn't wake up. Good-sized rug. Make a nice place for a bit of loving. Her hair was loose, blown by the sea breeze, wafting across her face. She was wearing a blue cotton dress with a white collar. Its high neck and modest skirt made her look like a teenager, an innocent girl. He wished she was. He didn't like to think she'd had someone else's cock inside her. He wanted to be the first, the only one.

'Hello, Audrey.'

She looked up, pushing hair out of her eyes, frowning, as if she'd never seen him before.

'Don't you know me? Sam Salter. We've spoken before.'

She glanced towards her son and then back to him. 'Oh, yes. I didn't recognise you. The sun's in my eyes.'

He moved nearer. 'I'm going on leave for a few days, thought I'd try and see you before I go. My car's up the lane, Jag SS1, 1939, nice little runner.'

Her eyebrows lifted. 'Goodness, more than a little runner, I think. Tommy would be envious if he were here; he's always going on about Jaguars. Doesn't SS stand for Swallow Sidecar and Coach building company? He'd be proud of me remembering that.'

He didn't want to talk about Tommy, and he didn't like being told things about his car he didn't know. 'Well it's Jaguar now. Perhaps you'd like to have a drive in it? I could take you into Ipswich if you like. We could have a bite to eat. Bring the kid, or perhaps your ma-in-law would look after him for a few hours.' He imagined driving with her by his side, all the envious glances as people saw the beautiful woman sitting beside the tall, handsome man in the expensive car.

Her face hardened and she started to get up. 'Thank you for the offer, Mr Salter, but I'm a married woman, and I wouldn't dream of going out with you, now or in the future. Please don't talk to me like that again. Good—'

Before she could finish her sentence, or get to her feet, he grabbed her and threw her on the rug. He'd have one kiss; she'd soon lose her hoighty-toighty manner when his arms were round her and his lips against hers.

He held both her arms against the ground and lay on top of her, revelling in the feel of her breasts against his chest and her wriggling body as she tried to free herself. He kissed her with all the passion he'd stored up over the last few months, drinking in the smell of her perfume and body. My God, he'd never wanted anyone so much. His cock was as hard as steel and he ground it into her belly. Had Tommy ever wanted her like this?

He released his hold, rolled off her, sure she'd want him now. He'd never been refused before, except by Patsy, holding out for a walk down the aisle.

315

'Like to go for that ride now? Or shall we stay here and continue what we've started?'

She pushed on his chest and then brought her arm back and slapped him so hard his head snapped back. 'You disgusting, cheap little man. I'll report you to your senior officer. How dare you treat me like that? Don't you ever come near me or my son again. I hope they throw the book at you.' Her voice was as sharp as glass, full of contempt and anger. Her cheeks flushed, her blue eyes deepening until he felt he would drown in them. She tried to get up.

He felt his face paling, blood sinking down, anger swirling up. Cheap. Little. She'd report him, would she? He bared his teeth and clamped his hands round her throat.

The contemptuous look disappeared; she was scared, her eyes bulging, mouth open, fighting for breath. He put his full weight on her body, pulled her arms above her head so he could hold both wrists with one hand, and continued to press her throat with the other, until she started to lose consciousness. When her struggles stopped he tore off her clothes and gathered her body to him

'Audrey, my love. My one true love.'

'Sam, Mr Salter, can you hear me?' His eyes had remained open, moving from side to side, eyelids flickering, and his lips quivered, as though he was speaking to himself. She bent her head closer to his. 'Sam, it's important you tell us what happened the day you saw Audrey Coltman and her son John.' She decided to risk it. 'The doctors are doing all they can for you, but you may not have much time left.'

There was an intake of breath, probably from the nurse, but she didn't butt in.

'This is your chance to make reparation. Please, I want you to try and talk to me.'

'Audrey, my love. My one true love.' His cracked voice full of deep emotion, made her back rigid.

'Will you tell us what happened?'

His eyes stared at her. 'Get Stephen. Bring him to me.'

Stephen was in a nearby room, being treated not only for the cuts on his chest, but for severe shock and also the trauma of discovering his father was a murderer and rapist. No one had suggested he should visit his dying father, but he'd been told of his condition. She turned and looked at the nurse. 'Is he fit enough to see his father?'

'Possibly, but he may refuse. We could bring him in in a wheelchair. Shall I see if he is willing?'

She looked at Frank. 'Could you ask him? Explain it's important.'

Frank approached the bed. 'Why do you want to see him, Sam?'

Salter's twisted mouth almost resembled a smile. 'Diamond, you here. I love him, want to say sorry.'

'I'll see if he'll come.'

He and the nurse left the room.

Laurel sat down by Revie. 'I hope to God Frank is right.'

'Do you think he is?'

'I don't know.' She went back to the bed. Salter's eyes were closed, his face pulled in a grimace of pain. 'Sam, if Stephen comes, what will you tell him?'

His eyelids flicked open; all she saw was pain.

'I love him. He was my salvation.'

He laid her body on the rug, covering her nakedness with her torn clothes. He couldn't believe she was dead. He hadn't meant to do this. What should he do? He wiped away the cold sweat covering his face. They'd hang him.

His mind went into a panic. No, that mustn't happen. Think. Think. He looked around. No one in sight. He must have been mad to do it here, in the open. Someone could have seen him. Someone did see him before he talked to Audrey. That wimp Hovell. He'd finger him for it. Think. Think.

If he got in first, could he pin it on him? He was a weirdo, a loner. Wandered about the shore and fields by himself. Evidence. Could he plant evidence? Her torn knickers. He'd tossed them onto her body with the rest of the clothes. Grimacing, he found them under her dress. He wiped them between her legs. He'd put them in Hovell's locker, his work locker. Easy enough to open, wouldn't be the first lock he'd picked. Hide them so Hovell wouldn't see them, then when her body was found, he'd make a telephone call, say Hovell was sweet on her and kept bothering her. Then they'd find the knickers. That would be it.

He needed to get away before anyone saw him, get back to London. Patsy would give him an alibi, say he'd got home several hours before the time of death. He looked at his watch, noting the time. Could he get back into the barracks without anyone seeing him? That was going to be tricky. If he was spotted, what would he say? Forgotten his present for Patsy. He put the knickers in his pocket and turned to leave. Then he saw John, still fast asleep in his pushchair. His pink cheeks moving as he breathed. What should he do about him?

Frank saw Stephen sitting in a wheelchair by the side of his bed with a young woman close to him in another chair. They were holding hands and her other arm was round his shoulder. She was speaking to him, but her voice was low and Frank couldn't hear what she was saying

'Stephen,' Frank said, 'sorry to barge in on you. I didn't know you had a visitor.'

Stephen looked pale, unhappy, tears not far away. His chest was heavily bandaged. 'Mr Diamond. Good to see you.' He didn't look as though that was the truth.

'Eve, this is Frank Diamond, one of the detectives who was working undercover. Mr Diamond, my wife, Eve.'

She was a slim, dark-haired woman, her face showing the strain of the last few days. 'Mr Diamond. I must thank you for saving Stephen. If you hadn't found him...'

'Mrs Salter.' He shook her hand. 'There were three of us: Laurel Bowman and Tommy Coltman. He rowed us over to Orford Ness. His knowledge was invaluable.'

Stephen gasped. 'Did he hear what my father said?'

Frank shook his head. 'No, we persuaded him to meet the search party before Laurel and I went into the pagoda. We did tell him later.'

Stephen looked at his wife. 'I still can't believe it. What does Mr Coltman think? It must be bringing it all back. Poor man, how he's suffered. I don't think I'll ever be able to face him. I'm so ashamed.'

Eve frowned. 'Stephen, that's ridiculous. None of this is your doing. Of course, you must see Mr Coltman and try to help him. But you have nothing to feel guilty about. I won't allow you to think like that.'

Stephen looked at Frank, a faint smile on his lips. 'Don't you love a bossy woman?'

Frank shook his head and laughed. 'No thanks! No offence, Mrs Salter, but my mother cured me of that.' She was just what Stephen needed, he thought. But not for me.

The nurse coughed and gave him a fish eye. Get on with it, her expression said. Another bossy one.

He pulled up a chair. 'Stephen. I know you're still in shock, but I'm going to ask you to see your father.'

Stephen recoiled, a look of horror on his face. 'No! I couldn't. Not after hearing what he did.'

Eve leant towards him. 'Why are you asking Stephen to do this? Is his father asking for forgiveness? How can Stephen do that?'

Frank hesitated. He couldn't tell them why he thought it was important. He could be wrong. He wished Laurel were here, she'd find the right words. 'I believe your father has more to tell us, facts that would be important to Tommy Coltman. If you are there I think he will do that. Mr Coltman has suffered for many years, but I believe what your father could tell us may help him. Will you do this for him?'

Stephen looked as though he wanted to escape from the room and from what was being asked of him. Eve looked grim.

'Please?'

Stephen swallowed hard. 'I don't know what to think. I loved my father, but how can I continue to love him knowing what he did? Not only the murder of a woman and her baby, but deliberately sending that poor boy to be hanged.'

'Has he got long to live?' Eve asked the nurse.

'He may die tonight. In my opinion he'll go in the small hours, or just before dawn. It's often the way,' she said.

Eve took Stephen's hands in hers. 'Darling, I think you must do it. Mr Diamond wouldn't ask if he didn't think it was important. He and his friends saved your life. It will be difficult, but this is the last chance. If you don't do it the truth will be lost forever. If it will help Mr Coltman, I think you should see your father and persuade him to talk to us.'

Frank felt like kissing her; perhaps there was something to be said for bossy women.

'Will you come with me?' Stephen asked Eve.

'If that's allowed.' She looked at the nurse.

'I don't see why you shouldn't be there.'

'Good.' Eve stood up and moved behind Stephen's wheelchair, gripping the handle. 'Let's get on with it.'

Chapter 29

Salter fought back the pain; he needed, wanted, more morphine, but he was afraid if he took it he would lose consciousness before he'd seen Stephen. Would he come? Would Diamond be able to persuade him? He clenched his teeth and thought about that day. The day he murdered Audrey Coltman. For those few brief minutes she'd been his: he'd held her, kissed her, loved her and then the dreadful realization dawned. She was lifeless. Her deep blue eyes gazed at him, unseeing.

There was a swish of noise and a faint current of air brushed his face. The sound of rubber wheels on the floor, and then a face came into his view.

'Mr Salter. Stephen is here and so is Eve. He's agreed to see you if you'll tell him what happened the day you met Audrey Coltman. Are you willing to tell him the truth?' Laurel asked.

Salter tried to raise his head to see Stephen, but it was too difficult. 'Pillow,' he croaked.

The nurse gently raised his head and shoulders as she slid another pillow under him. He groaned with pain. Now he could see him. Stephen, in a wheelchair, his poor chest covered in bandages, his face as pale as the white sheet Salter lay under. Eve sat beside Stephen, holding his hand. She'd be a great help to his Stephen. Good woman. Sensible. There was Frank Diamond sitting next to Laurel Bowman, and next to her, a man. Who was he? Policeman, Inspector something. The nurse sat by the door.

'Stephen. Come.' He wanted to hold out a hand to him, but couldn't. If only he could hug him, show how much he loved him, surely he'd be forgiven?

Eve said something to Stephen and he nodded. She got up and pushed the chair nearer to the bed.

'Stephen. I am sorry you had to hear what I said.'

Stephen nodded and a tear ran down his cheek. Eve bent over and wiped it away.

'I'll tell you what happened.'

He looked at the baby. He'd killed his mother. His father might never come home. John would be an orphan brought up by that snobby mother-in-law. Someone would find him. But when? What would he do when he woke up and found his mother lying dead beside him? Would he understand? He might fall out of the pram, crawl away and fall in the river. Or an animal, a fox, might attack him. He couldn't leave him. Where could he take him? He had to get off. Now. He started to walk away from John. He turned.

That's what he'd do. He'd take him, keep him. He couldn't have children. He hadn't wanted to adopt, let everyone know his shots were duds. Patsy wanted a child, and was willing to adopt. He wasn't. You never knew what you were getting with an adopted child – they could turn into right little bastards. He'd square it with her. Make up some story she'd believe. She wanted a kid so much she wouldn't ask too many questions.

This was Audrey's child. He'd always have part of her. He'd be a good father. Sort out the details later. Got to get back into the barracks and put the knickers in Hovell's locker, then get back to London. Make up a story about John while he was driving. Couldn't call him John.

Something beginning with S, like his name, there'd be two Salters. Stephen, yes, he liked that name. Stephen Salter.

He picked up the baby and held him gently against his chest. He glanced around again. No one in sight. He walked quickly to his car, which had an enormous boot; plenty of room for cigarettes and booze. He opened it and made a nest for Stephen, his Stephen, with a blanket he always kept there. Be prepared was his motto and you never knew your luck when you were dating a girl. Stephen was sleeping peacefully. Soon what memories he had of his mother would fade, and he'd never seen his father. Not until today. The thought of being a father, and his son being Audrey's son, filled him with joy and excitement. Now he must get to Hovell's locker and then to London. A birth certificate wouldn't be a problem, he knew just the bloke to fix that. He turned on the engine, and it quietly throbbed into life. He put it into first gear and smoothly backed out of Doctor's Drift.

Salter looked into Stephen's tearful eyes. He'd had a son for all those years. A son who'd loved him. Today he'd give him back to his real father.

'Stephen.' He wouldn't be Stephen any more, in a few seconds he would be John. 'Stephen. That day.' Stephen winced. 'When I said I threw John into the river, I lied.'

Stephen leant back. Eve turned to anxiously look at him.

'I took John home with me. You were that baby. You are John Coltman.'

What little blood was in Stephen's face drained away, his eyes widened, his mouth gaped. Eve put up a hand to cover her face. Miss Bowman was biting her lip and Diamond was nodding his head. He'd guessed.

'You... you are not my father?' Stephen whispered.

'No, Thomas Coltman is your father.'

'Mr Coltman?' He was shaking his head in disbelief. 'My mother? You killed my mother?'

Should he have told him? The boy was looking at him as though he was seeing a monster. Too late. 'Yes, your mother was Audrey Coltman.'

The look of horror turned to one of anger and loathing. 'You murdered my mother, then you kidnapped me. My father thought I was dead. You turned him into the man he is today. How could you do it?' He turned to his wife. 'Get me out of here.'

So, this was how it was to end. Did he deserve to die with the one person he'd truly loved hating and reviling him? Was there no one feeling any pity for him?

'Stephen, I love you,' he whispered as Eve pushed Stephen from the room; Laurel Bowman followed them.

Frank Diamond sat beside him. 'You did the right thing.'

He didn't reply.

'Can you hang on for a bit longer?'

'Hang on? For what?' he croaked.

'I think Tommy Coltman needs to hear this from your lips. I think you owe him that.'

'Why? I've said it. He'll know soon enough.'

'I think he deserves to hear it from you, before he's reunited with Stephen – John. Otherwise he may never be able to come to terms with what happened. Stephen's been taken from you, never to return. You've had his love for nearly all of his life. Those years should have been Tommy's. You've robbed him of all of Stephen's childhood, boyhood, his marriage and his grandchildren. He will never be able to get back those vanished years. You are hurting now at your loss. Think of what he must have felt when he came back from Java, a physical and mental wreck, only the thought of his family keeping him going through torture and humiliation. To return and discover what you had done. You owe him, Salter.'

Salter remembered Coltman's ravaged face, his stooped figure, as he walked about the holiday camp on his way to some menial task. He'd feel a twinge of guilt now and then, but he'd salved his conscious by thinking how he'd given Stephen everything, supported him in all his ambitions. Stephen would take over the running of the camps when he retired. Perhaps one of Stephen's children would follow on. A dynasty. Now it lay in ruins. Would Stephen want to run the camps? He doubted it. He'd a conscience, a real conscience. 'Send for Coltman, be quick.'

Diamond had a word with the Inspector who was at the back of the room. He left.

The nurse approached him with a syringe. 'Only enough to keep it at bay. I need to keep awake,' he whispered.

Diamond came back. 'I'll stay with you if you want me to,' he said.

He gave a nod. He didn't want to die alone.

Chapter 30

When they'd returned to Stephen's room, Laurel sat down next to him; she found it hard to think of him as John. Eve sat on his other side, holding his hand. Inspector Revie had barrelled in for a few minutes and told them Johnny Cottam was fetching Coltman, if he would come. He wished Stephen luck and barrelled out: important police matters to attend to, or was it all a bit too much for him? It was probably a bit much for all of them, but especially Stephen. She hoped Salter was still alive by the time Coltman arrived.

The tension in the room was high, and a sunny day outside and little ventilation in the room made for a claustrophobic atmosphere. She managed to open the one window, but there was hardly any air movement outside either.

'Stephen – do you still want to be called Stephen?'

He looked at her and shrugged. 'I can't believe it. I've always felt sorry for children who were adopted and didn't find out until they were adults, the people they thought were their mothers and fathers, weren't. Now it's happened to me, only a million times worse. How can I love my true father? I don't know him. I only know him as a part-time worker at the camp, a recluse, who wandered round the fields and near the river at night looking for the body of his baby son.' He looked as though he might lose control of himself, his throat working as he gulped down the sobs heaving from his chest. 'He was looking for me, for my dead body. What will I do if I can't love him when I meet him? He deserves so much from me. What if I can't give him that?'

Eve put an arm round his shoulders. 'Stephen, try not to intellectualise your meeting with your father, let it happen. Remember, he'll only have a few minutes to digest the truth before he meets you. Perhaps he may feel he can't see you straight away. It'll be a great shock. We don't know how he'll feel.'

Laurel didn't know whether to join in or not. It was a complex problem; it ought to be joyful, the reuniting of a father and son, but Stephen seemed to be afraid; worried how he'd react. Did he think he would have nothing in common with his father? Did he think Tommy was a weirdo? 'I haven't known your father for very long,' she said, 'but I can tell you what I think he's like as a man, and also how he helped us to get onto the Ness. I've also learnt from him something of his past life. I like him, and the way he reacted last night showed me the man he once was. A brave, intelligent, caring man. He loved you and your mother so much. Would you like me to tell you what I know of him?'

Stephen looked at her. 'Yes, I would.'

She told him everything she could remember from meeting him in the churchyard to the point when he left them outside the pagoda to meet the police on the quay.

'He was an architect? I didn't realise he was an educated man.'

'He's also a very competent boatman, and knows these waters well.'

'It must have been dreadful when he was accused of Bert's murder,' Stephen said.

'I think he deserves our respect, and if you find you can't love him as your father, then you must hide that, but hopefully it won't be necessary,' Eve said.

There was a knock on the door. Frank put his head round. 'Tommy's here. Johnny Cottam says he was reluctant to come. Cottam found him in his back garden burning all the boxes. He wants to speak to you,' he nodded to Stephen, 'before he'll see Salter.'

Stephen gasped. 'I can't see him, not until he knows.'

Eve gripped his arm. 'It's important he hears the truth from Salter. You must try, darling.'

Stephen took a deep breath and nodded to Frank. 'I'll see him, but not alone. Everyone must stay.'

Frank looked round. 'I'll bring him in.'

A few minutes later he opened the door and Tommy Coltman walked in, Frank following. When Tommy saw Stephen, white as the walls of the room, bandaged and with a worried face, he gasped and shook his head, concern written on his face.

'Mr Salter,' he said, 'I'm so sorry you had to face such a dreadful ordeal. I can't imagine how you've suffered, not only at the hands of Hinney, but to find out about your father. I want you to know if I can do anything for you, or help in any way, I will. The events of the past few days have made me realise it's time to accept the loss of my wife and son. I must try and bring myself out of the morass I've created. I am truly sorry for what you've had to endure.'

Stephen's eyes filled with tears. 'Thank you, you're very generous.'

Eve stood up and held out her hand. 'I'm Stephen's wife, Eve. Thank you for helping Laurel and Frank last night. You got to my Stephen in time. I can never thank you enough.'

Tommy took her hand. 'I must admit I enjoyed the first part of the night; for once I felt alive and useful.' He turned to Stephen. 'Your father has asked to see me. I hope you can understand why I don't want to meet him. I wanted to talk to you first. Is there any point in this meeting? What can either of us gain? I'm afraid if your father's looking for forgiveness, this is impossible. I am a Christian, I know I should turn the other cheek, but it would be false to pretend.'

Stephen gulped. 'Tommy, can I call you Tommy?'

Coltman smiled. 'Of course.'

'Tommy, I would like you to see him and to listen to what he says. He hasn't much longer to live. I want you to hear his confession. It's very important to me and I think it will be to you.' His voice was filled with tears.

This was so hard for Stephen; she was afraid he'd blurt out the truth.

Tommy frowned, then sighed. 'Do I have to? What will it achieve, except to make my blood boil and put murder into my heart?'

'Please.' Stephen held out his hand.

Tommy grasped it. 'Very well. I'll say goodbye. I won't want to speak to anyone afterwards.' His gloomy expression and drooping shoulders changed him back to the recluse he'd been. Frank followed him from the room.

Eve kissed Stephen's cheek. 'Well done.'

Stephen sniffed and blinked back tears. 'He seems a kind man, but I still can't believe he's my father.'

'I can see the resemblance. Can you?' Eve asked Laurel.

Laurel looked at Stephen. 'Yes, I can. Strange, I'd never seen it before, but when you were side by side... You've definitely got his nose.'

Stephen looked bemused. 'I like him.'

'I do, too,' Eve said.

Silence fell over the room as they waited. Would Tommy Coltman come back to see Stephen when he knew his son was alive and close to him?

As they waited, Stephen asked Laurel more questions about his father. Did she know anything about his years as a prisoner of war in Java? What was his cottage in Orford like? What was behind the strange boxes he'd made? She answered as fully as she could, often repeating the same facts, but Stephen seemed to need to hear them again and again, as if the repetitions would coalesce, form his own memories and make his father real to him. As they talked his eyes flickered and his face became animated. 'If only I could remember my mother, my real mother. I don't look like her, do I?'

Laurel smiled. 'She was beautiful. Your father showed me her photograph when I went to his cottage. You've definitely got your looks from your father, from Tommy.'

'I think you're dishy, darling. I wouldn't like you to be too handsome; I don't want to play second fiddle in the looks stakes,' Eve said.

Stephen laughed, winced, clutched his chest, then laughed again.

The door opened and Frank came in. 'You need to give him a few minutes. He's overcome.'

'Is he all right?' Stephen asked, his eyes wide, his face tense. 'I know how I felt. The shock will be even greater for him.'

Frank went to him and placed a hand on his shoulder. 'The doctor's with him, checking him over.'

'Oh, my God,' Stephen cried. 'Please don't let anything happen to him now. Not now. I couldn't bear it. He deserves peace and happiness for the rest of his life.'

Frank's grip on his shoulder tightened. 'He may look frail, but he's tough. He handled the boat last night like a young man. Well, perhaps there were a few groans from the joints, but that was all.'

Stephen's agitation didn't lessen. 'I should go to him. Eve, wheel me, please.'

She shook her head. 'Give him time, Stephen. Let him compose himself. I'm sure if there are any problems the doctor will let us know.'

'I can go and see him and come back with an update, if you'd like me to do that?' Frank said.

'Please,' Stephen said, nodding vigorously.

'Do you want me to give him a message, if I think he's ready for it?' Frank asked.

Stephen was silent for several seconds. 'Yes. Tell him I want to meet him. Not as Stephen Salter but as John Coltman, his son. Tell him this is a new beginning for both of us.'

Laurel bit her lip, trying not to let her emotions rise to the surface. This was their hour; she shouldn't force her feelings on them, but looking at Eve, tears trickling down her cheeks, Frank's pale face and Stephen's expression, a mixture of uncertainty and concern, it was impossible to keep the tears at bay.

Frank looked at her. 'Laurel, could you go to him? I think your skills are needed.'

She looked at Stephen. He smiled at her. 'Would you?'

She took a deep breath. 'Yes. I'm honoured.' She repeated the message he wanted Tommy to hear. 'Is that right?'

'Yes. Bring him back, if you can.'

Sniffing, she searched her pocket for a handkerchief. Frank passed her one, a wry grin on his face.

'He's two doors down, to the left,' he said, giving her arm a squeeze as she brushed past him. 'Good luck.'

Laurel knocked on the door.

A nurse opened it and stepped out into the corridor. 'Yes?'

'I've come with a message for Mr Coltman from his son. Is he well enough to see me?'

The nurse frowned at her. 'It depends what the message is.' She sniffed. 'What that poor man's been through! Well?'

What a dragon! 'It's a good message. His son is very concerned. He asked me to see how he is and to tell him he wants to meet him. It's been a great shock for him as well.'

'I'll ask the doctor. What's your name? Does Mr Coltman know you?'

'It's Laurel Bowman. Yes, he knows me.'

'Wait there.'

Laurel thought it was just as well it was her, and not Frank, who was dealing with Nurse Dragon.

It seemed an age before the door opened again. This time it was the doctor. 'Come in, Miss Bowman. Mr Coltman is well, he didn't need anything stronger than a cup of sweet tea.'

He ushered her in. Tommy was sitting by the side of a bed, looking bemused, tearful, but his face was full of smiles. 'Laurel, you know? You know John's alive? It seems impossible. I've seen him so many times, spoken to him, thought what a good young man he was, so different to his father. How could I not sense he was mine? Shouldn't I have instinctively known?' The words tumbled from his mouth, raw emotion ripping through the air.

'Tommy!' She went to him and gave him a hug. 'He's waiting for you. He's concerned about how you're coping with the news, he's worried you might be ill.'

'He is?' Tommy's voice was joyful and he clasped her hand, his own quivering with uncontrollable euphoria.

'He wanted to come and see you himself, but Eve, his wife – and your daughter-in-law –said you needed time to assimilate the wonderful news.'

'Eve. I met her. My daughter-in-law. She was kind, thanked me for helping on The Ness. How does she feel about all this?'

'They both knew when you saw them a short time ago.'

'Why didn't they tell me then?'

'They wanted you to hear the truth from Salter's mouth.'

He sighed. 'Yes, I can understand. It makes it real.'

'Ste– John, asked me to give you this message.' She told him.

'A new beginning,' he repeated. 'I mustn't expect too much, I realise that. Will he want an old failure of a man for his father? I know now I've wasted what talents I had. If only I'd known – but how could I have done? I've spent all those years grieving for my wife and child and searching the fields and river banks for his dead body so he could rest with his mother. Now I wish I'd resumed my career, then he could be proud of me. I'd possibly be a successful architect instead of a nobody.' As he spoke the joy in his face faded.

This wouldn't do. 'Tommy, this isn't like you. And this isn't the time for self-pity, this is a time to support your son. He needs you. He's had a dreadful time being tortured by Hinney, thinking he was about to die, then discovering Salter wasn't his father but was the man who murdered his mother. I think you should meet John now, otherwise he might think you don't want to see him. He'll be worried too, wondering if his association with Salter has put you against him.'

Tommy looked horrified. 'No! He couldn't possibly think that.' He looked at her for a few seconds and smiled. 'Ah! I see what you're doing. You're manipulating me.'

'Someone's got to,' she said. 'Ready?'

'Yes.' He got up and brushed away imaginary creases in his trousers. 'Do I look OK?'

Laurel stood back and frowned. 'Your hair could do with a comb.'

'Allow me,' the doctor said, taking a small comb from a top pocket and brandishing it at Tommy, who looked in a mirror and tugged at his greying hair.

The nurse stepped forward and brushed down his jacket with her hand. 'May I?' she asked, straightening his tie.

Laurel laughed. 'You're like parents sending off your child to his first day at school.'

Tommy's back was straight, his face determined. 'I'm ready.'

Frank silently told himself to get a grip. The tension in the room as they waited to see if Tommy would come to meet Stephen was growing exponentially. Stephen — he must start to think of him as John — was twitching in his wheelchair, unable to sit still and Eve had retreated into herself, her eyes downcast, her hands clasped tightly together in her lap. He wanted to say something to alleviate the atmosphere but couldn't think of anything that wasn't banal or bleeding obvious.

'I think I'm beginning to believe it,' John said. 'Now I can understand many of the things that puzzled me, both as a child and an adult.'

Frank's shoulders dropped with relief; they'd probably been up to his ears. 'Really? Can you tell us one of them?'

John looked at Eve.

'Sorry, I shouldn't have asked. I'm sure they're memories you don't want to talk about yet, especially with someone who isn't a member of your family,' he said.

John shook his head several times. 'No, no. It isn't that, it's just at the moment they're wisps of half-forgotten happenings; perhaps I'm trying too hard to find a meaning to everything.'

Eve stared at her husband. 'I know you told me how you never felt close to your mother, even though you were young when she died, and you felt guilty about it. Does it make more sense now? She might have guessed, or even known, she and Sam where keeping someone else's child, a child they had no right to. Is this something you want to find out, before...'

John's face was sombre. 'I don't want to see him again. I realise there are some things I'll never know, and I'm sure I'll be haunted forever by the thought of those lost years, but I can't say I had an unhappy childhood or that my fath– Sam, didn't give me everything I wanted or needed. He was determined I'd follow him into the holiday camp business: the business degree in the States, giving me responsibility at an early age and freedom to design the camp at Sudbourne. I'm beginning to imagine what it would have been like to have a different kind of childhood, a different education, different parents.'

Eve put a hand to her throat. 'Darling, have you realised? We might not have met? That's awful. Or perhaps you're also Imagining a different wife?' She laughed, but Frank wondered if the thought hurt.

John reached for her hand. 'Never.'

There was a tap on the door. John straightened, his hands gripping the arms of the wheelchair.

Laurel came in. 'Here's Tommy, here's your dad, John.' She stepped into the room and held back the door.

Tommy Coltman stood at the entrance. The shambling recluse was no more. He was standing straight, his broad shoulders back, no longer hunched. You could see the man he had once been: tall, strong, with an ascetic face, his short curly hair still thick and vigorous. He was having difficulty in keeping his emotions under control, his mouth moving, eyes blinking back tears. He stood there waiting for a sign, as if unsure what he should do.

John was looking at him, as though he too was searching for a sign. A smile slowly formed on his lips and rose to his eyes. 'Dad?' he asked, holding his arms wide.

Tommy's lips trembled, he blinked and holding wide his own arms went to his son, knelt down before him. 'John?' he asked as he enfolded him. Great sobs came from both of them as they speechlessly hugged each other.

Frank moved to the door and Laurel joined him. He grasped her hand and put an arm round her shoulder. She was crying and so was he.

'I'll come with you,' whispered Eve, wiping her eyes with a handkerchief. 'They need time to themselves.'

At the door Frank looked back at them. Tommy was staring at John. 'You have her eyes, your mother's eyes, and the shape of your face is hers. My boy, I looked for you for so many years, for your poor dead body, so I could reunite you with your mother.' He shook his head, overcome once more.

John pulled him to him and cradled his head on his chest, wincing and smiling in turns. 'Is my mother buried in Orford churchyard?'

Tommy looked up and nodded.

'The first thing we'll do together will be to go there, then she'll know I'm safe and you are at peace.'

Frank closed the door.

Chapter 31

Sunday, July 25, 1971

Stuart pushed back his chair, exuded a satisfied sigh and reached out for Mabel's hand. 'Nothing like a blackcurrant tart,' he said. 'Almost my favourite, but not quite.'

'That's the last of the blackcurrants.'

Stuart pushed out his bottom lip.

Mabel laughed. 'Won't be long before the apples are ripe, though I don't think the earlies make good pies.'

They were eating Sunday lunch in the kitchen of Greyfriars House, the only occupants at the moment.

'Like some cheese and biscuits?' Mabel asked.

Stuart rolled his tongue round his mouth, savouring the sweet, sour taste of the fruit and the contrasting bits of crisp pastry. 'For once, I'll say no thank you, love. I'm enjoying the after-taste.'

Mabel dimpled. 'Thank you, Stuart; makes it all worthwhile.'

'It's been nice having the place to ourselves for a bit, but I'm looking forward to everyone coming back. They all needed a holiday after that case.'

Mabel got up and started to clear the table. 'I was worried when I saw them; it took a lot out of them, especially Laurel, she looked drained.'

'Leave the dishes, I'll wash up.'

'Thanks, dear.'

'Mind if I have a smoke first?'

She stacked the plates and cutlery next to the sink. 'No. I think I'll have a cup of tea. Like one?'

He nodded as he packed his pipe.

She sat down again. 'Do you think she'll marry that Oliver?'

He held the match to the bowl of the pipe and sucked vigorously until a satisfactory glow established itself. He shook his head. 'I thought she was going off him, but this case has... I'm not sure how it's affected her. She wasn't like this when Nicholson tried to kill her, or that other bugger, what's his name? It's not like her, she's usually so positive.'

'You could see Frank was unhappy about it, though he wished her well when she said she was thinking about accepting.' Mabel pulled a face. 'She can't really be in love, or she wouldn't need to think about it, would she?'

Stuart gave her an old-fashioned look. 'Pot calling kettle?'

Mabel blushed. 'Fancy bringing that up! I loved you, still do, but I couldn't... I'm not going to talk about it.'

Stuart got up and encircled her with his arms. 'We manage OK now, don't we?'

Mabel kissed his cheek.

He ostentatiously looked at his wrist watch. 'Dorothy won't be back until tea-time, we've got time for a quickie.'

Mabel grabbed the dishcloth and flicked his face. 'Stuart Elderkin! It's the Lord's Day and I've got to get supper ready; Laurel'll be back this evening as well. Can't not give them a welcoming meal.'

Stuart released her. 'Temptress. What are we having for supper?'

She shook her head and poked his waist-line. 'I'm putting you on a diet.'

He sighed and sat down. 'Do you still want to move in here? If we let the bungalow it'll bring in a bit more money.'

She joined him at the table. 'I'm not sure. Supposing Laurel does get married? I don't think Oliver would want her to take on too many cases like the last one. Then there might be babies. Supposing she left the agency, would Frank want to carry on?'

'You think it could be the end of The Anglian Detective Agency? I'd be really upset if that happened.'

'I'm not sure. I don't think Frank would drop it straight away, but if he didn't have Laurel...'

Stuart tilted back his head and blew a stream of smoke towards the ceiling.

'Let's go into the garden; I shouldn't have let you smoke in here.'

The afternoon was sultry, with a little breeze. Lazy bumble bees explored clumps of phlox and landed on the lower lips of snapdragons, burrowing into the flower for nectar.

Mabel pointed to one. 'He reminds me of you. Heavy enough to force his way in for a square meal.'

He waggled a finger at her. 'He's a she. All the workers are. The males have more sense, they're flying round, looking for sex. Bet they don't worry if it's the Lord's Day.'

Mabel laughed and then flopped onto a bench near the bird bath. 'I think we ought to wait before we ask Dorothy if we can move here. Supposing we let the bungalow and then the agency fell apart. We couldn't stay here, could we?'

Stuart sat beside her, sighed and took the last puffs of his pipe. 'Yes, we'd better wait, see which way the land lies. I don't know about you, but the last year's been one of the best of my life. I don't want all this to end, not yet. I know we'd have each other, and that's been the best bit, but I do enjoy working with Frank, Laurel and Dorothy. I really missed not being more closely involved with the last case.'

'I'd miss Laurel. I bet her parents will be glad if she gets married and leaves the agency. I expect they've been twisting her arm while she's been with them.'

'Pity she didn't go for a proper holiday with one of her friends from that school she taught at in Ipswich,' Stuart said, tapping out the contents of his pipe into a flower border.

Mabel frowned at him.

'Good for the plants, the nicotine will kill the greenfly.'

'It'll kill you as well!'

He shrugged. 'It would have been even better if Laurel had gone on holiday with Frank. Then something really exciting might have happened.'

'I don't think so. You can tell Frank doesn't think of Laurel in that way. They're good friends and they work well together. Mind you, I'm not so sure of Laurel's feelings about Frank...'

'Then why is she thinking of marrying Oliver?'

'She's over thirty, Stuart. Mother Nature may be reminding her she'd better get a move on if she wants a family.'

Stuart groaned. 'I bet Frank comes back from Liverpool in a foul mood: tired of his mother bossing him about and his father going on about the trade unions. Let's hope Dorothy hasn't fallen for someone and wants to stay in Bournemouth.'

Mabel rocked with laughter. 'Dorothy in love! She's been faithful to her dead airman all these years, I don't think she's going off the rails at her age.'

Stuart gave her a fish-eye. 'She's not much older than you, Mabel. Perhaps her cousin lined up a few likely lads for her to cast her eyes over.'

'Her cousin's seventy-five; the best she'll be able to do will be to line up a few old dodderers for afternoon tea. I think we don't need to worry about Dorothy upsetting the applecart. It's Laurel; if she leaves, somehow I can't see the agency lasting.' She got up. 'Let's go in. I can start preparing supper while you do the dishes.'

He rose and put an arm round her shoulders and pulled her to him. 'I'm looking forward to seeing John Coltman christened. It was a messy case but that should be a good day. A father and son reunited after over thirty years apart.'

'They fixed the date?'

'Sunday before the August Bank holiday. At least we'll all be together for that. It'll give us a boost.'

Mabel slipped an arm round his waist. 'You old bumble bee,' she said as they went back into the house.

Chapter 32

Sunday, August 29, 1971

Frank sat next to Stuart; it was a tight fit: all the members of The Anglian Detective Agency in one pew. It was cool in St Bartholomew's church despite the heat of mid-day outside; the air in the huge, square space was redolent with the scent of lilies, beeswax polish and the dust of centuries. He moved uncomfortably against the hard, wooden pew and tried to loosen his collar; it was difficult – his tie had been efficiently knotted by Mabel before they left Greyfriars House. He hadn't worn this, his only suit, since her wedding to Stuart, and he also hadn't been in church since that day. Two church visits in a year, not bad. His mother would be proud of him. Or not.

Laurel was wearing the dress she'd worn at the wedding; in fact they'd all given their wedding outfits another airing. He looked around. The church was full. Pity the congregation hadn't given Tommy Coltman more support in the past, when he needed it: all the years he'd spent isolated and unloved, unable to sleep at night, wandering the fields and shores picking up shells and stones. Lighten up, Frank, he told himself. He was in a bitter mood. This was a day to enjoy, to rejoice, to see Stephen Salter finally laid to rest and to welcome John Coltman into the world.

Nellie Minnikin was a few pews back. She smiled at him ruefully, shaking her head, as much as to say, 'You had us all fooled.' How must she feel? She'd known Sam

Salter since childhood. There were other members of the camp staff: Cindy and Sally from the office, Jim Lovell and his wife, sitting next to the landlady of the Jolly Sailor. He couldn't see Charlie Frost. They must all be wondering what was going to happen to the camps. Would John decide to sell up? He didn't think it was in his nature to desert these people, at least not until he knew their jobs were secure. He wondered what Tommy would think if John continued with the holiday-camp business. He was jumping the gun; they probably hadn't come to any decision. He'd heard Nellie was in charge at the camp and enjoying the challenge. Revie was at the back of the church, with Johnny Cottam beside him. Good of them to turn up. He remembered Revie coming to Mabel's and Stuart's wedding, and chatting up a woman in a Carmen Miranda hat.

Chatter ceased as the vicar walked towards the font, followed by Tommy, John, Eve and two young children, both boys. About five and seven, he guessed, smart in school blazers and short grey pants. Tommy's grandsons. How would they cope with their new name and a new granddad? Tommy looked twenty years younger than when he'd last seen him; his carriage was erect, and there was a strange elegance to him in his well-cut suit, showing off his tall figure and broad shoulders; his lean ascetic face seemed less lined, and a proud smile played on his lips as he looked at his new family. They sat down in the pew before the font; its medieval panel showed old man God, holding between his knees a cross, with his son impaled on it. Did that resonate with John, and his ordeal in the pit?

The vicar, a lean, bald-headed man faced the congregation.

'Today we have gathered here to witness the christening of John Coltman. John has been previously baptised, and it is with the permission of the Bishop of Suffolk that he will be christened today. This is a unique service, there are no godparents and John will make the responses that would normally be spoken by them, or his parents.

'Let us start by singing a hymn together.' Prayers, readings, and psalms followed. Frank had always disliked the formality of the Church of England; however, it wasn't quite as bad as the Catholic Church his mother adored. He was with his father on this one, although he was just as bad with his rants on the positive benefits of Communism and the Trade Unions. He wished his father hadn't allowed his mother to give her children saint's names. Francis Xavier. He'd better make sure Revie never found out about the Xavier.

The vicar lit a candle in a cast-iron stand and held out a hand to John. He stood up and moved towards him.

'In baptism God calls us out of darkness into his marvellous light. To follow Christ means dying to sin and rising to new life with him. Therefore, I ask: Do you reject the devil and all rebellion against God?'

'I reject them,' John said, his voice quavering.

'Do you renounce the deceit and corruption of evil?'

'I renounce them.'

This was too close to the horrors they'd all witnessed. The evil of Gareth Hovell. The evil of the man who had murdered his mother, and become his father. John was pale, his voice trembling. Tommy Coltman stepped forward and stood by his son, taking his hand. The vicar nodded. John turned and looked at his true father.

'Do you repent of the sins that separate us from God and neighbour?' the priest resumed.

'I repent of them, 'John said, his voice stronger.

The questions and the replies followed in an orderly manner, but Tommy didn't leave his son's sid s e. The family joined them round the font.

Eve moved to John's side and one of the boys took Eve's hand, the other Tommy's. The look on his face as the small hand slipped into his made Frank gulp. He felt his mood lifting and he leant forward so he could see Laurel. She smiled at him, a triumphant smile, as though proud to have played a part in helping to save John's life and to reunite him with his father. He felt exactly the same. There was a splash as the minister dipped a vessel into the font, and John was christened.

The Coltman family stood with the minister in the vast porch, shaking hands and nodding as people expressed their congratulations and sympathy.

As they approached them, Frank leading the way, Tommy moved towards them, unable to wait. He shook hands with all of them, and was introduced to Dorothy, Stuart and Mabel.

'We're not having a christening party; none of us felt up to it and it didn't seem appropriate, but this mustn't be the last we see of each other. A celebratory meal is called for. Would the Oysterage suit everyone?'

Frank's mood improved a notch more. 'Excellent!'

There were positive noises from the rest of the team.

John shook Frank's, then Laurel's hands. 'I can never repay you for saving my life at the risk of yours,' he said to both of them. He kept hold of Laurel's hand. 'You saved my life a second time down in that damned pit.'

Laurel held him close. 'It's over. You've a new life, with a new father. God bless you, John. I hope all will go well.'

'Thank you.'

They all strolled to the car park opposite the Jolly Sailor. Laurel and Dorothy were dragging their feet, whispering to each other. If it wasn't Dorothy Laurel was plotting with, it was Mabel. His good mood was coming apart at the seams. What were they scheming? He found it difficult to talk to Laurel. What would she do? Would she marry Oliver? He was sure Oliver wasn't the right man for her. Who was? He knew what would happen: Oliver would get her pregnant and she'd have to give up her partnership. Could the rest of them continue? Would they want to keep going? Of course they would. But would he? He'd miss her. The agency could work well with Stuart and himself as detectives. Perhaps they could recruit someone else. He wondered if Johnny Cottam would be interested. He smiled. Perhaps he'd drop his name as a possible replacement to Laurel at their next meeting. See how she liked that.

Chapter 33

Monday, September 6, 1971

Frank reached out and switched off the alarm clock before it started ringing. Quarter to six. He might as well get up. He'd spent most of the night in a fitful sleep, images of the explosion replaying whenever he closed his eyes. He swung his legs out of bed and sat on the edge, his head slumped on his chest. Bloody hell, this wouldn't do. He'd have to accept whatever today's meeting brought.

He pulled back the curtains and looked out of his cottage's open window over the cliffs and the North Sea. The sea and sky were one colour: grey. It suited his mood. He breathed in the salt-laden air, filling his lungs, trying to energise himself. It didn't seem to be working. He groaned. There was only one thing that would get him going. A run along the beach. No. He decided on the heath. Today he couldn't bear the thought of running on pebbles, not after that night on Orford Ness. He'd have some water and leave breakfast until he came back. The meeting was due to start at nine-thirty. He didn't want to get there early; he wasn't in the mood for chit-chat or badinage.

Wearing shorts and a t-shirt, he ran across the Minsmere Road onto the heath. Although early, bees were busy in the heather flowers. The sandy soil was kind to his feet and he picked up speed as he ran away from the beach and cliffs down a bridle path and then onto the road that led to Eastbridge. When he reached the turning that led to the bridge over Minsmere River, he turned back: he hadn't time to run down The Cut and back along the beach near the bird reserve.

The Cut. At the end of it was the sluice where the body of Susan Nicholson had been found by Benjie Whittle. The beginning of it all. No, not quite the beginning. He'd first met Laurel in the mortuary in Ipswich when she came to identify her dead sister, in 1969. She was the catalyst: not only in playing a major part in bringing Susan's murderer to justice, but in helping him to take that vital step to resign from the police force and to form the detective agency. What would life be like without her?

It was only a year since he'd been assigned to that case, but in the time the case was solved, he'd resigned and with Stuart, Dorothy and Mabel, they'd solved three major cases, all of them complex and dangerous. Only a year. They seemed to have known each other for much longer. He headed back, stretching out his legs, trying to loosen his shoulders, breathing steadily.

The row of cottages came into view. He hadn't seen another soul. He'd half-hoped he might meet Laurel out for one of her runs; then he'd have invited her back for breakfast and she would have told him her plans. They were close friends as well as colleagues. He'd miss seeing her regularly, miss their matiness. It wasn't often you met a woman you could be close friends with, so close you forgot she was a woman, with all that entailed. She was Laurel, brave, intelligent, strong and good company.

As the water from the shower pulsed over his body he made a decision. She was a good friend and he should want the best for her. If the best was to marry Oliver and perhaps, eventually, or indeed soon, leave the agency, he should be glad for her and not selfish, wishing she'd stay because it suited him. He rubbed his hair with a towel; he didn't bother combing it, today he'd let nature take its course.

Laurel turned back off the Minsmere Road and ran through the woods towards Greyfriars House. She'd run along the beach as far as the sluice and on her way back glanced up towards the top of Minsmere cliffs, wondering if Frank was up. The sea air and her body's movement had increased her feeling of euphoria. Everything was wonderful, she was full of excitement and anticipation: she was in love, no doubt about it. What would Frank think? She grinned. He'd say she was mad. She didn't care.

Later, after a shower, she sat with Dorothy in the garden.

Dorothy put her cup and saucer on a nearby table and lit a cigarette. 'First one of the day!' she said proudly.

'What are you down to?' Laurel asked.

'Fifteen.'

'That's still too many.'

'Who says so? It's better than forty.' She looked at her watch. 'I'm all right for ten minutes, then I'd better go and get the papers on the table for the meeting.'

'Oh, Dorothy, I'm so happy. Thank you for saying yes.'

'You did ask Mabel?'

Laurel pulled a face. 'Of course, I did. She's happy for me.'

'Are you sure about telling Frank at the meeting? Don't you think you're being cruel?'

Laurel laughed. 'I can't help it if he's been moody and won't talk. Serve him right if he has a shock.'

Dorothy looked at her over the rim of her glasses. 'No Miss Sugar and Spice, then?' she sniggered.

Laurel laughed again. 'No, I'm in a Miss Salt-and-Vinegar mood.'

'Let's hope you don't get your chips!'

Smiling, they picked up their cups and went towards the house.

When Frank went into the meeting/dining room, Dorothy was busy laying out five settings of blotting paper, pencils, water glasses and the agendas for the meeting.

'Do we need blotting paper and pencils? No one uses either, we don't have a fountain pen between us,' he said.

'And good morning to you too,' she said, giving him a stern look.

'Sorry, I've been a bit of a bear with a sore head this morning. Didn't sleep well.'

She didn't answer, left the room and soon reappeared with a jug full of water. 'I like to set up the meeting as I used to set up the governors' meetings at the school. I didn't get any complaints from them, in fact I received compliments.'

Oh, Lord, this meeting is going to be a disaster. 'You're right, Dorothy. It gives a professional touch.'

She sniffed and left the room.

He picked up an agenda:

1. Minutes of the last meeting.
2. Finance report
3. Building projects
4. Possible new cases
5. Miss Bowman to speak
6. AOB

Great balls of fire! Miss Bowman to speak! Had it come to this? What was the matter with everyone? What had he done to be treated like this? He thought they were his friends as well as colleagues.

He dropped the sheet onto the table, looked at his watch — another seven minutes before the meeting started. He should have stuck to his original idea and arrived at nine-thirty, not nine-fifteen. He walked out of the meeting room and headed for the garden; at least the birds, slugs and snails wouldn't give him a hard time.

Mabel burst in from the kitchen. 'Frank. The meeting's starting soon. Where are you going?'

He stared at her. 'Thought I'd have a breath of fresh air. Dorothy's in a foul mood, so I decided to disappear.'

She grabbed his arm. 'Come into the kitchen, I'll make you a quick cup of coffee.'

He resisted and stood his ground. 'I've had far too much coffee already today, Mabel, but thanks for the offer.' He tried to move away, but she held on.

'How about a nice piece of fruit cake?'

What was the matter with her? Was he irresistible? It must be his hair, it was alarmingly curly after his no-combing routine. He grinned at the thought of Mabel lusting after him.

'That's better, Frank. It's the happiest you've looked for a good few weeks.'

'Got the hots for me, Mabel? We better not tell Stuart.'

She roared with laughter. 'I like my men placid, thank you. I told Stuart he was like a bumble bee the other day. Now you — I'd put you down as a wasp, or even better, a hornet. Fast and dangerous.'

'Talking about me again?' Stuart walked into the kitchen.

'Frank thinks I fancy him.'

'He's deluded. He thinks every woman is madly in love with him and wants to take him up to her boudoir and turn him into the perfect husband.'

'What? Like you, dear?' Mabel said

'I think I detect a touch of sarcasm.' Stuart looked at his watch. 'Time for the meeting.'

Mabel heaved a sigh of relief.

Frank grinned ruefully. What on earth was that about? He put an arm around Mabel's shoulders. 'He got to you first, Mabel, if he hadn't, who knows...'

She looked at him, a worried expression on her face. 'You'll be all right, Frank,' she said and patted his hand.

He'd be all right? The gnawing doubts returned. Somehow, he didn't think he would be.

Laurel couldn't contain herself, she was almost bouncing up and down in her chair. They'd got to item four on the agenda.

'There are two cases worth considering,' Dorothy said, then passed a sheet of paper to each of them. 'A landowner near Halesworth has had several farm machines stolen.'

'Why hasn't he brought in the police?' Stuart asked.

'He suspects his son-in-law, and as he's very fond of his daughter. He hopes if we investigate we can inform him if he is or is not involved. If he isn't he'll pass it over to the police.'

'He sounds a considerate person,' Mabel said.

'The second is a case of the owners of a posh hotel in Ipswich who also want a discreet investigation, they said they don't want "the plod" barging round and disturbing their guests.'

Stuart looked at Dorothy. 'As a former plod, I take offence at that remark, don't you, Frank?'

Laurel waited on his reaction. So far, he'd remained silent throughout the meeting.

He shrugged. 'It's a good job there are stupid people out there who underrate the discretion of the police: it gives us more work.'

He was in a bitter mood. Perhaps she should have told him before the meeting.

'Do you miss being a policeman, Frank? I've often wondered if you regret leaving the force,' she said, giving him a sweet, false smile.

He gave her a sour smile back.

Dorothy rapped her pencil on the table.

'So, you've found a use for it after all, Dorothy,' Frank said.

She turned the glare focussed on Laurel onto him. 'To return to the case, the problem is theft from guests. All the staff are long serving and they wonder if the thief might be one of the semi-permanent residents.'

'We can send Laurel undercover as a chambermaid,' Frank said, giving her a frosty smile. 'That is, if you're still around.'

Stuart looked from her to Frank. 'Shall we break for coffee and discuss these cases after? Got anything nice for us?' he asked Mabel.

Before she could reply Frank said, 'I think we ought to press on. We can have coffee when we've finished. Dorothy, please continue.'

Dorothy rearranged her spectacles on her nose. 'There isn't a great deal more to say. All the details are on the sheet of paper I gave you. I can't see any reason why we shouldn't take the cases.' She looked at Frank.

'I agree. Any objections?'

'I'm game, as long as you can guarantee there aren't any crazy murderers lurking behind combine harvesters or

355

sinister guests wandering the hotel in the small hours looking for victims,' Stuart said, obviously trying to lighten the mood.

'They seem straightforward cases,' Laurel said. 'Who will do what?'

'Stuart and I will take the farm machinery; do you think you can manage the hotel by yourself?' Frank asked.

'I'll let you know once I've done some preliminary investigations,' she replied.

'Right, that's settled,' Dorothy said. 'Item five, over to you, Laurel.'

'Thank you, Dorothy.' Frank wouldn't look at her, just stared at the blotting paper. 'I thought I ought to make my position in the agency clear. After the last case, which was distressing for all of us, I must admit I didn't know if I could cope with another case like that. As you know, Oliver asked me to marry him.' She paused. Now he was looking at her, his green eyes blazing. 'I like Oliver very much, he is an intelligent, thoughtful man.' His lips had started to curl. 'But now I realise although I'm fond of him and find him attractive—'

'For God's sake, Laurel, spit it out. Are you leaving or staying?' He looked attractively wild, his dark curls almost quivering with rage.

'Please, Frank let me finish.'

The other three were giving each other looks and Stuart appeared to be on the point of bursting into laughter. She knew she was being cruel, but... 'As I was saying, I've decided I can't marry Oliver and I've told him of my decision.'

Frank let out a long, relieved breath.

'However, something has happened recently. I've fallen in love and I hope you'll all be pleased to meet him. He's waiting outside.'

Frank's mouth was open. 'He's outside?'

'Yes, can I bring him in? Then we can all have coffee together.' She looked at Dorothy, who inclined her head.

As she went to the door she heard Frank questioning Dorothy. 'You knew about this?'

She didn't hear the reply.

She returned. 'Here you are. Isn't he gorgeous?' She held a black Labrador puppy in her arms. 'His name's Bumper, as that is what he's good at.' She walked over to Frank. 'Here's your Uncle Frank, Bumper.' She dropped him in Frank's lap. The puppy looked up at Frank, then started to nibble his hand.

'Christ, take him back, he's got shark's teeth.' Frank laughed, relief and another expression she wasn't sure about written on his face.

She picked up Bumper and kissed him. 'He can come with me for walks on the heath if you're unavailable,' she said.

'And if I am available?' he asked.

'He can come anyway.'

'He's too young to go anywhere,' Dorothy said, coming over to pet him. 'He's got to have all his jabs.'

'So, he couldn't go for a walk to the Eel's Foot this evening?' Frank asked, looking at Laurel.

She shook her head.

'I'll look after him,' Mabel said. 'It's lovely to have a dog again. It was nice of you to ask me, Laurel. I'll never get over Muffin being killed by that monster, but I've missed a dog's company.'

'You never told me that,' Stuart said. 'I'd have got you one, if I'd known.'

'Do you fancy a walk after supper?' Frank asked Laurel.

She smiled. It was the old Frank, quizzical, friendly, but perhaps a touch more... she mustn't read too much into

357

his expression. She lifted Bumper into the air, who squeaked and thrashed his fat little tail. 'I do fancy a walk, and a pint of Adnams.'

Frank nodded. 'Good. See you at supper. Dorothy, please accept the two cases. I'll start checking on the stolen vehicles. Want to come with me, Stuart?'

They left and there was the noise of Frank's Avenger being driven off at speed.

Laurel hugged Bumper to her. She had someone who loved her unconditionally. Perhaps one day...

THE END

Author's Note

In 2015 I visited an exhibition of the art works of Joseph Cornell at the Royal Academy, London. Cornell was a recluse, who never spent a night away from home. He rambled through the streets of Queens, a residential borough of New York, picking up detritus such as tinfoil and pieces of plastic. Using these, with pages cut from magazines, he created boxed assemblages of fantastic works of art. Some, I found disturbing.

This was the inspiration for Thomas Coltman's obsessive making of similar boxes to try and protect his dead wife, Audrey.

Author's note

In 1935 I visited the children of one Dr Lowery [?] in ... for retrieving the Royal Academy ... to ... Charge was a recluse who never spent a ... ... He rambled through the streets of ... ... honoured ... New York, picking up letters, stories and ... and pieces of ... ... right here and from stamps, he created boxes ... ... on a basic word-screen, string, hidden messaging.

This was the beginning of Charge's career of making ... of similar boxes to ... who profited handsomely ...

Acknowledgements

My thanks to:

The members of the Orford Ness National Trust team: the Warden, David Mason, and volunteers Bill Roberts, Mike Hawes and Guy Brown, but special thanks to Peter Whiley, who gave me the most comprehensive tour of the out-of-bounds areas of the Ness, regaled me with great anecdotes of happenings, and made suggestions on where to land a boat, places to hide a body and suitable explosives!

Simon, Gail, Oliver and Zara, for their help and love.

All members of my writing groups, but especially to the South Chiltern Writing Circle for listening patiently to this novel and for their friendship and helpful criticism.

All my friends for their fantastic support during a difficult year.

My editor, Jay Dixon, for her calm, professional approach as she helped to shape and polish this book, and her continuing dry wit.

Lastly, but certainly not least, my deepest thanks to Hazel, Katrin and Jamie of Accent Press, for their understanding and support.

Acknowledgements

The many staff of the Oxford West mercia, through the Wals.... David Mercer, and volunteers of Reform WMK shows, the ODY environhub... local charities to meet William ... books the urban recording renovation of the world-beaters areas ... the Neuve, reglied ... ... that ... ... imperative, anu ... who were to lend a kind place to ring a body and supply resources

We hope you enjoy this book. Please return or renew it by the due date.

You can renew it at www.norfolk.gov.uk/libraries or by using our free library app.

Otherwise you can phone 0344 800 8020 - please have your library card and PIN ready.

You can sign up for email reminders too.

NORFOLK ITEM

30129 081 714 678

NORFOLK COUNTY COUNCIL
LIBRARY AND INFORMATION SERVICE

Italian Royals

*Two royal medics—
can they find their perfect match?*

Take a trip through the cobbled streets of Venice
and discover the secrets that lie within them
in Annie O'Neil's decadent duet! When a
royal wedding is turned upside down it sets in motion
a truly unforgettable and unexpected journey
for Princess Beatrice and her best friend
and bridesmaid Fran.

Find out more in…

Tempted by the Bridesmaid

Bridesmaid Fran Martinelli's ideal
Italian summer goes south when she
turns up for work after the disaster
of her friend's wedding and finds out
the best man is her new boss!

Claiming His Pregnant Princess

When Princess Beatrice di Jesolo is jilted by
her royal fiancé, she must hide her secret pregnancy…
A great idea until she discovers her new boss is
The One Who Got Away…

Available now!